Praise for

## ALISSA YORK and FAUNA

"York is emotionally unflinching, and her writing is sharp-edged and intense." *The Globe and Mail*

"*Fauna* is the sort of rare novel that can change the way you see your world. Its cast of misfits and dreamers is united by their visceral connection to the forgotten animals surviving in the green patches of our big cities. This book is beautiful, unusual and memorable. And Alissa York is a daring and original talent." Jim Lynch, author of *Border Songs*

"Unique, compelling and hopeful." *The Record*

"Rich and strange and deeply satisfying. Whether she's adopting the voice of a homeless teen, a yuppy vet or a famished coyote, York writes with a spare, unsentimental fluency that connects strangers, enemies, species. *Fauna* reminds us of the life that swoops and slithers and lopes and pounces all around us, even in the most urban of worlds; a wild life we share and ignore at our peril." Annabel Lyon, author of *The Golden Mean*

"A tender and beautiful novel." *NOW* (Toronto)

"One of the novel's strengths is the way York turns her gaze from the human world to the world of Toronto's skunks, coyotes, raccoons and squirrels. . . . Even as she brings animals to life with her writing, she is clear about the terrible toll taken by everything from cars, to skyscraper windows, to live electrical wires." *Winnipeg Free Press*

"An extraordinary novel. . . . Daring and exceptional."
*Quill & Quire* (starred review)

# FAUNA

ALISSA YORK

*To Andy,*
*With all best*
*wishes,*

Vintage Canada

Library and Archives Canada Cataloguing in Publication

York, Alissa
Fauna / Alissa York.

ISBN 978-0-307-35790-8

I. Title.

PS8597.O46F38 2011      C813'.54      C2010-904893-8

Book design by Jennifer Lum

Printed and bound in the United States of America

2 4 6 8 9 7 5 3 1

for my brother, Ben,
and as always
for Clive

"Animals don't behave like men," he said. "If they have to fight, they fight; and if they have to kill, they kill. But they don't sit down and set their wits to work to devise ways of spoiling other creatures' lives and hurting them. They have dignity and animality."

—Richard Adams, *Watership Down*

# 1

# The City Book

She wakes to the sound of claws—a busy scrabbling on hardwood, not far from her ear. Pre-dawn darkness, a drift of warm, weak light from the bathroom down the hall. Slowly, warily, she turns her head. The mouse halts, whiskers quivering. Less than an arm's length from her face.

Letting her breath out in a thin, steady stream, Edal does what she can to soften her gaze. The mouse is unconvinced. It holds its position, flank pressed to the skirting board, fur jumping with the panic of its pulse. She knows better than to try soothing it with words; years of experience have taught her few sounds trouble the wild ear so much as human speech. A small shock, then, to herself as much as to the creature before her, when the sound escapes her lips.

"Hello," she says softly, and the mouse swivels and runs.

Looking up from the sink, Edal meets herself dripping in the medicine cabinet's mirrored doors. The centre seam draws a line down her nose, her unremarkable mouth. It separates her eyes, brown and large, already set slightly too far apart—a little odd, but not unattractive, perhaps the best feature in what she hopes could be called a heart-shaped face. Shoulder-length hair lies flat and brown against her skull. She would cut it short and be done with it, but she needs it to cover her ears. No one's ever told her they're too small—she reached that conclusion all on her own. They feel almost vestigial, like a dewclaw, or the ancestral nub of a tail.

Reaching for a towel, she thinks again of the mouse. Its ears are in fine proportion, sweet little petals folded neatly against its head, designed to lift a thousand times a day in alarm. There must be a hole behind the dresser—it shot back there and didn't show itself again. She should deal with it, find the breach and block it up.

Back in her bedroom, she folds open the closet door. Her work clothes take up half the space: short- and long-sleeved duty shirts, three pair basic cargo pants, two pair tactical pants, patrol jacket, fleece—all in peaceful forest green. She's only been off duty for three weeks and already she's starting to feel as though the federal wildlife officer uniform belongs to somebody else. As though she'd be committing an offence—*personating a peace officer*—if she tried any of it on.

She touches a summer-weight sleeve, laying a finger to the crest. She can remember exactly how it felt the first time she sported that blue and gold insignia on her arm—the mixture of pride and relief. And now, only five years on the job and she's living off a store of sick days, unsure when she'll feel steady enough to go back. It's one thing being off work because you've caught a nasty bug, quite another because you've broken down on duty, sat down on the floor and buried your face in your hands. At least the crying jags seem to be easing up. The choking sensation still comes, but it's been days now since her eyes ran like faucets. Some inner salt reservoir finally running dry.

She sweeps a palm down the front of the shirt. In the breast pocket, a familiar bulge. Her notebook, perhaps two-thirds full, every workday set down in its relevant details. She draws it up out of the pocket and flips to her final entry.

Canada Customs paged her first thing that morning. She made it to Pearson International in good time, arriving half an hour before the flight from New Delhi touched down. Anna-May Button had been flagged due to previous violations. She looked like a TV granny, a plump, apple-cheeked woman whose bags should have been crammed full of presents for the little ones back home. Instead, they were stacked with cardboard egg cartons—nine in her carry-on, twenty-four in the one she'd checked. Nearly four hundred little egg-shaped depressions, a juvenile Indian star tortoise in every one.

Those in the carry-on bag fared better: a third of them had suffocated and only two had been squashed. Those that had travelled cargo saw the worst of it. Edal opened carton after carton while the sweet-faced lady looked on. Every crushed carapace leaked colour, the cardboard soggy in places, swollen with blood.

Edal had seen as bad or worse. So why did the tortoises get to her the way they did? Why, as the day wore on, did she find herself gripped again and again by a sorrow so intense it threatened to close her throat? She fought it long enough to drive Mrs. Button back to HQ, take her prints and record a video statement. It was only later, when she was alone in the live evidence room, that the strangled feeling became more than she could bear.

She can't be sure how much time passed between the moment she gave in to it and the moment Barrett poked his head round the door. Even if she hadn't been crying too hard to speak, it would have been impossible to explain. By then she was beginning to suspect that the state she found herself in had less to do with baby tortoises than with the phone call she'd received the night before. She'd known something was wrong even before she'd answered—the hometown area code attached to a number she'd never seen. If she'd mentioned that call to her regional director, it would have been the start of a very long story indeed.

She tucks the notebook back into her duty shirt on its hanger. Pulling on a sweatshirt and bike shorts, she walks through to the kitchen, plugs in the kettle and drops a slice of multigrain in the toaster. When it pops, she takes the butter dish down from the cupboard—the last time she left it on the counter, the block showed diminutive whisker prints—and spreads a thin layer to the four corners of the slice. She eats standing up, gulping tea between bites. In a hurry. Only she's not.

*You've got the days banked, Jones. Why not use them?* She'd never heard Barrett speak so gently. Stress leave. The idea being that you leave your stress behind you when you go, only Edal seems to have carried hers home with her. Besides sleep, the only thing that helps is moving—walking or riding her bike. You might even say it's all she's good for.

Swallowing the last of her tea, she drops a greasy crust on her plate. It's irresponsible, she knows, inviting the mouse up onto the counter, laying out the bait without the trap. Childish. She'll have to stop.

Helmet and keys in hand, she eases shut her apartment door and takes the stairs softly. James and Annie won't be up for at least a couple of hours.

It's still dark out, porch lights and street lamps pitted against the last of the night. The maple trees stand shrouded. Within the hour they'll ring with the multi-toned strains of spring migration, untold species winging through.

Edal unlocks her bike from the porch railing and carries it down to the front walk. There won't be much traffic yet. She'll cycle south to Lakeshore Boulevard then east to the Beaches, ride hard along the lakefront path.

She feels better the moment she's on the bike, as though she's peeled away from her miserable self and left it standing. Partway down the block, she flushes a pale tomcat from beneath a parked car. It crosses the street in low, swinging strides, pausing to turn its broad face her way.

Wheeling onto Carlaw, she glides past ranks of tall brick homes that face the darkened park, young professionals and their babies interspersed among what's left of the neighbourhood's older families—mostly working class, mostly Greek. Edal thumbs her bell just to hear it. The land slopes gently, guiding her down to lake level as though she were one of the city's hidden streams.

At Langley, she changes her mind: she won't go east, but west instead, through the city's concrete heart. It's been months, maybe even a year, since she threaded a path through those glittering towers—not an experience she generally seeks, but this morning the idea of deserted glass valleys appeals.

From there she can cut down to the lakefront if the mood takes her, or carry on westward, maybe even as far as High Park.

Langley ends at Broadview, where Edal bumps across streetcar tracks and jumps the curb to ride overland. The grass is springy beneath her wheels. She rounds the looming statue of Sun Yat-sen and enters the deeper dark of the trees. The long bank of the Don Valley drops away. Giving gravity its head, she splays her legs wide and coasts, gathering speed.

She joins the path near the mouth of the Riverdale Footbridge—a quaint name for an arcing pedestrian overpass, all concrete and steel. Pedaling hard through the narrows where the bushes close in, she pumps up over the rise.

Halfway across the bridge, Edal brakes and slows. Balanced against the railing, she twists to look down on the slate glimmer of the Don River. Clumps of growth overhang the banks; a fallen tree rakes the current, waving a snagged plastic bag. The river has been straightened here, forced into the lesser form of a canal. The lit-up parkway follows one unnatural bank, the railway and Bayview Avenue the other. The tracks lie quiet, but already cars are speeding into and out of town, some seeking space, others forming small processions, nose to tail. Edal looks north, her gaze swimming against the flow.

Not far upstream—perhaps two city blocks—the Don begins to meander as a river should. Left then right, in wide, lazy turns. The roads keep their distance. Darkness opens like a rift between them, home to marshland, grassland, woods. Given half a chance, the land would revert, clawing back through time, tearing holes in the city's thin coat.

A path winds through the shadows, and she spots a solitary runner, visible between the trees. She can't make out his face, only that he's tall and thin, with a dark mop of curls. He pelts down the path as if something's after him, though as far as she can make out, he's alone. Either way, he's crazy. Edal's trained in personal protective tactics, and she would never run alone down there in the dark.

She hears a distant rumble and lifts her head. Farther up the valley, a subway train crosses the barred undercarriage of the viaduct. On the deck above, cars dart and flash between the netted cables of the bridge's span. Netted to dissuade jumpers. Edal looks down into the sluggish, reflective river, and wonders at its depth.

He's found another one—she can tell by his low, snuffling wuff. Lily loves the shape he makes, shaggy and substantial, true black against the Canada Trust Tower's glimmering granite wall. She knows a stab of pride. His coat is impressive, even here, in the eerie, aquarium light of the business district before dawn.

"Whatcha got, Billy?" Crouching down, she cups the ruched, wet-velvet edging of his lips. His breath is jungly. As she feels up over the points of his teeth, he relaxes his jaw, delivering the small feathered body into her grasp. She drops a kiss on his wet black nose.

"Good boy." She rises, closing the bird in her palms. It's alive, the certainty palpable. "Any more?"

He sets to work again, nosing along a planter's edge, disturbing ghostly petunias with his snout. Lily follows him to the corner, where Bay Street stretches north into spotlit gloom. She can make out the slow-swooping arc of a flash-light maybe a block away. A few minutes, no more, before they ought to be moving on.

Warming the bird a little longer in her hands, she turns to look west along Front Street, wide and quiet save for the taxi line out front of Union Station, shrunk to a mere three cars. Median gardens stand like skinny tropical islands, palm-leaf shadows, flowers lying low. Maybe they'll try there next, cross three deserted lanes to pick a path along the concrete rim. Birds that live through the impact often make their way to the nearest patch of green.

Across Bay, the Royal Bank Tower shows a sensible black hem of three or four storeys before rising in golden, knife-edged pleats. Its heights betray the first red hints of sunrise. Gulls are beginning to circle up from the lake; a fat one lands close by, stretching, then stowing its wings. It rotates its snowy head Lily's way, eyeing her carefully clasped hands.

"Fuck you," she murmurs, "fucking creep."

Pressing the stunned little body to her chest, she frees a hand and unsnaps her right cargo pocket. The hunting vest isn't much to look at—shit brown and big enough to hold two of her—but it's lightweight and warm, and all those pockets mean she generally has what she needs. The Tim Hortons bag is used but clean. She shakes it open and slips the bird inside.

Billy's growl is soft, the frequency felt as much as heard. Lily turns. At the curb, a woman in bike shorts and a pale sweatshirt stands astride a mountain bike. She's unusual-looking, built like a gymnast, pretty in a not quite human way. Lily flashes on the little tree frogs that used to cling to the siding beneath her bedroom window. Grey-green backs and pearly bellies. That trilling sound.

Billy eases up beside her, his growl rumbling in her kneecap, humming coldly in the steel shank of her boot. She touches a hand to her breast pocket, seeking the folded outline of her knife.

"Excuse me," the woman calls, "can I ask what you're doing?"

There's something of the teacher in her tone, maybe even the cop. Lily takes a step back.

"Don't be scared."

Lily spins on the spot and runs, Billy right behind her, keeping himself between her and the woman at the curb. The bike glints where she left it, propped in the recess of an emergency exit door. The crossbar means she has to swing her leg out over the back wheel, but it's better like that, you can bring your boot down pumping and tear away.

She burns down Front on the sidewalk, headed for the first glaring slip of day. For seconds she's on her own, then Billy pulls alongside her, a shaggy black bison on silent hooves. Lily grips the handlebars. The pair of them stampede toward sun-up, leaving the frog woman to choke on their dust.

Nothing in the kitchen traps this morning. They're getting wise to him, learning the heady scent of peanut butter can herald death. Maybe he'll have better luck in the yard.

For now, Guy sips his coffee, using the barbecue tongs to prod the frozen grey lump simmering on the stove. An inch of water in Aunt Jan's cast iron skillet—she'd kill him if she knew. If she wasn't long dead herself.

The mass in the fry pan is beginning to break up. Like the crust ice beside a riverbank, it develops seams along which to divide. Softening, it reveals heads and slender tails. Bodies separate, becoming distinct. Limbs loosen and seem to swim.

Good enough. Guy plucks the mice from the water one by one, arranging them like furry sausages on the tin pie plate in his hand.

Letting the screen door slam behind him, he stands for a moment on the concrete step, looking out across the yard. Howell Auto Wreckers, also known as home. The place always looks its best in the morning—the sun cresting the metres-high piles of wrecks along the eastern fence, winking through missing windows and gilding crumpled hoods.

Behind him, the house stretches long, living quarters down this way, cinder-block office at the other end. All that stands between it and the sullen, mud-coloured Don are the sloping ruins of Aunt Jan's garden, the high back fence draped in creepers, the on-ramp to the parkway's roar.

A whiff of warm, wet mouse calls him back. He walks south along the wall and rounds the corner. A narrow chain-link enclosure runs between the house and the southern fence. Setting the plate down on the ground, Guy feels for the key on the chain around his neck, opens the padlock and steps inside.

Down the far end, the dead oak looms. It was a big job, sinking the trunk two feet deep and bolstering it with a pair of engine blocks; he couldn't have done it without Stephen's help. It's handy having a live-in employee, especially one so keen to learn. It was the first time Stephen had laid hands on a chainsaw, and as usual Guy only had to show him once. Stephen took his time, measuring the oak's limbs before stunting them. When they stood the tree up on end in its hole, it grazed but didn't breach the cage's roof.

At the near end, they rigged up several of the cut-away boughs. Guy has to stoop to avoid them as he drags the mesh door closed, and for a moment he feels a sense of winter forest, barren canopy overhead. Between the branches and the tree they came from lies a run some twelve metres long. A stump stands at the midpoint. Guy sets the pie plate down on the round, ringed surface and steps back.

Invisible until this moment, the enclosure's inhabitant appears. Forsaking its private branch at the back of the oak, it stretches one yellow, reptilian leg along a leafless side limb, then the other. Talons gripping bark, the hawk balances. Its gaze sweeps the cage, touching briefly on Guy before returning to the plate of mice.

Guy catches his breath when the bird takes to the air. It's over in seconds—only a half-dozen pumps before it reaches out with its feet and lands, retracting its long, mottled wings.

The hawk settles on the edge of the stump then begins to sidle round, showing Guy its layered back, the rusty, spreading wedge of its tail. Shrouding the tin plate with its wings, it huddles and bobs. In no time it's bolted the mice into its crop. Taking flight again, it falters ever so slightly, flapping clumsily to regain the branch.

As the bird hunches to bring up the mice, Guy pulls a sandwich from the breast pocket of his heavy Mack shirt. Nothing fancy, ham and bread. Uncle Ernie liked his sandwiches simple—a taste he managed to pass along.

The hawk dips its bright crown and tears into a mouse. The sun is warm; it rests like an open hand at the back of Guy's neck. He stands and watches. After a moment he remembers the sandwich and eats.

As a rule, Lily coasts the last half block to the dead-end foot of Mt. Stephen Street, but this morning she rides hard to the last, jams her boot down on the pedal brake and skids to a halt. Billy gallops past and turns a sloppy U to come panting to her side. She takes pains to prop the bike against the fence, hooking a handlebar through the chain-link so the front wheel won't fold, taking the old paper-boy basket along for the fall. Its cardboard banana box holds precious cargo, a collection of rustling paper bags.

At the gate, she lays a hand on the painted plywood sign. HOWELL AUTO WRECKERS SINCE 1966. The key hangs on a bootlace around her neck. She fishes it out and jams it into the padlock with nervous hands. It's stupid. She must've looked over her shoulder a hundred times during the ride—there's no chance the woman followed them all this way.

She's careful not to bump the bike on her way through the gate. Billy follows, nuzzling the small of her back.

"Hold your horses." She shoves the gate closed and fumbles again with the lock. He drops into a sit, releasing a soft, impatient whine.

"Okay, go on."

Billy whirls, his blunt head trading places with his behind. He lopes across the yard, past the two trucks sitting idle, the bunker-style office with its shabby add-on house. She watches him disappear around its far corner, hears his bright, delighted bark. Amazing how he knows exactly where to go, his brain-map of the yard sparkling with streams of scent. Lily wishes she could sniff people out. Smell them coming before they get close enough to do any harm.

She runs a hand through the choppy, hot pink inches of her hair, turns back a moment to peer through the gate up the lightening street. Nobody. She guides the bike forward, following Billy's trail.

Guy steps out of the flight cage as she rounds the corner of the house, and Billy greets him with puppy sounds, his dark mass rippling with joy. Lily watches her dog best the jumping-up instinct she trained out of him. It felt a little cruel, saying no over and over like that, but she hadn't any choice once he reached full size and started knocking her to the ground. It was easy teaching his Newfoundland retriever majority—bred to work and generally eager to please—but there was the other portion too, the muscular mystery breed responsible for his height, his shortened muzzle and steely jaw.

Guy doesn't let him suffer long. He drops into a crouch, grasping Billy by his furry jowls. "Hey, Billy. Hey, Billy-boy." Billy licks him on the cheek. Lily taught him that too. No kissing on the lips.

Down the far end of the cage, the hawk mutters, fussing along its branch. It humps its wings, directs its gaze at Billy and releases a prolonged, peevish shriek. Billy parts his jaws, but Lily nudges his back end with the wheel. "Quiet, you."

"Hi, Lily." Guy stands, glancing down into the box. "Not so many this morning."

"Nope."

"Any live ones?"

"A few."

"Good stuff. Bring 'em in and we'll take a look." He leads the way, waiting while she leans the bike against the house and lifts the box free. "You want a hand?"

"I'm okay."

He holds the screen door open for her and Billy, leaves a gap before stepping in after them and letting the door slap shut on its spring. She likes the weird little house. It's more like an oversized trailer than anything, the kitchen flanked by Guy's bedroom and the can on one side and Stephen's room on the other. No denying the hum of the parkway, but she's used to that after the last couple of months; she'd have trouble getting to sleep without it.

Standing in the bright patch where the door lets in the morning, she watches Guy open the Living section of the *Star* and spread it out. She's fond of the table too. It's the old fifties kind, with shiny metal legs and a scrubbed pink surface that used to be red. He always leaves the centre leaf in, even though the edges don't quite meet up.

"Let's see what you've got."

He stands at the other end of the table with his arms folded, and for a moment Lily feels like she's in school—that same sick dread. Only Billy's here with her, not chained up waiting at home. Not nosing for crumbs around the kitchen counter like any other dog, either, but right beside her, leaned up against her leg. She sets the box down and fishes out the Tim Hortons bag. See to the living first.

The little bird lies motionless in her palm, but she can feel the quickened beat of its breathing, the faint sensation of warmth.

"Another ovenbird," Guy says.

"Yeah." At the shadowy foot of the tower, she could be certain of little beyond general colouring and size. Here in Guy's kitchen, she can make out the speckled belly and pinkish legs, the Mohawk stripe at its crown, the white rings around its tightly closed eyes.

"He's a beauty," Guy says quietly. "Needs a little longer, I guess."

"Yeah."

She slides the ovenbird back into papery darkness. Laying it carefully on the newspaper, she reaches into the box again.

Edal can feel something crawling on her—one of the leggy millions that feed and multiply and die in the foxtail grass. Whatever it is, it's making a pilgrimage up her calf. An ant, maybe, or a spider. A tick. She reaches down without looking to brush it away.

She's only partly hidden by the plywood sign, one half of her face pressed to the cool chain-link. It was no mean trick, hanging back while keeping the girl in sight. Upon arriving, she heard a distorted screeching that seemed to originate from the far corner of the yard—some kind of pulley or rusted hinge. She listened for it to come again as she laid her bike down in the weeds. Nothing. Then the girl rounded the corner in the company of a red-haired man—him leading, holding open the screen door, her following with bent head, canine shadow and banana box.

Edal doesn't ask herself why she followed the girl and her massive dog back to Howell Auto Wreckers—or why she lingers after they've gone inside. Instead, she wonders about the girl. There are people who comb the business district during migration season, many of them members of FLAP, an organization formed to draw attention to the deadly lure of the tower lights—but the girl doesn't look the type to be a member of anything.

And what about the man? Presumably a Howell or an employee of one, but who is he to the girl? A boyfriend? Unlikely. Edal saw no hint of the loaded current that runs between lovers' bodies. In any case, he's Edal's age, or near enough—late twenties at least—and the girl can't be more than sixteen. Older brother? If so, there's no resemblance. The girl is rail-thin, fine-featured, her skin watery, a shade of whey. Her hacked-off hair could be any colour under the dye, but Edal doubts it was ever a match for his.

She's never seen that shade of red on a human, dark as an old penny with new-penny flashes when he moved. Only slightly shorter than her own hair, it feathers back from his broad-boned face—a style common where Edal comes from. He wears a green and black Mack shirt, a relic of sorts in the city. She had a red one when she was growing up. Sometimes she slept in it—soft as a chamois, smelling of herself.

Definitely not a brother. A friend, then. Edal can only guess at what they're up to, now that they've gone inside. Still, there's plenty to observe.

The wrecking yard sits on a deep lot that butts up against the Dundas Street on-ramp. Three-metre-high fencing lined with banks of crushed cars. Just inside the gate, a flat black pickup stands beside a baby blue tow truck long past its prime.

In fact, none of the equipment looks anywhere near new: a front-end loader scabbed with rust, a limbed thing like a digger with a grapple in place of a scoop. A third corroded machine sits amid a field of broken glass. Composed of an open-jawed block mounted on a long metal bed, it resembles a child's cereal-box construction more than an assembly capable of crushing cars. Because that's what it must be; something flattened all those stacked-up wrecks.

Besides a small tool shed, there's only one building: a cinder-block bunker trailing a long clapboard extension. The yard's a mess, hard soil deadened by chemical runoff, mud healed into ruts, puddles showing rainbows of gas. Here and there a shock of grass perseveres. It's the kind of place that makes Edal uneasy, a place where things collect. To be fair, though, the longer she looks, the more a rough species of order becomes clear. Steel-mesh baskets brim with seemingly sorted parts. Tires in a tidy mountain. Engine blocks like a cache of pirate chests.

"Looking for something?"

Edal jumps, jamming the bridge of her nose against the mesh. The pain is brilliant, fierce. She holds a hand to it and turns.

The voice was a man's, but the tall, muscular creature before her is still part boy. Twenty, maybe twenty-one. Jet-black hair hanging down over dark, lashy eyes, cheekbones that look almost rouged. He's holding something in his hand. A brick? No, an innocent carton of half-and-half.

"Are you okay?" he asks.

She feels it then, the warm, wet trickle snaking down her upper lip. Bunching her sweatshirt sleeve up at the wrist, she holds it to her nostrils while she pinches the tender bridge.

Why won't he do the decent thing and look away? As long as he keeps staring like that, she can't help but see herself through his eyes. If she were in uniform, it would be called surveillance, but she's not; she's somebody with nothing better to do.

"I'm fine." The thickness in her throat alarms her. She can't possibly be about to cry.

"You want me to get you some ice?"

"No, I'm fine." She checks her sleeve to find a sizable splotch of blood. Stooping for the bike, she becomes aware of a trembling weakness in her legs.

"Hey, are you—"

"I'm *fine*." She hears the shrillness and knows there's only one conclusion he can draw. She's unbalanced. Unwell. She lifts the bike with difficulty, as though unearthing it. He gives her room.

"Was there something you wanted?" He says it quietly, perhaps even kindly, but Edal can only think of getting away. She doesn't dare swing up onto the bike; no choice but to push it beside her in a pathetic retreat.

"Hey," he calls after her.

She doesn't answer, doesn't look round. By the end of the block, she's steady enough to ride. Climbing on, she hazards a backward glance. He's still standing there. Still refusing to look away.

Back in his bedroom, Stephen stands by the window, looking out. His day is off to a shaky start. First the woman with the bloody nose, and now this: Lily down on her knees in the back garden, burying her birds. Her grubby vest and narrow, rounded back. Whoever decided it was a good idea to make bodies so fragile? Bones so close to the surface you can see them. Blood threading just beneath the skin.

It helps a little when Billy, sitting solemnly alongside the shallow graves, looks up and returns his gaze.

"You get the cream?"

He turns to find Guy framed in the doorway. "Yeah, sorry." He points to where the litre carton lies on its side on his bed. It's a high four-poster—the kind that ought to be draped with a handmade quilt, not made up tight with a single camp blanket. Drilled-in habits die hard.

Guy leans up against the jamb. "You all right?"

"Uh-huh."

"Kits okay?"

Stephen nods, his mind going to the four chubby little raccoons asleep in their dog-carrier den beneath his bed. They'd be dead if it wasn't for him. *Stop it.* Starved or eaten or both, plucked out of hiding and picked clean—a crow, maybe, or a feral cat. *Stop.*

"There was this woman," he hears himself say.

"What woman?"

"I don't know, I never saw her before. She was looking in at the gate when I got back."

Guy cocks his head. "Did she say what she wanted?"

"No."

"Huh. What did she look like?"

Stephen thinks. "Pretty. Kind of short. Around your age, maybe a little older." He pauses. "She had a nosebleed."

"What?"

"She hit her nose when I came up behind her. I startled her, I guess."

Guy steps into the room and reaches for the half-and-half. Doesn't leave with it, though. Instead, he sits down on the bed and balances the carton on his lap, lifting his gaze to the collection of framed photographs on the opposite wall. Stephen can't see them from where he stands; no matter, he has the images by heart.

The largest shows a sixties bride and groom in black-and-white. They're nowhere near hippies—his hair is pomaded back, hers rises in a modest hive—but there's something of the time in her racy hemline, the way he's pulled her in close against his side. Guy's Uncle Ernie and Aunt Jan.

Then there are the true parents, the ones Guy lost first. The second wedding portrait is a vivid colour shot. The groom's purple cummerbund matches the clutch of artificial flowers behind the bride's ear. Her dark red hair is huge, like one of those branching fans they snap off coral reefs. Her eyes, ringed with more purple, are fixed on the man she loves. Stephen knows Guy's dad was around his own age when the photo was taken, but the broad-shouldered tux and clownish cummerbund make him look closer to twelve than twenty-one. Very close, in fact, to the teenage boy in the neighbouring frame.

That one's Stephen's favourite: Guy standing in front of a gutted Dodge Dart with an oversized tabby cat draped around his neck. The others are good too—Guy as a toddler, pushing a toy tow truck the same powder blue as the one he would come to drive; Guy as a sturdy boy, standing alongside his uncle, one hand on his fishing pole, the other holding up a sad excuse for a fish—but the cat photo takes the prize.

"You don't have to leave those up, you know," Guy says. "We could find another spot for them, let you put up some stuff of your own."

Stephen flashes on a pair of prints on his parents' living room wall: an airbrushed man morphing into an eagle, his hazy mate in the process of becoming a wolf. His-and-hers shamans, both plainly Caucasian, though rendered in soothing, earthy tones. If memory serves, there were no actual photos around while he was growing up. Grade after grade, he was the only kid who didn't order any school portraits— not even the poor-family package of one five-by-eight and four handy wallet-size. *Photos are about holding on to the past,* Mica told him when he asked. *Your father's right,* Ariel added. *Life happens in the now.*

"It's okay," Stephen says. "I like having them there."

"Your call."

"Unless you want them in your room."

"No, no."

"You should have the bigger room anyway. I feel like I'm—"

"Hey, I told you, I've been sleeping in that room since my bed had rails around it. I doubt I could sleep anywhere else." Guy turns the carton upside down as though testing the seal. "Besides, you've been here, what, a year and a half now?"

"Just about. Since December 2006."

"Okay, then, I'd say this is your room." He stands. "I've got Ted Price coming to pick up a load of parts around noon. Maybe you could get started stripping that Vette."

"Sounds good."

"Coffee first, though."

"Yeah." Stephen turns back to the window. Billy's leaning up against his mistress where she kneels, patting the earth flat. Stephen feels a tightening sensation in his chest—sometimes it happens like this, no shock or exertion required. He may not be lying flat on his back in St. Mike's anymore, but his heart is far from the young organ it was.

"She's found some live ones too," Guy says behind him.

"Huh?"

"Lily. She's found a few that survived." He pauses. "Come on, buddy. Come and see."

Edal stands in the shower, her eyes shut tight. The needling water draws her out of her mind and into her tingling skin—until the needles begin to turn cold. She has yet to soap up or lather her hair; she's just been standing here, emptying the hot water tank. It doesn't matter. She can shower again later, or not.

She steps out of the enclosure and sees herself in the divided glass. Her nose is swollen, but only slightly. No sign of bruising. She presses it lightly and feels only tenderness, nothing sharp. Her sweatshirt lies soaking in the sink, cold water for blood, as every girl learns. She can't remember being told—it's not the sort of thing her mother would've managed—so she must have read it somewhere. *Harmon's Household Hints* or *Are You There God? It's Me, Margaret*. The sweatshirt looks bloated. It looks like something tragic, a baby elephant's ear.

She confiscated an elephant-skin drum once. It's still lying in the evidence room at HQ, alongside an umbrella stand made from a hollowed-out foot—giant toenails and all—and scores of yellowing curios carved from tusks. Banned parts and products are bad enough, but they're nothing to the living finds: the trio of hyacinth macaws with taped grey beaks and frantic eyes; the Jamaican yellow boa stuffed into a matching backpack; the California condor some sick bastard had folded up like a sports coat, breaking its magnificent wings.

She'll never forget the double-deep briefcase Security yanked off the belt because it was emitting a sinister hiss. She brought the snake-handling kit to that call but ended up putting it aside. The briefcase belonged to a balding, middle-aged man in leather pants. He held his tongue while she questioned him, but she caught his look of misgiving when she popped the case's lock.

Standing back, she extended her baton to its full length and pried up the lid. For a moment there was nothing. Then out came a hairy, segmented leg. Edal dropped the lid, severing the limb. Covered in fine, coffee-coloured fur, it contracted in a final beckoning gesture before it lay still.

"Now see what you did," Leather-pants said.

She turned to him. "What is it?"

"You're the expert. You tell me."

Goliath bird-eating tarantulas, she checked the species identification books once she'd transported the briefcase back to HQ. Only three out of a dozen were still showing signs of life. Of the dead, several had nourished their fellow travellers, their insides turned soupy before being sucked dry.

Edal shakes her head, absently towelling herself dry. She should eat something, keep up her strength. Still hugging the damp towel about her, she pads out to the kitchen, opens several cupboards, stares down into the steely sink. A single mouse turd—a dark, seed-shaped offering—curves like a comma beside the taps. She lets it lie.

The clock on the stove shocks her. It can't possibly be only 8:38. It seems as though a week has passed since she woke to meet the mouse's gaze, and yet the day in all its emptiness remains.

It's full morning by the time Lily returns to the valley floor. No sign of the nightlife beyond the usual fresh graffiti tags and empties, the odd abandoned shoe. Somebody's been stapling up yellow flyers—probably some pervert or religious freak. She doesn't bother to take a close look. Day-timers pass Billy and her on the footpath—runners and cyclists, people who keep their dogs on leads. She looks through them until she's safely by.

Her pockets are alive. Seven survivors this morning, the whole vest bursting with birds. She waits until they're north of the viaduct before wading out into the weeds; might as well get clear of the most obvious obstacle.

The first bag comes from the right cargo pocket. The ovenbird is lively, definitely ready to try. Lily parts the paper and reaches in, closing her fingers around its breast. The peck it gives her scarcely registers, her hands drunk with the silken overlap of its feathers, the fluttering protest of its heart.

As always, there comes the moment of doubt as she cradles the bird in her closed hands. "Ready?" she whispers through her fingers. "One, two, *three!*"

It's like scooping up water when you're a kid at the lake, watching it break open the light. Billy barks as she flings the bird skyward. She doesn't blame him—it really is something to see.

Ever since Stephen showed the workers at the Valley Animal Shelter he could handle the troubled dogs, that's all he ever gets. Which is fine, because they need to get out as much as their neighbours do—maybe more, when you consider how rarely they're chosen to be taken home.

Today's dog is Tiger, a Staffordshire terrier mix with a striped coat and a tendency to snap and piddle when approached. He lunged repeatedly at Stephen's feet the first time they went out together, which was how Stephen knew the man in Tiger's former life had been the kind that kicked. Once they'd made it down to the valley path, he fixed Tiger's leash to a sapling and bent to remove his boots. While the quivering dog watched, he dropped a liver treat down each one. Then stood back in his stocking feet to wait.

Tiger was easily distracted. He erupted into paroxysms of barking at the sound of a chipping squirrel, then again at the flash of a passing bike. Eventually, though, he honed in on the scented message of the treats. He had to shove his stubby snout deep to retrieve them—no tasting the gift without tasting the man who gave it. The next treat came from Stephen's hand, the cup of which Tiger snuffled into long after the dark morsel was gone.

They're good buddies now—which doesn't mean Stephen can let down his guard. As they leave the shelter lot for the sidewalk, he keeps Tiger to a tight heel, placing himself between potential violence and passersby. The occasional bonehead overlooks the obvious and attempts to make friends. Stephen has found it's best not to mince words. *He bites* does the trick every time.

The bridge is all sun and car horns, the Queen streetcar squealing on its rails. Metal stairs carry them down to sweet relief—the shady, beaten earth of the valley floor. They walk north. Stephen lets some slack into Tiger's lead on the lonely stretches, reels him in tight at the first sign of life.

Today they enjoy relative solitude—only two cyclists and a small pack of lunchtime runners between the Queen and Dundas Street spans—leaving Stephen free to take stock of the burgeoning world.

The air is sweet, car fumes a distant second to the scent storm of an advancing spring. The valley's looking good, trees filling in nicely, undergrowth rising up to hide a winter's worth of trash. All around him, weeds are doubling their number, stretching their thin green skins. A swath of white, knee-high flowers catches his eye, and then something else new—a bright yellow flyer bearing the black stroke of what appears to be a single phrase. Upon closer inspection it turns out to be a URL:

coyotecop.blogmonster.com

Whoever's posted it has little regard for trees: he's stapled the page directly to living bark, and Stephen can see others fluttering on trunks along the path up ahead. He folds the first one he tears down, slipping it into his back pocket before moving on. The rest he collects in a loose sheaf under his arm—two dozen or more before they peter out just south of the viaduct, and he and Tiger can turn around.

Edal wakes in late afternoon. Twenty minutes pass before she sits up. Another five before she can force herself to rise.

To begin with, she showers properly, washing and even conditioning her hair. She dresses and makes a mug of tea, sits down to tackle the two-day-old Saturday *Star*. Not one head-line grabs her, but she forces herself to keep on. Between features, she plays with the idea of checking her email for the first time in a week. Voice mail, too. At the very least, she should turn the ringer back up on the phone. Which would be worse, finding messages or finding none?

Around five, she begins to feel vaguely nauseous, an unpleasant reminder of the body's unrelenting need for fuel. There's food in the fridge, much of it too far gone to consider— squashy bags in the crisper, yellowing bacon, a litre of lumpy milk. She should have a good cleanout. The garbage cans go out tonight, so it's the ideal time to start fresh.

Edal slips on her shoes. She descends to street level, crosses the park and takes the quiet streets to Loblaws. The IGA is closer, but the walk is half the point.

She makes herself a proper meal when she gets home, chicken breast sweating in the oven while she assembles a complex salad for its bed. She could eat in front of the TV, but it seems wise to maintain at least some of her rules. It's not easy, though, just sitting at the kitchen table, lifting the fork over and over to her lips. Before long she can scarcely stand the sound of her own chewing. The chicken gives out a soft, fleshy clicking; the chunks of red pepper squeak. Romaine collapses against her palate, a series of watery, crumpling spines.

She leaves more than half her dinner uneaten. Considers wrapping it up, but can't imagine ever wanting to look at it again. Bending to scrape the plate, she spots the crust she left out for the mouse. Idiot. She drops that in the garbage too.

Lily never liked tuna casserole until she tried Guy's. She'd gladly have it tomorrow too—only tomorrow's her turn to cook.

Tonight she washes while Stephen dries.

"You guys want to stick around when you're done?" Guy says as he shoves the leftovers in the fridge. "Maybe hang out a little?"

"I have to feed the kits." Stephen slides a saucepan into the drawer beneath the stove.

"Yeah, and I need a smoke."

"Okay, so after that."

While Billy noses along the vine-draped fence, Lily settles on a hummock not far from her graveyard of birds. The smoke is rich in her mouth, incredibly good. Only one left in the pack, and not enough money for more, but she might go ahead and smoke the last one too. She feels at ease in the long back garden—hell, anywhere inside the wrecking yard's high mesh fence. Strange, considering she's only been coming here for a month and a half.

She and Billy had been calling the Don Valley home for nearly two weeks on the morning she met Guy. It was early, but she'd already broken camp and stashed her stuff. She was threading through brush, heading south toward the viaduct, when Billy tore away from her side. The Newfoundlander part of him knew better, but once in a blue moon his unknown fraction caught a glimpse of movement in the grass and took off.

"Billy!" She hated having to cry out like that, advertising her girl's voice to any creep within earshot, but whistling never worked when he really lost his head. "Billy!" she yelled again. "Come!"

It was incredible how fast he could move. Shading her eyes against the early sun, Lily saw what had set him off. The rabbit was giving him a run for his money, showing above the grass, plunging and showing again. It must have felt its pursuer gaining; why else leap like that, springing wildly to one side? Billy wasn't fooled. He swerved, snatching it mid-spasm from the air.

It was stupid of her to scream, stupider still to stumble through the dewy weeds while Billy shook his prey to death. She caught up in time to see him curl his lips in a slobbery, rabbit-squeezing smile. The cottontail's back was broken— she could tell by the way it draped over Billy's bottom jaw. He looked up at her in triumph. She brought her fist down on his back. "Bad dog! Bad dog!"

When he shrank from her, dropping his prize, she felt her legs give way. Down on her knees beside him, she suddenly understood: he was hungry; starving, even. She hadn't fed either of them since the morning before. The tears blinded her at first, but soon she saw through them to brownish fur and grass. She laid a hand on Billy's head. "It's okay, boy. Go ahead." Still he hesitated, so she pressed down with her palm, guiding his snout to the kill. "It's okay. Eat."

He breathed the rabbit in—at least that was how it looked. Sound was another matter. No mistaking the crunch of itty-bitty bones.

She felt someone approaching before she heard it, the ground trembling in her bones. Still on her knees, she turned to see a red-haired man pounding toward them across the field. Billy whirled and began barking, his mane standing on end. The man slowed to a stop.

"I heard a scream," he called.

"Quiet. Quiet, Billy." Lily stood up, wiping her eyes.

"Are you all right?"

"Yeah." They faced each other like a pair of surveyors, twenty metres between them.

"Okay if I come over there?"

"Why?"

"I won't hurt you."

She felt for her knife. "Okay."

He advanced slowly, stopping again when he was still several paces away. Didn't step in close to pat Billy. Didn't even pat his leg to bring Billy to him. "Was that you screaming?"

"Yeah. Sorry."

"Don't be. You're okay, though, right? Did somebody—"

"No. Nobody."

"Good." He nodded, and she saw that he too was shaken.

"It was a rabbit," she blurted. "My dog—he killed a rabbit."

"Oh." She saw his eyes searching the grass.

"He ate it." Again the tears threatened. "He was hungry."

"Ah." He nodded again, slowly this time, thoughtfully. "Well, that's good."

"Good?"

"Not that he was hungry. That he got himself something to eat. It's better than some dogs. People too, for that matter. Killing for fun."

Lily felt the small hairs stand at the back of her neck. So far he'd restricted his gaze to her face, but it was an unnerving gaze all the same. She glanced down at Billy, surprised to find his fur lying flat, his posture relaxed.

Turning her attention back to the man, she realized he was older than she'd thought, maybe as old as thirty. He was dressed young, jeans and All Stars, a green and black Mack— the first Mack she'd seen in the city that wasn't paired with a hard hat. Not bad-looking, but in a way where he might not know it. If he was vain about anything, it would be that hair.

"I'm Guy," he said. "Guy Howell."

She nodded. Why was he still there?

"You like rabbits?"

The question caught her off guard. *Not especially* was what she wanted to say, but it was hard to lie to somebody who wouldn't look away. "I guess."

"Me too." He looked around then, as though he was scanning the grass for long ears. Or else making certain there was nobody close at hand.

Lily clutched the folded form of the knife inside her pocket. The bear spray was tucked in the wide game pocket that ran along her lower back. Billy was pressed up against her. Besides, this particular man—this Guy Howell—had come running when he'd heard her scream.

"You like books?"

It was the last thing she expected him to say. It stunned her—thirty, forty seconds until she figured out what it meant. *Bait.* But how had he figured her out so fast? How had he picked up on the only thing she'd been missing, the little blue bookshelf in her room? She'd found her way to the Riverdale Library on her third day in town, but Billy wasn't allowed in, and they wouldn't let her take anything out. You had to have an address to get a library card. You had to show ID.

"Not especially." She managed to say it out loud this time.

"No? Huh. Somehow I figured you for a reader."

Billy was really listing now, settling his black weight against her. She clenched her hands. "I am."

He smiled. "Thought so." Reaching into his back jeans pocket, he produced a small pad and pen. Wrote for a moment, then tore off the page and held it out. He let her be the one to step forward and take it.

Billy rose up the way he always did when she made a move, but still he stood easy, seemingly unconcerned. The note showed an address and a roughed-in map. *Howell Auto Wreckers* underlined twice.

"That's my place. Gate's locked, but you just buzz." He returned the pad and pen to his pocket. "I've got plenty of books."

Lily kept her head down, holding the little map in both hands, studying it.

"You're welcome there any time, you and your dog."

It turned out to be true—about the books, but also about the welcome. Neither Guy nor Stephen has ever tried to mess with her. More than that, they've treated her like a friend.

Both of them are sitting at the table when she and Billy walk back in. In Guy's hand, an old book with an elephant on the cover, some guy in a turban grinning down from its back. The title tells her nothing. *Kipling: A Selection of His Stories and Poems.*

"What the fuck is this," she says, "storytime?"

"You guessed it," says Guy. "Pull up a chair."

The raccoon is old. He's lived through more snowed-in sleep and green return than most of his kind ever know. Little wonder—he's stronger than most, and wilier. He knows how to bide his time.

She will come. Any moment now, the human will emerge, unhook the containers from their moorings and drag them to the path. Until then, he wears the bushes like a mask.

Other raccoons have come this way recently—he can smell the fresh rub-mark of a yearling male. Cats, too. A pale tom, not paying sufficient attention, set a soft foot down behind him not long after he took up his post. It froze when he turned his eyes its way, backed out into the open before he even so much as hissed.

His vantage point is good, but he'd see even more if he sat up, leaning back on the stub where his tail used to be. It troubles him still, the absence more than the scarred-over lump itself. He'd known bites before—a male is called upon to fight for his share—but never so dirty or so deep. He saw the interloper off, only to find the damage had been done. The ringed glory of the old male's tail turned septic. He dragged it rotting behind him for a time, then chewed free of it one frost-hardened day. When he crawled out from under the brush pile that evening, the tail curled stinking where he'd lain.

It was a trick learning to balance without it; more than once he wobbled on a fence rail or slid from a branch, clumsy as a kit. The following winter, he felt the true measure of his loss. The fat he might have stored in its fluffy length, he made do without. Worse still, he had nothing to tuck around the chilled tip of his nose, the near-naked extremities of his feet. And yet he lived. Come mating time, he took on three young rivals and won. The female welcomed him, tail or no.

And now the world is new again. The kits he started that night are denned up with their mother somewhere—unless they and their mother are dead. Either way, the old male sits and waits.

The dragonfly doesn't spot him, despite its bulging eyes. Intent on the hunt, it hawks and dives, hovers and dives again. Soon it wavers close to the bushes, as though daring him to snatch it from mid-air—which he does, his hand shooting out like the sticky-tipped tongue of a frog. The catch struggles in his fist. He opens his fingers in increments, rolls the kicking creature between his palms. Pressing the ruin of it to his nose, he feels a lone, still-twitching leg play over his whiskers, thin as a whisker itself. He opens his jaws, welcoming the veined resilience of its wings. Its head is a bitter nut. Its body's bright armour guards the thinnest of meats—enough to rouse his hunger and make it cry.

He has a clear view of the containers now—two slim and two sturdy—huddled under their wooden den. The slender ones interest him most. For several nights in a row they've resisted him, thwarting his hands while they wafted a maddening scent. The treasure they guard is ripe: chicken bones and pig fat, softening apples and half-eaten ears of corn. Some smells he doesn't recognize yet finds appealing. Others speak of scraps he will cast aside.

The human has bound up her treasure tight. They use a kind of stretchy, spotted snake—only snakes are good to eat, and these are sour and impossible to chew. Hooks in place of their heads and tails, they hold the fragrant containers closed. Worse, they hold them fast to the slats of their enclosure, so he can't even tip them on their sides. He can wait, though. He can watch and he can learn.

And here comes the teacher now.

She leaves her door wide open—tempting, but almost always more trouble than it's worth. Besides, she's brought a fresh bag to add to the cache. Already he can make out strains of cheese and bread, something fruity, something with leaves. Eggs—probably only the shells, but each jagged little cup holds a glossy tongueful.

Setting the bag down, she bends to the nearest container. The old raccoon rises up on his hind legs; even this he has mastered without the tripod leg of his tail. Human hands are subtle, terribly strong. Even a slight female such as this makes short work of the hook-headed serpents, releasing the container from their grip. He works his fingers in an echo of hers, but there's a trick to it he's missing—something about the give in that patterned length.

Never mind. Tonight's the night when the lonely, feast-filled vessels stand unguarded, fastened with nothing but a clip any yearling could undo. He'll wait until the street is quiet before making his move. A flick of the fingers, a well-placed push and, one after another, they'll spill.

The raccoon kits are finally quiet, tucked into their carrier after the day's last ramble around the room. Stephen lies on his side on the bed above them. He hasn't bothered to undress; he's exhausted but knows he won't sleep yet. His mind is alive with the jungle, the story of a boy raised by wolves.

Guy read the entire first chapter, doing the voices and everything, even singing the songs. They heard how the child Mowgli evaded the lame tiger, Shere Khan, and came to live among the Seeonee pack; how he became the pet of Bagheera the panther and Baloo the bear. Stephen had never seen Lily sit so still for so long.

He rolls onto his back, a papery crackle reminding him of the folded flyer in the seat pocket of his jeans. Sitting up, he digs for the yellow sheet and opens it. Half a minute more and curiosity trumps fatigue.

Stephen rises, passes through to the office and flattens the flyer alongside the keyboard. A wiggle of the mouse wakes the screen. He opens the browser and types in the URL.

**Coyote Cop's Blog**

**Monday, May 26, 2008**

Well Toronto and whoever else this is my first blog ever so welcome. Why start now? Because this city is in trouble. I have one word for you. Coyotes. And if you think I'm joking you better think again.

Maybe you know about the damage they do on farms.
Ask any farmer and he will be glad to tell you how
many lambs or calves or chickens he has lost to
coyotes this year. Maybe you have even heard about
cats going missing in the suburbs or even some of
the smaller dogs. Thats right. Coyotes have come to
town and not only in L.A. or Vancouver where you will
know if you watch the news they are running bold as
anything down the open roads and biting the legs of
joggers and stalking into peoples backyards to
snatch not just the pets but the children too. And
don't forget those western coyotes are smaller than
the ones we have here. In the old days the eastern
coyote used to be called a brush wolf so that should
give you an idea of how big they get.

And we're not just talking about the suburbs anymore.
Ever been to the Don Valley? I mean the lower Don.
I mean practically downtown. Ever felt like you were
being watched while you walked along the path down
there? Well believe me you were. Maybe your thinking
but isn't the whole idea of cities that we don't live
out in the wilderness with the animals anymore?
Sure. Only cities aren't airtight. You can't screw
down the lid on Toronto the way you do on a mason
jar. They get in. And its our job to get them out.

Maybe you know about what happened with wolves down
in the States. They wiped them out. Why not the
coyotes? Don't think they didn't try. So how come in

L.A. of all places coyotes are multiplying like rats? Because thats the thing about vermin. They are damn hard to get rid of. But damn hard doesn't mean you don't even try. Some things are worth fighting for and I don't know about you but when the city I have chosen to call home is getting overrun by what might as well be rats as big as dogs I figure its time to do something. And one more thing. I'm going by Coyote Cop for now but you can bet one day my real name will be known. In the meantime if any of you are wondering it starts with D.

*POSTED BY Coyote Cop at 8:10 PM*

# 2

# Ring of Dark Timber

There was a time when Letty Jones still read a portion of the books she dragged home. Edal loved to watch her mother run a finger down a rank of spines until a particular title caught her eye. Letty would tilt her head and grow still, like a bird listening for creatures inside the bark of a tree. If the title exerted sufficient force, she would hook her finger over the crest of its spine and work it free.

Often she read where she stood, minutes, half an hour even, before she slapped the book closed and wedged it back into place. Occasionally, though, the story held sway, and she walked slowly, head bent over its pages, to the nearest seat.

Even more occasionally, she felt moved to read aloud. Only a certain kind of story, and only if Edal kept very, very still. If distracted by a question—even a finger pointing to the page—her mother might well set the book aside and wander off. Edal practised sitting beside her like a stone.

*Ring of Bright Water* may be the only book Letty ever read to her in full. In any case, it's the one Edal envisions—blue spine, cover photo of a boy and his otter on a beach—when she calls up her mother in that rare, forgiving light.

Letty's face was prettiest in profile. Her hair slipped forward, every strand of it still dark, still young. She would tuck the hank behind her ear six, seven times before giving up and letting it hang. Edal longed to sweep it back with her fingers, maybe even hold it in place—her hand a pale, decorative comb—but a stone would never do such a thing.

The story began with a man named Gavin sitting in his *kitchen-living room* and an otter sleeping like a baby among the sofa cushions nearby. They were in a house called Camusfeàrna, in a place Edal had never heard of called the Highlands. If it hadn't been for the cover—a photograph and not a drawing—she might have thought the whole thing was made up.

Her mother explained nothing, and she left nothing out. Countless words slipped Edal's grasp and swam away, but they swam beautifully, some darting, others wagging long and languid lines. *Pinnacles* and *glacial corries. Filigree tracery* and *tide-wrack rubbish-heap. Clairvoyance* and *manna* and *quarry. Purloined.*

Letty didn't spare her the part where the hooded crows pecked the eyes out of a living lamb, nor did she skip the fatal rhubarb-leaf poisoning of the nanny goats. She read straight through the pneumonia that almost killed Jonnie the dog, and on to the cancer that got him in the end. Jonnie, whose *fleecy flank* Gavin had so often used as a pillow when the two of them went out together in the boat.

Letty didn't cry when such things happened, but when Jonnie lay down under the vet's needle, she turned from the page to look her daughter in the eye. "Everything dies, Edal. Everything and everyone."

It wasn't news to Edal. She may have been only seven, but she'd already lost Nana and Grandpa Adam and, before them, the father she'd never met. Letty wouldn't talk about the boy who'd gotten her in trouble, so Edal's knowledge of him was patchy, stitched together from scraps her grandparents had let slip. He wasn't a bad boy, just a little wild. He'd seen sense after a talk or two, agreed to make things legal and grow up fast. Too bad he didn't do a little of that growing up before deciding to take his father's Ski-Doo out on the lake. The ice was nowhere near ready to bear that kind of weight.

So, no, Edal didn't need reminding about death. All the same, she couldn't help crying a little, but she did so silently, in order that she might not miss what came next. Jonnie's end brought the end of a chapter. Gavin couldn't imagine owning another dog—that corner of his heart had sealed over. He could, however, imagine owning something else.

He found the first otter in another place with a made-up-sounding name: the Tigris marshes of Iraq. Edal fell in love with Chahala just as Gavin did—and who could blame them, when she had *more charm per cubic inch of her tiny body* than any other infant. Where a kitten would've mewed, Chahala chittered—a word Edal understood instantly via its sound. Gavin made a daughter of Chahala. He nursed her from a bottle, carried her inside his shirt, taught her to know her own name. When she was old enough, he fed her the flesh of two dead sparrows—sad, because Edal knew sparrows, could picture them puffed and twittering among the sunlit branches of the back hedge; but also exciting, because it meant Chahala was growing like any baby, trading milk for solid food.

Then came the food that killed her. Digitalis was another deadly plant, and men in the Tigris marshes used it to poison fish—which, in turn, became poisonous themselves. Chahala lay on her back among the water flowers, looking as though she were sleeping. Her death ended another chapter, and when Edal lay in her small bed later that night, she felt her own hands floating webbed and lifeless by her sides.

The second otter was a boy, Mij, and unlike Chahala, he lived. He survived a gruelling trip by plane and car back to Gavin's home, though he fought the box that held him until his face and paws were wet with blood. Mij chittered too, but he also had other ways of making himself understood. A simple whistle-chirp. A harshly whispered *Ha!* or *Hah?* upon entering an empty room. He burbled to greet a bathtub full of water, hummed a serious warning and wailed to herald a coming bite.

He was clever in other ways too. He could untie knots and turn on faucets, carry a marble or a flower or a shotgun cartridge for miles. He played like a child in the bathtub, and swam in the *burn*, which was another word for a creek— though the burn in the book ran brighter and deeper than the one that crossed Edal's own back woods. Mij learned to catch his own food there, and soon he moved on to swim in the pounding sea. Once, he got trapped in the shadowy ravine above the waterfall. Once, he went missing for so long, Gavin imagined him eaten by a killer whale. All this and more Mij survived. Then, after a year in Gavin's company, he went wandering and met a man called Big Angus working on the road. By then he knew no fear of humans. He didn't even flinch when Big Angus lifted his deadly pickaxe and brought it down.

Edal feared that would be the end of animal companions for Gavin, a loss too great to chance repeating. She never dreamt another could take Mij's place.

It was a charmed meeting. Gavin—a man with an otter-shaped hole in his life—crossed paths with the MacDonalds, a couple who were most anxious to find a home for their unusual pet. "'Everyone admires her,'" Letty read in the voice of Dr. MacDonald, "'but when they come to the point of actually owning her they all shy off . . . Poor Edal—'"

Edal squeaked. She couldn't help it. Letty met her gaze, her brown eyes mild, unblinking. Then she nodded, and Edal knew she'd heard her mother right.

Edal was a girl otter, and she was different from Mij in other ways too. She shared some of his language; other sounds were her own. The hum Mij had threatened with, she used to ask for the food in a human hand. By then Gavin had a helper, a boy named Jimmy Watt. Edal loved Jimmy fiercely, scolded him often and followed him when it suited her mood.

She learned to fish for eels in the burn as Mij had, and to swim in the sea, though at times the depths sent her panick-ing to shore. Her hands had no webbing, so she was capable of even greater feats: picking pockets, peeling boiled eggs. The boy on the cover could only be Jimmy, so the otter in that picture had to be her. The description fit. Where Mij had been a dark, luxurious brown all over, Edal was silver-headed, with a snowy throat and chest. Her skin was several sizes larger than she was, and she turned inside it as Edal the girl might turn in a sleeping bag, or in Nana's old rabbit-fur wrap.

The book ended happily enough, but it felt unfinished somehow. Edal watched the spot where her mother pushed it into its row, and took it back down the first chance she got. The photographs came as a shock. Letty must have pinched the slick pages between finger and thumb and turned them as one, eager to learn what happened next. Edal turned them singly, holding her breath.

Camusfeàrna was about the same size as the house Letty and Edal shared, but instead of crouching amid trees at the end of a gravel driveway, it sat in the open on a grassy coastal field. Edal had thought she and her mother lived far from their neighbours, but Gavin had only the land and the sea.

Gavin wasn't a real father, but he had a fatherly look about him—worried while he was awake, a little less so while he slept. In one photograph he wore a skirt, but Edal thought she knew something about that being all right for Scottish men. In another, the boy Jimmy stood naked at the top of the waterfall. He looked to be shouting or laughing, but the picture was taken from too far away to be sure. Edal looked long and hard at the happy, blurred figure, wondering what it would be like to swim without her blue suit between her and the water, to stand in her skin like a tree in its beautiful bark.

There was Mij—chewing his towel, tossing an apple, kissing a woman on the lips—and there was Edal. Her throat really was white as snow. She lay across Gavin's lap as he slept; she lolled in the rowboat, deciding whether to slip into the sea. The photographs Edal the girl went back to again and again, though—the best ones in the book—showed Edal the otter in Jimmy's arms.

In the first, he cradled her like a baby, his strong right hand cupping her supple back. The second was more grown-up. She lay beside him on a hillside, her tail draped over his thigh, her forepaw folded in his loving grip. She looked into the camera for the baby shot, but her gaze was soft and somehow private in the one where they lay together on the flowering hill. Behind them lay the view—black cattle grazing, a crust of rocky shore—but Jimmy was looking at Edal. He couldn't tear his eyes away.

# 3

# The Chronicles of Darius

Darius had never been kept in at recess before. Mrs. Gamble's eyes looked weak and watery behind her glasses, but it turned out she noticed things anyhow. Things like the way Darius couldn't stop yawning and laying his head down on his desk. The way, when he wasn't sleeping, he was scratching himself, hard.

"Darius, honey, when is your bedtime?"

"Eight o'clock." Scratch.

"And do you fall asleep right away?"

"Sometimes." Scratch, scratch. He had his red and blue sweatshirt on. It was hard to get through to his arms. "But then . . ."

"Then what, Darius?"

"I get woken up."

Her eyes closed, a blink longer than most. "Who wakes you up, honey?"

Darius wasn't sure he should say any more. He and Faye had never even spoken about it between them. He looked down at Mrs. Gamble's shoes. "The biters."

"The biters?"

He nodded and scratched his arm.

Mrs. Gamble breathed out a long breath. "Darius, push up your sleeves."

They walked together down the long, deserted hallway to the school library, Mrs. Gamble leading him by the hand. The book had a green and white striped caterpillar on the cover. Mrs. Gamble let him carry it to a nearby table even though it was heavy, big enough to show every bug that ever was.

"These ones?" she asked, after finding the page she wanted. "They're small, almost like specks. You see them hopping."

Darius shook his head.

She turned the pages, glassy wings and antennae flashing past. "These? About this big?" She pointed to the nail on his pinky finger.

Darius peered into the book, and there they were—the red-brown, shiny-backed biters that found him no matter where he lay down. They were worst on the couch that was his bed, but the carpet wasn't safe either. He knew not to bother seeking refuge in Faye's bed; she liked sleeping alone, and, anyway, they'd found her too. He'd seen the marks on her thin white skin. It might have been why she spent so much time in the bathtub, lying motionless until the water cooled, then digging the stopper out with her toe and running the water up to her chin again.

"Does your mother know about this?" Mrs. Gamble asked.

Darius said nothing.

"Darius, what does your mother say?"

———

Faye wasn't mad at him for telling—at least, she never said she was. As usual, she said very little at all. Even when the lady in the light brown raincoat came, his mother mostly listened, nodding her head slowly, as though she could scarcely manage its weight. The raincoat lady was their first-ever visitor, but she wasn't their last. The men in dark blue jackets and matching pants came next. Darius and Faye weren't allowed to stay in the apartment while the men were there. The raincoat lady was late coming to pick them up, so they crossed the street—Darius reaching for his mother's hand— and sat together on the curb, watching as Darius's couch and Faye's grown-up mattress were lowered from the apartment window on ropes. They landed in a black Dumpster the men had wheeled into place.

"Where will we sleep now?" Darius asked, but Faye didn't hear him over the passing cars.

The answer was somewhere called The Miskes.

"They're very nice people," the raincoat lady said, twisting to smile at him over her shoulder when they came to a red light. "You'll like them."

Darius held his tongue. It seemed wrong to speak up while Faye was strapped into the front passenger seat, keeping her thoughts to herself.

Mr. and Mrs. Miske turned out to be older than Faye, but they were stronger-looking too. Muscles moved under the skin of his arms; smooth, solid fat under hers. The first room they showed Darius and Faye was the bathroom. The toilet, tub and sink were pink as cupcakes, the towels a frosty green.

"You can put your clothes in this bag," Mrs. Miske said,

smiling. "Just go ahead and put everything in there and hand it out to me. Then you can have a nice hot shower, the pair of you. There's a fresh bar of soap in there, and a couple of wash-cloths. Shampoo, the works."

Darius had never taken a shower, at least not one he could remember. At first it was too hot, and frightening in its force, but once Faye adjusted the taps, he warmed to the feel of the water-fingers combing his hair. Faye stood in the tub with him, even soaped up a washcloth for him to use. He'd seen her naked before, of course, but always lying down in the rust-stained tub. Standing up, she looked even less like a mother than usual. He scrubbed hard behind his ears while he counted the ribs in her side.

When he was as clean as he could get, she handed him one of the peppermint towels and bent to run herself a bath. He wrapped himself up and perched on the toilet, watching the water rise up about her ankles, her shins. When she lowered herself into the steam, he rested his head against the lip of the sink.

"Hello?" Mrs. Miske's voice through the door roused him. "You two all right in there?"

Supper was what Darius would've hoped for if it had occurred to him to hope. Tomato-rice soup and hot dogs. They had everything—fluffy buns, ketchup and mustard, as much as he liked.

Mr. Miske stood at the open fridge and asked what everyone wanted to drink. "Milk? Grape juice?"

"Oh, go on, George," Mrs. Miske said. "I think tonight's special enough for pop."

"Right you are, Missus." He held out two bottles. "Coke or cream soda?"

The jewel-red liquid called to Darius, and somehow Mr. Miske knew. He waggled the bottle. "Good call." Then, because there was another guest at the table, he added, "Faye?"

Darius looked at his mother then, sitting with her hair draped wetly down her back. Alongside Mrs. Miske, she looked like someone who was barely breathing, someone who could be mistaken for a ghost. He looked back to the man of the house, waiting patiently in the drift of refrigerator light. Nobody to compare him to at all.

"Faye?" Mr. Miske said again. "Something to drink?"

"Oh." She started as though shaken from a dream. "Water." Then, after a moment, "Please."

"Water." He closed the fridge door. "I believe that can be arranged."

# 4

# The City Book

Darius takes the stairs up out of the valley at a sad-sack pace. He's been up all night, with nothing to show for his trouble but grazed forearms and grass stains on his jeans. They're just unlocking the doors at Castle Frank Station when he arrives; he's the first to shove his token in the slot and descend. He waits at the edge of the platform. After a moment a grubby mouse shows itself, scavenging between the tracks.

It bolts for unknown quarters when the train pulls in. Darius steps aboard and lingers in the doorway's hollow. Turning his back to the handful of other passengers, he catches himself in the glass. His reflection startles him: a twelve-year-old's face on a tall, nineteen-year-old frame—still only one shave a week and that mess of brown baby curls. It's enough to make a man lose track. Make him think he's back in the mountains where that boy's face used to belong.

He braces himself as the train begins to move.

He loves crossing the Don Valley. It's been the highlight of every subway ride since he arrived in the city five months ago—that moment when the train leaves its dank tunnel for the viaduct's airy cage. He always makes it his business to stand in a doorway, even when it means shouldering someone out of the way. North-facing on the way downtown, south-facing on the way home—always the side with fewer girders, the clearest view down.

It made him giddy in those early days, feeling the long ravine open up beneath him. Much as he'd told himself he was done with backwoods life, there was something about that remnant of river stretched in its scrubby bed that caused the blood to thrill in his veins. When it was light out, the trees showed him their crowns, still black and bare; winter worked like an X-ray, the space between branches revealing riverbank and brush, trash-strewn campsites, snow and broken grass. When it was dark, the sunken forest grew. The river glinted. The roads—however jammed, however sparkling—were secondary. Some nights, they almost seemed to disappear.

Now, as the train makes that familiar leap, Darius feels the drop of the valley distantly. The trees have filled in, concealing the ragged camps. A girl and her dog are walking along the path below. He looks down on the pink shock of her hair, the wide black sway of the animal's back. Pressing his forehead to the glass, he twists to keep them in view until the train burrows underground again.

As they pull into Broadview Station, he backs away from the door and sits, closing his eyes. Why this sudden stir of feeling, as though he's caught sight of someone he knows? The girl is a stranger to him, and he's seen scores of dogs passing below the train—dark or pale or one of a dozen middling shades. He's watched them charge into the bushes or keep like furry trams to the path. The owners are never far.

Except once, when there was no owner at all.

It must be two months ago now—the trees showing an early green haze of leaves—when he looked down from his doorway and spotted a canine with no true colour of its own. Its coat was made of the same clean, shifting light as the sky. There was something different about the way it moved too— none of the nose-down, empty-headed zigzag dogs tend to favour when forsaking a human path. This creature had knowledge of the field it was crossing. It advanced at a steady pace, its stride an easy median between a lope and a stroll.

It wasn't Darius's first. Having grown up in the Rockies, on the verge of a national park, he'd come across their scat more times than he could count, glimpsed flashes of pale fur between boughs. He'd even watched that mated pair on the gravel flat where the Bow River took one of a thousand turns. Grandmother had been the one to spot them that afternoon, pointing and holding her finger to her lips. The animals caught wind of them soon after. Stood stiff-legged, returning their stare.

Just let one of them try looking at him like that now.

He's first off his car at Main Street Station, up and out into the breaking day. Half a block and he's back under artificial light—the grey-blue lobby of his building, the panelled, vaguely pissy elevator to the twelfth floor out of twenty-six. The door to 1208 sticks like always; like always, he persuades it with the heel of his boot. No point opening the blinds, he'll just have to close them again when he hits the sack. He crosses to the table. One chair for his backside, the other to hold up his feet. He ought to get himself an armchair, some middle ground between sitting up straight with rails at your back and lying with nothing but two inches of foam between you and the wall-to-wall.

It takes a minute for the PC to come to life, several seconds more to bring up the blog. Six comments—more than he expected, given that somebody's already torn all his flyers down. Only two of them talk any kind of sense: scum-hunter and #1lacrossemom. The others are weak-minded, the worst kind of sheep. One bleats loudest of them all.

*soldierboy wrote . . .*

Have you really seen coyotes in the Don Valley? Because I haven't, and I'm down there just about every day. Either way, I have a hard time seeing what the problem is. You say coyotes are vermin and I guess you're right, because if you think about it vermin is just a word for creatures that do well where we do. Mice get into grain silos or stocked-up cupboards. Cockroaches love all the warm houses we build. Some people might include raccoons on the list, and don't forget pigeons and gulls. Of course there's the example you already thought of, rats. And you're right there too—rats and coyotes aren't really all that different. Both are smart and resourceful, both thrive by adapting, both are warm-blooded and bear live, helpless young. Can you think of anything else like that? Or anyone?

POSTED AT 10:37 PM, May 26, 2008

Darius feels a sudden chill in his spine, right where he

harbours the insidious beginnings of a stoop. How can words do that, leave you literally, physically cold? He's tired, is all. He rubs his hands to get the blood into them, extends both index fingers and begins to type.

**Coyote Cop's Blog**

**Tuesday, May 27, 2008**

Thanks to all of you who wrote comments. Well most of you. But while we are on the subject lets get something straight. This is not some kind of conversation. This is a public service. Got that soldier-boy? And by the way are you sure thats such a good name for a bleeding heart like yourself?

So your down in the valley every day. I wonder if you know anything about some flyers that have gone missing. Well I'd like to see you try and tear down this blog.

In answer to your question hell yes I have seen coyotes and plenty of them. They are down in the Don Valley and in just about every other park around town digging their dens and having their poor little helpless babies. If you want to sit around thinking about how much you have in common with them and your other rat and roach buddies be my guest. Eat all the garbage you like. Maybe even find yourself a carcass you can scavenge off. I for one know the difference between a man and a beast.

*POSTED BY Coyote Cop at 6:47 AM*

*Bleeding heart.* There's probably no point responding. *Boundaries, Stephen,* Mica would say. *It's his stuff, not yours.* Which was always a bit of a mindfuck when you lined it up alongside the idea of oneness with all beings. In any case, he ought to be giving the kits their morning feed, then checking in with Guy to see what needs doing around the yard.

soldierboy wrote . . .
Which part of my name do you think doesn't fit, the
soldier or the boy? Because you can take it from me,
soldiers bleed plenty, from their hearts and every-
where else. And as for boys, not all of us spent our
time blowing up frogs and trying to stone birds out
of their trees.

Seriously, though, I'm not trying to say we're exactly
the same as coyotes, only that we're not so different.

You said I should find some garbage to eat. Ever hear
of junk food? And that's not even getting started on
all the people in the world who crawl over landfill
every day in search of a meal. As for scavenging,
when was the last time the meat you ate was meat you
killed? And anyway, where would we be without the
vultures and the carrion beetles and, yes, the
coyotes? Up to our necks in rot.

Look, I'm not trying to be an asshole. I'm just
trying to make a point. I figure if you get that a
coyote's not so different from you or me, you might
also get that it has a right to be here. To live out
its life in the Don Valley or anywhere else.

*POSTED AT 7:21 AM, May 27, 2008*

There were fewer birds this morning: a balanced half-dozen,
three buried, three tossed up to the lightening sky. Just like
Guy promised, the spring migration is easing off. They'll be
safe now until fall—from high-rises, anyway. Nothing Lily
can do about pesticides and picture windows, airplanes and
slingshots and guns.

After all his good work, Billy's earned himself a swim. Lily
watches him from the bank. He's up to his belly in the river,
splashing like a fat kid, so happy he could be stoned. Still, it's
Billy who spots the woman first. He lifts his wet muzzle
sharply, sees that the stranger isn't male and relaxes back into
the flow. Lily hesitates for a moment before stepping out from
between the skinny trees.

"What a beauty." The first thing she hears the woman say.
Black shorts and a blood-red T-shirt, dark ponytail down her
back. "Newfie cross?"

Lily nods, the two of them standing side by side on the
bank, watching Billy flop over in the muddy shallows and roll.

"I'm Kate," the woman adds.

"Lily." It's out before she can bite it back.

"Too bad it's not deeper for him," Kate says after a moment. "Looks like he'd love a proper swim."

"Yeah."

Lily's sweating. Not the warm sheen of exertion Kate shows—every pore open and clean—but a secret, slippery chill, confined to the armpits and palms. It gets worse when she steals a glance at Kate's face. She forces herself to look back at Billy. "You like dogs?"

"Love them."

Lily looks around. "You don't have one?"

"No, I inherited a couple of cranky old cats." Kate interlaces her fingers, stretching her arms out in front of her before swinging them up over her head. "I work with dogs, though."

"Yeah? Doing what?"

"Vet tech. Veterinary technician." She releases her grip, letting her arms fall. "We do something like physiotherapy where I work."

"Physiotherapy."

"Uh-huh."

"For dogs."

"That's right."

Lily's not sure what to say to that. Luckily, Billy's sociable side gets the better of him then, and he leaves the water of his own accord. As he lumbers up the muddy bank toward them, Kate shows none of the usual caginess a wet dog inspires. When he shakes, soaking them both, she laughs out loud. Billy brightens at the sound.

"You giving me a shower, boy?" Kate crouches down to his level, setting his hind end wagging. "You think I need a shower?"

Lily stands at a little distance, blinking to clear away the image that's slipped into her head. It's not X-rated or anything, just the ponytail untied, the dark hair loose beneath the spray. She focuses on the scene before her: Kate rumpling Billy's ears.

"He likes you."

"I like him." Kate stands up, begins bouncing on the spot. Keeping her blood moving. Soon she'll be gone.

"My friend has a hawk." Lily had no idea she was going to say anything, let alone that. Some sly, fast-acting part of herself pushing into the driver's seat, grabbing the wheel.

"A hawk?" It's a funny look, a blend of curiosity and concern.

"It's not a pet or anything." She hears herself talking quickly, as though her ration of air is running out. "He's just looking after it until it can fly."

"Oh." Kate smiles again.

"You want to see it sometime? I could take you."

"Sure."

It's the response Lily's hoping for, yet it looses a wave of rich discomfort in her gut. For a second she thinks she might actually hurl. The wild, driving part of her doesn't care. "Any day's good. Around suppertime—that's when I'm usually there." She fumbles in her breast pocket and produces Guy's scribbled map. No reason to keep it when she knows the way by heart.

Stephen lies on his bedroom floor, hiked up on one elbow so he can watch the kits sleep.

It's hard to credit how much they've grown since the day he carried them home. Their eyes were open then, but only just—that eerie, unfocused stare. Now they track his every move, gaze up at him like lovers after every feed. Their guard hairs are coming in, making them more alike, but he still thinks of them by the variation in their undercoats: the grey twins, the tan big brother, the chocolate brown runt.

He should leave them be, push the carrier back into the peaceful shadow beneath the bed—and he will. Any minute now he will.

They'd be dead if it wasn't for him.

*Don't.*

It's okay, he saved them, didn't he? They're safe. Unlike their mother. Their mother he let die.

He was on his way home from returning a half-blind bulldog to its cage when he spotted the raccoon descending a tree. Unconcerned with gravity, the animal clambered head-first down the rutted trunk to re-establish itself on the ground. Stephen froze to let it pass—and therein lies his guilt. If he'd kept on like a normal human being, claiming the right of way, the raccoon would have crouched among the tree roots, waiting. And while it did so, the minivan would have passed.

As it was, it chittered softly, crossed the dark patch of lawn to the pale strip of sidewalk and trundled out into the street. The minivan backed out fast. Stephen's voice fell back down his throat, useless; the raccoon was already rolling, already resting against the curb. He squinted to get the plate number. What for? *Officer, I want to report a hit and run.*

Ten steps took him to the body. There was no blood—at least none he could see—yet there was little doubt. He touched its back gently with the tip of his boot, then crouched and touched its belly with his hand. His index finger found the nipple, dark and swollen, damp. *God, oh God.* He hadn't run like that since Pashmul; no IEDs or skinny gunmen to worry about now, just his own weak and whining heart.

Guy was standing at the stove when he got there, pork chops hissing in the heavy pan. He flipped one after another, waiting for Stephen to catch his breath. "Did you see which tree it was?" he asked, once the story was out.

Stephen nodded.

"I'll get the ladder." He turned off the heat and covered the pan. "You grab us some coveralls."

"What? Why?"

"Nobody hassles a man in coveralls. Uncle Ernie's words to the wise."

It turned out to be true. A young woman slowed her stroller when they lifted the body into the bin, but she asked no questions, saying only, "Poor thing." The old guy sitting on the porch opposite watched mildly as they leaned the ladder up against the tree. Stephen had assumed he'd be the one to hold the legs steady, but Guy surprised him by stepping aside.

"You know what you're looking for?"

"Me?"

"Yes, you."

"Not really." Stephen stared up into the branches. "A hole?"

"You got it. Look for a hole."

He was almost out of rungs when he found it—a shadowy depression in the cleft of a sizable limb. He unzipped the coveralls to just below his breastbone, braced himself and reached in. He'd never felt anything so private. The kits were like warm, lightly furred organs in the torso of the tree. They scratched the hand he closed around them; it came out smudged with his blood.

Backing down, he curved an arm up under the shape they made inside his coveralls and held them trembling in its crook.

It was daunting, taking on those four small lives. Guy offered advice and more: the heating pad tucked under one end of their carrier-den; the bed of paper towels instead of the flannel pyjama top Stephen had in mind. *The lint can plug up their noses when they're little like that.* Rooting around in a kitchen cupboard, Guy produced two doll-sized baby bottles and a jar marked *KMR*. It turned out to be powdered kitten milk replacer left over from various four-footed orphans he and his aunt had tended over the years. Many of which hadn't made it, he told Stephen gently. More than half. Stephen nodded, but inside he said firmly, *No.* Not half, not even a quarter. Not one of them would die in his care.

He got them fed, got them settled in their new home. Then went round back to where Guy was digging their mother's grave. It wasn't the first burial Stephen had witnessed in the long-lost garden. He knew the words and spoke them quietly with his friend.

He should really introduce the kits to the backyard too— start getting them used to the great outdoors. It pains him, though, the idea of setting their carrier down in the grass and opening the door. What if he can't keep track of them all? The big tan has already shown himself to be an avid climber, and he's perfecting a stumbly run. What's worse, the hummocky back garden will only be the beginning. In another month or so Stephen will have to carry them out into the wide, wide world—or at least the scruffy strip of it that borders the Don. They may well find their way up to the fish ponds and garbage of the city, but he wants to make sure they get a grounding in the basics. He's the only mother they've got; he owes them a proper start.

He's been reading up on the subject on sites like wildbabies.ca and littleorphananimal.com. It turns out instinct is only part of the picture. Mammals learn by aping their elders. Like a baby with his first blunt spoon, the kits will need to be shown.

It'll be hot by then, the valley brimming with green. One early morning, Stephen will strap the carrier to the old bike's basket and cover it with a towel. He'll ride as slowly, as gently as he can, carry the bike down the stairs on his shoulder to spare them the frightening tilt. He has a spot in mind, well screened from the path, the water wide and reedy, a gradual bank. To begin with, he'll let them watch him through the bars. Crouch down and lower his net into the sluggish flow. If the river brings him a fish, he'll flip it onto the bank, whack it on a rock until it shows a glassy eye. If he can manage to scoop up a crayfish, he'll hold it by the tail while beating it senseless, making a show of keeping clear of the claws. Once he has the kits' attention, he'll let them out to line up alongside him on the bank. He'll wet his hands; they'll wet their paws. Together, they'll feel for life among the pebbles, clutching at whatever moves.

Sooner or later—on the third trip out, maybe the fourth—the kits will begin to move off on their own. One after another, they'll paddle out into the shallows, causing his heart to shrink. The big tan will be the first to scramble carelessly up a tree, but the others will watch and follow suit. Then one day, when they're sufficiently fat and feisty, Stephen will leave the carrier lying open under some brush, pick up the bicycle and ride away. One or more of them may watch him go, but he mustn't hope for that. Ideally, they won't give him a second look.

He'll return with supplemental rations for a couple of weeks—less food every day, placed in the carrier at first, then farther and farther afield. He might catch sight of one of them, though the chances of that happening are slim. If he's lucky, he'll spot a track in the muddy bank—hind paw like the foot of a long-toed infant, forepaw like the infant's clutching hand. Tapered release, it's called, at least according to littleorphananimal.com—the tried-and-true method of the wildlife rehabilitation set. *Tapered.* Which means something that gets thinner and thinner until it's gone.

The air inside the flight cage is special—Guy felt it the first time he set foot in there, a faint, crackling charge. If anything, it's growing stronger over time, as though the red-tail has been electrifying the space with its repeated passage.

Stepping all the way inside, he pulls the cage door closed behind him. No plate of poached bodies this morning, only a grey plastic box—the first live mousetrap to get lucky. "Hey, Red," he says softly, "guess what I brought."

The hawk watches him from its branch.

Guy moves closer, some five or six steps. Crouching down,

he sets the box on the ground. His fingers find the catch. "Sorry," he whispers, lifting its little door.

It happens in the blink of an eye—the mouse shooting from the trap like a tiny greyhound to run a mad scribble beneath the red-tail's falling form. In a flash of rodent genius, it cuts left, scrambling for the border of the cage. Guy stumbles back, meeting the mesh door with his shoulders as the hawk angles its caped wings to brake. Feet outstretched, it strikes hard, meeting the mouseless ground.

The hawk's scream could be a child's; it cuts Guy to the heart as though he were the father. He takes a step toward the humped and staggering bird, then stops himself with a jerk. Not the father. The red-tail's eye reminds him. This creature is wild. Wild and, very possibly, hurt.

"Okay." He eases back toward the door. "I'm going."

The hawk works its wings, rising in a convulsive rush. Guy knows a wash of blind panic, his animal body taking control, shielding eyes with arms, soft organs with the bones of the back. He drops to the ground, contracting. It's like being beaten with heavy silk. The talons tear through his Mack and T-shirt, just grazing the flesh beneath. The pain is nothing; it's fear that makes him yell out in that echoing, feathered cave.

Suddenly the bird no longer beats against him. It's a thing of sound now, the discreet, rhythmic squeaking of flight. Guy cracks an eyelid, peeking out from beneath his elbow as the hawk makes contact with the oak. It's an awkward landing, reminiscent of the first few times he exercised the clumsy, undernourished bird. The red-tail takes a moment to compose itself on its branch. Guy doesn't notice until the bird comes to stillness—it's standing on one leg, holding a foot against its belly, the way a child might cradle an injured hand.

Panhandling isn't Lily's favourite thing. It pays okay—especially when she and Billy make the trek up to Danforth Avenue—but it also gives any passing asshole an excuse to squat down beside her and talk.

Today they've been sticking to the less lucrative patch around Broadview and Gerrard. She's heard there's a bigger Chinatown somewhere on the far side of the city, but in the two months since they landed in Toronto, she's never been west of the centre of town.

It's weird how life steers you. That first bewildering afternoon in the city, she said goodbye to the last of four hitched rides, hiked the duffle bag onto her back and called Billy to a close heel. Together they let the crowd carry them down Yonge Street to the outside corner of a mall. Standing with her back to the glass, she steadied herself between duffle bag and dog. After a minute she drew a smoke from her pack, lit it and tried to think.

She saw them coming from a good way off; drab and shambling, they stood out from the downtown colour like a pair of leaf piles come to life. The guy was holding hands with his grubby girl—no guarantee that he was all right, but it made him a slightly better bet. Also, they had a dog.

Lily could spare the smokes it would take to meet them; the pack in her pocket was only five down, and she had half a carton in her bag. She'd stocked up before heading out to stand on the shoulder of the highway in the early morning dark. It wasn't stealing when you only took what you needed— what you were owed. The smokes, the mummy bag, the camo tent, a few other small necessities. She left the real treasures alone: the wall of graphite rods in the garage; the Excalibur crossbow patterned like tree bark; the Browning A-Bolt, pitch-black save for the trigger, a tempting sliver of gold.

She waited until the young couple and their skin-and-bones dog were close before drawing the pack from her pocket like a lure. Billy stiffened at the other dog's approach.

"Be nice," Lily murmured.

"Hey," said the girl.

"Hey."

"Spare a smoke?"

Jen was the girl's name, the boyfriend was Darryl. They gave her directions to a nearby shelter. She couldn't stay there with a dog, but she could get a coffee and something to eat. Lily might have hung out with them longer if it hadn't been for the smell. It wasn't the fact that they were dirty—she wasn't so big on bathing herself. It was the sugary, deathbed scent Jen and Darryl shared. She didn't know exactly what it meant—they were her first junkies—but she was sure they were letting themselves and their skinny dog die.

An hour spent hanging around the shelter doors with the gathering supper crowd told her the regulars all had bugs; the only creature she'd seen scratch itself that hard was a squirrel that had lost half its fur. Every new arrival wanted to touch Billy—she made a note to brush him extra well once they were alone. Most were savvy enough to extend a closed hand for sniffing first, though one solvent-stinking old guy went straight for a head pat and raised a warning snarl. Lily gave a sit-stay order when they opened the dining hall door, hoped nobody would be fucked up enough to get themselves bitten before she came back.

She filed along with the others, filling up her tray. Took a corner seat at a corner table, ate her beans and drank her burnt coffee and stood to go. Not before she learned something, though. Eyes down, ears open. There was a ravine not too far from there where people sometimes camped. It had a highway running through it, but it had a river and a forest too.

The Don Valley has turned out to be a dream come true—all that good cover, and you can climb up into the city whenever you like. Walk the streets and watch the people, stare through shop windows at treasures you can't possibly buy—and the occasional one you can't resist.

It's the red book that initially catches Lily's eye, but once she's inside Mei King Co., weighing the brocade-covered journals one after the other in her hands, it's clear she has to go for the black. The dragon pattern is what settles it, a dozen lovely monsters spun from pink and green thread.

She shows it to Billy when she steps outside. "Pretty, huh? No drooling, now. Remember what I told you about books."

Baby, the brain-tumour Shih Tzu, puts the fear of God into other dogs. At first Kate and her assistant, Sandi, put it down to the little dog's bark—a high, strangled garble that thins to a guinea-pig scream—but whether Baby vocalizes or not, certain fellow patients set eyes on the silky little dog in her basket and start barking hysterically, while others simply turn tail and flee. It's not as though Baby could come after them. Even when the tremors are mild, she has little balance left; whenever they swim her in the tank, Sandi has to keep a good grip on the back of her doggy life jacket to stop her lolling like a harpooned seal. More to the point, Baby's hind legs are all but useless. The best she can manage is to lever up on her forelegs and sway.

She's been day-boarding at the rehab centre for a week when Kate finally figures out what the problem is.

"Look," Sandi says, folding a towel against her chest, "Baby's doing yoga."

Kate glances up from the screen to see Baby doing a shuddery rendition of the cobra pose. Never mind the fur and the floppy ears, Baby looks like a fat black-and-white serpent making ready to strike. The Australian shepherd they have coming in this afternoon is one of those most upset by the little dog, and now Kate understands why. A breed shaped in the outback is bound to have a healthy fear of snakes.

"Do you mind carrying her back to the shower room?" she says. "I don't want Blue to see her and freak."

"Sure." Sandi bends from the waist to scoop up dog and basket; she does yoga too. It's handy having a fit assistant. Sandi may be petite, but she can lift anything up to an adult Doberman with ease.

Blue is late as usual, which isn't the right way to think about it, Kate knows; it's not Blue at the wheel of the Suburban. His owner, Joanne, is on her cell when they finally arrive. "I know. I told her. I know."

Kate steps out from behind the desk, patting her leg. Blue comes to her, lifting his nose to the treat pocket in her vest.

"Hey, Blue. How's that knee?"

He nuzzles the pocket.

"I'm there now," Joanne says loudly. "I know. *I know.* I'll call you back when we're done." She snaps shut her phone. "Oh my God, Kate, you should have heard how he was crying after the last session."

"Crying?"

"All the time."

Kate reaches back to take hold of her ponytail; since childhood, she's comforted herself by gathering it up in her fingers, running a hand down its dark length. "He cried non-stop?"

"Well, whenever he'd try and get up, you know."

"Uh-huh." Kate counts to three in her head. "And how long did he keep that up?"

"The whole first day. He was just miserable."

She transfers her attention from Joanne's face to Blue's. "Well, there's bound to be some soreness, but that sounds like it's within normal range."

"I guess so, but—"

"Let's get you working, huh, boy?" Kate turns and heads down the hallway to the tank room with the dog at her heel, leaving Joanne to follow.

Blue's used to the tank; he ambles up the ramp, tucking round to face the front pane as it hinges closed. He keeps calm as the water begins to rise, even ducks his head to lap a chlorinated mouthful or two. Kate takes up her position on the bench that runs opposite the lateral view. The water creeps up Blue's legs, narrowing them to their actual size. His mottled coat is even lovelier when wet.

When he's half submerged, Kate nods to Sandi, who stands by the controls near the tank's back end. She stops the flow. A moment for Blue to get comfortable, and then Kate nods a second time, and the whirr of the treadmill begins.

Blue has no trouble keeping up with the starting speed, his steps light, almost jaunty. He keeps his nose to the pane with ease, egged on by Joanne and her zip-lock bag of marrow bone treats. She's slipped him three already. He'll have had three dozen before they're done.

Kate watches him walk on the spot through the tri-panelled side of the tank. Good balance, and he's favouring his strong side only slightly. "Up a notch," she tells Sandi, who nods and presses the *Faster* button. Kate had to bite her lip to keep from grinning the first time Dr. Kelleher demonstrated the controls. Four fat red buttons: *Slower, Faster, Fill, Drain. Slower* doubled as "stop" when punched repeatedly. *Fill* both started and halted the tap.

Blue slips a little with the increase in speed. In the corner of her eye Kate sees Joanne delve into her zip-lock. It's one of the trickiest topics to bring up, especially when the owners are on the heavy side themselves. She can't avoid it, though— every ounce over the optimum puts a strain on a TPLO case like Blue. Though routine, the operation is anything but simple: the bone plateau of the tibia levelled in order to compensate for the ruptured cranial cruciate ligament. Odds for a return to pre-injury function are good, but only if everyone involved takes the recovery period seriously.

"How's his eating?" she asks as Joanne hangs a treat-filled fist down into the tank.

"Oh, it's great. His appetite is really good."

Blue speeds up and snaffles the marrow bone. Chewing slows him down. His hindquarters bump up against the end of the tank.

"So you're sticking to regular mealtimes?" Kate rises and steps up onto the ramp to stand alongside Joanne. "Two feedings a day?"

"Well, sometimes if he's really mopey I give him a little snack."

Kate nods. "Come on, boy, you can do it. Keep up." He works a little in response to her tone, his head and shoulders returning to the front third, where they belong. "Good boy, Blue." Beside her, Joanne reaches into her bag again. Keeping her eyes on the dog, Kate spreads her elbows across the top of the tank. "How about exercise? Are you getting him out for walks?"

"Mostly." Joanne presses the bag to her chest. "He has his good days and his bad days."

"Right. But most days you get him out."

"Sure. Yesterday he was really perky. He took off after this guy on a bike. I let him go for it. I mean, if you ride in the off-leash area, you're pretty much asking for it, don't you think?"

*One. Two. Three.* "Okay, but remember, we talked about how he shouldn't be running yet?"

"Well, sure, but this guy came out of nowhere."

Kate closes her eyes. "It's just something to keep in mind." *If you don't want to cripple him all over again. If you don't want me to cripple you.* She hops down from the ramp and returns to the bench to check on Blue's gait. Still close to even, still going strong. "Up another notch," she says, and watches Blue take the challenge in stride.

When she glances up, Sandi catches her eye and smiles. It's the kind of look Kate would have misread only months before. Hard to believe now, the hours she spent fretting over a casual comment, an innocent hug. For a time her nights were haunted—Sandi with a towel-swaddled poodle in her arms, Sandi slipping treats to a shivering Italian greyhound with fractured front legs.

Kate was no stranger to the hopeless crush; she'd suffered through seven or eight of them by the time Lou-Lou taught her the delights of requited love. *What's a beauty like you doing wasting herself on straight girls?* The infatuations had rarely lasted more than a few weeks, and thank God, Sandi proved to be no exception. It helped, being invited to her wedding. The official kiss raised hoots and wolf whistles from the crowd, Sandi finally twisting her face free, lips swollen, eyelids heavy with heterosexual love. It was the shock Kate needed. She learned her lesson, once and for all.

Joanne rattles her bag. She digs for a marrow snack and dangles it, and when her dog trots up like a charger, she lets out a happy little laugh. Blue nips the treat from her fingers, this time lagging only slightly before getting the better of the belt again. He's making progress, this creature that had to be carried into the centre not so long ago.

"Attaboy," Kate murmurs, and feels a swell of something like laughter herself.

Lily and Billy have made their way north past the library, past the high, blind wall of the Don Jail, the decrepit face of

Bridgepoint Health. East Riverdale Park. You can see out over the valley from here: the vast platter of the playing field, then the parkway, then the wild and wandering Don. She's chosen one of the benches by the statue of Dr. Sun Yat-sen. He's pretty white-looking for a guy that has to be Chinese, but she likes the bronze swell of his dress.

It's a good spot—quiet enough to concentrate, with sufficient foot traffic to keep the pervs away. Billy takes up the other three-quarters of the bench, so she doesn't have to worry about anyone sitting down. Most people know not to talk to you when you're reading, but not all. Persistent types get to view Billy's sunlit canines, his dark lips curling to show glimpses of gum.

Since he got chopped, Billy shows little interest in his own kind. His chin, stretched across her thighs, lifts only slightly to acknowledge a passing boxer, a pair of grubby-faced Westies on matching leads. For her part, Lily glances up whenever there's movement, then returns to the novel in her hand.

Hard to imagine how she would have lasted this long without anything to read. She fretted for days before taking Guy up on his offer, made several aborted approaches to the wrecking yard gate before finally laying her finger to the bell. From the first he left her alone to make up her own mind. It wasn't easy. At the school library she could take her time, maybe test-drive a page or two. Standing on her own before Guy's bedroom bookcase, she chose quickly, going by title alone.

The first one jumped out at her from eye level: *Wild Animals I Have Known*. When Guy saw what she'd picked, he made a face she couldn't quite read.

"What?" She crossed her arms.

"Nothing." He smiled. "You'll see."

It wasn't until the second chapter—"Silverspot: The Story of a Crow"—that Lily understood the meaning of his look. "Get this," she said to Billy. "'Old Silverspot was the leader of a large band of crows that made their headquarters near Toronto, Canada, in Castle Frank, which is a pine-clad hill on the northeast edge of the city.'"

Castle Frank was the name of the subway station at the western end of the viaduct. Silverspot had lived in the Don Valley, just like her.

And he wasn't the only one. Redruff the partridge had lived there too. He'd hatched out of his egg and drummed on his log and met Brownie, his mate—only to wind up dangling from a snare, dying for days until an owl finally came and finished him off. Probably the same owl that had left Silverspot in a bloody heap. Cheery tales. The animals almost always croaked in some brutal way—one dog because he ate poisoned horseflesh, another because he killed sheep and bit the girl who fed him. Lily didn't buy that one, just as she didn't buy the one about two wolves taking down 250 sheep in a single night. There was one chapter she couldn't help swallowing whole, though, even if it was the least likely of them all.

The title made it sound like a story for babies. She thought about skimming "Raggylug: The Story of a Cottontail Rabbit" or even giving it a miss, but the first illustration changed her mind: Raggylug's eye huge in terror, the snake drawn up above him, showing its ribbon of tongue. Lily took a breath and turned back to the opening line. The scene was mushy as hell—the fluffy baby bunny screaming *Mammy, Mammy,* as the snake tightened its grip—but when the mother rabbit came bounding to save the day, Lily found she had to stop reading and wait for the blur in her eyes to clear.

Raggylug became Rag when he got older, which made the whole thing easier to take. He learned everything he needed to know from his mother; he could outwit dogs and foxes, hawks and human snares. *No wild animal dies of old age*, the author was kind enough to point out—*its life has soon or late a tragic end*—yet Rag somehow managed to beat the odds. His mother drowned, but Rag lived on to rule the swamp, overpopulating it with his bucktoothed seed.

Reading that rare happy ending by the light of her camp lantern, Lily couldn't help but remember the broken-backed rabbit in Billy's mouth. "Hopefully not Raggy Junior, huh, boy?" she said, but Billy snored on.

"What did you think?" Guy asked her when she came to trade the book for another. He was bent over an open car hood, his hands black with grease.

"It was okay."

"That all?"

"Yeah, well, he's kind of a sick fuck."

Guy straightened up. "Who is?"

"The writer." She stared at a spot between Billy's shoulders. "I mean, he gets you feeling all sorry for the animal in one story, but then the next minute he's chaining up a baby fox or torturing some poor wolf."

"Huh."

"And it's supposed to be some kind of freedom when the mustang gets run off a cliff—what the fuck kind of logic is that?"

"I never thought about it like that."

She glanced up to see if he was messing with her. He looked

thoughtful, though, almost concerned. "Yeah, well," she said, "it was cool, though, those parts about the Don Valley."

He nodded.

"You mind if I pick another one?"

"Go ahead. There's a bag of dog food just inside the door."

Billy perked up as though his name had been mentioned, though Lily had yet to give even that much away. She wasn't sure what the dog food meant. "Thanks," she said finally, making for the screen door.

"Hey," Guy called after her, "leave that one on the table, will you? I want to read it again."

It was a lame thing to feel happy over, but when had anyone ever given a shit what she thought about a book? She poured a generous helping of kibble into the chipped brown bowl beside the bag. The white enamel basin beside it held water that looked to be fresh, though there was no sign of any pet on the premises besides her own. The little corner was for visitors. For Billy. When he stuck his face in deep and started gobbling, she left him to it and went to stand in front of the bookcase again.

She must've picked out a dozen books in the weeks since. The one in her hand is different, though. It's the first one chosen for her by Guy.

"You remember *Wild Animals I Have Known*?" he asked her this morning, when she came back into the kitchen after burying her birds.

"What am I, eighty? Of course I remember it."

He laughed. "You were right, it's pretty weird."

"Yeah."

"I like that one about the rabbit, though."

She said nothing, her hand seeking Billy's head, taking hold of the nearest ear.

"You too, I bet."

It was only a simple question. More of a comment, even. So why did it make her feel like running? Guy moved past her to his room. He returned with a book and laid it on the table, alongside the three surviving birds tucked up in their little bags. She'd noticed the odd title more than once, but never so much as laid a finger to its spine.

The cover illustration was of a rabbit, soft and brown, with a quick, intelligent eye. She picked it up, slid it into her cargo pocket and patted the Velcro flap down. One of the bags gave a rustle. "Guess I better be going," she said. "Set these little fuckers free."

She's thirty-five pages in, and already she knows the book will change her. Fiver, the twitchy little rabbit, has persuaded Hazel and the others to escape the doomed home warren and make their way into the terrifying woods. In the past, Lily wouldn't have known what to do with words like these. Now, she draws the dragon book from her pocket and turns to the first blank page. Holding the novel open against her thigh, she digs for her ballpoint and pulls the cap off with her teeth.

> Since entering the wood they had been in severe anxiety. Several were almost *tharn*—that is, in that state of staring, glazed paralysis that comes over terrified or exhausted rabbits, so that they sit and watch their enemies—weasels or humans—approach to take their lives.

It helps having copied it out. She lets the dragon book flutter closed and feeds the pen back into its cap. *"Tharn,"* she says softly, and Billy cracks his black muzzle to yawn.

Edal's managed to keep herself busy for most of the day— cleaning up the spray of garbage on the front walk, doing the vacuuming, taking two unread novels back to the library and checking out three more. She might have kept on along the same sensible lines if it hadn't been for a certain sound. It comes to her upon waking from her second nap of the day: a mental echo of the rusty wrecking-yard screech. Only now, with her temple warm and slightly damp against the pillow, she recognizes it as the cry of something alive.

She doesn't exactly think it's a good idea, going back there. It's downhill most of the way, though, so in effect the bike does the thinking for her.

She coasts past the wrecking yard gate to where the asphalt ends, hides her bike in the grass and picks a path along the bottom fence. Virginia creeper has already come in thick over the winter dieback. At the southwest corner of the lot, she pushes her hands into the mess of vines, parting greenery gone dull with exhaust. Her fingers find chain-link. With the on-ramp rumbling at her back, she leans in close and puts her eye to the leafy hole.

She sees the droppings first, chalky splashes down the trunk of the lifeless tree. Then, drawing her eye upward, leg feathers so white they look bleached. Golden feet. A coppery tail.

The hawk has heard her. Its head orients back and down, finding her eye among the spring growth. It's an adult red-tail, maybe half a metre in length, though it looks a little thin. She's guessing male, but it's difficult to say. Its cage is substantial—only a few metres wide but at least a dozen long. Still, it's a cage.

Laying her cheek to the leaves, Edal angles her gaze along the back of the building. Only the nearest window reveals any depth of scene: a single bed, the far wall lined with books.

A strip of untended yard lies between the building and the back fence—mostly weeds and grass, but she spots the splayed reach of a squash plant, a rampant burst of mint. Here and there the growth is thinner, the earth dug over recently, as though someone has attempted a flower patch and given up. Nothing so unusual about a garden let go, but what's with all the hubcaps? Embedded on edge at regular intervals, they rise up out of the grass like the bright, cresting combs of waves.

A small disturbance draws her attention back to the cage. The red-haired man is standing at the far end, busy with the lock. His Mack is gone, replaced by another relic, a rawhide jacket dyed the same shade as his hair. There's something theatrical about the way he enters the cage—the star of a hippie musical preparing to belt out the theme. Slowly, dramatically, he lifts his arms out at his sides, revealing banks of dangling fringe. Edal has to remind herself to inhale. When he lunges forward, it's all she can do not to let out a cry.

He runs toward her, arms flapping, face set—a madman attacking a caged bird. The penny drops only when the bird leaves its branch. Not attacking it, Edal realizes. Forcing it to fly.

She can make out every splayed-feather finger at the tips of the hawk's retreating wings, every strip of fringe along the man's open arms. When he pivots and runs back the way he came, the hawk drops from its far branch and comes swooping. It's a narrow miss—the thrust of its wings showing in the lift of the man's hair—yet he doesn't flinch, only turns in a whirl of suede and, before the bird can settle, comes pounding again.

His face is changing, beginning to reflect the chase—lips parted, eyes shining, wild.

This time he touches the bark of the dead oak like a boy touching home-free. Gaining speed on the turn, he drives the hawk harder, so it scarcely lands before it's away again. When he wheels beneath the branches to follow it, he wears a wide, unthinking smile. Edal can't help but mirror him. For a moment she imagines shinning up the creepers, showing her friendly face above the leaves.

"Hey."

This time greenery saves her nose. The muscular young man with the pretty face has her bike by its handlebars.

"Come on." He turns. "You'd better come with me." His tone is one of invitation rather than coercion. A note of resignation, perhaps, an older brother giving in to a tagalong little sibling. Still, he keeps a firm hold on her bike.

At the gate, he leans his forehead against the painted sign, reaches down the front of his T-shirt and draws out a key on a loop of kitchen string. He has to stoop to fit it into the padlock. Pushing the gate open, he motions Edal into the yard.

She stands to the side, hands balled up in the pocket of her sweatshirt, while he secures the gate. "Think I could have my bike back?"

"It's okay." He walks on. "I've got it."

He leads her past the old trucks, past the cinder-block office, to where the clapboard extension begins.

"Wait here." He pushes her bike to the end of the building and rounds the corner out of sight. "Hey, Guy," she hears him call out, "can you come here a sec?"

"Now? I'm flying him."

*Guy*—the name suits him somehow, as does the voice. Edal imagines the younger man gesturing, attempting to mime *crazy lady at the back fence.*

"Okay, I'll be right there."

Her escort returns empty-handed.

"Where's my bike?"

"Don't worry." He stands with his hands clasped behind his back, feet slightly apart.

"I'm not worried. I just—"

"What's up?" Guy comes alone, leaving his hawk behind. Of course he does—as if he'd come wearing it on his arm like a medieval prince. His eyes rest on her with a strange familiarity. "Who's this?"

She can smell the jacket—warm hide, traces of the animal that wore it originally. That and the aroma of something good wafting out the screen door.

"I found her outside," the young man says simply.

"Yeah? Well, I guess you met Stephen already. I'm Guy. Guy Howell."

He holds out his hand. It takes Edal a moment to extend hers in return. His grip is callused, firm. None of the false weakness most men imagine women require.

"Edal Jones. I was just—"

"Edal?" He grins. "You mean like the otter?"

It comes as a bit of a shock. It's been years since her name has elicited anything more than *That's different* or *What kind of name is that?* "Yes," she says, "like the otter."

"Man, I loved that book."

She nods.

"I'm named after Lafleur," he adds. "Nobody ever says it the French way, though."

She nods again. Why is she like this, shamed by the simplest human exchange? Stephen looks at the ground. They're not sure what to do with her—she can see it. They're beginning to wonder when she'll leave.

"You hungry?" Guy says.

Stephen brightens. "Yeah."

"I know *you* are—what else is new. I was talking to Edal."

"Me?" Hungry. For the first time in days, she suddenly is. "I guess so. Why?"

"Why? It's suppertime, that's why." He steps past her to open the screen door. "Come on."

Edal hesitates for a moment then follows, Stephen falling in step behind. Inside, the smell is even better. She recognizes grilled cheese.

It's a deep room. Two doors break up the southern wall; one gapes to show a polka-dotted shower curtain, the other—which can only give onto the little bedroom with the bookcase—is closed. A third door divides the northern wall. Painted a bright shade of green, it too stands closed. Beyond it, countertop and cupboards that date back to the seventies, double sink, tall, mustard-coloured fridge. Down the far end, a girl stands at the stove, her back to the room. Pink hair, drooping vest. She looks round, spatula in hand, and scowls.

"What's she doing here?"

Guy crosses to the sink. "You guys know each other?"

The girl snorts. Guy turns on the tap, reaches for the dish soap and begins lathering up his hands. The frying smell darkens, on its way to burning.

The girl turns back to the pan. "She's the one who followed me."

For a moment Edal considers making a break for it. Abandon the bike if necessary, scale the gate. Only Stephen is still behind her—between her and the door.

"I'm sorry, I saw you with the birds . . ." She falters. "I was curious."

The girl says nothing.

Guy dries his hands on a dishtowel. "She thinks you're a cop."

"What? Why?" No one answers. "Well, I'm not."

"Fair enough. Edal, this is Lily. Lily, this is Edal. She's going to eat with us."

"I only made enough for three," Lily says.

"Come on," Guy says lightly, "there's plenty."

"Whatever."

Stephen moves past Edal to wash his hands, drying them on his jeans. Unsure what else to do, she takes her turn at the sink.

"You want to set the table, Stephen?" Guy opens the fridge. "Anybody want a beer? Lily? Stupid question."

"I'll have milk," Stephen says, pulling open a drawer.

Edal dries her hands, resisting the urge to sniff the dishtowel before using it. "Beer's good."

Guy tucks the milk carton and two beers between his arm

and his chest. Twisting the cap off a third bottle, he hands it to Lily. She accepts it in silence, keeping her back to the room. He crosses to the table, where he opens the other two, pocketing the caps. "Have a seat, Edal."

There are six chairs, chrome and vinyl, still the bright cherry red the table must've been. Stephen's laying out four places—plate and bowl, soup spoon and glass. Edal chooses the spot nearest the door.

Still standing, Guy takes a brief swallow of beer. "Where's Billy?"

"Out in the garden." Lily moves to look out the window. "He's okay."

Edal imagines another young man, a twin of sorts to Stephen, digging among the hubcaps and unruly grass. Then remembers the dog.

Lily turns to hand Stephen a plate piled high with browned sandwiches. Following him to the table with a saucepan in hand, she begins ladling out chicken noodle soup. Up close, she smells unwashed.

Guy drags out the chair at the head of the table and sits. "Help yourself." He nudges the plate of sandwiches toward Edal.

"Thanks." She takes a half.

"Go on, don't be shy."

She takes another. Stephen settles in across from her. Lily sets the pot down on the table and slides into her seat.

"Looks good, Lily," says Guy. "Thanks."

"Yes, thank you." Edal hears herself. She sounds like a permed pensioner, fresh from church, still in her hat and gloves.

"Thanks, Lily." Stephen finishes his first half sandwich and starts in on a second.

Lily nods and bends to her soup. The sandwiches are perfect, buttery and ever so slightly burnt. Cheap orange cheese, the kind Edal grew up with and no longer allows herself to buy. She can't remember the last time anything tasted so good.

When the food's all gone, the companionable quiet persists. Guy leans back in his chair, pushes a hand into the front pocket of his jeans and draws out a Swiss Army knife. Picking with his fingernail, he teases the bone-coloured toothpick from its sheath. It can't be. Edal searches her mind for when she last saw a man pick his teeth.

Guy practises the polite form of the transgression, covering the lower half of his face with his left hand while he goes to work with the right. Edal looks away, but she can still hear the minute scraping of plastic on enamel—a private, probing sound.

Finally, he lowers his hands. She watches as he wipes the toothpick against his sleeve, like a tiny blade on a whetstone, then threads it back into its slot. He glances up, catching the tail end of her expression before she can wipe it away. It's in her mouth mostly—at least, that's where she feels it. A little pinch of judgment. She smiles to cover it, but the smile, too, is pinched.

He pushes back to clear the plates. When she rises to help, he says firmly, "Sit, finish your beer."

Across the table, Stephen is intent on his milk glass, filling it again to the rim. Lily stands and drains her beer, then heads for the door. It slaps shut hard behind her.

"Is she going?" Edal asks Stephen.

"Just getting her dog."

Guy piles the plates in the sink and leaves them. Without a word, he crosses to the small bedroom and disappears behind its door.

Stephen drinks his milk in one long, lazy go, watching her over the glass. He wipes his mouth. "You live around here?"

"Not far." It feels a little mean, holding back when she's the stranger among them, but Stephen seems satisfied with her reply. Edal inspects her hands. She feels the dog's arrival in the floorboards, looks up to see two bright eyes in a wall of black, advancing fur.

"Hello, boy." She holds out the back of her hand. "That's me."

"It's okay, Billy," Lily says, though he's showing no aggression—quite the opposite in fact. He's nuzzling Edal's fingers as though she's been handling raw steak.

"Hey, Billy," Stephen says quietly, and the dog shoves past Edal's thigh, jostling the table as he tunnels beneath it to lay his chin in Stephen's lap.

Lily gives them all a wide berth on her way to the fridge. She gets another beer and resumes her seat. It's clear both she and Stephen are waiting; they sit unnaturally still, like children who've been promised ice cream if they're good.

Guy's hiding something when he reappears, one hand tucked behind his back. "Everybody ready?" he says.

Lily and Stephen nod. *Ready for what?* Edal wants to ask. Guy flashes her a smile and shows the tattered hardcover in his hand. She looks for a title but finds only the author's name.

"We started last night," he says, "but the chapters stand up pretty well on their own."

"Oh. Okay."

He's a better reader than Letty ever was; he even does the voices, shifting subtly from bear to boy, with not a hint of Disney in Bagheera's liquid panther drawl. Edal closes her eyes and sinks into the story, a willing captive—at least until Mowgli falls into the hands of the Bandar-log.

Kipling didn't specify species—in fact he confused the matter by referring to them as both *the Monkey-People* and *the grey apes*—but it's an Indian jungle, so the Bandar-log are probably langurs. All the same, Edal envisions a different primate, one she's come to know through her work. Mounted with its long fangs bared, the baboon hangs just inside the evidence room doors, strategically located to give newcomers a scare.

Having entered that room full of oddities, her thoughts are inclined to remain there. As Baloo and Bagheera chase through the jungle after their beloved man-cub, her mind's eye moves over confiscated grizzly rugs and black bear galls, a dried tiger penis, a leopard-skin coat. When they make an ally of Kaa, the massive rock python, she can see only wallets and handbags, hideous pointy-toed boots. She manages to focus again during the great battle at the ruined city known as the Cold Lairs, but only until Mowgli tumbles down into the abandoned summer house and lands among the hissing hoods of the Poison-People. Why would anyone shove a cobra down inside a bottle and pickle it? More to the point, why would anyone spot such a monstrosity in a marketplace and long to possess it, let alone attempt to smuggle it home?

Edal forces herself to concentrate, if not on the story then at least on the sound of Guy's voice. By the time the battle comes to a close, she finds she no longer has to try. The Dance of the Hunger of Kaa is what does it, something inside her *swaying forward helplessly* alongside the hypnotized Bandar-log. She escapes in the company of Mowgli and his creatures, returning to the vivid, living jungle, leaving the evidence room and its dust-covered dead behind.

Guy switches deftly from prose to verse, finishing with the "Road-Song of the Bandar-log." It's startling, the quiet confidence with which he sing-songs his way through the lines. By the end of the first stanza, he's keeping time with the heel of his hand. Soon they're all beating out the meter— Edal with the tips of her fingers, Stephen open-handed, Lily with a white-knuckled fist.

The fox is light on his feet—soft toes, softer fur between. The roadside gravel bears little mark of his passage, save for the sweet scent of his prints.

Cars come thundering. No longer the downpour roar of early evening, now each rolls out a singular din of its own. He feels their wind in his flank fur, keeps his tail to their stupefying light.

Trot while they deafen you, pause to listen during the lulls. The grass along this particular stretch is worth it, tall and weedy, teeming with food.

*There.* The leeward ear finds it first, its partner swivelling a hair's breadth behind. Incremental adjustments now, flicking, flickering. Another car brings several seconds devoid of sense. Then a clearing, a locking-in.

No mistaking the fat-bodied scuffle of a vole. It's not far, no more than a tail's length from the border where the grass begins. The fox tenses, a trembling in his long hind legs. Until now, he's been a mere facet of the rustling, hundred-scented night. Springing, he becomes a thing entire.

The angle is all: too wide and he'll land beyond his quarry, too narrow and he'll fall short of the mark. He registers a shiver in the grass from on high, contracts a fraction tighter at the crest of his pounce. Forepaws and nose lead the jabbing descent. He pins the wriggling, pissing vole, snaps it up in his jaws and tosses it high in the air. Catching it, he tastes the night's first blood.

It's a start. The fox's stomach is small, but a vole is smaller—and when the stomach stretches to its limit, there remains the planned promise of the cache. His territory is dotted with bodies, each deposited in a tidily excavated hole. Covering the dead is a careful business. Push the loose earth in, pausing to pack each layer flat with the nose. A sweep of the whiskers to clear away any sign.

Some caches he will find again by landmarks, others by smell. Of these last, a certain number will lie empty, raided by creatures as bold as or bolder than he. Which is why there must always be more than enough. Why, full or empty, a fox must hunt.

He lifts his nose to find the breeze has turned back on itself, delivering unwelcome news. Coyote. A dog-plain whiff of its urine, and now, not so distant, a waft of its recent scat. How do they abide such a stink? His own slim form creates only pleasing smells—from the vivid scat-spray, to the subtle chin gland, to the flower-scented patch on his tail.

No sense chancing another shift in the wind. When coyotes kill his kind, they kill as humans do, with little or no thought for food. The fox turns neatly in his tracks. His pupils shrink in the sudden glare.

Edal should be on her way, but she's loath to be the first to speak.

Lily beats her to it. "Come on, Billy." She rises, her dog at her side.

Guy looks up. "You coming by tomorrow?"

"Maybe."

"Okay. See you then."

"It was nice to meet—" Edal begins, but they're already gone, the screen door slapping Billy's rump.

"Don't sweat it," Guy says. "She takes a while to warm up."

Edal's saved from responding by the muffled ring of a phone—a nostalgic *brrrring* reminiscent of the mechanical age. Stephen pushes back from the table. "I'll get it." He turns and opens the green door, revealing a partial view of what looks to be another bedroom. Edal hears a second door open, after which the phone falls quiet, replaced by the murmur of a brief exchange. Glancing up, she finds Guy watching her. She searches for something to say. *How about that python. Wish I was brought up by wolves.*

"Roy Tanner," Stephen says, returning. "Says you're supposed to be picking up his LeBaron."

"Right." Guy stretches, his T-shirt rising to show a strip of belly, hair a shade lighter, redder than Edal expects. "Duty calls."

"Oh, right, okay." She stands quickly, almost knocking over her chair.

"I'm going online," Stephen says. He pauses in the doorway. "Bye, Edal."

"Bye-bye." Something about his expression makes her say it gently. *Nighty-night.* "Online?" she adds once he's gone. "Doesn't really go with that ring tone."

"Yeah, he set all that up." Guy grabs his Mack from a hook by the door and shrugs it on. The back's torn where Edal could swear it wasn't yesterday.

"You don't have a cell?" she asks, following him out.

"Nope. You?"

"Just for— Not really. I used to."

"I'll grab your bike," he says over his shoulder, heading for the corner of the house. He's back before she can decide whether to follow. "It's gone."

She stares at him. "What do you mean, gone?"

He stoops to pluck up a stray spark plug. "I guess Lily took it."

Edal fights a sliding sensation of fault. She's done nothing wrong—nothing except let her guard down among people she knows nothing about. It's not that far to walk home, maybe half an hour, but she's suddenly very tired. She'll have to take the streetcar—only she has no tokens. No cab fare either. "Great."

"She'll bring it back." He smiles.

She's beginning to think he does that a little too often. She crosses her arms. "How do you know?"

"Trust me, she will."

He pivots on his heel, draws his arm back and lets the

spark plug fly. It cuts a high, tumbling arc, lands with a ping on a shadowy heap of scrap.

"Where do you live?" he asks.

"Me?" Edal says, still watching the spot where it hit. "Pape and Danforth."

"Come on. I'll drop you on my way."

She's never ridden in a tow truck before. The cab is cleaner than she would've imagined—no coffee cups or balled-up burger wrappers, only a few duct-taped tears in the pearl grey seats. Roomier, too. There's space enough behind them for two large Rubbermaid bins and a clutter of tools, including a pair of bolt cutters, a shovel and an industrial jack. She watches in the passenger-side mirror as Guy hops down to close the gate behind them. Like Stephen, he wears his padlock key around his neck.

She expects him to take Mt. Stephen Street to Broadview and head north from there, or else follow Gerrard to Carlaw. Instead, he turns right, making his way via back streets to the on-ramp for the northbound parkway. It's an odd route— he'll have to double back and cross the viaduct to take her home.

He speeds up to merge then keeps to the slow lane, taking his time. He's watching her again. At first she thinks it's her imagination—but no, she can feel his eyes repeatedly sliding her way. They pass beneath the footbridge. Moments later he flicks on his signal and begins to slow, already drifting right.

"What are you doing?" There's hardly any shoulder, but he glides in snug against the guardrail. "Why are we stopping here?"

He jams the truck into park and frees his belt. "This won't take long."

With a quick glance in his mirror, he throws open his door and drops to the ground. Edal twists to watch him rummage behind his seat. He grabs the shovel by its blade and drags it toward him.

"Come on," he says. "I could use a hand."

"With what?"

"Grab the bin behind you." He backs out and swings shut his door. Shovel in hand, he walks along the shoulder, heading back the way they came. Edal stares straight ahead for several seconds. Then reaches down to unbuckle her seat belt.

The bin is light. She doesn't lift the lid to check what's inside, just holds it close to her belly so she can walk without it bouncing against her knees. Oncoming headlights blind her for seconds at a time, Guy's figure taking shape in the gaps between cars.

Midway between two towering lights, he halts and drops into a crouch.

The grass around him is coated in dust; it shows pale with every wave of glare. As Edal draws near, the lights of a lumbering cement truck pick out another colour—the shade Guy must've spotted from the driver's seat. Because he was looking for it, she realizes. Not looking at her after all.

As she hunkers down beside him, he draws a thin flashlight from his breast pocket and switches it on. The fox's coat is the colour of new bricks. Its tail is substantial, a slim second body, the tip lily-white. White throat, too—spotless. Four sooty, sparrow-boned legs. It could almost be sleeping, if it wasn't for the fact that no fox would bed down so close to passing traffic.

"Broke his back," Guy says.

Edal nods.

"Sometimes they're still alive. There's the odd one you can save, but most of them are too far gone. The shovel comes in handy then too." He stands, his flashlight spilling its narrow beam. "Can you take the lid off?"

She looks up at him, his face in shadow, hands at his sides. "What are you going to do?"

"Take him with me."

She straightens to stand beside him. "Why?"

He stoops for the shovel. "Anything that comes to feed on the carcass stands a fair chance of getting hit too." He directs his beam along the small, bright body, letting it rest on the pointed face. "Besides, look at him. I can't just leave him here."

She watches as he nudges the shovel's blade beneath the animal's ruined back. He's careful—bizarrely so, given that the fox is dead.

"Christ," he says, "he barely weighs a thing."

The truck is crowded now, full to bursting with a musky presence, as though the fox's spirit has turned to pure scent. They pass beneath the viaduct's barred shadow, cliffs of concrete rising on either side. Guy keeps his eyes on the road now, and Edal does her best to follow suit. When he enters the loop that will lead them up out of the valley, her mind takes a turn of its own.

A grey, daytime road overlays the lanes before her. Her mother is a bad driver. She tends to drift, the road a river, the Chevy a makeshift raft; no wonder the undercarriage is practically rusted through. She's doing it now, sober as a judge but weaving, groping in her handbag for a cigarette.

"I'll get you one, Mom."

"It's okay," she says, still fishing, "I've got it."

Edal hates the handbag. Squeezed between the two front seats, it's crammed with crap, like everything Letty owns. The back seat of the snub-nosed car they ride in is crowded with boxes and plastic bags, plus the scaly old Hoover and matching grey pails that are the organs of her mother's work. Down on her knees in the homes of half a dozen nearby towns.

It's a lovely stretch they're on, hay bales and horses, the Chevy the only blight on the landscape for miles. The centre stripe dips and rises, endless. Save there, where the bright line breaks.

"Hey," Edal says, pointing, "what's that?"

"Hm?" Letty's got the du Maurier in her mouth now.

"What's that on the road?"

Her mother squints. "I don't know." She has to talk around the filter, gripping it between her lips. "A rock."

Maybe, only they're closer now, and Edal could swear the rock just moved. The head is what gives it away. Edal cries out, but her mother's busy digging for the lighter. The bump is minor, as though they've driven over a book, or a girl's first jewellery box.

"What? What?" Letty says, her unlit cigarette bobbing.

Edal wrenches round in her seat. The turtle lies broken on the road behind them. Its colours will haunt her. Green— dark green, like the pond where Edal knows to look for them, lined up basking on a log. Also, smeared by the Chevy's wheel, the loveliest, ugliest red.

---

"You said Pape and Danforth, right?"

Edal blinks. They're already at Carlaw, idling three cars back at a red light. She's missed the rattle and rush of the viaduct, plus a good portion of the Greektown strip. "This is fine," she blurts. "I'll get out here."

He looks at her, surprised. "I can take you."

"I'd better go." She cracks her door. "The light's going to turn."

"Okay. Come by for your bike tomorrow if you like."

"What bike?"

He laughs. "She'll bring it back, you'll see."

Edal checks for cyclists and slides down off her seat.

"Besides," he says, "you want to hear the next chapter, don't you?"

She turns and closes the door gently. "It's green," she mouths through the glass, pointing to the light, the traffic already leaving him behind.

Edal's bike is a treat to ride after Guy's junkyard clunker. Lily burns along the darkened valley trail, Billy working for once to keep up. She barely slows for the tight spots, the blind turn before the culvert that runs beneath the tracks. Corrugated pipe closes in, too dark to see the scribbled tags that mark its metal ribs. She could cream somebody coming the other way, wipe out and trash the bike—maybe even trash herself. She passes the marsh, the stands of lion-tailed rushes where blackbirds like to flash their red shoulders and cry. Pumps harder. By the time she shoots under the viaduct, her thighs are burning. Glancing back over her shoulder, she sees Billy lagging, a good way back. She slows, glides a wide loop through glowing, knee-high blooms—stalky white flowers that scent the night. Back on the path, she brakes and stands astride the bike, bringing a thumb and forefinger to her lips. Billy pours it on when she whistles, galloping with everything he's got left. She knows a corresponding jolt of joy. Nothing sweeter than the sight of that black bulk coming on like a train.

He's with her in seconds, crashing through the weeds, using the drag of them to slow himself down.

"Hey, Billy," she pants.

He sidles in to push his heaving flank against her. Looks up bright-eyed, breathing hard.

"What do you think, boy?" She tucks a hand under his jaw. "Think I broke any records?"

He tilts his head, his tongue wetting her wrist.

"You thirsty? I bet you're thirsty."

She steps off the bike, turns the handlebars and leans into them, pushing a path through the growth. There's little hope of hearing the Don, what with the surrounding traffic and the viaduct's overhead hum. She can smell it, though, and so can Billy, lolloping ahead of her now, turned puppyish at the promise of a swim. Nothing like water for a water dog; it's the oldest song he knows, the one forever singing in his skin.

There's no way she should let him go in, not when the two of them will be sharing a tent within the hour. When he hesitates at the bank—and he will, he's that good a dog—she should be firm with him, tell him a drink is all he gets.

She draws up behind him at a muddy slip between two clumps of sedge. The smell is stronger here, equal parts natural and not. The sight of the water is strangely calming. This close, she can hear it sighing in its bed.

Billy stands quivering.

"I know, boy."

He twists to show her the look in his eyes.

"Okay," she says. "Go on in."

It's never easy breaking ground in the old garden; Guy could be digging down through a pile of soggy jute mats. He's fixed on a spot just inside the back fence, where a twist of morning glory pushes up through the creepers. He has no need of a lamp. Warm light reaches back to him through the kitchen window, overlaid by the on-ramp's chill.

Eventually he cuts through to pure, dark dirt. He rests a moment, leaning up against the wall of vines. The morning glory shows no flowers as yet; even if it were in bloom, the day's effort would be wilting by now, preparing to drop to the ground.

The second jag of digging goes faster. He doesn't cut corners, though—the hole has to be wide enough so the fox can lie down and rest. *You want them standing to attention down there?* Aunt Jan knew how to plant an image deep.

When he's sure there's sufficient room, Guy opens the bin, flooding the night air with musk. He takes a deep breath, his eyes watering, and stoops over the fox. For a moment he holds its foreleg, feeling through fur to bones both sturdy and slight.

Over time, he's learned the gentlest way to deliver a creature into the ground is by kneeling at the graveside and making a hammock of both hands—fingers laced beneath its belly or its back, depending on how it lies. It can be awkward, even a strain, but it's no great feat with the fox. When Guy's knuckles meet soil, he holds still a moment—head over the pungent hole, armpits wedged against its grassy lip—then he loosens his fingers and withdraws.

Infilling is the easy part, at least after the first couple of spadefuls have obscured the fox's fine coat. He tamps the mound gently with his sole. No need to come up with the right words in the right order—Aunt Jan got it right long ago. Guy props the spade among the creepers, shoves his hands into his pockets and bows his head.

"Fox, beautiful fox. Goodbye, fox."

Billy smells more like a swamp than a river, but Lily lets him crawl into the tent just the same. He always goes in first— that way he has room to buckle round and face the open end. The first couple of times, he wanted to sleep in a curl the way dogs do, but she's taught him to stretch out long like a human being. The camo tent is meant to be a one-man affair; lucky thing Lily's so thin.

Unstuffing the mummy bag from its sack, she flings it out along the narrows between Billy and the flimsy wall. She's tried leaving the long zipper open, but the nights are sometimes still too cool. There's a trick to worming down inside the bag. You have to think of it as something you're returning to, somewhere you belong. Otherwise the puffy confines can fuck with your head.

The smell of the bag was something else she hadn't planned on. The body it had known before hers was still present in the weave—no amount of aftershave sufficient to cloak its overactive glands. During her first couple of weeks in the valley, the odour was strong enough to give her nightmares. Time and again she woke writhing, Billy upset beside her, the tent closing in. She considered burning the bag, but survival required a tougher turn of mind. It was only a smell. It would fade. Turns out she was right; these days she only ever catches the occasional whiff.

The vest was never a problem that way. It was brand new, ordered online to replace the khaki one that had been around for years. She could almost pretend it had been meant as a gift for her, only somebody clicked on *XL* when they should've chosen *S*. In any case, she's come to appreciate its shapeless bulk.

The ground is hard beneath her shoulder blades, the twin bony points of her butt. Not many rocks, though, or roots, and the cover is good—thick enough that she's called the spot home for more than a single night. It's a rough, limb-scratching hike in, only the ghost of a path. Tonight's passage was even more laboured than usual; she did her best to protect the bike's paint job as she followed Billy deep into the blind-dark scrub. When they finally reached their little clearing, she laid the bike gently on its side in the grass.

"Duffle bag," she told the shape that was Billy, and he bellied in under a clump of bushes and dragged it out. She lit the Coleman, turning the flame down low. The tent she could do by feel in the dark, but she needed light to rebuild the scrim of loose brush.

Now, tucked into the mummy bag, wreathed in a fug of damp dog, she twists over onto her belly and reaches out through the flaps to draw the camp lantern close. One more thing she needs light for. One task left before she can sleep.

The knife is in its pocket, trapped between her small breast and the ground. She thumbs the snap and prises it out. It's a pretty thing, the beaten aluminum hilt warmed by a swish of wooden inlay, natural against the palm. It was nowhere near the largest in the collection case—the blade maybe eight centimetres, the whole thing under ten folded closed. She couldn't believe her luck when she opened it by flashlight in the darkened den. There was a butterfly on the blade, *BENCHMADE* printed across the span of its wings, *U.S.A. 440* beneath its tail. She knew then it would be gentle. A fluttering you could scarcely feel.

Always the smooth surprise of its action. Billy whines at the snick of the blade locking open, then again as Lily rises up on her elbows and pushes back her sleeve.

The month of April filled her left forearm; now she must work awkwardly with her left hand to mark the right. She's not sure what she'll do when May comes to an end and she runs out of room on this side. She hasn't thought that far.

Tonight being her fifty-seventh night of freedom, she's partway into a group of five. The fifth cuts are the tricky ones, slashing down across the previous four. They require a deeper breath, an extra-steady hand.

She touches the flat of the blade to the back of her wrist. It takes more guts than she possesses to slash the fish-belly flesh of the underside, risk nicking a vessel and letting some serious blood. The way Lily does it, nobody gets hurt. Score out the new mark with the tip—just a scratch—then drop the blade, flicking inward for a neat, clean line. She has to press a little harder these days, the knife duller than it was when she began.

*There.* Practice makes perfect. Not much blood, but enough.

Billy whimpers.

"It's okay, boy. It's not serious."

He wriggles in tight against her, nosing, then licking, the wound.

# 5

# Ring of Dark Timber

To begin with, Letty kept her books on shelves like anybody else. On weekends Edal trailed after her through the auction barn or napped fretfully in the passenger seat while Letty trolled the yard sales for "proper wood." By the time she turned eight, her mother had burned through the small savings Nana and Grandpa Adam had left behind, and even a set of used veneer shelves had become a luxury. Letty still slowed for every hand-painted roadside sign, but now all her pennies went on books.

It turned out bricks and chipboard planks could often be had for the price of carting them away. What was more, they could be altered to fit any space. Letty unlocked the disused tool shed and rooted out her father's saw. Her first attempts were uneven, but she soon got the knack of a tidy cut.

Edal helped when she wasn't in school. She could carry three red bricks at a time, and she often took up one end of a big grey one so her mother wouldn't have to manage it alone. Together they lined the front hallway, stacking the makeshift shelves higher than Edal's head. Then came the upstairs hall. It was narrower up there, and once both walls were lined, it took on the feel of a secret passage. Darkness added to the effect when Letty built over the window. The single pane had let in a surprising amount of light.

Edal was confused when her mother suggested they do the spare room next. Since when was Nana and Grandpa Adam's room spare? It wasn't that Edal went in there often; in fact it took a rare state of mind to get her to crack that door. They had both died in there, in the big maple bed—Grandpa Adam first, then Nana, not even a year later. Pneumonia was a disease old people caught when they were sad. Edal's mother told her this, her face wet and streaky, and Edal wondered how old was old, and whether Letty was trying to tell her she too would soon be lying down forever in the maple bed. She didn't, but for months Edal kept watch whenever her mother mounted the stairs.

Wasn't the room somebody had died in supposed to be special somehow? And didn't that go double if it was two people? Letty didn't seem to think so. She closed both windows and covered them up. When Edal took a rest from carrying bricks up the stairs and stood still in the middle of the room, Letty turned and said, "Nana and Grandpa Adam would want us to have all this nice space."

There was space going to waste in the living room too. Letty cut shelves to fit on either side of the mantelpiece, then in between Grandpa Adam's chair and the sideboard that held Nana's tea set and very best plates. After that she took her measuring tape to the kitchen. A good three feet lay between the refrigerator and the back door—and then there was the door itself. "It's silly, right?" Letty said. "Who says a house needs two ways in?"

Edal began to make excuses when her mother asked her to help: she had to get started making supper, she had a project due the next day. Not being there worked best of all; Letty rarely came calling for her in the woods.

Not long after she lost her helper, Letty stopped constructing shelves. The books stood in piles then—*Historic Hairstyles of the World*, *A Guide to Grouting*, *The Good Earth*. Edal grew accustomed to clearing a space when she wanted to open the fridge, or run a bath, or watch one of two stations that came in striped and blurry on their rabbit-eared TV. One afternoon she came upon a Canadian Club box full of Trixie Belden mysteries sitting on the stovetop, directly over the pilot light. *I only set them there for a second, Edal. I was coming right back.*

Edal was eleven when she took the small brass key from its hook and eased the fat padlock from the bolt on Grandpa Adam's shed. The light in there was brown, like ditchwater, and the smell was like an old tin can fished out of that same ditch. She ducked under the cobwebs and found a screwdriver and a handful of long, biting screws. The bolt gave her a little trouble, the screw heads rusted tight, but she kept at it, raising blisters on her palm, until it finally came away.

Her mother must have noticed when she found herself locked out the next time she came to Edal's bedroom door with an armload of drab local histories or bright travel guides—but she never mentioned it. Maybe she knew by then, as Edal did, that there was a word for what was happening in their house. It wasn't a word Edal said out loud to anyone; she saved it for herself, for times like when she woke from the dream that Letty had bricked her in, the upstairs hall packed solid with books. Alone in her bed, Edal would whisper the word aloud. "Crazy." Sometimes once wasn't enough, and she had to repeat it—*cra-zy-cra-zy-cra-zy*—until finally she slept.

# 6

# The Chronicles of Darius

Darius was used to his mother spending forever in the tub. *I'm going for a soak,* she might say, *you be a good boy.* Or she might say nothing, and he would know from the moan of the pipes, the faucet's coughing stream.

The second round tended to use up whatever hot water was left. Sometimes she'd drag her pale feet up to keep from getting scalded; sometimes she'd let them turn pink under the flow. Occasionally she just lay there, letting the water go icy cold. When Darius was really little, it made him nervous. He'd pretend he needed to pee so he could come in and check she hadn't let her head slip under the surface, forgetting her need to breathe. By the time he was six, even when he did need to go, he'd hold it. Rather than see her long, waterlogged hair, her small, floating breasts and upturned hands, he'd pee in her lonely, long-dead plant.

He knew something was different the night she slipped and fell. For one thing, there was the sound. She often dropped things—not out of clumsiness so much as an abiding fatigue—so he told himself she'd dropped the chipped Chinatown cat their toothbrushes stood in. Only the cat would've smashed, making a splintery noise. Maybe the toilet tank cover. She'd lifted it up after jiggling the handle hadn't worked. Relaxed her grip and let it slide.

After a time, he peed in the plant. Perhaps an hour later, he decided it was all right not to brush his teeth and turned the TV down low to help himself drift off.

In the morning, he folded his blanket away beneath the big brown cushion like always and visited the plant again, leaving a yellow puddle in the saucer beneath the pot. He was good at getting himself ready for school. Cereal in the blue bowl, milk if there was any, otherwise dry. Sometimes just bread. Or if the bread had turned green, then a can of SpaghettiOs; he could work the opener just fine. There was always something if you checked every cupboard. There had never been nothing at all.

It was one thing going to bed with dirty teeth, but he couldn't see going to school that way, risking that Mrs. Gamble might catch a whiff of sourness when he opened his mouth at attendance to say *Here*. He tried the bathroom door and found it open. There was no blood—the edge of the tub wasn't sharp enough to cut. There was a bump, though, bubbling out from her skull. She lay naked on her back like usual, only for once her green eyes weren't closed.

After standing for a time gripping the sink, Darius backed out of the bathroom on tiptoe. He made two baloney sandwiches—one for now, one for lunch—and he went to school, leaving the door to the apartment ajar.

He never did learn whether it was the super, Mr. Kane, or maybe the old Indian lady down the hall who noticed the open door. Somebody called out to see if anyone was home, then pushed the door wide and went inside. Somebody telephoned the police. Not from the apartment, though; the phone on the kitchen wall had been dead for as long as Darius had understood about phones.

The officer who came to his class had a lady with him. She was old like Mrs. Gamble, but her silvery hair was cut short instead of wound up like a doughnut and pinned to her head. She asked him about his family.

"There's only us," he told her. And then, remembering, "Only me."

But it turned out he was wrong. After only a few days back in the happy canned-soup smell of the Miskes' house, the short-haired lady came again. This time the man at her side had no uniform, though he stood as though he might be wearing one under his stiff tan coat. He was the wrong size for the Miskes' crowded kitchen, his shoulders the width of their refrigerator, his forehead reflecting a white slash of fluorescent tube. His hair was the colour of metal. Slicked close to his skull, it was long enough to curl over the collar of his coat. His eyes, when he brought them closer, bending awkwardly at the waist, were a familiar green.

Darius didn't notice the woman at first, but when she eased out from behind the big man, he saw that she wore his mother's mouth. She was older than Faye, though, and she had more flesh on her bones. She looked as though she just might last.

She knelt down before him on the Miskes' kitchen floor. She was like a dog then. Darius had never had one of his own, but he'd talked to plenty of them in the parkette. The woman looked at him the way they all did—the secret streak of wildness, the well of bald, beseeching love.

It was a long drive back to his grandparents' home, soft light in the foothills, abrupt night once they truly began to climb. While he could manage to stay awake, Darius maintained a fair grasp on things: he was in the cab of a truck, wedged between the man and woman who had made Faye. She'd never spoken of them as far as he could remember, but then she'd tended to keep her thoughts to herself. Anyway, the fact that he'd never heard of Ron and Agnes Grimes didn't mean they were strangers. Mrs. Miske had told him so that very morning while she'd helped him dress. *They're family, sweetie. They're your flesh and blood.*

The road wound on and on, the Rocky Mountains crowding close. Try as he might to keep his wits about him, Darius succumbed to a rumbling sleep. *Flesh and blood, flesh and blood*—his dreaming mind made a taunt of the words, and then a horror. The woman on his right became *flesh*, pinkish-white and formless. The man on his left—hard-thighed, hard-sided—became a brilliant crimson rush.

Once, when they hit a pothole, he jolted awake for the space of a brief exchange.

"Slips in the bathtub and dies. *In the bathtub.* Can't even manage to take a bath."

"Ron—"

"Ron what?"

"He might wake up."

"What if he does? Boy's got a right to know what his mother was."

———

They roused him from both sides as the truck juddered to a stop—a gentle *Darius*, a hand dropping from the gearshift to close on his knee. In the headlights' beam, there stood a small, solitary house. It was made of logs, and for the first time ever, Darius saw wood for what it was: the bodies of fallen trees.

His grandfather cut the engine, making the naked bulb above the front door the only light in the world. Darius would learn the next morning that the source of all that spongy, whispering darkness was nothing more sinister than trees. He'd never imagined they could grow in such staggering numbers. Never seen them cross branches and block out the stars.

Inside, the house was no larger than the apartment where Faye lay floating. No, Faye was down in the dirt now, remember? She'd never have a good soak again.

Darius assumed one of the two inside doors led to a bathroom, so the other one had to be for his grandparents' room. He would sleep on the couch like always, and that was a small comfort in itself. Except it turned out there was no bathroom, and certainly no tub. During the night you went in a big white bowl with handles by the back door—the pot, his grandmother called it. In the daytime you went out to the backhouse. Which left a door unaccounted for, the door that opened onto his very own room.

He could scarcely believe it. There was a bed, a desk and a chest of drawers—not exactly child-sized, yet somehow not fully grown. His grandmother stood beside him on the braided rug. "We'll get your things put away in the morning. Come on now, pants off and let's get you into bed."

She turned the covers back while he worked his elastic-waist jeans down, stood aside while he climbed in. He saw then that the walls of his little room cut off before they reached the ceiling's peak. Rafters and the shadows they made. Until then the only ceilings he'd known had been flat. Water-stained in the apartment, pocked in school, brushed with stucco swirls at the Miskes'—but flat.

"This was her room." Her voice so low he could barely hear it. "Her bed."

Darius nodded. He could feel the slight dip his mother's body had made. Not just girl-like then, but an actual girl. He wished his grandmother would leave, preferring the threat of the unknown dark to her miserable hovering.

"We won't talk about her, though. Not when he can hear."

He nodded again.

"You must be tired." She patted him through the blanket, the same knee her husband had clutched in the truck. "Good night, Darius." She sighed his name, as though the sound of it made her sorry.

"Good night . . ."

"Grandmother. You call us Grandmother and Grandfather." She found the whisper again. "I like Grandma, but he won't hear of it." She bent in close, her words more breath than sound. "You be sure and mind him. Mind everything he says."

# 7

# The City Book

Metal, Guy thinks. His first thought of the day. Someone striking metal with—not a hammer, the sound has a slipping quality to it. A chisel? He sits up, blinking. Dawn, but only just. It's not like Stephen to be out in the yard this early, and Lily always comes quietly, bearing her terrified birds. Who, then?

The sound rings out again, and he rises in his boxers, stepping to the window and sliding it open wide. Head and shoulders in the morning air, he turns. A blue jay bobs on top of the red-tail's cage. It spots him and squawks again.

The hawk twists to turn a malevolent eye skyward. The jay must feel that look along its pale underparts, but it's a brainy bird, well aware of the barrier it stands on. Its fourth gloating cry elicits a murderous shriek. Guy feels the hawk's note in his neck bones. Reaching back for the blanket, he drags it up over his shoulders like a shawl.

The jay takes a jaunty step. It turns up its tail—flick, flick—then parts its beak and releases a perfect echo of the hawk's cry.

The red-tail takes the bait: doubling its volume, it pumps on the branch like a set of bellows, blasting the jay. No sign of yesterday's sore foot, much to Guy's relief. The hawk's tormentor answers, and the pair of them let rip with a skirling duel.

It's a hell of a racket to start the day on, but he can't help smiling to see the red-tail give as good as it gets. For days after he first installed the diminished hawk in its temporary home, it endured vigorous protest from the local birds. A robin tutted from the bushes; waves of indignant sparrows came chipping; a pair of house wrens stalked and whistled along the top of the cage. Through it all, the red-tail hunkered glumly, prompting Guy to wonder if its spirit was broken beyond repair.

Suddenly, the screeching halts. A standoff? Could be, only the hawk's holding itself like a victor, the jay merely holding still. It may just be the angle of the day, but the balance of colour seems to have shifted too. The blue jay's blue is waning, while the red-tail's red seems to pulse.

Guy turns back to his empty, rumpled bed. If Carlotta were still coming to see him from time to time, she might be lying there now, snoring gently, dead to the world. Nothing could wake her when she wasn't on duty. Strange, given how alert and attentive she'd been with Aunt Jan—dozing like a guard dog on the cot Guy set up alongside the old four-poster, stirring at even the slightest moan. She'd worked the morphine drip like an artist, finessing the dosage so the dying woman could keep her wits about her while they still mattered and then lose them when they were no longer any use.

The first time Carlotta climbed into Guy's bed, he knew it could only be because his aunt didn't need her anymore. It wasn't love—not for either of them—but that didn't mean it wasn't good. When she was awake, Carlotta was more awake than most. The sex was vigorous, therapeutic; it left him feeling contentedly weak. How often she visited depended on the requirements of her latest patient. Then came Mr. Havelock, her most demanding patient of all.

"He's got this big old house over in Rosedale. You wouldn't believe it, Guy. There's so much ivy, it's a miracle the place can stand." She took a breath. "He's going to be sick a good long while. He's going to need more than a nurse." After a moment she touched him on the arm. "You understand?"

"Yeah." And in a way, he did.

Guy stoops to pull the sheet straight, then swings the blanket down from his shoulders and smooths it flat. Still no sound from the warring birds—which reminds him, the hawk must be hungry. He should see if there's anything new in the traps.

**Coyote Cop's Blog**
**Wednesday, May 28, 2008**
A right to be here. Thats funny coming from a guy like you soldierboy. You don't seem so concerned about peoples rights. What about the right a little kid has to play in his yard without wondering when a pair of jaws is going to snap shut on him. I bet you grew up watching nature shows and feeling sorry for the poor prisoner animals when your mommy took you to the zoo. Well guess what. While you were standing there thinking oh what a pretty polar bear

why can't he be free that polar bear was looking back at you and thinking food. Thats all. Food. Some of us know a thing or two about wilderness soldierboy. We know its always there and we know its the enemy. And hey if you understand so much about soldiers and blood then you ought to know what you do with the enemy. Or did you miss that day of basic training? Well nows your chance to catch up.

*POSTED BY Coyote Cop at 4:56 AM*

*soldierboy wrote . . .*
Maybe you're right. Maybe I don't get the whole enemy thing. Take coyotes—that's what this blog is about, right? Farmers say they're the enemy because they kill livestock. So how come a study out in BC found that mutton made up only 0.2% of the diet of so-called sheep-killing coyotes? Less than half of one percent, and even that could have come from scavenging.

In case you're wondering, 70% was small rodents (something else farmers don't like), and other wild animals and plants made up the rest. So coyotes are the enemy because they eat sheep—only it looks as though they hardly ever do. The same goes for attacks on humans. Seriously, how often does it really happen? Rover and Fido are more of a worry. And you know who attacks people even more than dogs do? Never mind murder, way more people die by suicide than by any kind of animal attack. Which means the average human being has more to fear from his own hand than from any coyote's jaws. In which case, maybe you can explain to me what this war of yours is really all about.

*POSTED AT 9:08 AM, May 28, 2008*

Stephen rises and crosses to the Naugahyde couch. It squeaks when he stretches out on it. He hooks an arm over his eyes. It's a question he can't seem to get shut of—a stupid question, really. What is any war about?

As a boy, he was taught not to sully his karma by using physical force. Beacon Hill Alternative wasn't so different from other elementary schools in Victoria; there was violence on the playground—everything from dodge ball with intent to Indian burns—but being the biggest kid in school meant he could sidestep the worst of it. When weaker kids required protection, he wasn't so much the sheepdog as the sheltering tree. Ruby Hopper found her way to that shelter more often than most. Home-schooled until her mother remarried and reconsidered her ideas, Ruby wore whatever she felt like wearing, said whatever she thought.

Things changed with the move to junior high. Here was a forest rather than an open field; Stephen was surrounded by trees taller than himself—grade tens in hoodies or, worse, in rugby jerseys gone wet beneath the arms. He became a master of passive resistance. When slammed into lockers, he righted himself and stood with his fists at his sides.

He made it to grade ten without ever lifting his hand. Then, one afternoon during his final semester at that unhappy, piss-yellow school, he walked around back to unlock his bike and came upon Ruby Hopper in the centre of a crowd—girls and their boyfriends, maybe a dozen in all. Ruby had spoken her mind, or worn something she shouldn't have, or done nothing, absolutely nothing at all. Stephen saw her drop, saw the Nikes and ballet flats and boots of the group draw back. He didn't actually bare his teeth and come bounding on all fours—it only felt that way. In truth, he ran headlong into the cluster, taking as many of them down as he could.

He would find out later about the damage he'd done—a shattered elbow, several chipped teeth, countless abraded hands and arms—but at the time he knew only the vicious intimacy of the fight. He raged on for a minute or more, until one of the boyfriends got his bearings. Stephen felt his head hit concrete and bounce. From the depths of the ensuing darkness came stars. Then Ruby, bursting out of the carnage and sprinting for the school's back door.

Kline let him sweat. Left him alone in the office marked *Vice-Principal* to nurse his sore head and think about what he'd done.

"I had to close the store," Ariel told him when she finally showed. "You know Mica's leading a workshop today."

"Mrs. Carnsew." Kline stepped in behind her, closing the door.

"Ariel."

"Sorry?"

"Ariel. I don't use my last name."

"Ariel, then."

But Stephen could remember a time when her name was Mom, even Mommy—back when she and his father were still Amy and Mike. They'd wanted to hear their new names as often as possible, so they'd told Stephen to start using them too. *You can change yours if you want,* Mica said, but Stephen decided to stick with Stephen. It felt safer if one of them stayed the same.

"Stephen," Ariel said, still standing, "you know how Mica and I feel about violence."

It was hard to look directly at her—the clear blue eyes, the brown hair loose and natural, like a girl's. He stared at his skinned knuckles instead. "I know, but they were hurting her."

"Hurting who?"

"Ruby."

"Ruby who? Who's Ruby?"

Kline cleared his throat. "Your son was protecting a friend of his. A girl who doesn't . . . well, who doesn't fit in."

"Is this true, Stephen?"

Stephen nodded.

"Unfortunately," Kline went on, "things got a little out of hand. Well, a lot out of hand, actually. Several students had to be taken to the walk-in clinic."

"Stephen." She said his name quietly, almost gently. "You know how to deal with negative feelings."

"It wasn't a feeling."

"Pardon me?"

He looked up. "It wasn't a feeling, it was a situation. It was an emergency."

"Okay." She took a breath, closed her eyes for a long moment before opening them again. "Try and come into the now, Stephen."

"I am in the now. Jesus, I just—"

"I don't think this environment is helping." She reached for the door handle.

"Mrs. Carn—Ariel," Kline said, "I'm not sure you understand. This incident is far from over. I'll have to speak to the other students, as well as their parents, before I decide on the appropriate course of action."

Stephen saw his mother's eyes close again. Her breath slowed and became even. He could almost hear the litany of restorative thought.

She said little on the drive downtown.

"Why can't I just go home on my own like usual?" he asked after several silent blocks.

"Because we need to process this."

"Process what? I saved a girl from getting the shit kicked out of her." He'd never spoken to her like this, his voice hard, almost ugly. He took a breath. "It's just, Ruby, she's this weird, sweet girl. She wouldn't hurt a—"

"Stephen, breathe."

"I am breathing."

"You know what I mean. Focus on your breath, follow it inward."

Stephen tried. He followed a breath until it bumped up against his struggling heart, and held it there for as long as he could. By the time they pulled up in front of the store, he'd gone quiet inside. Quiet and dark.

The sign caught him off guard. He came close to laughing, though he'd never found the name funny before. *Sage.* It was perfect—part spiritual quest, part soothing interior design.

It fit the place—fit his parents, for that matter—like an Andean alpaca wool glove.

Ariel unlocked the door and held it open for him. Fairy bells and a face full of sandalwood. She brushed past him on her way to the CD player. Strains of airy flute came floating, making his head hurt all over again.

He looked down into the brassy shallows of a Tibetan prayer bowl. "Two hundred bucks." He felt giddy. "That's some markup, Mom."

She turned to look at him. "Why don't you go spend a little time in the meditation room."

"Go centre yourself," he muttered.

"Mica should be back soon," she added.

"Just wait until your father gets home." He headed for the back of the store.

"If you speak, speak clearly, Stephen. Own your words."

"Ohm," he chanted loudly over his shoulder. "Ohhhhh-mmm!"

Slamming the door to the little white room felt right. He threw his backpack down and stood motionless, his fists clenched. When that got old, he sat down, centring his ass on the yin and yang rug.

Yang—that was the warrior energy, wasn't it? So what was so terrible about accessing your inner yang when the yinnest person you knew was about to get her kidneys kicked in? He already knew what Mica would have to say on the subject, some tai chi nugget about inner discipline triumphing over external force. Which was fine when you were waving hands like clouds, but not much use in the face of a bloodthirsty mob.

Stephen didn't know how such thoughts had leaked into

his mind. Maybe the fight behind the school had changed him. Maybe now was the time to pick a new name—Rocko, or Spike. His head felt a little better. He closed his eyes and lay back on the black and white rug.

Mica woke him by nudging the door in against the soles of his sneakers.

"You asleep?"

Stephen sat up, blinking. His head made an internal whimpering sound.

His father's gaze was mild. "Ariel told me what happened."

"Yeah? How would she know?"

"I don't follow."

"She never asked me anything about it."

Mica nodded. "You know, Stephen, everyone has their own path."

"What's that supposed to mean?"

"It means you may believe you can alter another person's experience in this life, but that experience is something he or she has created. This girl today—"

"Ruby." Stephen stared at his father's knees, baggy in white cotton pants.

"Okay, Ruby." He said it as though they were agreeing between themselves to call her that. As though it wasn't really her name. "The point is, only Ruby can change the path she's on. Only Ruby can alter the energy she puts out into the world, the energy she attracts."

"You mean she asked for it."

"That's not what I said."

"Yes it is. You think she asked for it. Like she's some kind of fucking freak who wanted to get wailed on. Like she hoped those assholes would be waiting for her when she went to unlock her bike."

"Stephen, that's your stuff, not mine." Mica glanced over his shoulder at the tinkle of the front-door bells.

"Don't let me keep you."

Mica looked at him then, one of his probing, reflective looks that only went one way. "There's a lot of anger in this room, Stephen."

"You don't say." Stephen stood up, the whimper in his skull spiking to a howl. He steadied himself before stooping for his pack. "I'm going home."

He was only fifteen, but when he straightened, he met his father face to face. It was like looking at a snapshot of himself a couple of decades down the road, still tall and handsome, but hollowed out somehow, his gentle face bearded, lashes blinkering his eyes. When Mica stepped aside to let him pass, it was as though the photograph flipped over, showing the blank on its other side.

Stephen walked slowly up Fort Street that afternoon, each step echoing in his tender head. Those blocks were familiar to him—known by heart—and yet they had a strange, almost enchanted feel. Had there always been that many homeless hunkering in doorways? That many hanging baskets dripping blooms? Not long after crossing Blanshard, he noticed something else that had eluded him before. In among the antique shops and the happy little cafés, one storefront stood out. Canadian Forces Recruiting Centre.

Several posters hung in the window, but Stephen saw only one: the soldier in filthy fatigues, an even filthier child in his arms. He knew he was too young to do anything without his parents' permission. Still, it couldn't hurt to go in and ask a few questions. Maybe even pick up a brochure.

It's hard to pass by Bill's Lobsters without stopping to look in. The window tank is crammed with sluggish creatures, their claws clamped shut with white rubber bands. It's a slow struggle, the brutes rising to the top while the ones on the bottom gradually give up. As always, Billy whimpers at the sight.

"It's *Bill's* Lobsters," Lily tells him. "Not Billy's. Besides, they're gross."

He has less interest in the supermarkets—Fu Yao and Trinity and Cai Yuan—but Lily likes the outdoor mounds of scaly, nameless roots, the bags of sweating green beans long as licorice whips. Who knew there were so many kinds of oranges? Leaves, bruised and slippery, litter the ground. A massive, knobby squash has a wedge chopped out to showcase its bright insides.

Around the corner on Broadview, Billy grows hopeful again. The Sing Sing BBQ House makes him cow-eyed. Pork quarters hang like fatty, gathered curtains alongside orange mini-monsters with tentacled legs. Lacquered ducks dangle from the hooks wound through their necks, eyes like seed pods, beaks and leg nubs charred.

Five doors and an alleyway along, a pair of porcelain happy-cats wave from the window of the shop both Lily and her dog adore. Miao Ke Hong Bakery. If she has even a little change in her pocket—and today she has three loonies plus—she never passes the place without going in.

She chooses a coconut bun for herself and a ham-and-egg bun for Billy. Doesn't spot the patrol car until she's halfway out the door and both heads inside it are swivelling her way. Blood thunders in her ears. A moment's frozen, light-headed panic, and then Billy shuffles close, looking up at her in hungry hope.

"Not yet, boy." She stuffs the bag in her vest pocket. "Come on."

They walk north, past plastic bins full of dried beans, dried sea creatures, dried mushrooms like scraps of suede— back into the condensing crowd. The cops follow, creeping along on the far side of the parked cars, now and then nudging their bumper into Lily's peripheral view. She can just about hear the description they'll be working from.

*Thin. She's terribly thin.*

*You mean skinny. You'd hardly know she was a girl.*

*And she has long black hair.*

*Looks like shoe polish. Natural blonde and she goes and dyes it.*

*She's still pretty, though.*

*Pretty stupid. Pretty goddamn selfish, putting her mother and me through this.*

Would they have a picture too? Not one with the pink hack job—she'd done that in the bathroom at the mall, sawing off hanks in the end stall before glopping on the goo, dragging her toque down over the stinky mess and going outside to sit with Billy while the colour burned. Of course, it's Billy himself who's the giveaway. Maybe she should've bleached his beautiful coat while she was at it. Turned him brassy, then rinsed him clean in the filthy Don.

Traffic backs up behind a streetcar, slowing, then halting,

the cops. Lily keeps to an even, unhurried pace. One hand twisted in Billy's mane, she weaves through the dozen or so disembarking passengers, makes the corner and turns. The alley's only a few doors down. She turns again when they reach it, and then, only then, she runs.

Billy lopes along easily beside her. If only he were a little bigger, she could jump up onto his back and be gone.

They take a hard left where the alley turns, hammering along behind the businesses that face Gerrard. They've walked this way maybe a dozen times, Lily lifting the lids of the green garbage bins in search of morsels Billy might like. She's gotten used to her own hunger; it hurts her belly worse to think of him going without.

Running flat out, she spots a dark blue Dumpster and veers. There's just enough room between the bin and the restaurant's back wall. Lily sinks down, shoulder blades pressed to the Dumpster, knees drawn up against her chest. Billy squeezes in beside her and leans.

They hear the patrol car when it comes. Idling. Trolling. Idling again. Lily reaches for Billy's forepaw and works her fingers in between his toes, feeling for the webbing there. He lets his tongue slip out and hang. She counts in her head, one hundred and fourteen before the cops move on. They could be squatting at either end of the alley, though. Better to wait.

She wouldn't risk smoking even if she had some, but the thought of it makes her remember their treats. Billy makes a baby sound when she pulls the ham-and-egg bun out of the bag. He mouths it carefully from her fingers, tosses and snaps, swallowing it in one. Lily peels the coconut bun from its tinfoil circle. Nibbles a third before giving him that too.

He nuzzles her cheek.

"Ack, dog breath."

He grins at her. Then suddenly, softly, he growls.

She hasn't heard the back door of the restaurant swing open. The man standing on the cement stoop is short, wiry, old. A shock of snowy hair under a white peaked hat.

"Hey," he calls, "you eat garbage?"

"Quiet, boy." Lily stands, sliding up against the bin. Looks round its corner as casually as she can. No sign. Stepping out into the open, she feels Billy's nose butt the back of her thigh. "Hold your horses. Heel."

"Well?" the old guy says.

"Well what?"

"You eat garbage?"

"No."

"Good." He pulls a pack of Marlboros from his apron pocket. Lily feels a nicotine pang that apparently shows. He holds them out. "Want one?"

What's he going to do, knife her? String her up like a portion of pig, a charred and naked duck? Not with Billy beside her. Not with her own knife weighing her breast pocket down.

She walks over to him and pinches a yellow-ended smoke up out of the pack. The stoop is three steps up, but he hunkers down, bringing his face level with hers. Pretty good knees for a grandpa. He lights his own then hands her the lighter. Good—she hates it when they cup a hand around the flame and make her bend in close.

He says nothing, smoking, keeping his ash tidy with an occasional flick of his thumb. After a minute or so, Lily considers moving on. Which way, though? The cop car could be long gone, or it could be waiting like a cartoon cat by a mouse's cut-out hole.

She decides to stay awhile, smoking in the late morning sun. Maybe he'll make the best of his break and light a second smoke off the first. If so, he might offer her another one too.

Sensing her intention, Billy drops into a sit.

"Good dog," the old guy says.

"Yeah."

"Good manner."

"Yeah."

He takes a deep drag, blows it out in a needle-thin stream. "My name Chin."

She looks at him.

"You know chin, right?" He thumbs his own as though feeling for stubble.

She nods.

"You got no name?"

She looks away.

He grinds out his cigarette, drops the butt off the side of the stoop. "You need job?"

Lily takes a drag, aware of the slight tremor in her hand.

"I think you hard worker."

"I don't know." She lets the butt fall from her fingers. "I guess so."

"You know how wash dish, right?"

"Right."

"Okay." Chin rises, no hand on the iron pipe of the banister, just the strength of his own stringy thighs. "Come on."

"What about my dog?"

"He good dog. He lie down here." He points to the stoop. "I bring him lunch."

"Lunch."

"Lunch for him, lunch for you, plus eight dollar an hour cash."

She looks down at Billy. He seems happy enough.

"Come on, no-name-girl," Chin says, turning to go in. "Work to do."

The Joel Weeks Parkette is a good spot for a rest. It's an oddly peaceful place, given the origin of its name. Stephen wondered about it for months before he finally remembered to look it up on the Web. The little wedge of land is dedicated to an eight-year-old boy who drowned—not in the murky Don River, not even in the chemical blue of the neighbourhood pool. In a sewer. A moment's inattention, an open manhole that ought to have been closed.

Stephen often comes here after ducking into the Pizza Planet on Queen for a coffee and a slice. There's a bench in amongst a few young maples, tucked away behind a stand of pines. Close to the quiet alley, it's sufficiently lonely to be almost always free.

The light here is subtle and sweet. Tiger lies in the slatted shade beneath him; Stephen can feel him panting, pressed up against his calf. Lungs inside ribs inside skin.

Only one kid on the basketball court today—fourteen or so, the bones showing painfully at his elbows and knees, as though he's recently been stretched. He's worked up a sweat playing against himself, deking and dribbling low, whirling to show unseen opponents his back. His dark arms gleam as the ball leaves his fingers and flies. Stephen wonders if he could still sink a basket. He could ask to join in, just for a layup or two, but what would he do with Tiger? Besides, he can't be certain a white boy would be welcome on the court.

Growing up in Victoria, he couldn't help but register if somebody was black. There were exactly four African-Canadian kids at Vic High, and two of them were brother and sister. Of course, there were black guys in the Forces, more among the American units—but it's best not to wander down that path in his mind. It only ever leads to one colour: the shade every soldier wears on the inside.

He eases the lid from his coffee and lays it upside down on the ground near Tiger's nose. Drawing two creamers from the bag, he empties them into the lid. Tiger drives his brindled snout into the little puddle. When the cream is gone, he favours Stephen with a doe-eyed glance, then commences shoving the lid about with his tongue. The pizza slice is Hawaiian. Stephen peels off a half-moon sliver of ham to share.

When he straightens up, a photograph stands before him. It's the only way he can make sense of the young woman's looks: someone has scissored a picture out of a magazine and blown it up large as life. Her lips turn up at the corners, wet-looking, silvery-pink. Her hair, thick and blond, falls like a bright cloak about her arms. A black T-shirt tight as a bandage, golden cleavage in the V of its neck. Stephen is staring. Some part of him registers the fact that the kid on the court has stopped dodging and leaping. The kid is staring too.

Stephen lifts his gaze to find hers has fallen. It rests on the beast at his feet.

"Aw," she says, dropping into a squat.

"Careful." He shoots an arm down between them.

"It's okay." She reaches past him to lay a hand on Tiger's brow. "Dogs love me."

It's a common, often foolish, claim, but this time Stephen feels the truth of it in Tiger's rippling flank.

"What's his name?"

"Tiger." Stephen takes a breath. "I'm Stephen."

"Kyla." She keeps her eyes on the dog. "Tiger, huh?" She works her long, white-tipped nails around the base of one striped ear. "You like that, boy?"

Her hair is glowing—Stephen can almost feel its reflected warmth—but the crown of her head tells a different story. The black half-inch stripe at her part shocks him. Her true colour the same as his own.

"Your hair." He hasn't meant to say it out loud.

She looks up at him. "What about it?"

"It's . . . pretty."

"Pretty fake." There's something muscular, almost reflexive about her smile. "I know, I need to do my roots."

"Do you like it?" Something reflexive about his speech too, bypassing all the usual controls. "Better, I mean. Like that."

She turns her attention back to the dog. Stephen forces himself to look away from the black strip that halves her skull, a scorched path through a blinding field. He focuses on her hand; she's moved over to the other ear now, keeping things balanced, fair. Tiger gives vent to a sigh, reeling the sound out steadily through his nose. She won't answer now—it's been too long a pause. He never should have asked.

"I don't know." She gathers Tiger's thin-skinned ear in her fist and gives it a tug. "It's not really *for* me."

"Your hair?"

She releases the ear, her body seeming to coil as she rises, as though she were made of smoke. "I better be going. My shift starts about now."

Stephen makes the calculation: If she's supposed to be at work already, how far away can it be? Three, four blocks at most. He can make note of which way she turns at Queen and narrow the field further still. It can't be an office with the way she's dressed. A waitress? He begins running through nearby restaurants in his mind.

Tiger scrambles out from under the bench and stands trembling, his nose pressed to Kyla's knee.

"Aw, look. He doesn't want me to go."

And now Stephen stands. He's taller than her by a hand's breadth. He looks down along her scalp as though sighting his mark, until the line tips back and he's looking into her eyes. "Where do you work?"

She closes her eyes as though remembering, and he sees that her eyelids are shiny and green. A black slash marks the lash line, the lashes themselves unusually long.

"Jilly's," she says.

"Jilly's?"

She takes a step back and regards him. "Yeah, you know, over at Queen and Broadview. Jilly's."

"I don't think so. Is it—"

"Christ, everybody knows Jilly's." Her gaze is suddenly hard. "I'm a dancer there."

"A dancer?"

"That's what I said." She looks down. "Bye-bye, Tiger."

Sensing another betrayal, Tiger barks.

"Quiet." Stephen closes a hand around the dog's collar as Kyla turns on the sharp white heel of her boot. She walks away quickly, a short block and a half before she rounds the corner onto Queen and disappears. "It's okay, boy," Stephen murmurs.

The dog sits back on his haunches and howls.

It's incredible, the way some of them come back from the brink. Mitzy was dragging her hind end when she first came in, the classic dachshund scar still fresh alongside her spine. Now, a mere four weeks later, she's stepping lively and half wagging her tail, good for fifteen minutes on the treadmill followed by a two-minute swim. Kate still has Sandi diaper her to be on the safe side, but it's been three full treatments since she let go in the tank.

She's too small to be in there on her own, so Sandi stands over her with her feet planted on either side of the running belt. Mitzy only needs a few centimetres of water to buoy her up, but Sandi's rolled her scrubs up above her knees. Bare feet, bare calves—no denying she has nice legs, but the sight of them no longer causes Kate pain. Besides, she's intent on four stubby little limbs at the moment, down on her side on the tiles alongside the tank, evaluating Mitzy's diminutive stride. There's no sign of a drag, not even the slight skipping she was showing last week. Kate reaches for the camera and snaps a series of stills.

"Smile, Mitz." Mrs. Greenbaum has planted her chair at

the base of the ramp where Mitzy can see her. Dressed head to toe in fuchsia velour, she's the brightest thing in the room. "I just can't get over it," she says.

"I know." Kate smiles up at her. "We'll measure her later, but I can already tell her muscle mass is up."

"Just look at those drumsticks," Sandi croons, reaching down to centre Mitzy on the track.

"Have you noticed her face?" Mrs. Greenbaum says.

Kate sits up. "Her face?"

"Her expression. She always used to look so cranky. Hell, she *was* cranky. It's like she's a completely different dog."

"Did you see her with Baby when she came in?" says Sandi. "She went right up and touched noses."

"I *know.*" Mrs. Greenbaum taps the front pane. "Come on, Mitzy, come on. That's my girl." She sits back. "When I walked her in the hallway the other day, she didn't even bark at the cocker spaniel from 3B."

"It's the pain," Kate says, noting the first hint of a slow-down in the dog's hind legs. "Once they feel better, it's easier to be nice."

"Poor Mitzy," Mrs. Greenbaum sighs. "All this time Daddy and I just thought you were a little bitch."

Kate laughs, rising to hit the *Slower* button then squatting to see if Mitzy's gait improves. A little, but she's clearly getting tired.

"Okay, girl, not far to go now." Kate picks up the camera again and centres it on the back legs alone. Sandi's toes are in the shot—tanned and well tended, the nails a glassy pink.

What must Lily's feet look like? Thin, of course, and pale. Certainly in need of a long soak, a healthy scrubbing. Someone to bandage the blisters and trim the curved nails with care.

"Think she's had enough?" Sandi says.

"Huh?"

"Mitzy. That's fifteen minutes now."

"I'm getting pooped just watching," says Mrs. Greenbaum.

"Okay." Kate stands and steadies herself with a hand on the tank. After a moment she lays a palm to the *Slower* button and depresses it again.

This time it's Guy who lets Edal in. She doesn't even have to buzz—he appears in the office doorway seconds after she shows herself at the gate.

His jeans are faded, worn to strings at the left knee. A green checked shirt sets his hair blazing. He walks like no one she's ever known, hands in pockets, a kind of springing stroll.

"Hey," he says, drawing near, "you came."

She nods. "My bike back?"

"Not yet." He reaches down the front of his shirt and draws out his key on its silver chain.

She looks away, peering up the street as though she hopes to find her bicycle there.

"She'll show up soon." Guy draws back the gate.

"Yeah?" She steps inside.

"Yeah."

If this was the old country—any old country—they'd know what to do next. Clasp hands or kiss each other on the cheek—once, twice, even three times, bobbing together like a pair of preening birds. As it is, she stands side-on to him in silence, both of them surveying the yard.

"You want the tour?" he says finally.

"Sure." Too quick—she should at least pretend to think about it.

"Okay." He sweeps an arm grandly across the scene. "Loader. Link-Belt. Big old dirty oil drums, big old dirty pile of tires." He grins. "Over here, these are my trucks. The funny-looking one's a tow truck and the other one's just regular."

"Okay, okay." She points to where a mangled white sedan sits mounted on the boxy machine. "What about that?"

"That's an Acura."

She gives him a look.

"Oh, you mean the thing it's sitting on. That's the crusher."

"That's what you call it?"

"What else? Hey, you want to see something worth seeing?"

"Sure." Again, the unhesitating assent. She'll have to work on that.

The hawk is hiding. Guy presses up against the cage door, fingers hooked in the chain-link on either side of his head. Standing behind him, Edal can't help but remember the last time she patted a suspect down.

Customs was on the lookout for a different breed of smuggler coming off the Bogotá flight, but that didn't stop one of them noticing the crusts of white crap on the suspect's shoes. He was pacing the holding room when Edal arrived—nineteen years old, a skinny, unthinking kid. She frisked him gently, halting when she discerned the first lump on his thigh. He did as he was told, standing up on the chair and stepping carefully out of his wide-legged jeans. The pant legs had been rigged up with a series of hammock-style slings; each one held a red siskin—pretty little finches prized for their crimson plumage and trilling song. There were males and females, living and dead. Their keeper stood on the chair in his grubby briefs, eyes fastened on the floor.

"Ah." The sound Guy makes is soft, little more than a sigh. He glances back at her over his shoulder. "Look who's decided to show himself."

The red-tail peers round the trunk of the dead oak. After a moment, it stretches out one foot, then the other, grasping hold of the broken side branch. It looks steadily at Guy, then cuts its eyes away. Guy motions for Edal to step forward, the hawk watching her now, gauging her intent. Guy gives a low whistle. Again the bird looks away, turning its head sharply aside this time, as though piqued.

"You're no fool, are you, Red?" Guy says. "He knows I haven't got anything for him."

"He?"

"Well, he hasn't laid any eggs, anyway. At least not yet."

The hawk's head is in motion now, as though buffeted by hairline variations in the breeze. Countless trajectories extend from the curved midline of its bill, pointing up the minutest of movements and sounds.

"I could swear his colour's getting better," Guy says. "Especially his head."

"It probably is. Their hood feathers brighten up in spring."

She's spoken without thinking. When he turns to look at her, she keeps her eyes forward, pinned on the hawk. "I've got a couple of bird books."

"Uh-huh."

"Red, huh?"

"Yeah. It's not a name, really. More of a nickname. Makes it harder if you name them, you know, when it comes time to let them go."

"You won't keep him?" She hears herself trying to sound merely curious.

"Only till he's strong enough to make it on his own."

"Where'd he come from?"

"Farther up the parkway. He was hopping around like crazy in the grass, looked like he was trying to hunt. I let him wear himself out before I got close."

"How'd you catch him?"

"Threw my coat over him." He shakes his head. "You could feel how skinny he was."

"When was this?"

"Must be a month ago now."

The red-tail makes a sound of its own then—*Awk*, or, with a slight stretch of the imagination, *Hawk*.

"Aawk," Guy says back to it, and it shifts from foot to foot on its branch, seemingly pleased.

"So," Edal says after a moment, "why'd you keep him? I mean, aren't there places?" She's actually lying now. She knows there are places. She has their numbers in her cell, knows the names of the people who would pick up if she called.

"I take good care of him." Something's shifted in his tone. A hint of distance, possibly even hurt.

"Oh, sure," she says quickly, "I can see that. It's just, I mean, how'd you know he didn't have a broken wing or something?"

"I told you, you could tell what the trouble was. He was starving. Anyway, I felt his bones to be sure. His breastbone was like a butter knife, all the muscle shrunk away. I figure somebody tried to make a pet of him, maybe in one of those condo towers along the valley. Maybe they weren't feeding him right, or else he just wouldn't eat. I have this picture of him making a break for it from a balcony, you know, leaping off and finding out he was too weak to really fly."

"Could be." She leaves another small pause. "What do you feed him?"

"Mice. I started with dead ones, but just lately I've switched to live. You know, get him hunting again."

She nods. "Sounds like a good idea."

"Speaking of food, you can stay for supper if you like."

"Oh." She feels herself flush. "I don't know. I don't want to eat you out of house and home."

He laughs. "I wouldn't worry about that. It's Stephen's turn to cook, so it'll be something with lentils—about seventeen cents a plate."

"I don't know."

"Lily usually shows up to eat. You don't want to go home without your bike again, do you?"

"No. Well, if you're sure."

"I'm sure."

It turns out to be beans rather than lentils—a fragrant stew served over fluffy brown rice. Lily shows up when the three of them are already seated.

"Hey, Lily," Guy says.

"Hey." She dumps a helping of kibble in the bowl by the door. Billy buries his snout and starts crunching.

"There's plenty in the pot," Stephen tells her. "Help yourself."

"Thanks." She heads for the stove.

Edal's playing over the ways in which she might broach the subject of the bike when Guy says simply, "You bring Edal's bike back?"

Lily takes her seat. "Do I look like a thief?"

"Okay." Guy takes a swallow of beer. "Maybe next time you could ask."

"I don't see what the big deal is."

"Who's making a big deal?"

"Whatever."

It's Edal's turn to say something—the right thing, if she can figure out what that might be. "What did you think?" She meets Lily's gaze across the table.

"About what?"

"The bike."

Lily shows the briefest of smiles. "It's pretty sweet." She bends over her plate, eating quickly, catching up. When she stands and begins clearing the table, Edal rises to help. "It's okay, I've got it."

"I don't mind."

"No, really, it's okay."

Last night it would've been a rebuke, but tonight Edal's fairly sure it's a kindness. She resumes her seat, watching Stephen fold Billy's black ear in his palm, causing the dog's dark eyes to close with pleasure. Guy leans back and fishes out the knife. The toothpick slips out easily, and he goes to work behind the curtain of his hand.

"You mind?" Edal asks, reaching for the knife.

"Be my guest."

She's always loved them—the smooth casing, bright and candy-hard, the neat white cross. She fits her thumbnail to the first dark groove and folds out the larger of the two knives. He keeps it sharp, she's strangely pleased to see, and clean. She digs out the scissors next, the combination screwdriver–can opener, the awl. File, small knife and corkscrew. It's silly, but she has to get the tweezers out too. Lay them down alongside the bristling whole.

She glances up to find both men watching her. How long has she been playing with the knife, marvelling open-mouthed like a child or a chimpanzee? She snaps its appendages back in place quickly, feeling the nip of the little blade's point in the pad of her thumb. Guy takes it up a moment after she sets it down. He slides the toothpick into place. Cups the knife as though weighing it before shoving it away.

Guy's body is tired—deep in his bones, but also the fragile, creeping fatigue that lives in the skin. His brain, on the other hand, is wide awake.

Is it his imagination, or was Edal in a rush to get away? Maybe she hadn't liked tonight's reading. "How Fear Came" is a little slow compared to the other chapters. Or maybe it wasn't the story at all, but the fact that he was reading it aloud.

He feels for the bedside lamp, the push-through toggle of the switch. It's the gentlest light he knows. Aunt Jan often complained it wasn't strong enough, swore she was ruining her eyes.

She always sat in the same spot, crossways at the foot of the bed, walking her buttocks back until her shoulder blades met the wall. Once she was settled, Guy liked to work his feet out from beneath the covers and rest them against her thigh. The older he got, the more he had to tuck his legs up to give her room. When Uncle Ernie wasn't out on a call, he'd light a smoke and draw a chair up to the bedroom doorway, balancing the ashtray on his lap. Sometimes, when his bad disc was bothering him, he'd lie on his back on the floor.

*Everybody comfortable?* Aunt Jan would say. *Now, where were we?*

When Brother the cat came to live with them, it was Guy's turn to read aloud—not the whole chapter, as Aunt Jan had done, but bits and pieces, the passages too good to keep to himself. *Listen to this—White Fang's getting picked on by the dogs. "To keep one's feet in the midst of the hostile mass meant life, and this he learned well. He became catlike in his ability to stay on his feet."* Sometimes Brother curled up in Aunt Jan's old spot and listened. Other times, when the kitten part of his brain took over, he batted the book's cover, or wormed his way in between Guy and the page.

Now there's nobody to keep Guy from reading. Also, no question which book he will read. It's been on the nightstand since he took it down last night. He sits up against his pillow and reaches for it, opening to where the story begins.

I sit in a pitch-pine panelled kitchen-living room, with an otter asleep upon its back among the cushions on the sofa, forepaws in the air, and with the expression of tightly shut concentration that very small babies wear in sleep . . .

Edal lies on her back, the futon hard beneath her. Why, despite all her years of gainful employment, has she never invested in a proper bed?

No sign of the mouse, the lone turd by the kitchen faucet its only message. It's deserted her. Left by a rodent. Ridiculous but true.

Doubtless it's made its way down through the walls to James and Annie's place, where it can nose out two people's crumbs. They probably let their dirty dishes lie—at least on those nights when they turn their music up loud. French dance hall tunes, or rhythmic gypsy guitar. Sometimes, in the quiet between songs, Edal catches a scrap of laughter, or worse.

They've laid down traps—Annie told her last week when they met up in the front hall. Edal said yes, she'd noticed them too. She made sure to say "them," not "it." Everyone knows there's no such thing as a single mouse.

Annie said they were using the regular wooden snap traps with cheese, only they hadn't caught anything yet, and the guy at the Home Hardware—you know, the cute one with the beard—said to try peanut butter, so they might do that. The cute one? Edal flinched inwardly. Annie had James, and yet she still kept an eye out for bearded boys. Maybe they weren't so happy after all. Edal had heard them fight, not often, but they both raised their voices, and sometimes Annie cried, really howling, like a child. But that was normal, wasn't it? Was it? Edal could scarcely imagine. Yelling at someone— really yelling—and standing your ground, or collapsing, or both when he yelled back. Then, the next morning, kissing that same someone deep and long. Standing on the front walk and kissing so you don't hear your neighbour on the porch behind you, forcing her to call out *Morning!* in a strained and cheerful voice, and scuttle past you with her bike.

Not glue traps, though, Annie said, they could never do that. What are you supposed to do when one of them is stuck there, squeaking its little head off—squash it with a frying pan? She pulled a sick, fearful face, and for a moment she was no longer a beauty. Snow White, Edal thought the first time they met, and she can't help but believe Annie's apple-blossom skin and thick black curls have something to do with the abandoned sounds—happy and unhappy—she plugs her ears not to hear.

She can see them now, falling together into bed. Maybe Annie pushes James down onto the duvet, or maybe they don't even make it that far, but stay where the music plays in their little living room, him easing her down on the sofa, or lower, the blood-red rug Edal's glimpsed through their open door.

Turning on her side, Edal draws her knees up and hugs them. It's pathetic. She's crying now, wetting her pillow with tears and even a thin stream of snot, because a common house mouse has forsaken her home for another.

In the beginning, she told herself she watched it with the eye of a naturalist. She'd known it was there for some time, but had never actually spotted it until her first day home on leave. It left the shadow beneath the refrigerator boldly, sniffing the air only briefly before darting across the kitchen floor. It expected her to be at work, not lying useless in the adjacent room. She'd been awake for an hour, trying to think of something—anything—she wanted to do.

Warmth was what she felt. She could call it delight, but gratitude would be closer to the truth. She lay dead still for what remained of the morning, watching the little creature whisker its way over her kitchen floor.

Here among the trees, the leaf litter lies thick and driven through with shoots. Fallen branches hide grubs. There are mice, and there are ground nests brimming with eggs. On lucky nights, the odd nestling, bird or squirrel, drops from the thin cover above.

The skunk snuffles. Scenting a cache of grubs, he halts, listening hard for their soft-bodied sound. In the distance, a human yelp, followed by the bark of a dog. The ground slopes down from here to the field where they gather—the dogs gambolling like puppies, returning time and again to feed from their masters' hands.

The skunk has no master. He relies on his own curved claws.

Turning an ear to the ground, he discerns the subtle music and digs. The night is generous—not only grubs writhing in the sudden air, but there, slipping out from beneath a rotten limb, a snake. As a rule, the skunk doesn't hurry. He must act quickly now, though, before the bright-sided slither plays tricks with his eyes. A lunge, a single bite to the head, and the snake lies still. So smooth to the nose's touch, the scent still delicate, no time to panic and release its stink. It's a good length—his own measure and more. The chewing will take some time.

He's a fine hunter, young but able, no trace of the blind kitten he once was. The memory lives in his senses: the massed, many-hearted comfort of the den; the return of the mother's pungent coat and sweet-smelling teats. Soon she brought them more than milk—the first leggy mouthful of spider, the first pretty pink worm. Eventually she led them to the source of all things good and wriggling, the wide-open night of the world. The skunk remembers in the red hollow behind his eyes the striped, winding column he and his siblings made as they followed the lovely brush of her tail. They were adept at raising their own tails by then, though the glands that would afford them special standing had yet to swell with their precious yellow oil.

It's the best kind of weapon to have—the kind that rarely comes into play. Here where the humans live packed so close, the only cats to be found are skunk-sized and smart enough to give him a wide berth. On occasion the call of an owl lifts his hackles, but it's rare to feel the silent-feathered wind of a swoop. Foxes are only a problem when famine gets the better of their good sense. There was one, not long after the skunk left the living column to hunt alone. All bone and mange, it stalked him with a dull-eyed desperation he'd never encountered before. It ignored all warnings. Taking the initial blast head-on, it recoiled but held its ground. The skunk fired again into its blinded face, again and again, and still the snapping jaws came on. Only when he loosed the last doubled jet he could muster did it finally turn tail and run.

Hunger comes to them all. The skunk has known frozen nights devoid of a single scrap, stark contrast to this scene of bounty, this scaled and tender feast. The snake is half gone. The skunk works the next fine-boned section back between his teeth, chews and swallows, then stills his noisy jaws.

Panting. Rustle in the undergrowth, the thud of heavy paws.

The skunk wheels, letting the raw remnant of his quarry drop. The dog is tall, long-nosed and dark, its coat no thicker than a newborn's but slick with an unnatural sheen. It lets out a whine—a submissive signal belied by the pointed intent of its ears. Looking to its tail for clarification, the skunk finds only a mute black stump. Best to be on the safe side. He sends a gentle message to begin with, standing terribly still.

Beyond, in the meadowy open, a human calls. The dog pays no heed. Steps forward when any sensible creature would step back.

The skunk stamps his feet. The dog whimpers and crouches low. The skunk arches his back and chatters, the dog inching, beetling close. The skunk growls, an utterance the dog doubles and returns. The human bellows again, and still the dog remains deaf to all but its own dim purpose. Up comes the black and white signal of the skunk's tail, the tip still limp, a slim and final chance.

The dog reads it wrong. As it lunges, the skunk twists his hindquarters round, his tail stiff to the limit now, pointing up through the darkened canopy to the sky. The dog leaps back when the spray hits, a single round more than enough.

It wants its human now. Blind and howling, it crashes away.

After a moment, the skunk lowers his tail. He draws a deep, rich breath, finding the little wood altered, the very air his own. Dropping his snout, he noses out what's left of the snake.

Kate wakes to a smell, the animal base of her brain dragging her up out of a dream. Silhouetted down the end of the bed, the cats lie like a pair of Chinatown lions, noses lifting to the message wafting their way.

Pushing back the quilt, Kate crosses to the window and brings it down. It's a coolish night, and she finds herself wondering if Lily's warm enough. Is it possible she really sleeps out there, among the twigs and trash of the urban woods? At least she has Billy with her. Thank God for the devotion of dogs.

She turns back to the bed to find Smoke and Fire watching her in the gloom. "Skunk," she tells them—as if they didn't know. Climbing back under the covers, she takes care not to prod their soft bellies with her feet.

It'll take a while for the room to clear. In the meantime, she reaches across the empty half of the bed to Lou-Lou's nightstand. Drawing open its little drawer, she feels inside. A paperback, a hardcover, a pair of the drugstore reading glasses Lou-Lou wore. In one corner, the bottle of massage oil, still greasy around the cork. In another, the second, smaller bottle her fingers seek.

She sits back against both pillows, twists off the cap and holds the bottle to her nose. Suddenly the skunk is gone.

She's in a darkened garden in France. Forget France—she's in her own back garden, not last summer but the summer before, when Lou-Lou was still around to make things thrive.

Upending the bottle against her finger, Kate touches the scent to her upper lip. *Lavender moustache.* Lou-Lou's helpful hints.

She returns the little bottle to the drawer and wriggles down, her skull rediscovering its own impression, reminding her where she was before the reek of a passing creature found its way to her nose. She was in the kitchen with Lou-Lou. Not a sex dream—the kind that started up like some kind of cruel joke on the night of the funeral and haunted her for months. Not a nightmare either. There have been fewer of those— always coming home to find her lying in the hallway; always touching her hand to find it cold.

Tonight's dream was nothing so dramatic. It was the kind of scene you live without a thought: Lou-Lou making pancakes while Kate sits at the kitchen table reading out crossword clues. The waking mind forgets, but the mind of the night sees the glow around the woman at the stove. It knows a delight akin to affliction upon hearing her murmur answers to the most baffling of clues. *Ocelot. Kingpin. Rapt.*

Maybe it was because Kate was so much younger that it never occurred to her to consider an end. It wasn't that she treated Lou-Lou badly. She was good to her, wasn't she? Of course she was. In every way but one.

For more than a year, Lou-Lou was Kate's housemate as far as Mummy and Daddy were concerned. Even that was too much for Daddy. *Housemate, never mind housemate. What about mate?* One Sunday dinner when Kate went on a little too long about the herb bed Lou-Lou was putting in, Daddy forgot the manners that were so important to him and pointed at her with his fork.

"Always you are talking about this housemate." The fork quivered in his hand. "Will housemate look after you the way I look after Mummy?"

Yes, Kate said inside, and no. Not like you look after Mummy. Not at all.

"That's the way they do things nowadays, Vic." Mummy never called him Vikram. As far as Kate knew, no one did. "Young people like to have a bit of freedom before they settle down."

"Freedom." Daddy waved the fork before withdrawing it. "Nothing but freedom in this country." He shook his head. "And look what you get."

He fell into a peevish silence—no need to utter aloud what the three of them already knew. Kate's unspoken love was the gravest of her transgressions, but it was far from the first. She'd let her father down in countless ways, not least of them being her choice of career.

Daddy had been top of his class in dentistry school back home. Too bad nobody told him teeth were so different in Canada that his training wouldn't count. Okay, so he would work nights for Mr. Malcolm Dysart, Denturist, and attend classes during the day. Simple. Or not so simple. Not when the red-haired girl behind the counter at the Country Style Donuts met his gaze and held it every time he came in. Not when he found himself walking into City Hall holding that same girl's hand, having already posted the letter that would break his parents' hearts. He wouldn't talk about the one his parents sent him in return; Kate knew only what Mummy told her—that the envelope was blue, and that Daddy never replied.

But Daddy's story wasn't about the old life in India; it was about the new country, and the way things happened here. It wasn't so easy to say no to extra hours when Mr. Dysart started staying home with shooting pains in his legs. Or when he tired of leaving his bed altogether and offered to sell the business to his one and only employee for half of what it was worth. Who could say no then, with one fat-cheeked baby at home and the red-haired girl already swelling up with another? Nobody, that's who.

Things might have been different if that first baby had lived long enough to become a man. Mummy wanted to call their son after his father, but Daddy wouldn't hear of it. *He's stuck with Prabhu. Don't burden him with Vikram too.* So Mummy settled for the next best thing.

Victor Prabhu was born stubborn like his father. Worse, he was born without an ounce of fear. Kate can remember Mummy laughing about the way he would climb down out of his high chair in seconds, or run full tilt for the nearest road the moment she let go of his hand. In grade one, he knocked himself out cold twice, once by dropping straight down onto the crown of his head from the monkey bars, then again when he lost control of his bike while riding it down the slide. In grade two, he rode that same bike out into the street and disappeared under the wheels of a U-Haul truck.

If Vic Junior had kept to the sidewalk like he'd promised, Daddy would've made him a gift of his precious dental tools. As it was, Kate inherited the tiny mirror, the various picks and probes.

She was in high school before she realized none of the other kids knew a bicuspid from an incisor. Career day at the end of grade twelve confused her. The aptitude test was too hard. She began by trying to check the boxes that felt true, but the process made her anxious, so she erased all her choices and started again. The second round of responses was designed to add up to what she already knew, that she would spend her working life with her hands in other people's mouths. Or, as Daddy put it, she would be busy fixing smiles.

When the bell went, her test was nowhere near complete. Half an aptitude, if that. Mr. Talbot stopped her at the door. "Stay behind a minute, will you, Kate?" He waited until they were alone in the classroom before he held up her test. "What gives?"

"What do you mean?"

"I mean, what happened here?"

She didn't want to cry, didn't even know she would until she was a snot-nosed mess. She told him everything—the lost grandparents in Goa and her father's little tools and Victor not looking both ways before he flew from the curb.

"You won't tell them, will you?" she wailed.

"Tell who?"

"My parents. My father. About the test."

"You're not being graded here, Kate. This is supposed to help."

"Oh."

"Here." He pinched the test by its corners and tore it in two. "Forget about the test. Forget about your parents for a minute if you can. What about you?"

"Me?"

"Yes, you. What do you want to be?"

"I . . ." She'd never felt so stupid. "I don't know."

"Okay, let's put it this way. What makes you happy?"

She didn't need to think to answer that one. She'd scarcely been able to believe her luck when Mr. and Mrs. Dove from down the block had asked her to look after their pets over Christmas break. Besides the two cats, Karl and Kitten, there was the Lassie-dog, Sally, and a cockatoo named Roger, who screamed whenever she set foot inside their door.

Daddy didn't like it one bit. More often than not, when she scooped the Doves' house key from the bowl in the front hall, he called out from the kitchen, or the armchair where he sat watching the flickering news, *The zookeeper is off again.* And when she came back, *Ah, the zookeeper returns.* His commentary grew more colourful as the days wore on. *Did you wash your hands, zookeeper? Who knows what nastiness you're touching over there.* Or, *I hope you're not sitting down on their sofa. I don't want any fleas in this house.*

She couldn't help but answer back from time to time.

"They don't have fleas."

"Oh, no? And how would you know, miss? If you know so much, tell me this: why don't these people have any children, the way nature intended? Why so many animals and not one single child?"

Kate spent as much time as she could on the job. She took her time walking Sally, adding another block to the snowy circuit whenever they went out. She washed the food and water dishes every morning before filling them, even though Mrs. Dove had said every few days would be fine. She even fashioned cat toys at home—barrettes like silver butterflies clipped to lengths of dental floss. Roger stopped screaming at her and began to talk. He mostly said *cocky*, but once there was something that sounded a lot like *Kate*.

"Kate?" Mr. Talbot was watching her, waiting for her reply.

"Animals," she said. "Animals make me happy."

He smiled. "Okay, now we're getting somewhere."

Daddy said nothing when she told him about the veterinary technician program at Seneca College. Not one word. He kept it up for three months, by which time her classes had already begun. *Tell your daughter she should eat a better breakfast. Ask your daughter where she put the remote.*

She thought that was as mad as he could get, but now he won't even speak to her through Mummy, and it's already been more than a year. Little wonder it took her so long to work up the guts. There were moments when she came close to spilling the beans—her head a tightly packed jar, a dip of the chin all it would take to release the clattering stream. Somehow she maintained the seal. Month after month she promised herself she would tell them—would tell Mummy, at least—when the time was right. Even after Lou-Lou died, she managed to keep it all in. When Mummy offered to go with her to the funeral, Kate spoke evenly into the receiver, assuring her there was no need.

The shock made it almost easy. From the moment she'd let herself in the front door to find Lou-Lou dead of a massive brain aneurysm, Kate had entered an underwater world. She was walking, sitting, lying on the ocean floor.

Then came the second shock. In her grief, Kate hadn't given a thought to the house. Lou-Lou had. She'd changed her will seven months after Kate moved in. She'd been that certain, even then. Even though Kate had gone to the clinic's annual picnic without her, saying it was a staff-only event. Even though they'd spent every Sunday dinner and all of their first Christmas apart.

There was only one way to be worthy of that kind of love. The following Sunday, when Daddy asked her, "Why so glum?" and Mummy said quietly, "Vic, you know her friend passed away," Kate felt herself coming up for air.

"Not friend, Mummy." She turned to look her father in the eye. "I'm sad because I loved her, Daddy. I'm sad because my lover died."

It's not the only time Brother's come to Guy in his sleep, though it is the first time in years. In life he made more sound, butting the bedroom door open when it was cold enough for him to be kept in at night, scrambling up the clapboard outside Guy's window during the other three quarters of the year. Either way, he invariably announced his arrival with an emphatic *mrrrph*, the sound of a living engine turning over, the first, vibrating hiccup of his home-safe purr.

Ghost-Brother, by contrast, comes in silence, swimming through the darkened room to find Guy lying on his side. The living Brother would wait for a groggy Guy to pat the mattress—that springy-soft, welcoming sound—but the phantom cat needs no such invitation. He knows that the space between Guy's body and the edge of the bed belongs to him.

He rises with a flick of his tail, not a hop but a hover.

His four white feet touch down where the sheet hammocks against Guy's belly, his silvery weight drawing it taut. Guy stirs—not into wakefulness, but into the reality of the dream. Brother has come to sleep alongside him. His beloved pet has returned.

Both of their bodies remember. Brother makes a brief knot of his length, then unties it and lays it out long. The back of his skull rests against Guy's collarbone; the pads of his hind feet touch Guy's knee. His front paws cross like a pale prisoner's hands, extending beyond the mattress into air.

Guy's right arm is tucked away beneath his pillow. His left curls down as Brother settles, his hand landing where the belly fur lies thickest, where the skin can be gathered up gently and held. The purr is soundless, but Guy can feel it humming in his fingers. The warmth of a long-dead body. For a time the sleep they share is sound.

# 8

# Ring of Dark Timber

Jim Dale was tall—the tallest man Edal had ever seen. His hair and beard were black, but in the cold classroom light they showed purple like the slash on a duck's wing. His age was hard to pin down; he acted like a dad while he told them about skinning a moose, but grinned like a kid during his joke about two squirrels and a bear. Her mother was thirty—Edal's twelve years plus the eighteen Letty'd had under her belt when she'd given birth—but it was difficult to compare women and men. One thing was certain: Jim Dale was old enough to know everything worth knowing about the natural world.

When Grandpa Adam was still alive, Edal would sometimes join him on his daily walk through the woods, the pair of them passing hand in hand through the gateway formed by the twin red pines. He spoke rarely once they'd left the yard. When something took flight overhead, or slithered across their path, he would give her fingers a squeeze, pointing out the flash of feathers, the disappearing slip of tail.

Once he was gone, she went alone. Short forays at first—
she was only six—but Nana was too sick to mind, and Letty
was too busy looking after her to notice, so Edal ventured
deeper by the day. She remembered which trees stood where,
even if she had no names for them, and she mourned the
fallen after every storm. She knew only the simplest words for
the creatures she caught sight of, *mouse* or *squirrel* or *bird*.

They learned a little in school—*bear* and *moose*, *birch* and
*maple*—but it wasn't until the proprietor of Jim Dale
Outfitters on Dogleg Road came to visit her class that Edal
awoke to the mass of all she didn't know. It weighed on her
like shame. She fretted over it on the school bus home, three
rows back in her usual spot, the seat beside her unclaimed.
The walk up the winding driveway only made it worse. Maple
trees lined the margin, but what kind? Jim Dale had mentioned sugar, white and black, as well as several others she
couldn't recall.

The solution came to her as she pushed her key into the
front-door lock. The house was lousy with knowledge. Surely
in all her mother's sprawling, dust-furred jumble there lay
something she could use.

Little light penetrated the front hall—a single column
from the frosted window in the door and, down the far end,
dim spillover from the panes above the kitchen sink. Edal set
down her backpack and squinted to read the spines of the
nearest stack.

She found four books in the hour or so before her mother
came home. Nothing from the front hall, but the mound
behind the couch yielded up *Trees, Shrubs and Flowers to Know
in Ontario* and *Tracking: The Subtle Art.* Upstairs on Nana's

dressing table, *Canada's Many Mammals* was a brick in the untidy pyramid that hid the oval mirror from view. The last discovery was in rough shape. *Ontario Birds* was one of several dozen swollen paperbacks piled up between the toilet and the tub.

Letty didn't like her books to leave the house, but Letty would never know. *Ontario Birds* wasn't a field guide as such, but it helped Edal narrow down what to look and listen for, depending on where she stood. Ovenbirds called *preacher* in the undergrowth; grackles squawked like neglected hinges down where the creek mislaid its purpose and became a waterlogged stand of stumps. *Wick, wick, wick* could be a yellow-shafted flicker, but *wack, wack, wack* meant a pileated woodpecker, drummer of the woods.

There were line drawings in black ink: an osprey snatching up a fish from the shallows, a chimney swift clinging to brickwork, a ruffed grouse tilting to land. Edal found herself returning to the pair of turkey vultures on page sixty-four—one soaring in the distance, the other hunched in the foreground, meeting the reader's eye. *The Turkey Vulture builds no nest. It deposits two, sometimes one or three eggs on the ground beside a stump or within a hollow log or cave in some wooded wilderness.*

She dreamt of coming upon such a cache. A single egg would be best, *creamy white, blotched with rich reddish brown and pale lavender.* She wouldn't touch it, but she would return every day, creeping close in time to witness the hatching, the bare black face and downy body slick with yolk. Eventually the parent birds would come, banking down between the trees to land heavily on the shadowed ground. Neither would cry out to its young; they were silent birds, save for the odd croak or hiss. They would bring food in their mouths, their throats, even their stomachs—*tidbits from the putrefying carcass of a horse or hare.* Looking out from the brush, Edal would understand what the book's author had understood before her, that *what seems a gruesome ritual may in fact be a labour of love.*

Throughout the book, the body parts of certain species appeared in isolation: the heron's beak a massive darning needle, the cormorant's foot a webbed and sinister hand. Figure Six showed a flying gull, and beneath it, the same bird in the same attitude—only plucked. Edal had held many feathers to the light, but the naked gull was what made her see. Plumage allowed for streamlining, waterproofing, warmth. Not to mention beauty. Not to mention flight.

Perhaps oddest of all, Figure One presented a crow's skeleton standing upright as in life. It took pride of place opposite the first chapter, with its question of a title: "What is a Bird?" The bone-crow offered only a partial answer. Animal and not animal. Not entirely of this earth. In evolutionary terms, birds could be thought of as reptiles with long, elaborate scales. Except for a certain four-chambered creation. The bird heart was close to mammalian, cousin to the quartered organ that kept time in Edal's own chest.

*Canada's Many Mammals* helped her get her bearings too. She hadn't far to look: porcupines gnawed the porch steps; cottontails lived in the back brush pile; raccoons mined the compost, retreating to keep watch from the cottonwoods whenever Edal came bearing the ice cream bucket full of scraps. The large, moon-coloured rat she'd watched trailing its many babies across the yard was in fact a Virginia opossum; if she were ever to come upon one curled motionless on its side, she'd know better than to believe it was dead.

It appeared she'd been safe enough trusting the woods. The weasel family were consummate killers, but were bent on smaller prey. Lynx were the ghosts of the forest, and she'd have been lucky to get within a stone's throw of a coyote, let alone a wolf. Foxes could be a problem when rabid, but she had yet to see one come wobbling with foam on its lips. As for bears, they were out there, all right, but they tended to be shy. She could remember going with Grandpa Adam to watch them paw over the dump. *Just be careful you don't surprise one. Be sure and let him know you're there.*

She longed to come across an otter, but suspected the creek was too shallow to sustain such a find. In the meantime she made do with the beaver pond. It was a long walk—beyond the culvert that fed beneath the highway—but well worth it. Surrounded by sharpened stumps of standing-beaver height, the pond featured a good-sized dam, as well as the grassy mound of a lodge. Flat tails slapped warning. Dark bodies slipped between lily pads, came slithering down muddy banks.

It turned out the maples along the driveway were sugars— you could tell by the dark grey bark in long, erratic strips, the smooth-topped leaves with U-shaped notches between their lobes. The more Edal learned, the better. When she met Jim Dale again—and somehow she felt certain she would—she'd amaze him with all she knew.

# 9

# The Chronicles of Darius

The first time Darius laid the table for Grandmother, he was surprised when she told him to set it for four. Someone was coming to join them, and for a minute his baby mind let him believe it could be Faye. But why would his poor mother be allowed at the table if even her name was banned? And anyway, his poor mother was dead.

It turned out the fourth place was indeed for someone no longer among the living, as near as Darius could make out. He'd never been to church, and there wasn't much talk about such things in school, but he knew a little from staying with the Miskes. God was like a man and he wasn't; he had a long white beard and he lived in the clouds. His son was even more human. His beard was shorter and the colour of gold, and even though his father ran the world, the son was nailed up under that father's nose and left to die. What Darius didn't know was that the younger man-not-man—the dead one—could sit down across from you when supper was served.

Except that they started without him. Grandfather planted his elbows alongside his knife and fork, interlaced his fingers and rested his forehead on their knuckled ridge. Grandmother did the same, but not before shooting Darius an urgent glance that told him to follow suit.

"Bless us, O Lord," the old man began. "Bless this house built by Your grace and by the sweat of my humble brow, and bless this land that stands between it and all the wickedness of the world. Lord, in all Your might and wisdom, protect us from the governments that would run us down like lambs to slaughter, and from the Churches that make a mockery of Your holy name." He drew a noisy breath. "Bless this food we are about to receive, and keep it clean from all contagion. And Lord, bless this boy beside me, who is returned unto this house by Your righteous and merciful hand."

Grandmother made a sound then, so slight it might have been the sound of a heart pausing then picking up again.

"As ever, Lord," Grandfather went on, "we reserve the place at my right hand for Your Son, Jesus. We do this to honour the sacrifice He made, and to remind ourselves that He is with us throughout every trial and tribulation of this earthly life. Amen."

"Amen," Grandmother echoed, her slippered foot making contact with Darius's shin. He did his best to weigh the word down as they had, but it came out squeaky and small.

Jesus never made it to supper that night, nor any other. Every time Grandmother stood up to clear, she took Jesus's full plate first, carrying it in both hands and tipping the untouched portion into the garbage pail. It hardly seemed fair, given that Darius had to eat every scrap he was served.

*There's half a pig left on that bone, boy. Pick it up. That's right,
use the teeth the Lord gave you.*

He'd never had meat with bones in it before. Faye had
favoured boiled wieners, baloney. Once in a while, on days
that were bright and friendly, they would walk to the store
together for bacon. She liked to cook the whole package in
one go, set the pan down on the table between them so they
could pluck the fragrant strips direct from their fatty pool.
Darius always ate long after he stopped feeling hungry. He
couldn't help it—Faye smiled at him every time he reached
into the pan.

Jesus must have been hungry, missing supper every single
time. Maybe he did make it sometimes, only he got there too
late, after everyone was already in bed. Maybe it wasn't animals
Darius could hear outside his little window, shuffling past the
backhouse, lumbering up to the locked shed. The garbage
cans stood side by side in there, stinking. There was always
something scratching at its door.


Darius woke up needing to go. He thought first of the old
bathroom, Faye's grubby soap ring in the tub. Next, he
remembered the dead plant by the window. Finally, upon
waking fully, he realized he was in his mother's childhood
bed, in the log cabin she'd left behind. No bathroom, no
plant. Only the pot by the kitchen door.

He couldn't have been asleep long; the coals were still
showing colour through the grate of the stove, and he could
hear the old couple moving around in their room. Their door
stood ajar. He should've kept his eyes to himself as he passed,
but their bedside lamp was on, and the dark of the room he

was passing through lay thick. Grandmother was already in her nightgown, but Grandfather had yet to undress. Or, as it turned out, to be undressed. Like a baby. Even Darius had been pulling on his own pyjamas since he was three.

Standing before the old man, Grandmother reached up and undid the top button of his denim shirt. Grandfather let his chin drop. Another button, and he made a gurgling sound, like something slipping away down a drain. One more, and then Grandmother slid both hands inside his shirt. After working at something for a moment, she began gently to pull.

The cord was long. She seemed to be drawing it from between Grandfather's ribs, but that was wrong, Darius knew; if it came from inside him, it would be bloody, or at the very least, wet. Instead, it looked dry, almost dusty, and flatter than it had first appeared. A strip more than a cord. A ribbon. If ribbons were meant to make things look ugly instead of nice.

Whatever it was, Grandmother looped it several times around her thumb and elbow then set it aside on the bed. Grandfather turned and bent over the greyish twist, as though he too were trying to determine what it might possibly be. He made an odd, nonsensical picture: head and shoulders curling forward while his shirt kept its shape, seeming to stand up straight on its own. Darius wondered if this was the first distorted hint of a dream—if he'd somehow fallen asleep on his feet.

Grandmother stood behind the old man now. She hugged him around the middle to reach the last few buttons then eased his shirt off, the way men sometimes removed women's coats on TV. Darius caught his breath. The board stood stiff as a fence post, jutting up from the back of Grandfather's pants. The man it had held upright braced himself, hands flat on the bed. Bare arms brown from the midpoint down, the rest pinkish against the old-tooth white of his undershirt.

Faye's houseplant had needed help standing too; it came tied to a dark green stake with three hairy slips of twine. Long after the stem had given up trying, the stake still held it in place. It seemed cruel. One day, after he'd wet its dead roots with his pee, Darius brought the big knife from the middle drawer, sawed through the three loops and let the poor thing lie down.

It seemed Grandmother was doing the same. She reached around Grandfather's middle again and unbuckled his belt. Fumbled at his pants button, his fly. Took a small step back and closed her fingers around the board.

"Easy," Grandfather said hoarsely as she lifted it up and away. He drooped further with it gone, arms giving way at the elbows, forehead kissing the quilt.

Grandmother set the board at an angle against the wall. Turning back, she caught sight of Darius through the crack in the door. Her eyes opened wide. Despite the soft drag of her cheeks, he could clearly make out the muscled contraction of her jaw.

He didn't dare continue on to the pot. Turning in place seemed an equally foolish idea, bound to cause the floorboards beneath him to groan. Walking backwards was the thing to do, stepping silently into the invisible tracks he'd made.

Faye's bed may have been old, but it had been built to last. Two-by-fours bolted tight, no springs in the foam mattress to cry out. Darius lay down like a leaf on a river. His bladder complained, but he knew from experience he was a long way from losing control.

# 10

# The City Book

**Coyote Cop's Blog**

**Thursday, May 29, 2008**

Ever notice how when common sense tells us life is one way theres always some smartass who looks up a bogus study and uses it to deny the plain truth? Just like when theres dirty work to be done and that same smartass stands around making up excuses. Well some of us see through that particular brand of bullshit soldierboy. Some of us can't be fooled.

*POSTED BY Coyote Cop at 7:57 AM*

The female is grey, but her belly is palest gold—the colour of a fresh peanut freed from its shell. His own coat is black, pure calm, save for the point of white awareness at the tip of his tail.

The grey ones tend to be flighty. She's taken refuge in a tree hole for the time being, but he can still make out the twitch of her pretty tail. Between them, a chain of hopeful suitors jostle on the branch. The white-tipped male holds back. When the female leaves her hidey-hole to lead them in the next leg of the chase, he'll be well placed to head up the queue.

He wasn't the first to answer her silent, scented call, though he's played that part with others in the past: the days-long, tentative dance; the first hard-won sniff; the wild morning when she emerges with her perfume fully blown. Her *quack* is a soft question, his *whick* the only possible response. Little can match the thrill of that initial burst of speed, the sight of her ripe hindquarters bounding away.

That's the best of it, though; first on the scene rarely seals the deal. No female wants the nearest male, a dull neighbour who might well be her own close blood. She wants the fleet-footed outlier, the squirrel she barely knows. She wants him.

And now, forsaking the tree hole in a flurry of softness, she offers him his chance.

Following the trunk's impetus, she breaks for the leafy heights. The other males—a black-and-tan, two greys and a straggler with a reddish tinge—follow her like a multi-toned tail. Meantime, the white-tipped male rises handily, limb to limb. Foresight pays off: he's the first to fall in behind her when she angles back along horizontal lines.

The high branch bucks and sways, bearing her weight, then his, then the mass of the other males—trailing for form's sake now, the long race all but won. They're closing in on the female's territorial core. Any moment now she'll show him how fast she can really run. She'll put a last, maddening distance between her bright body and his, then crouch and await him at the heart of her own home ground.

First, though, there remains the small matter of a road. The female may be skittish, but she's no fool. She keeps to the high pathways, springing from her twig to the black line of a human wire. Absorbing her after-bounce, the white-tipped male lets go on the upswing and sails splay-legged through the air. He lands in an echo of her landing, walks hand over hand in her steps. Her balance is a thing of beauty. She runs with a confidence bordering on madness, her small feet singing to him through the wire.

She's a short hop from the pole when the others crowd onto the line behind him. He anticipates a leap to the nearby tree—her coat disappearing against its bark as she descends— but she surprises him, scrambling up onto the storm-coloured swelling that's fastened to the pole. He freezes, clinging to the wagging wire. Something he knows and doesn't know has hold of him—some dim loop of memory, his own or older, wiser. His rivals bunch up behind him and still he doesn't move.

The female rises up on her hind legs, showing a glimpse of her golden front. Reaching beyond a second, smaller growth, she gropes for the dark link to the highest of the human wires.

The screen goes blank. It's unsettling, as though Stephen's posting itself has somehow blown the system. He stares mutely into the monitor's empty frame. Several seconds pass before it occurs to him to test the desk lamp. Nothing. He rises, feeling awkward, almost ashamed. He hasn't closed the window, let alone the browser. Everything left lying open inside the silent machine.

He finds Guy in the kitchen, looking mournfully at the coffee maker. "Power's out."

"Yeah." Stephen thinks for a moment. "Wonder if it's working on Broadview."

"Maybe."

"I'll go to the Rose." He opens a cupboard and stares into it. "Where's the Thermos?"

"Right there."

"Where?"

Guy reaches past him for the squat, plaid-patterned flask. "You okay?"

"Sure."

"You seem a little—I don't know, freaked out."

"No." He's not sure why he hasn't told Guy about the blog—why he doesn't do so now. "I'm fine." Thermos in hand, he turns and heads for the door.

"Hey," Guy says behind him.

Stephen busies himself with his bootlaces. "Yeah?"

"Get me a sub, will you?" He fishes the wallet from the back pocket of his jeans. "Barbecued pork with everything. Extra chilies."

"For breakfast?"

"Yeah, why not." Guy slides out a twenty. "Get one for yourself too."

"It's okay." He's out the screen door before Guy can reach him. "It's on me."

Darius is about to shut down when a new comment appears. First time the two of them have been at their keyboards together. He feels a prickling in his spine.

*soldierboy wrote . . .*

One more thing about that study. Like I said, the coyotes were eating plenty of mice and the like, but they were also eating raccoons and muskrats, opossums and rabbits, plants and even bugs. There's a word I came across while I was looking (not making) things up. Generalist. See, it's the creatures who only eat one or two things that are in trouble when change comes. The generalist, on the other hand, is a survivor. And speaking of that, here's something else I came across in my wanderings. There's a Native American saying that when the rest of the world's creatures are gone, the coyote will be the only one left. Pretty scary if you look at it one way, but change the angle a little and you might just see something you can admire.

POSTED AT 8:01 AM, May 29, 2008

*Admire?* Darius can't let that one go, and he won't. He'll set the poor sucker straight—just as soon as he's had some sleep.

It usually kicks in around now, once she's descended the foot-bridge stairs and started northward along the valley path. Kate knows all about endorphins, but there's more to what she's feeling than a simple chemical rush. Running is something the body longs for, like light or water. Like love.

Funny that it brings her so much pleasure, given that she was initially drawn to it through pain. Those early mornings when her mind still insisted Lou-Lou was alive, and woke her to the feel of no one beside her in bed. She began by walking, but Lou-Lou's absence walked alongside her, so, on the second or third morning, she began to run. Amazing the strides a body can make in a year. Ten kilometres a day is what her heart demands of her now; anything less and she risks growing antsy, uncomfortable in her own skin.

She crosses the old plank-and-girder span to the eastern bank, each step feeding the next. The parkway hums in one ear, Bayview Avenue in the other—neither of them equal to the internal music of the run.

After the straightaway where the Don cuts a wide bow away from the path, she enters the viaduct's swath of shade. Overhead, a subway train judders and squeals. She emerges into the morning again.

To her right, a buffer of scrub between her and the embankment; to her left, a clearing studded with trees. She's always been fond of this stretch, but it's only over the past couple of days that she's begun to make note of a particular spot. *Here,* she tells herself as she passes a certain spiky stump, *right here.*

It was the dog that caught her eye that morning. Normally she kept to the path, maintaining a steady stride, but there was something about that dark, four-legged form appearing and disappearing between the trees that slowed her to a halt. Even at a distance she recognized the swivel-hipped hustle of a Newfoundland retriever, and yet something about the profile didn't fit. Another breed in the mix—Rottweiler, or even mastiff, given the dog's size—something bull-headed, with a substantial jaw. No sign of an owner, but surely a dog that big and beautiful couldn't be a stray. A runaway, then, on the lam from some poorly fenced yard.

When it slipped away down the riverbank, she felt the tug just as surely as if she were holding its leash. Less than a minute of cooling muscles, and she decided it couldn't hurt to get a better look.

The grass was dewy, wet against her calves, laced with some coarse, tangled weed that threatened to trip her up. As she neared the river, she caught sight of the creature again, motionless in the greenish flow. More bear than dog in that moment. She half expected it to draw back a paw and swipe a writhing salmon from the murk.

The girl stood unmoving as well, camouflaged among the scrappy saplings that fringed the bank. The dog heard Kate coming, or else caught a whiff of stranger on the wind. It lifted its head and only then, when the girl turned to follow her dog's gaze, did Kate see her. The grey toque, the shapeless, dun-coloured vest, the skinny legs. She might have passed for an underfed boy if it hadn't been for the delicate features, the fine white throat.

Something told Kate to advance slowly, being careful to

make no false moves. That was no ordinary dog eyeing her from the shallows. And this was definitely no ordinary girl.

The grass is deep here. Lily lies with her head on Billy's flank, enjoying the warmest morning in the valley so far. Cash from yesterday's shift in her breast pocket, *Watership Down* in her hand. Life may not suck so hard after all.

It doesn't take long before a passage stops her cold. She closes her eyes, breathing carefully, feeling for her dragon book and pen.

It's important to get it down perfectly, remaining faithful to Fiver's tale of life in the warren of snares—the fat, sleek rabbits with their redolent fur, the man and his shining wires.

> They knew well enough what was happening. But even to themselves they pretended that all was well, for the food was good, they were protected, they had nothing to fear but the one fear; and that struck here and there, never enough at a time to drive them away.

A flash of movement lifts her gaze—there, where the path comes winding out of the wood. The runner emerges at a good clip. Only her top half shows above the sea of grass, so that she seems to hover, propelled by her pumping arms alone. Lily could sit up and see more, but she'd rather not give herself away. Weird, given that the woman's known to her.

Even before the face comes clear, Lily recognizes the dark, swinging ponytail, the shapely arms.

Billy knows who it is too. *"Hrrrr,"* he says.

"Quiet." She reaches back to clamp his mouth closed.

It's fucked, she knows, lying low in the grass while her new friend passes her by.

The morning before last, she watched Kate's entire body running off down the valley path—not just the top half, like today. And now even that partial view is gone. Billy knows she's not far, though; Lily can feel him wriggling in his skin, a trembling so violent it moves through her body too. It's only natural that he'd want to go after Kate, catch up and see her turn and smile. But natural isn't always smart.

"Stay, Billy," she tells him firmly. "You stay."

Edal holds her eyes shut against the late morning light, listening for the mouse. Nothing. Three long, bewildering days without a single scritch.

She should get up. Just for an hour or two, then she can go back to bed.

Hauling herself up from the futon, she shuffles into the kitchen and turns the kettle on. Sits in her tank top and plain white panties to wait. Downstairs, a swell of music, the slow, throaty pump of a tango drifting up through the floor. Who the hell tangos at eleven in the morning? The mouse could be down there, swaying along to the accordion's draw, overshadowed by James and Annie's fused form. Or it could be lying broken-backed in one of the old-fashioned snap traps the bearded boy recommends.

Maybe she should get a pet. A python or a sleek black panther. A hawk. Crazy. Even a dog or cat would be unrealistic; she has time on her hands now, but she mustn't forget what her real life—her working life—looks like.

A dog would be nice. Nothing too big, maybe a terrier of some kind. She could take it for walks in the park, stoop with her hand gloved in a bag when it did its business, stand with the other owners at the edge of the off-leash zone. The conversation would be dog-centred, easy. She could call out to the terrier when it got overly feisty—she can see him more clearly now, black-eyed and bouncing, with grizzled fur. She could name him after one of the neighbourhood streets, Chester or Logan or Wolfrey. Then some other human being standing there might smile at her and say, "That's my street." It's the kind of thing people do—people who belong to the place they live in, and don't just adhere to it like some tide-washed, clinging thing.

Why doesn't she have a pet? Why has she never, in all her thirty years, had a pet?

It's tempting to blame her mother. Letty said animals make a house stink; plus, dogs chew the place to pieces and cats shred anything they can get their claws on. It was the part about the smell that got to Edal the most. All those blocked-up windows, the trapped air heavy with smoke and mould.

Pets cost money, too. "There's the food," Letty told her, "and the vet bills. Do you have any idea how much a vet costs?"

No, Edal thought, and neither do you.

"Animals are always getting sick, Edal, or cutting themselves on old tin cans."

"Maybe you should buy a book about it." Edal's not sure if she spoke the line clearly or mumbled it, or just thought it with force.

In the end, she contented herself with the animals she came to know in stories: the otters at Camusfeàrna; Black Beauty and White Fang; the ever-expanding collection of a boy named Gerald, whom she envied to the point of pain.

Still, she hasn't lived under Letty's roof for over a decade. Maybe a petless childhood has the power to shape a person for life. Except—*oh God*—she did have a pet. Not for long, but she did.

The memory stands her up like a leg cramp. She moves into the living room, passing the navy blue loveseat, the blind grey eye of the TV. Standing at the front window, she stares out into the whispering heights of the elm. The thinnest of breezes enters the room. It brushes against her and is gone.

Guy's a rare breed. Most bosses would let the junior man strip and sort while they sat up high in the cab of the Link-Belt, but there he is, bent over the Lumina's open hood, severing engine bolts with his blue-tongued torch so Stephen can reach in and pluck out the block.

Working the pedals to track into position, Stephen keeps the boom in tight, letting the grapple hang. Just like Guy said, it really does get so you can work the controls without a single conscious thought. It's practically his own long arm now, his own massive, grasping hand. Imagine having a magnet for a palm; four steely, contracting claws. You could right a flipped vehicle and set it back on the road where it belongs—back before that road exploded in a geyser of shrapnel and dust. You could feel down over a courtyard wall and gather up rifles like a fistful of twigs. Turn sentries, even snipers, into ordinary men.

On the ground before him, Guy straightens and kills the torch. He stands back, giving the signal: *thumbs-up-and-away*.

Stephen brings the boom round with his left hand while extending the middle cylinder with his right. Opening the grapple wide, he rotates it a quarter turn, centres the magnet and floats it down onto the engine block. It rests there a moment until he wakes the charge with his trigger finger. The block gives a little jump, letting go of the mount with hardly a wiggle, a baby tooth loose at the root. He closes the grapple and raises the boom.

In the corner of his eye, Guy nods his approval. Stephen would love to flash him a grin but knows his attention should be cabled to the task at hand.

With a glance in the rear-view, he presses down with both heels, tilting the pedals to reverse. He tips the toes of his right boot forward to turn, then joins with the left to track straight for the engine pile. The block of the Lumina swings. It finds its own spot, like a fieldstone fitting into a wall. Stephen releases the magnet and opens the grapple in one. A place for everything and everything in its place.

Earlier this morning, they were faced with three unprocessed wrecks; now all three stand stripped to the axles and gutted, ready to be drained. He'll lift the Lumina onto the crusher first, then check if Guy wants to drop into the pit and chisel holes in the tank and oil pan, or if Stephen should take care of it himself.

Tracking back to the wreck, he spots Guy signing the *shut-'er-down*. He brakes, tucks in the boom and cuts the engine. Plucks out his earplugs and lets them hang around his collar on their string.

"Man," Guy calls, "you're getting to be a demon on that thing."

Stephen lets himself have that grin. Working the Link-Belt is a gas, the loader too—even the crusher, now that he knows what kind of racket to expect. His heart raced uncontrollably the first time the rusty-toothed track hauled in a wreck; he had to squeeze his eyes shut to keep from hitting the dirt. Nowadays, though, the scream of the buckling steel delights him. He laughs out loud when the windows go— that sudden crystalline spray.

Only her second day on the job and already Lily has the dish pit well in hand. She never suffers a buildup, no matter how many grey bus pans the busboys bring. There's a rhythm to it. Two trays on the slide at all times—a flat one for cups and cutlery, a pronged one for plates and bowls. Set the big items aside—pots and woks and stainless steel bowls—run them through whenever the pace drops off. When a tray's fully loaded, reach up for the dangling shower hose and blast away the surface crud, then shoot the dishwasher door up on its runners and shunt the clean tray out with the next in line.

She's been using the rubber spatula to scrape the plates since partway through yesterday's shift, when Chin noticed her scooping scraps into the garbage with her hand.

"Tch, no-name-girl," he said, grimacing, "you never hear of germ?"

He pulled the same disgusted face later on, when he caught her shovelling half a plate of black bean chicken into the to-go container by her feet.

"What this?"

She straightened. "It's just going to waste."

"You eat garbage again?"

Kenny, the youngest of the busboys, set a bus pan down and left grinning.

"No." Lily drew down the hose and sprayed the standing ranks of side plates. "It's for Billy, okay?"

"Billy? I told you, I give him lunch already."

She let the hose spring from her grip. "For later. For tonight."

"Tonight." Chin shook his head. Then he turned and dragged the colander from beneath his chopping-block counter. Shouldering Lily away from the sink, he took up the scraps and dumped them into the colander. "Dog can't eat black bean, barbecue. Too salty. Too much spice."

She stood back, watching him spray the meat clean.

"Now he know what you give him. Chicken, pork, beef. See here, even crab." His cheeks creased with a smile. "That one lucky dog."

When he comes to stand beside her today, she carries on with her work, saying nothing.

"Your sleeve," he says, pointing. "Why you no roll up your sleeve?"

She's wearing the white kitchen jacket she changed into at the start of her shift. Both sleeves are wet past the elbow, the cuffs ringed with orange grease.

"No reason."

She lifts the dishwasher door and slides in a tray of soup bowls, shoving a bleach-scented load of pans out the other end. Slamming the door back down, she hears the resulting rush.

"No reason, huh?"

She turns to find him regarding her steadily.

"You a junkie?"

"No." She dumps the cutlery tub out over a tray, chopsticks skittering. "Why, are you?"

He plucks up a ladle from the pile, plays its cup against the cup of his palm. "Not for long time." He sighs. "Not since Shanghai."

For once, no one's booked the after-lunch slot. Sandi's gone for lattes; Kate sits with a stack of files in front of her on the desk. Days like today—when the dogs are all getting better, and the humans are getting along—she can't believe how much she loves her job.

She wasn't always so sure. The position at the clinic's new rehabilitation centre came with a raise and regular hours, but it troubled her that the centre dealt solely with canine patients. Kate loved dogs, but no more than she loved cats and rabbits, parakeets and hedgehogs and snakes. There were days when the main clinic came close to a kind of paradise, so infinite was the variety of cries.

Still, it could be hard. The first time she wrapped a cat in black plastic and carried it back to join the other bodies in the deep-freeze, she faced the wall in that chilly corridor and wept. Shifts in Emerg left her footsore and dazed; there was rarely time to dwell on any one case—always the bleeding creature before you, the burned one waiting in the next room. Chemo duty was quiet by comparison, though the last shift she pulled in that cramped, brightly lit room was undoubtedly one of her worst.

The golden retriever had already lost one back leg; he lay down missing limb first, tucking the loss away. Tina was one of the best Animal Care Attendants on staff. She knelt down beside the dog, then sat with her legs folded to one side and gathered him into her lap. Like a woman in one of those painted scenes, Kate thought as she pulled on her paper gown—a woman in an elaborate hat cradling her lover on a grassy bank. Only the woman was a sturdy teenage girl in a mask and faded scrubs, and the golden-haired lover was a dying dog.

Tina knew the golden would require little more than a comforting embrace, just as she'd known to immobilize the miniature husky that had come before him with a nylon muzzle and full-body hold. It was the husky's first treatment, and once Tina'd gotten the better of him, Kate had no trouble getting a good stick. Long needle, deep in the vein on the second try.

The golden, on the other hand, had already been in half a dozen times. Kate had been surprised to learn of the breed's particular vulnerability; it seemed unlikely—almost cosmically wrong—that such sweet-tempered beauties should so often harbour tumours beneath their coats.

This one, Pickles by name, seemed fairly calm. A faster than normal pulse and the panting to match, but otherwise calm. Some patients got trickier with every treatment— became wrigglers or biters, backed into corners or broke for the door—but breeds that were docile to begin with generally chose to submit.

Kate knelt down beside Tina and the dog and pulled the cap off the needle with her teeth. Mask up, goggles down. She'd chosen a long needle to start, though she doubted whether she'd have any luck getting it to go in. The golden already had substantial scar tissue in both front legs. The left was played out, but she would try the right, lower down to begin with, though again, she knew her chances were slim.

The first attempt wasn't promising; she had to jab harder than she liked to, and even then she only made it a few milli-metres up the vein before she hit a valve. Tina looked up at her. Kate shook her head and felt a little farther up the shaved foreleg. The higher she went, the fewer viable vessels the golden would have left. On the other hand, if she kept on too long at the distal veins, she risked shutting down circulation in the entire limb. Which would mean the end for Pickles—if the owner could be made to see sense. More likely, given Eileen Brody's teary track record, a second amputation. Dog in a basket. Dog pulled in a wagon around the park.

Discerning a potential vein with her forefinger, Kate took a breath and jabbed. A little deeper this time, but not much. Again, the valve closed against her. She withdrew, moved higher, tried another spot. Pickles lay unmoving, eyes at half-mast, resisting her on a vascular level alone. Over and over, that faint, collapsing *no*.

Tina smiled sadly down at the dog while Kate swallowed the thickness in her throat and made a fourth unsuccessful attempt. She was past the high crook of the ankle now, approaching the knee. She switched to a shorter needle, a final resort before giving up on this leg. The golden's breath came fast, and Tina murmured, "Good boy, Pickles. Not long now."

Kate steeled herself and spiked the vein. No good. The valves could see her coming a mile off; they were flinching shut like so many minuscule eyes. She didn't want to move on to the left hind leg—the only untouched limb Pickles had left—but she hadn't any choice. Her jaw ached. The floor beneath her was cold.

"She should have to watch this," she said.

Tina glanced up.

"Mrs. Brody. She should have to watch me stick him over and over. Maybe then she'd let him go."

"Yeah."

Kate hooked a finger over her mask and dragged it down, bit the cap off a fresh needle and spat it aside. The hind leg still had that lovely elastic angle. She stroked it once before stretching it out long. Tina had shaved a section of fur just in case—a small comfort to know she'd seen it coming. Feeling for the lowest possible entry point, Kate slid the needle in without a fight. The relief was overwhelming. She felt like howling, burying her face in Pickles's silken fur.

Edal's starting to feel like the local stray—feed her once and you'll never get rid of her.

She glances at her watch. Just after two, not a bad time for a drop-in. It would be easier if she didn't have to buzz for permission to enter. If, like a stray, she could insinuate herself under the fence's springy hem.

She watches the office window for signs of life. Presses her palm to the sign for a long moment before her finger finds the buzzer. This time it takes him a minute or so to appear. His walk is already familiar—she would know him a long way off.

"Hey," he says, letting her in.

"Hi." She can't help crossing her arms. "I was just passing."

He nods.

"Is this a bad time?"

"No, in fact, I was just thinking about you."

"Oh?"

"Yeah. There's something I forgot to show you on yesterday's tour."

"Oh."

"Yeah, oh." He smiles. "Come on."

He leads her past the trucks, down to where a tall hedge runs at right angles to the bottom fence, connecting up to the office's facade. Edal remembers the overgrown garden, sees now how it's cut off from the yard. The hedge is healthy, thriving in a shapeless way. Guy approaches it without pause, as though he expects it to part and allow him passage. When he turns hard right and disappears, it takes her a moment to see the trick: not one hedge but two, staggered to form a narrow point of entry in what appears to be an impenetrable wall. She slips through the opening to find Guy on the other side, holding back a switch that would otherwise have caught her in the face.

"Thanks." He lets go the branch, stepping back to give her room. She surveys leafy ruins. "Wow."

"Yeah, I know."

"No, I like it." Her eye follows a row of planted hubcaps to where it butts up against the bottom end of the flight cage. If the hawk's in its tree, she can't see it. Guy clears his throat and moves to stand beside a mound of freshly turned earth. A clean hubcap rises from its centre.

"Well," he says, hands clasped behind his back, "here's our fox."

Staring down at the odd little scene, Edal feels her neck hair lift. She begins a silent count of hubcap headstones, reaching twenty-seven before he speaks again.

"It was my aunt's thing. Aunt Jan. I don't know when exactly she got started. She never really did much driving while my uncle Ernie was still alive. He did the pickups, she held down the fort—you know, kept the books, took the calls." He bends to remove a snail from the hubcap's rim, sets it down in the grass. "After he died, it was her or nobody—I still had a few years to go before I could get my licence. I took over in the office. Sometimes I went out with her on calls."

"What about school?"

"What about it?"

"You didn't go?"

"Off and on. Pretty much off after Ernie was gone. He was the stickler. Aunt Jan didn't mind so long as I kept on reading."

"How old were you—when he died, I mean?"

"Thirteen. It was a heart attack, first and last. He wasn't even doing anything, just walking out to the truck. Nobody saw him drop. Ten minutes later Aunt Jan noticed the truck was still there and went out to see."

Ten minutes—an eternity to the one who lies dying. A week was the estimate for how long Letty had been dead before the local constable forced open the front door—but how long had she lain alive at the foot of the basement steps, leg jackknifed beneath her? How long between breaking her body and leaving it behind?

"Jesus." It's all Edal can manage.

"Yeah, she beat herself up pretty good about it, figured she could've given him CPR. The doctor told her, though, it was a big one. He was likely gone before he hit the ground."

"Jesus." She hears herself say it again, helpless.

"Better fast than slow, that's what I figure." He nudges a tuft of grass with his boot. "With her it was cancer. Stomach, liver, lungs. Took forever."

Edal opens her mouth and shuts it. She can't say *Jesus* a third time. Can't say what she's thinking either, how sometimes it's both slow and fast: slow for the one who suffers in secret, the dizzy spells rare to begin with; fast for the one who hasn't been around to see it coming, the one who takes the late night call. If she says that much, she might not be able to stop herself saying more. About the house and all it harbours. About the bag or box or urn—she can't remember which one she agreed to—the *container* of ashes she has yet to pick up. Safer to keep the story about him.

"So they raised you, your aunt and uncle?"

"Uh-huh. My dad was Ernie's little brother. They died when I was a baby, him and my mom." He looks away. "They got married in a hurry, you know, never got a chance at a honeymoon until I was eleven months old. Niagara Falls. Classic, right? Seven cars and a semi. Everybody but the truck driver died."

"God, I'm sorry."

"Yeah, well." He glances at her. "Anyway, we've got just about everything back here—skunks, raccoons, opossums, rabbits, crows."

"Foxes."

He nods. "Foxes. There's even a couple of deer. Aunt Jan hauled back a doe one time, and I found a fawn." He stuffs his hands in his pockets. "They're not all roadkill."

"No?"

"Lily buries her birds out here, and there's a few baby squirrels that fell out of their trees, that kind of thing." He points down to the far end. "You see that big one, the one with the spokes?"

Edal spots the hubcap in question. Double the size of its neighbours, it arcs up out of a thicket of weeds.

"That's Brother." He lets her hang for a few seconds. "My cat."

Edal hears herself laugh. It's only a short burst, a twist on an inner release valve, but it's loud, and anyway, no kind of laughter should follow the mention of a dead pet. "Sorry." She bites her lip. "You called your cat Brother?"

He nods. "Only child." He says it plainly, without the slightest hint of self-pity.

"Yeah," she says after a moment, "me too."

Stephen should get up. There's more to be done in the yard, and after that there are dogs in their cages, waiting to be walked.

Edal must have gone; he can no longer hear her and Guy talking through his bedroom window. He wasn't listening in, exactly, just sitting on the floor, keeping an eye on the kits as they wandered the room. It gave him a twinge—just a small one—to hear his friend tell another his secrets so soon.

He's given the kits their afternoon feed and gathered them back into their carrier. Now, as they settle into sleep beneath him, he lets himself close his eyes. The power's been back on for a while now; he could switch on the clock radio and listen to people calling in about their gardens or their kitchens or their kids. Or he could just lie here. It's not really a nap if you stay on top of the covers. At worst it might be called a snooze.

The fatigue is never very far. He's come a long way in his recovery, but his heart will never pump the way it ought to. Hard to believe a body could change so profoundly, so fast.

It happened while he was sleeping. They'd leaguered up in the open that night, LAVs and G-Wagens circled around sand flea–bitten bodies on the ground. Stephen woke before dawn, feeling feverish and sore. Afraid he might have rolled over on something venomous in his sleep, he took a soldier's rapid inventory of his parts. No localized pain or swelling, only this all-over, worrisome ache. By mid-morning he was having trouble breathing. In the chopper back to Kandahar

Air Field he began to rave. The field hospital smelled of raw plywood, antiseptic, blood. Harsh light and clamour. Fear.

He slept through much of the flight out. Landstuhl Regional Medical Center may have been a U.S. Army facility on German soil, but the doctors who came to listen to his chest were Canadian as often as not. It was there that he learned what had happened to him. Apparently certain viruses had it in for the human heart; the infection began with inflammation but progressed quickly to where the red muscle had to struggle and stretch. Myocarditis. The pathogen was out of his system now, but the damage—*the considerable, lasting damage*—was done.

His transfer back to Canada posed a further problem. Any number of civilian hospitals were equipped to facilitate rehabilitation, but the perceived wisdom held that injured personnel tended to recover best close to home. Stephen had two—the one he'd grown up in and the one where his unit was based. Neither appealed.

Notwithstanding Mica's Monthly Mandala group email, he'd had little contact with his parents since he was foolish enough to visit during his pre-deployment leave. They'd allowed him into the scented sanctuary of their home—and it was *theirs* now, though he'd moved out less than a year before—but the welcome was nowhere near warm. A working dog, no matter how well trained, still bears the wild, ancestral taint; every step Stephen took put a ripple through the woolly flock. Ariel in particular maintained a buffer of physical distance—a peck on the cheek at the airport and nothing more. Maybe she would have hugged him if he'd changed out of uniform before boarding the flight.

He'd felt easier at CFB Shilo, but six months' training with his unit had done little to make Manitoba feel like home. Besides, why locate himself close to the base when he doubted he'd ever serve again?

One of the nurses on his ward had worked for a time in the cardiac rehab centre at St. Mike's in downtown Toronto. She'd liked it there, but she liked it fine at Landstuhl too. Hardly a rave review, but Stephen clung to it. Toronto was the largest city in Canada; logically, it would offer the most chances to belong.

He was still an in-patient at St. Mike's when he learned he no longer met the universality of service standards. It came as no surprise: a body that suffered palpitations and shortness of breath while shuffling from hospital bed to hospital bathroom could scarcely be expected to "deploy on short notice to any geographical location, in any climate" and "perform with minimal medical support." *Illness or injury incurred in theatre.* The phrase never failed to bring a grim smile to his lips. He saw himself clad in doublet and tights, stabbed in the chest with a trick dagger but dropping to the boards for real.

After six weeks, the in-patient became an out-patient. A basement bachelor apartment not far from St. Mike's, checkups every week, then every month. It turned out a bewildering array of services awaited the soldier no longer fit to serve. He might have taken advantage of the Canadian Forces' Vocational Rehabilitation Program if only he'd had a clue what he wanted to be. He could read the frustration in the eyes of those assigned to guide him; in some it bordered on disgust. Either way, it did little to help him decide.

Once the official medical release came through, he was in line for further rehabilitation under the aegis of Veterans

Affairs. So many levels of assistance—financial, medical, psychosocial, vocational—yet nothing could seem to put right what had gone wrong in his chest. No matter how many counselling sessions and job placement workshops he attended, no matter how his physical condition improved, he remained quietly sick at heart.

What energy he had, he spent on reconnaissance of his new hometown. He walked until the exhaustion kicked in, then boarded the nearest subway, streetcar or bus. It was incredible how much he saw: single houses that could hold an entire Kandahar village, goats and all; a man—old, or perhaps only weathered—squatting to relieve himself off the edge of a curb; women wearing the hijab, even the full-body burka. Women wearing as little as the late fall weather would allow.

It's hard to say what made him pause one frosty morning and watch the red-haired man at his work. Tow trucks had never held much interest for him before. It might have been the wreck, a mangled silver Mini with a streak of what could only be blood down the driver's-side door. Or it might have been the way Guy met his gaze and straightened. The way he nodded hello.

"Disgusting to make, delicious to eat." Aunt Jan never made meat loaf without saying it, so Guy says it too, bursting a yolk in each fist and working the goo into the mix. Maybe that's why Edal didn't stay—not everybody wants a meal mushed up by a mechanic's hands. He doubts it. More likely it was a simple case of too much information. Did he have to tell her about every dead relative he had?

Then again, maybe it was the pet cemetery that threw her. Or maybe she just had other plans.

He digs into the pinkish mass, squeezing fat ribbons of meat between his fingers. As he mashes and scoops, evening light falls across his forearm, illuminating a silvery scar. He lifts his hand free of the bowl and turns it. The mark curves like a third of a bracelet. No forgetting what the body knows.

Brother was long, built more like a fish than a cat—not the sluggish, muddy things Guy and Uncle Ernie used to drag up from the Don, but the kind men set their hooks for on TV. He had the white underbelly of a fish, the dark ridge of spine, the black and silver stripes best suited to underwater light. Glimpsed weaving between tires or slipping deep into a forest of weeds, Brother glinted, sometimes even flashed.

He was a short-haired domestic tabby, or so the lady at the shelter said. Uncle Ernie had been dead three months when Guy and his aunt crossed the bridge to look over the animals that had no homes. About time, Aunt Jan figured, for the pair of them to start taking an interest again.

"Dogs are a lot of work," she told him. "What we could really use around the place is a champion mouser."

There were dozens of caged cats, some calling out to them, others speaking with their eyes alone. Only one stretched a paw through the bars to bat Guy's shoulder as he passed.

When the lady opened the cage door and lifted the tabby down, Guy saw the full extent of him, a size somewhat at odds with his still-kittenish face.

"He's a teenager," Aunt Jan said, "like you." She laid a hand on his shoulder. "He the one you want?"

Guy nodded, and the tabby gave a low utterance, not unlike the cooing of a dove.

"Hear that?" the lady said. "We've been calling him Pigeon."

"Pigeon." Aunt Jan gave his shoulder a squeeze. "What do you think?"

Guy held out his arms, and the lady smiled and handed over the cat. "Support him under his backside. That's right, don't let him dangle."

Guy didn't need telling. He cradled the tabby's length against his chest and, for a long, stupid moment, felt as though he might bawl. "It's okay," he said, when he was sure he could speak. "I already picked out a name."

From the first, Brother knew to keep his claws in with Guy. There was only one time when he forgot, and even then it wasn't really his fault.

It was the screaming that did it. Guy knew better than to get between a carnivore and its prey, but the pitch of pure distress made him lose his head. The squirrel was a big grey, not a hint of mange in its full, frantic tail. Brother was heavier by then—they'd had him a couple of years—but he was nonetheless testing his limits by taking the squirrel on.

By the time Guy threw open the door, broom in hand, Brother had abandoned cat tactics and was shaking his victim terrier-style. Guy brought the broom down edge-on, aiming for the seam between Brother's bunched-up nose and the squirrel's spasming back. It was a clumsy tool, but the right tool for the job: Brother sprang back hissing from the bristles; the squirrel lay stunned for a moment, then scrambled to its feet.

Working interference with the broom, Guy blocked Brother's spitting lunges while the bloodied squirrel made tracks. When Brother let out a scream of his own, Guy threw a look over his shoulder and caught sight of the quarry clawing an erratic path up a poplar's trunk. It would've been nothing for Brother to follow; Guy had watched him scale that tree and countless others with no greater incentive than the chance at a vertical run. What the squirrel needed was time. The thing to do was to get Brother inside.

It was there that he made his mistake. Still working the broom with his left hand, he stooped to grab Brother with his right. Brother wasn't himself in that moment, at least not the self Guy had come to know. Even so, he managed to keep his front claws sheathed. It was the back feet, attempting to kick free, that did the damage. Thick and dull, the hind claws don't often break skin. When they do, they leave a nasty mark.

Guy stumbled to the door, pressing the mad, thrashing body to his chest while he somehow managed the latch. The pair of them fell together across the threshold, the door springing shut in their wake.

Brother was never more fishlike than in that moment of release—all muscle and whipping spine. His nose was at the door crack in seconds. For a moment there was quiet, then came the howl, this time more plaintive than enraged.

"Sorry, buddy."

Brother butted the door with his forehead, then stood up on his hind legs and began scratching the screen.

"No, Brother. Hey, quit it." Guy reached again to interfere, and only then did he notice the blood.

It wasn't so bad—the claw had found purchase in the meaty edge of the wrist, only grazing the vulnerable core. The idea was there, though, Brother's blunt, curved nail plucking the tendons like guitar strings, twanging the fine blue veins.

Guy closed a hand over the bleeding and stood staring down at his cat. All four of Brother's paws were white. Guy had often seen the front two pink with blood, Brother like a kid with a pair of strawberry cones, tonguing one then the other, as though they might melt and drip down his grey fur sleeves. Never a bloodied back foot, though. Not until now.

Aunt Jan was out for groceries, but Guy was no baby. He knew to wash the wound with as much soap as he could stand, knew where the Dettol and bandages were kept. It took five Band-Aids laid out side by side to cover the gash.

By the time he came back into the kitchen, still applying pressure to be safe, Brother had given up on the screen and was sniffing the weatherstripping along the door's bottom edge. Guy hooked a chair out with his boot and sat, resting his pulsing forearm on the table. Aunt Jan would be pissed when he didn't come out to help with carrying the bags, but she'd forgive him pretty quick. He closed his eyes and breathed quietly, listening for the sound of the truck.

Edal can't think of a thing she'd like to eat. Two days of having dinner made for her and she's forgotten how to feed herself. She walks from the kitchen into the living room, drops in a sprawl on the loveseat.

It's a worry, that graveyard of his. She doubts whether he's ever called in a find, and provincial regulations regarding roadkill are clear: acquisition of big game carcasses must be reported immediately, fur-bearing mammals within two days.

She could call the office. It's not federal business, but there would be procedures in place. At the very least, Barrett would want to pass the information on to the Ministry of Natural Resources. She can see him sitting behind his desk, his broad, sun-browned face growing still the way it does. The last time she saw that face, she was in tears. *Take the time, Jones. Hell, take a holiday if you think it'll help.*

*It won't,* she wanted to tell him. *Trust me.*

She's only ever been on one true holiday; her vacation time always went to Letty, three days' visit plus another week spent recovering in her own apartment. Then came the year when she couldn't face it—last year, in point of fact. It's amazing, the power of a blue and white poster when viewed in the right bleak light. After years of living just south of Greektown, she decided the real thing was a reasonable bet.

She went for ten days—Athens, Mykonos, Athens, home. Saw the Acropolis and its crumbling cousins, the markets of Monastiraki, the grass-topped windmills and flagstone streets—filling her camera's memory card. She recalls other details with her body: drinking wine that tasted of Pine-Sol and stripped her tongue, and then drinking more; dancing in a dizzying circle with the other pale, clumsy souls at her hotel, the black-haired waiters corralling them, their muscular arms in the air.

There was a teetering moment when she leaned back into one of them—the youngest, or so he seemed—and the wine in her blood turned from uplift to down. She was sensible, took up her purse and began a careful ascent to her room. He appeared alongside her on the stairs. *Miss Jones, I help you.* He didn't actually press up against her—didn't go that far— but she can remember his arm coming down like a toll bar at the landing's turn. It was a fine arm, dark against its crisp white sleeve. She stared down at it for a stupefied moment. All she had to do was touch it, lay a single finger on the jutting wrist bone, or the elbow's inner curve.

"I don't need help," she said in her work voice. It would've been easier to let his arm drop, but the waiter lifted it, a small show of defiance, the edge of a threat. He left her to manage the final flight on her own.

Edal stares at the shadowy ceiling. The house is quiet, no music moving in the apartment below. They've probably gone out to dinner, Annie reaching across to try James's lamb, James refilling Annie's wine. For once she wishes she could hear them—dancing, fighting, anything to let her know there was someone home.

The sound when it comes is subtler than any human might make. Inquisitive, interior. It's back. Her mouse is back, charting a twitchy, hidden course behind her head. She closes her eyes. Softly, ever so softly, she lays her palm to the wall.

The maple tree provides good cover. Darius might more easily have hidden in a bush, but it makes sense to get up off the ground, where there's no way one of the furry buggers can catch him unawares.

His position affords a decent view: clots of blackness that are clumps of trees, a gunmetal twist of river, the ashy expanse of the field. Unlike the shallow, snaking Don, the low-lit path runs straight between the viaduct's massive feet. Darius stares south along its length, watching the girl and her dog pass through the great graffitied arch. It's like something out of a movie, the lost daughter and her guardian leaving the ancient city's gates.

It's the first time he's met them in the valley. Or not *met*, exactly. Not yet.

The girl is familiar to him, and not just from the lone aerial sighting. It's in her walk—the swift, scissoring stride, arms held rigid, shoulders pinched up high. Faye walked like that. She was always forgetting his legs were shorter, forcing him to run and stumble or else chance being left behind.

Having cleared the viaduct's gloom, the dog peels off into the adjoining field, its steps echoing those taken by the coyote months ago. Coincidence? Darius has come across no further sign hereabouts, but then his senses are only human. For all he knows, the dog could be following a freshly scented trail into the enemy's midst.

He can picture it now, the pack filtering out of the trees, most of them falling on the dog, leaving the helpless, tender-skinned girl for the alpha pair. The male would be the first to bite, the female latching on seconds later to help drag the victim down.

Darius calls out to warn her in his mind but manages to keep his flesh-and-blood mouth shut. As though in answer, she raises a hand to her lips and whistles, turning the dog in its tracks, drawing it back to her side. Together they carry on northward along the path, passing not far from the foot of Darius's tree. Holding both moving shadows in his sights, he dangles, then drops. The stoop has taken hold during his vigil. He feels it shaping him as he lands.

No fighting a family defect: he's not yet twenty and already he can feel the spine softening inside him. He straightens, forcing his shoulders back. One day he'll have to do something drastic. For now, though, he can still get the better of it. When he hunches to follow the pink-haired girl, he does so entirely by choice.

Lily's glad Shere Khan is dead, trampled to stripey shit by the *slaty-blue buffaloes* with Mowgli on the back of the biggest bull. It was fierce, the way the jungle boy managed the herd with the help of his wolf companions, the loyal Grey Brother and Akela the wise.

She throws an arm over Billy. "You'd make a kick-ass herd dog, wouldn't you, boy?"

He sighs in his sleep against her, his breath spicy in the close quarters of the tent. Normally she wouldn't sneak scraps from Guy's table, but she knew Billy would love the meat loaf the second she tasted it. Besides, Guy had made a ton. Probably hoping Edal would show. Lily missed her too. It's weird, how quickly things become routine at the yard.

It's taking a chance, lighting the camp lantern again, but a person can only lie staring into blackness for so long. The book has been calling to her since before she marked the fifty-ninth day and wiped the butterfly knife clean, before she made herself extinguish the light. Now, less than an hour later, the flame stands shivering again. Lily rises up on her elbows, opening to the bright yellow bookmark Guy let her keep. It's low light for reading; she's probably fucking her eyes up beyond repair.

She's come to a terrible part in the story, where Fiver and the others learn what became of the home warren after they left. Escape holes plugged, gas spreading through the tunnels like poison in a body's veins, rabbits piling up in the runs. Terrible. And yet, somehow, a source of wretched comfort. Fiver was right, and the others were right to believe him. They had no choice but to leave the old place behind.

She's reaching for the dragon book when a twig cracks. Only one, but it shakes her like the report of a gun. Billy wakes, stiff with listening at her side. She does her best to listen too, but hears nothing over the sickening rush of her pulse.

*Nothing.*

Maybe it was nothing.

A rat or a raccoon, but nothing with any motive beyond feeding itself and its young. Just in case, Lily recites her levels of protection in her head. *Camouflage, dog, bear spray, knife. Camouflage, dog, bear spray, knife.*

Camouflage does the job nine times out of ten—but not when you're stupid enough to leave a light burning. She should turn out the flame, but that would mean stirring, which could mean missing the crack of a second twig. Billy has relaxed a little beside her, but he has yet to lay down his head.

*Dog, bear spray, knife.*

Three times since she came to the valley, her tent has been found. The first creep only came close enough to get Billy barking before he took off. The second, made bold by the drink he reeked of, had to be chased. Lily was up and breaking camp by the time Billy returned with a scrap of black leather in his mouth.

The true test came with the third intruder. Whatever he was on, it made him worse than bold. He swung at Billy with a length of pipe, kicked through the tent flaps until Lily, still trapped in the mummy bag, shot a blast of bear spray up into his featureless face. Even then he kept on. Blind and gasping, he dropped to his knees, one hand flailing out behind him with the pipe, the other grabbing for Lily where she squirmed. Billy circled round and flew at him from his unprotected side. The pair of shadows became one, Lily heard a tearing sound, and then a new note came into the choking—the first high note of fear.

The tent was toxic, more pepper than air. Wrestling free of the bag, she thrust her head out into the night and saw through her tears how one half of the doubled shadow was attempting to drag itself away. The sound it made now was almost pitiable—harsh, coughing sobs threaded along a keening wail. Billy showed no mercy; he held on tight, snarling through fabric and flesh.

"Get off me!" the shadow screamed. Then the sound of crashing in the waist-high brambles. "Get off!"

Lily struggled to her feet in time to hear the fall. It was like a young tree coming down, the forest disturbed but left standing. Except a tree lay still once it had fallen, instead of thrashing and howling aloud.

By the time Lily got the mummy bag and tent stuffed away, the struggle in the bushes had slowed, each sorry cry more muted than the last. She couldn't let Billy kill the guy, could she? *Could she?* She brought a thumb and finger to her mouth. Whistled over and over, until he separated from his victim and came lumbering back.

Later that same night, far from their first unlucky camp, she clung to him in the dark. His body felt new to her, his muzzle wet against her cheek. At first light she stashed their gear and led him down to the Don. While he waded and drank, she dipped a pair of clean panties and wiped at her face and neck. Wherever Billy had nuzzled, the underwear came away red.

He sighs out his nose, as though remembering that bleak morning with her. Lays his chin down on his paws. A soft surrender comes over his body, nose to rump. His dark eyes flutter and close.

It really was nothing. No one here but a girl and her dog, the pair of them blissfully alone. Her heart is slowing now; she might even get lucky and drift off. She should turn out the lantern. Only she left off reading partway down the page. She'll read to the bottom—to the end of the chapter, maybe, but no more.

# 11

# Ring of Dark Timber

The claw-foot tub was an eyesore—cracked enamel, years of rust and crud. The kitchen window gave onto the weedy patch where it stood. Whether Edal was bent over long division at the table or scouring the carbonized mess of Letty's most recent attempt at a meal, all she had to do was look up and there it was, wallowing in the yard like a shabby old sow.

There was no family member—or even family friend—to haul the thing away, and the idea of Letty Jones paying to have such a thing done was a joke. Besides, that kind of wishful thinking often gave rise to a depressing mental inventory: clogged eavestroughs, leaky roof, black mould messages scrawled on the basement walls.

The best Edal could allow herself was to imagine the tub transformed. Another kind of mother might bring loads of soil in a bright wheelbarrow and turn it into a planter, might even get her daughter to help. The two of them would pore over catalogues, agreeing on what they would plant—something pink and bushy mixed with something purple and tall.

There was nothing to stop Edal from taking the project on by herself. It was true that they had no wheelbarrow, but she could use a bucket, dig soil out of the rift of exposed earth where the yard was subsiding down back. No way she'd get Letty to buy plants, but she might be able to talk her into a few packets of seeds.

It was a Saturday morning when Edal looked out the kitchen window and saw something moving in the old tub. She couldn't make out what it was—the angle was wrong—but it was black and it was definitely alive. Probably a crow, come to pick a meal of bugs from the dead-leaf sludge that gathered about the drain.

She took pains to work the front door quietly, not for her mother's sake—Letty rarely kept her bed later than six—but for the sake of whatever it was that was grubbing around in the tub.

She got a fair idea the moment she stepped out onto the porch. It wasn't the full eye-watering cloud, just the cabbagey musk that threatened worse to come. She stood up on the porch chair to see. The skunk was pacing the length of the tub, now nosing about the drain's dirty mouth, now turning to take a run at the slick enamel slope. Edal thought she could hear a low muttering issuing from its muzzle. She broke from her fretful trance when it scrambled halfway to the lip and toppled back, releasing a wretched squeal.

As always, she tried first to solve the problem by herself. No sense attempting to tip the tub—she'd never been able to budge it an inch. In any case, if she came too near, the skunk would spray. Even if she could somehow keep on through the fumes, it would surely bite her if she tried to pick it up. Edal ran through half a dozen possible approaches in her mind, every one of which ended with her reeking and dripping blood.

The skunk squealed again, a sound like a baby snatched up by someone or something cruel. Edal panicked and ran looking for her mother. She found her where she often did, down in the basement, bent over a musty box.

"Oh, Edal, good." Letty straightened and plucked up the cigarette she'd balanced on the edge of the utility sink. "Give me a hand with these, will you?"

"There's a skunk in the tub."

"What?"

"Outside. There's a skunk in the old tub."

"Oh." Letty took a drag. "I thought you meant it was in the bathroom."

"It can't get out." Edal swallowed the beginning of a sob. "It's trapped."

"What do you mean, it's trapped? It got in there, right? How did it get in there?"

"How do I know how it got in? Jesus, Mother!"

That other mother—the one with the wheelbarrow—might've gotten angry then, flashed her eyes and said, *Just who do you think you're talking to?* But Letty clamped her smoke between her lips, looked down into the box and began lifting out the top layer of books. "It'll get out the same way it got in, Edal."

If she had any other great advice, Edal didn't stick around to hear it. In the kitchen she cried properly, hunched at the table with her face buried in her hands. For two whole minutes, maybe three, she let the hot tears slide down her wrists. Then, in the quiet that followed, she had an idea.

Years of phone books were stacked up beneath the wall-mounted phone. He answered after half a ring. The sound of his voice—familiar, though she'd heard it only once—worked on her like a soothing hand.

She'd thought about what to say. "Mr. Dale, this is Edal Jones. You came to my class." She heard herself chirping like a six-year-old and tried to slow down.

"Uh-huh. What can I do for you, Edal?"

"I've got a problem." She took a breath. "There's a skunk in the old bathtub in our yard." Bathtub. In our yard. There was no other way to say it.

"Stuck in there, is he?" Jim Dale said.

Edal felt a swell of gratitude, almost enough to restart the tears. "Yes."

"Where do you live?"

Edal worried her mother would show herself at the sound of the truck—her hair dragged back into a greasy ponytail, track pants and Wasaga Beach T-shirt patterned with dust—but the boxes and their contents held sway.

Jim Dale unfolded his long body from the cab of his mushroom-coloured truck, held a hand up in greeting, then put his finger to his lips. Edal nodded, and that made them partners. She knew for certain she'd done the right thing.

He cast his gaze about the yard, spied a pile of scrap wood no good for bookshelves and made for it on silent feet. Fishing a length of one-by-four from the tangle, he headed for the tub.

For a long, horrible moment, Edal thought he was going to kill the skunk. Bash its skull in from a safe distance and lift it up by the tail—or, worse, leave the little striped body for Edal to dispose of herself. Then she remembered how he'd stood at the front of the class, drawing the outlines of leaves on the blackboard in yellow chalk. Just because he was a hunter didn't mean he'd brain an innocent skunk.

Jim Dale moved like the high grass he passed through, the same wave and hush. When he came within range, he reached the one-by-four out like a feeler and touched it to the tub, just where the back of a bather's head would rest. When no whiff of alarm rose on the breeze, he began sliding the plank forward and down. The skunk huddled by the drain. Edal was keeping a safe distance, but she could make out the twitching tip of its tail.

When the plank met the far end and angled up out of the tub like a ramp, Jim Dale let go of it and backed away. Edal tiptoed over to meet him at his truck.

"He ought to be able to figure it out," he said, swinging up into his seat. "You be sure and call me again, though, if he's not out of there by nightfall."

He was leaving. Edal had a sudden urge to tell him something—anything—but she only nodded and stepped back.

After he drove off, she settled into the porch chair to keep watch. She didn't have long to wait. Not ten minutes passed before the skunk realized its good fortune and came grappling up the plank. Edal sat forward in her seat. The skunk hesitated at the tub's rounded lip. A shiver animated the dark stripe along its spine. It held its breath—or so Edal imagined— and it jumped.

# 12

# The Chronicles of Darius

There were two Grandmothers: the wordless one for when Grandfather was home, and the talking one for the two slim hours between the school bus drop-off and the tires-on-gravel grind that signalled Grandfather's return. She always came to meet Darius where the bus slowed to a stop on the shoulder, and this was their secret. Grandfather had an idea that Darius should walk the long track down to the cabin on his own. *Never too young to get comfortable in the woods.*

Most days, Grandmother started talking the second the bus doors hissed shut. It might be about a bird she'd seen through the kitchen window that morning, or even an elk; or it might be about the meat loaf she planned to make for supper. Too bad it wouldn't be her own mother's recipe, with whole boiled eggs inside like hidden treasure. Grandfather didn't like it that way.

If the day was fine, they might drop Darius's backpack by the door and carry on down to the river, though they never lingered there long. Either way, once they were inside, there was no TV to listen to, so it made sense for Grandmother to keep on talking while she scraped the carrots or beat the steaks so they wouldn't be tough.

"Can I try?" Darius asked one afternoon when he'd been living there long enough for the ground outside to be dusted with snow. She drew up a chair for him to stand on beside her, and handed him her little kitchen mallet, its silver face covered in pointy teeth. "It chews the meat," he said.

"Well, yes, I suppose it does." She smiled at him, her brief, dissolving smile, and he felt a flash of pride. "You can hit it harder than that," she added.

"I can?"

She nodded, her mouth twitching up at one end. "Give it hell."


Sometimes she said more about her own mother than just meat loaf.

"Thirteen children she had. Can you imagine that, Darius? And those were just the ones that lived. Little wonder I wanted out of that house." She fell quiet for a time, down on her hands and knees, rubbing her rag over the floorboards.

The kitchen chairs were turned legs-up on the table, so Darius was sitting high up on the counter, dangling his feet. He pointed his toes in their wool socks as she shuffled closer, came within centimetres of grazing her back.

"Funny thing, I ended up wanting a whole big brood of my own." She sat back on her heels to drag the bucket after her. "I suppose you get used to what you know."

Darius nodded. He'd been used to the apartment, now he was getting used to this.

"I only had the one, though." She dipped her rag, swishing it through the greying suds. After several passes, she lifted it and let it drip. She didn't drop back down onto her reddened hands, though. Just knelt there, as though she were gauging the cloth's sodden weight.

Darius held his tongue for as long as he could bear it. Until it was like holding a toad behind his teeth. "Faye?" he said finally, letting it escape.

She looked up in surprise, as though she'd forgotten he was there. As though the stewpot or the coffee can had spoken her daughter's name.

"Yes," she said, blinking. "Faye."

The question had always been with him. He'd never put it to Faye—she'd had a terrible habit of letting his queries hang. Grandmother, on the other hand, generally did her best to respond, especially when the two of them were alone.

*Grandmother, what's that noise?*

*That's a red squirrel. He doesn't much like us walking through his patch.*

*Grandmother, what are you doing?*

*What's it look like? I'm washing the clothes.*

*But, where's the washer?*

*We don't have one, Darius.*

Of course not. There wasn't even hot water in the taps. She set the kettle on to boil a dozen times a day. Still, he kept on.

*Not even at the laundromat?*

*Not even there.*

She was making bread, punching the dough down in its bowl, when he began edging up to the big one.

"Grandmother?"

"Mm-hm?"

"With bears, there's a mother and there's the cubs."

"That's right, and you know if you see cubs, you need to watch out—the mother's never far."

"I know. But there's a father too, right?"

She paused, her fist mired in the dough. "That's right, but it's the mother who watches over the cubs."

"Do I—did I have a father?" He breathed carefully as Grandmother withdrew her hand from the bowl. The air between them was yeasty, close.

"You did, yes."

"Was he—"

"He was a man your mother worked for."

"Faye had a job?"

"She did. She was a cashier at the Tomboy Market in town."

Darius tried to see it. Faye with her hair tied back and one of those jackets that were really more like shirts. Green maybe, the same as her eyes. Or red. Faye smiling as she set a bag of apples on the scale—the yellow kind she liked. Fingers thin on the number keys, but nimble. Maybe even strong.

"She worked Saturdays mostly. After school now and then, but your grandfather didn't like her missing the bus home. Well, he didn't much like her working there, period."

"Because of my father?"

"Not exactly. Not at first, anyway. Afterwards, certainly." She looked down at her gooey hand. "He—the manager—he wasn't very kind to your mother. Not once he'd got what he wanted." She rubbed at her palm, rolling up little pills of dough. "She told us he gave her no choice. That got her in enough trouble, but I always wondered if maybe she wasn't fibbing. Not that I blame her. It got her out of here."

"What did?"

"You did, Darius." She looked at him then, her gaze hungry. "Sometimes the only way to get something done is to let it happen. Do you understand?"

He managed to unfreeze his neck and nod.

"Good." She turned back to her bread. "Good."

It wasn't Darius's fault. If Grandmother had never told him, he never could have let it slip.

Grandfather was late coming home from the mill that day. It was nothing to worry about; Grandmother had given him a list of what Faye and Mrs. Miske had called groceries but Grandfather called supplies. Darius had an idea that women generally did the food shopping, but when he'd asked Grandmother about it once, Grandfather had backed through the kitchen door with an armload of wood and answered for her. "Have to drive to get into town."

"I can drive," Grandmother said.

He dumped the wood alongside the stove. "That's a matter of opinion."

She flushed. "Well, yes. I don't . . . I haven't had a licence in years."

Now, as the truck came nosing down the snowy drive, she said only, "Go on out and help."

Darius dragged on his coat and boots, slipped out into the cold and presented himself alongside Grandfather's sawdusty thigh.

"Come to make yourself useful, I see." He dropped the

tailgate so it lay flat, pulling against its chains. Darius saw a crowd of brown paper bags, two open-topped boxes and a sack of flour the size of a second child.

"Yes, sir."

The old man bent as far as the board at his back allowed, snapping forward at the waist like a shotgun breaking open to take its load. Darius had watched Grandfather crack his twelve-gauge and push the shells in both barrels with his thumb. *It'll be yours one day, Darius.* The old man's face softened when he said it, the way it did whenever he ate something sweet. *The Lord help you if you lay a finger on it before then.*

The tailgate tucked into his lap, Grandfather snatched a bag by its scruff and dragged it toward him over the rutted deck. "See if you can manage that."

Darius held out his arms. The bag was heavy—three sloshing bags of milk and more—but he hugged it to his chest, shuffling to the front step so nothing could trip him up. Grandmother met him at the door, taking the bag just as he feared it might fall. "Good boy. Back you go."

Darius didn't drop a thing. His thin arms cried so he could almost hear them, but he helped and helped until the truck bed lay bare and Grandfather shut the tailgate with a clang.

Inside, Grandmother was busy unpacking. "Here, Darius." She set him up on a patch of floor not far from the wood stove, giving him the job of flattening the bags.

"Pack of thieves," Grandfather said, angling himself down into his chair.

Grandmother twisted the lid off the flour jar. "Who's that?"

"Them at the co-op."

"Oh."

"Jack up the prices for the skiers, never mind folks who actually live here."

Darius tucked the sides of the first bag in neatly, the bottom closing up tight like a jaw. Grandmother snipped the flour sack's cat-eared corner. Setting the jar down on the floor in front of her, she hoisted the sack up between her knees and began to pour. When the spout jammed, she bounced to get the flour moving again, like the sack was a little white pony and she was going for a ride.

"I've half a mind to take my business elsewhere," Grandfather said.

It wasn't telling. You had to mean to do it if you were telling, and Darius didn't even know he was going to speak. "You could go to the Tomboy Market."

"What?" Grandfather generally took a minute to rise from his chair, but by the time Darius looked up, he was already on his feet. "What did he say?"

"Ron—"

"Shut up."

"He just—"

"I said, SHUT UP!"

Grandmother dropped the sack, flour sifting over the floorboards. She stood up straight, chin down, hands working in her apron's folds.

Darius fought the urge to open one of the paper bags and crawl inside—head first, and somehow the rest of him would have to fit. Grandfather seemed to be made of nothing but boards now, the way his limbs creaked and swung. He walked stiffly into his bedroom, and for a moment Darius thought it might be all right to breathe. Then the old man was back, stalking straight for Grandmother, his fist doubled, wound up in something dark. The buckle gave it away. Pronged and bright, it matched the one still gleaming at Grandfather's waist. The old man couldn't strip his belt from its loops with a flourish; the board at his back might slip. He needed a second belt. A twin.

When he hooked his arm around Grandmother's shoulders and manoeuvred her out the kitchen door to the backhouse, Darius knew a leavening streak of relief. At least he wouldn't have to watch. He learned soon enough that listening could be just as bad. Covering his ears did little. He felt every lick of the leather, every piteous yelp.

Grandmother wouldn't look at him when they traded places, him rising in Grandfather's grip, her slipping to the floor. He took his punishment as he imagined she had, pants down, hands braced on either side of the seat. The sulphurous breath of the open hole.

The second belt didn't come out often; long stretches went by between transgressions gross enough to warrant its use. Sometimes Grandmother was the one to slip, as when she forgot to turn the stewpot down and wasted two whole fresh hares. Sometimes it was Darius, letting the fire die when he was meant to be feeding it, or sneaking a scrap of chicken skin during a particularly long grace. There were times, too, when Grandfather took them both out to the backhouse again, folding one then the other under his wing; usually when they'd been in on something together—baking a batch of coconut squares and wolfing them all before he got home, washing the pan but forgetting about the toasted, tropical smell. Darius never knew which order to hope for. Grandfather might tire and lighten his hand after the first beating, or it might just serve to warm him up.

On the whole, though, the pair of them did their best to behave, and so the belt often lay coiled on his grandparents' dresser for months at a time. Darius took to stealing into their room to check if it was still there. The first half-dozen times he only looked, but by the time he turned nine, it had become necessary to make contact with his hand. The buckle a bright chill. The leather slick, surprisingly warm.

# 13

# The City Book

**Coyote Cop's Blog**
**Friday, May 30, 2008**
Your not the only one who can look things up on the web soldierboy. The indians or whatever your supposed to call them had something else to say about the coyote which was that he was always sneaking around and messing with peoples minds. So think about that.

You just don't get it do you? Damn right coyotes are generalists. They have made a meal out of just about everything out there and now they are coming for us. Watch your pets Toronto. Watch your kids. Hell watch your step. Only I guess the problem is most of you don't even know what to watch out for.

Some of you have been asking how to be sure what your looking at is a coyote and not something else.

Well if your out in the country theres a slim chance
its a wolf. Of course coyotes tend to be smaller, but
theres not much difference between the biggest
eastern coyote and the littlest algonquin wolf. That
said, there are a few dead giveaways. If the tail
stands straight out when it runs chances are its
a wolf. Coyotes keep theirs hanging straight down.
Also watch out for ears that look too big for the
head they belong to. The main thing though is
the feeling. I have only ever seen a wolf from
a distance but I can remember just how it felt. And
more to the point just where. It was in my neck.
Coyotes I've seen up close and the feeling is nowhere
near your neck. Down low in your guts is where you
feel it. As low as they go.

In the city it gets a little harder knowing whats
what. Theres not much question with most dogs but
anything with husky in it can be confusing. Especially
with coyotes mixing their dirty blood up in things.
Anyway here again the tail is a good bet. Dogs most
often keep a curl in theirs.

Wherever they live coyotes are good hiders. You can
be standing a couple of paces from one and never
know he's there. They leave clues though. Maybe you
think those are all dog tracks in the park. Take a
closer look sometime. Coyotes leave oval tracks with
the front nails pinched together and the side nails
tucked in tidy so sometimes they don't even show.

Dogs make a rounder print with the claw marks splayed. Also, dogs leave a sloppy trail running all over the place the way they do but a coyote knows what he's about. Look for those neat little tracks laid down in a definite line. Maybe you think no way it can't be because the trail runs right by the swings where you take your kid to play. Well think again. And pay attention to the turds you come across too. If you see one left in the middle of the path and especially where 2 paths cross chances are its coyote. It might be all dark and wet or it might be full of hair and bones but either way it will smell more like skunk than dog shit. This time of year you should be on the lookout for dens too. Those bushy slopes all along the Don Valley are just about perfect. If you see a pile of dirt look for the hole it came from and if you find one be sure and let me know.

Oh and one more thing. Another coyote calling card is the way he gets into his kill. If you find a deer carcass that has been eaten out under the tail you can bet coyotes are to blame. Think about what they would do to your body given half a chance. This means you soldierboy. Think about what they would do to you.

*POSTED BY Coyote Cop at 6:17 AM*

*soldierboy wrote . . .*

Believe me, I know all about how soft human bodies are, my own included. So coyotes go in under the tail. So what? Nobody's going to take the deer to the butcher for them, are they? Maybe it is kind of rough, but it's nothing compared to what humans do.

The cursor blinks. There's more to be said on the subject, Stephen knows, but he seems to have hit some kind of wall. A mud wall. Dust-coloured where it isn't spattered with blood, waist-high in some places, higher in others. It's hot to the touch while the sun beats down on it, cool when the passage of untold hours brings shade.

Stephen's hands are trembling. He posts the comment, clicks to quit the browser and stands. *Are you sure you want to quit?* He clicks again. Yes, quit it. *Quit.*

Passing from the office to his bedroom, he lowers himself to the floor. After a moment he stretches a hand beneath the bed. The kits cry weakly as he works the latch, woken from the deep comfort of a post-bottle sleep. His remorse is sudden, almost crippling in its strength. Why can't he just leave them be? The big tan is the first to open its eyes. He can't help but reach for it. Its fierce little body is getting stronger, more substantial with every feed.

Edal's walking around Withrow Park when she spots the pigeon. It must have taken the wheel head-on; its insides have been pushed out in a smeary skirt around its feet. Rock dove—the most variable plumage of any species. This one is caramel-coloured, softening in places to a dusty, speckled pink. Iridescence floats across its flattened shoulders, loops tight around its twisted neck.

Edal lingers on the sidewalk, staring down. When a car approaches, she fights the urge to step out in front of it, stand over the body and force the driver to swerve. As luck would have it, it's a narrow miss. What about the next one, though, and the next? The pigeon could be carried off in the tread of a hundred different tires.

She turns and walks quickly back to the house. Upstairs in her apartment, she fishes a plastic IGA bag from the box beneath the sink. She has no shovel, James and Annie being the keepers of the yard. She drags open a drawer. The spatula will have to do.

The pigeon lies unchanged where she left it—still lovely, still grotesque. From the park comes the clatter of a skateboard, the Tagalog murmur of nannies gathering in the shade. Overhead, the garble of starlings. Another car comes—this one hugging the curb to soften the speed bump, leaving her no choice but to step out into the street, her spatula extended like a crossing guard's sign. The driver slows obediently. She waves him round.

She hasn't got long; already a dark SUV is turning onto Carlaw at the top of the block. Crouching down, she takes a deep breath and works the spatula under the pigeon's head. She loosens one wing, then the other. Folds the body like a feathered omelette and slides it inside the bag.

Feeling shaky, she stands and takes a step back onto the sidewalk, allowing the SUV to pass. Now what? Having saved the pigeon the indignity of the road, she can't possibly tie up the bag and drop it in a garbage can. Nor can she take it home for burial in James and Annie's Mediterranean vegetable plot. She hasn't been planning another visit to the wrecking yard; she can hardly show up there four days in a row—five, if you count the nosebleed incident. Maybe not under normal circumstances, but she stepped outside normal the moment she chose not to pass the dead pigeon by.

Again she doesn't get a chance to buzz. Billy's lying in the shade of the pickup. He catches sight of her and comes galloping, pressing his nose to the mesh.

"Hi, Billy." She spreads a palm out for him to smell. "You know me, don't you. Yeah, that's me."

Lily comes after him, her mouth flinching up at the corners when she sees who it is. Edal feels her heart do a little jump. They're happy to see her, both of them happy she's come.

"Hey, Edal." Lily fits her key into the padlock.

"Hi, Lily." Edal steps past her into the yard, Billy snuffling the bag in her hand.

Having secured the gate, Lily turns. "Manners, Billy." He looks up at her, and she pushes her fingers into the thick fur at his neck. "So."

"So."

"What's in the bag?"

Edal hasn't thought this part through. Any possible reply seems flippant, unequal to the truth. *Pigeon. Dead pigeon. Unfortunate bird.* In the end she holds the bag open, letting the contents speak for themselves.

"Aw." Lily's utterance draws a matching one from between Billy's teeth. "Poor thing."

"Yeah."

"You want to bury it?"

"You think we should?"

Lily says nothing.

"I guess so. Yes, I do."

Lily nods. "Come on."

Billy seems to know what they have in mind. He leads the way down past the office, sidling through the gap in the overlapping hedge. While he sniffs a winding path from hubcap to hubcap, Lily reaches for the spade where it leans against the cinder-block wall. Headed for the corner where fence meets hedge, she says over her shoulder, "Guy set a patch aside for me. You know, for my birds."

Edal comes to stand beside her, staring down at the neat rows of minute graves. It's heartbreaking, the way she's marked each one with a simple upstanding twig.

"We can put it here if you want," Lily adds. "There's room."

Suddenly Edal's not sure she can trust her voice. It's crazy, fighting back tears at a roadkill funeral. Maybe she should see about counselling after all. "Okay," she says finally. "Thanks."

Lily does the digging, which leaves Edal to stand with her head bowed, hands clasped before her, holding the pendulous bag.

"That should do it." Lily steps back and leans on the spade.

Billy joins them for the interment, lying down with his nose at the edge of the hole. It feels wrong to upend the bag and let the pigeon drop, but where would she pick it up—the neck? Lily and her dog sustain a patient silence while Edal kneels and sets the bag down on the grass. The spatula is fairly kind as kitchen implements go, designed to be eased under fluffy batter, the delicate, frilled edges of eggs. She slides the blade gently beneath the pigeon again. Tilts it slowly into the waiting grave.

Following Lily and Billy back out through the hedge, Edal feels easier, almost calm. The sensation lasts for several paces, until Guy steps out of the office door.

"Edal." If Lily smiled to see her, he positively beams.

"Hi, Guy."

Lily looks from one to the other. "Come on, Billy, time to go to work."

"Work?" Guy raises an eyebrow.

"Yeah, you know, you show up, you do shit, you get paid."

"You have a job?"

"Of course I have a job. You think I'm some kind of bum?"

"No, I just never—"

She spins on her heel. "See you, Edal."

"Bye, Lily. And thanks."

Lily waves without turning around. Guy and Edal stand together like young parents, watching her go.

"Thanks for what?" he says as the gate clangs shut.

"Oh, I had a . . . I found a bird. Lily let me put it in with hers."

"Wow. You should be honoured."

From anyone else it would be a joke. "Yeah," she says, nodding, "I am."

He looks away toward the flight cage, then back. "I was just going to feed Red. Want to watch?"

Fixed on its branch, the hawk eyes the small grey box in Guy's hands. Not even a glance at Edal as she shoves the cage door closed behind him. Maybe it can hear movement inside the trap, squeaking, even a pitiful wail. *Stop it.* The red-tail is a predator, the rodent a species of prey. Mice breed in the numbers they do for precisely one reason—to blanket the world with food.

Still, her heart sinks as Guy sets the trap down in the dirt. Lifting its little hatch, he backs away quickly. She opens the door a crack to let him squeeze out.

The mouse has been locked up for who knows how long. Still, it knows better than to burst from the trap into the dangerous light of day. It pokes out its nose, whiskers working. Black eyes now. Translucent ears. It emerges in unbearable increments, front paws groping, as though the creature they belong to is blind.

Edal forces herself to look away, transferring her attention to the bird. It hasn't moved—not a feather—and yet it is changed. The difference between a closed hand and a clenched one. She's conscious of Guy breathing beside her. Feels fleetingly, absurdly, as though he's breathing for her too.

Movement splits her focus—the mouse making a break for it, the hawk lifting off, becoming its own killing gaze. A second later the red-tail brakes with its wings, strikes hard with its reaching feet. The mouse is stabbed through, strangled. Wholly dead as the hawk gathers it up in its claws.

Edal expects the hawk to rip into the mouse—either that or bolt it down and carry it back to the dead oak in its crop.

Instead, it holds the little body to its breast and lowers its head.

"Wheep," it says softly to its food. And again, this time scarcely audible, "*Wheeep.*"

Guy lets out a low whistle—of admiration or plain release—and the bird looks up sharply. Staring, it lowers its kill to the ground. It stands motionless for several seconds, one foot on the mouse, before it moves. Hop, pivot, hop—an awkward, counter-clockwise shuffle. The red-tail is showing them its back.

Incredible that spoken language should ever have evolved, when even a bird can communicate so clearly without words. The hawk stoops forward and opens its wings, halting at half their span. The message is mixed, part tenderness, part sinister intent.

"Guess he'd like a little privacy." Guy hooks the padlock in place and snaps it shut. "You okay? You look a little pale."

Edal nods.

"Want a coffee?"

"Coffee." She considers the hawk's hunched form.

"Okay, then, how about a beer?"

Stephen's walking out to the loader when a mouse makes him jump. It's gone before he can get a good look, disappearing down the chute of a truncated tailpipe into a warren of scrap. *Gone.* But the sensation it evoked remains.

The camel spider made him jump too.

No one had warned him how much of his tour would be spent standing around, trying to keep alert in the heat. It was a tough slog for a boy from the wet west coast—white-hot mornings, forty degrees before your boots even hit the ground. Come the full of day, troops unable to keep to the shade started dropping, drunk with sun. He'd never dreamt his body could call for so much water—half a dozen litres on milder days, triple that when the sun did its worst.

It was blistering, the day the camel spider appeared in the corner of his eye. His platoon had been briefed on the big arachnids and other indigenous fauna upon arrival at KAF, the sergeant making a meal of the topic the way only an east-coaster could. *It'll feel like the bugger's stalking you, but he's only after your shade. He can give a healthy bite, right enough, but only if you go asking for it, messing him around. Even then there's no venom to speak of. No, it's the vipers you want to watch out for, and wouldn't you know it, the filthy fuckers like to hide.*

Four months in, Stephen had yet to lay eyes on one of the deadly snakes, though he'd seen his share of Afghan animal life. Pigeons or something close lined the rafters of the old Russian-built hangar at KAF. Horses were in short supply throughout the region, but there were always the hobbled, hopping donkeys, the reeking, skin-and-bones goats. Once, during a cordon search of a village, he came upon half a dozen rabbits in a corner courtyard. He didn't spot them at first, their fur the same powdery brown as the little baked houses, the many winding walls. *Fresh meat,* one of the others said hoarsely behind him, but Stephen could think only of scooping one up and holding it. Clutching it to his hammering chest.

Once he got over the small shock of the camel spider's presence, Stephen decided to test the shade theory for himself. Stepping to one side, he found the creature came too, riding the slim carpet his shadow made. Another step saw it dog him again. He'd heard they were big, and sure enough, this one was the size of a toddler's hand. He'd heard they were ugly too, but that wasn't strictly so. There was a delicacy to the way it fingered along after him through the sand. It was pale, soft grey and ivory, with pointed feet and a fine, almost formal design. Not so much a child's hand as an X-ray of that hand come to life. The longer he watched it, the lovelier it became.

It stuck by him throughout the long afternoon, even followed him back to the LAV when the order to move finally came through. He considered pointing it out to his fellow soldiers but thought better of the idea. It would only take one startled soul, one boot brought down with a nervous laugh. He lagged a little, making sure he was the last one up the ramp. The camel spider kept on alone. As it vanished into the gloom beneath the LAV, Stephen said a rapid, silent prayer. Let it keep clear of the wheels, he thought. Let it live.

He's forgotten what he was doing, where he is. The sun on his face is confusingly pleasant, the armoured vehicle before him all wrong. The fork is what sets him straight. Loader, not LAV. He's on his way to shift the cars he flattened earlier, start a new stack along the eastern wall.

Talk about a cheap date—one beer and she offers to make dinner? She's not the world's worst cook, but when was the last time she made a meal for other people? Guy didn't protest the way anyone else would have. If he had, Edal might have come to her senses and backed out.

She left to go shopping without thinking to ask what he and the others might like. Loblaws came close to defeating her, her mind a bright void as she wandered the aisles. In the end it was a chicken breast that saved her. *Fajitas.* She may have cried the actual word—several people looked round—or it may have been pure, unintelligible sound.

Strangely, everything seems to be going okay. They could be a family, and a modern one at that—Edal at the counter chopping garlic, Lily outside smoking, Stephen online in another room. Guy's already set the table. He sits there reading, the book unknown to Edal, something about a pilgrim and a creek. Whatever the story, it holds his attention almost entirely. *Almost.* Earlier, while she was slicing the green peppers, she caught him watching. He met her look, held it briefly before returning his gaze to the page.

Now, as she crosses to the stove, she catches him in a moment of distraction again. This time, though, he looks toward the screen door, where Lily can be heard calling across the yard.

"Hey, Kate."

At least Edal thinks it's Kate, the single syllable muddied by Billy's welcoming woof. *Kate.* It's not a name she's heard mentioned—but then, why would she? She's only known him—them—for a few days. She scarcely knows them at all.

A second female voice now; Edal can't quite make out the reply. She can make out the laughter, though—the first time she's heard anything more than a snort from Lily. Bright, almost childish in tenor, it finds a counterpoint in the other, sustained and warm. Edal becomes aware of the wooden spoon in her hand. She twists back to the stove and balances it against the hot lip of the pan.

When she turns back to face the room, Guy has laid his book face down on the table. The screen door is a portal, now empty, now holding a woman turned hazy by the fine steel mesh. Guy stands as she draws it open, coming clear.

First, there is her skin. The colour of caramel sauce, it glows against the ice cream white of her T-shirt, the black of her high-cut runner's shorts. Then there's her hair, far longer than Edal could ever grow hers, not a full blue-black but not what anyone would call brown either. Dark, most people would say. Long, dark hair. The high ponytail has swung forward to cover a shoulder, a breast. It lies there like a pelt, as though it might just as easily end in the sharp little face of a mink.

"Who's this?" Guy says, as Lily and Billy follow the new-comer inside.

"This is Kate." Lily looks at the floor. "I told her she could come and see the hawk."

"If that's okay." Kate's voice matches her laugh. The mouth it issues from is red and full. Edal feels herself swivel back to the spitting pan.

"Sure," Guy says warmly. "Hey, Edal, come and meet Kate."

She angles the spoon against the pan again, but it slips, splattering the stovetop, an oily spray. She hates herself for what she does next. She's tucked her thin hair back to keep her face cooler as she cooks. Now she reaches up to free it. It falls in two flimsy curtains as she turns, hiding the flaw she's come close to forgetting, her unfortunate little ears.

Something's up. Guy may not have known many women, but unless he's very much mistaken, something has rubbed Edal the wrong way. She's not what you'd call a big talker in general, but tonight she hasn't said word one—not even when he told her everything tasted great. It's true, too. He's had Mexican before, but never like this—the fresh green bite, the soft tortillas in their corn-scented steam. He helps himself to seconds, taking his time.

Too much time, it would seem. He's still working on the last fragrant bite when she stands to take his plate.

"Uh-uh." He swallows. "You cooked."

She stands still, as though admonished. Cuts her eyes toward the door.

Kate balls up her paper-towel napkin and rises. "I'll wash. You want to give me a hand clearing, Lily?"

Billy whines, and Lily slides down in her chair, bringing her nose to his. "Billy's gotta go."

"Maybe Stephen can take him." Kate reaches across Guy and he gets a whiff of the runner's sweat in her T-shirt. Honest sweat, Aunt Jan used to say. *You can always smell a phony, Guy. The pores don't lie.*

"Come on, Lily," she says. "You can dry."

"Yes, ma'am."

Stephen stands and pats his thigh, drawing Billy after him to the door. Edal watches them go. She still hasn't sat back down.

"Take a seat," Guy says.

She twists her hands together. "I thought I might get going." She says it as though she's a stranger among them. As though she doesn't know what happens next.

"Don't you want to hear tonight's chapter?" He means to say it lightly.

"I'm tired."

And he sees now that she is—not weary so much as sleepy. Somebody ought to pick her up and carry her to bed, tuck her in before she begins to cry. She would be easy to lift; he knows this in his arms, his chest.

"It's 'Letting in the Jungle' tonight," he says. "Mowgli gets his own back on the villagers." Ever so slightly desperate. Even he can hear it, and still he keeps on. "I'll give you a ride home after if you want."

She tilts her head, as though she can't quite make out his meaning. Then nods and resumes her seat—but not before grabbing a section of the *Star* from the table's far end. Aunt Jan used to read in different ways for different reasons. When she opened the paper, it meant she'd rather be left alone.

Guy takes his time fetching the book, sitting down on the bed and reaching first for *Ring of Bright Water*. Should he take it out to show her? Something tells him no, at least not yet. He lets it fall open to a page he's favoured. A man not much older than himself has fallen asleep in his chair. On his lap, a large, white-throated otter lies wide awake.

By the time Guy returns to the table, Edal's set the paper aside, folded her arms into a pillow and laid down her head, her face turned away from his chair. The others sit quiet and alert. Guy eases into his place, slips his finger in behind the bookmark and begins.

Having learned to hate man, Mowgli's back in the jungle, where he belongs. His friends counsel him to forget the village, but how can he when he knows Messua, his human mother, is to be put to death for having harboured him in her home?

Guy keeps his voice low to begin with, but allows himself to grow louder as Mowgli forms his plan. Louder still as that plan comes into effect.

Once Messua and her man have escaped, the jungle is free to do its worst. The wild pigs lead the way for every horned and hungry thing; soon the ripening crops are no more. With nowhere to graze, the village herds wander off to join up with their wild cousins. Ponies lie broken in the laneways, marked by a certain panther's paw. In the end, Hathi the elephant and his sons run mad, plucking roofs off the little mud houses and kicking through crumbling walls.

In the midst of the havoc, Edal turns to lay the other temple down on the back of her wrist. He can see her face now, her eyes still closed, the lids bluish, soft.

"'A month later,'" he reads, "'the place was a dimpled mound, covered with soft, green young stuff; and by the end of the Rains there was the roaring Jungle in full blast on the spot that had been under plough not six months before.'"

He leaves a pause before finishing with "Mowgli's Song Against People." When he falls silent, Edal makes a small sound in her throat, like the click of a CD reaching its end. She lifts her head and opens her eyes. Her cheeks are flushed.

"That was amazing, Guy," Kate says, stretching her arms up over her head. "The dinner was great too, Edal. I only ever cook Indian, and I even cheat at that."

"I love curry," says Stephen.

"Yeah? I should make some for you guys."

"You're on," Guy says. "How about tomorrow night?"

Edal rubs her eyes roughly and pushes up out of her chair. "Well, good night, everybody."

She's at the door before Guy can stand.

"Bye, Edal," Stephen and Lily say together, and Billy huffs out a sigh.

"Nice to meet you," Kate calls.

"You too." She says it over her shoulder, not looking back.

Guy slips out after her. She's walking fast, already coming alongside the trucks. "Hey, wait up." She slows a little but doesn't stop. He catches up to her at the gate. "What're you going to do, scale it? Hold your horses."

He feels for the chain at his neck and pulls up the key. Once he has it in hand, he finds that hand less than steady. Whatever's upset her, it seems to be catching.

He busies his hands with the lock. "No bike tonight?"

"No." She says it softly, almost sadly, her tone confusing him further.

"You want a ride?"

"No."

He frees the lock but keeps his other hand on the gate. *Never.* Aunt Jan's voice like a buzzer deep inside his skull. *Never, ever bar a woman's way.* It was mostly a joke, him blocking the office door that day, trying to keep his aunt from taking the call he wanted for himself. But he was taller than her by then, and it was anything but funny when she looked up at him with blazing eyes.

He steps back quickly, drawing the gate with him. Edal turns side-on to ease through the opening.

"You coming by tomorrow?" he blurts.

"I don't think so."

"Not a big curry fan?" He pauses, and when she doesn't respond, he fills the silence again. "We don't have to have—"

"It's okay. It doesn't matter. I'd better be getting home."

"I'll walk you," he says, a little too loudly. "If that's okay."

It takes her a moment to answer. "Yeah." Her expression is impossible to read. "Okay."

Despite her size, she's a fair match for him in pace and stride. She swings her arms as she walks; he stuffs his hands in his pockets. They head east toward Broadview, silence stretching along the first short block. Guy searches his mind. There ought to be something he can say about the street where he grew up.

When was the last time he walked along it with a girl? It must've been grade seven, because he was still making his way to school most mornings. If he timed it right, there was a fair chance Shelley Tang would fall in beside him when he passed her house. She was a grade older, but still the right height to look him in the eye. Other Chinese girls wore their hair in ponytails or shiny, blunt-cut bobs, but Shelley preferred to shave away handfuls and bleach what was left behind. "It's Shao-lin, actually," she told him one wet spring morning. "My folks figured nobody'd notice I was a Chink if they wrote Shelley on the admissions form." So far as Guy knew, he was the only one she'd ever told her real name. In turn he offered her the lost, hockey-great pronunciation of his own.

It can't have been long afterwards that the sign showed up on Shao-lin's narrow front yard. *For Sale* one week, *Sold* the next. "Richmond Hill, here we come," she muttered on their last morning together. The street was slick, the sky pearly. "No more cockroaches and fresh lychee for Shelley Tang."

He hasn't thought about Shao-lin in what feels like forever, despite the fact that he passes her old place every time he goes for a paper, or to the Rose for a sub. Now, coming alongside the little row house with Edal, he finds himself gesturing toward it. "A friend of mine used to live there."

She slows for a moment, regarding its drooping porch. Not much of a response, but to be fair, he hasn't given her much to respond to. He and Shao-lin used to point things out to each other as they walked: the yellowish, long-bottomed panties the old woman on Hamilton Street strung out along her line; the corner yard crowded with strollers—they counted nine of them, nine empty strollers catching rainwater and growing grey blankets of mould. On Broadview they charted the stains left by bleeding streetcar transfers, the vomit splatters outside the Lucky Lotus bar. Standing before shopfront stalls, they stooped over the bright, stinking bodies of dried shrimp, watched the pink-footed pigeons scramble over mounds of bok choy. The same stalls he passes with Edal now.

It comes to him as they turn onto Gerrard—maybe there is something he can show her after all. It's not a sure bet, but a good one, given that it's just gone dark. "Hey," he says, a few doors along, "let's go down here."

She halts, framed in the alley's mouth. "Here?"

"Uh-huh."

She glances over her shoulder. "How come?"

"You'll see."

She hesitates for a moment before leading the way into the

relative gloom. They walk south along the Trinity Supermarket wall then turn with the alley and travel eastward again.

Over on Gerrard, the light is rich—shop signs in Christmas colours, restaurant windows showing neon creatures of the sea. Blades of crimson-edged gold and peony pink reach back to them along the narrows, but for the most part the laneway light is halved: dim and domestic from the line of backyards on their right; variable from the string of businesses on their left—here a sink of shadows, there a flood of greenish white from a propped-open kitchen door.

The first Dumpster they pass stands tank-like and quiet. Half a dozen industrial green bins alongside it show no sign of life. The second is more promising. Guy hears a low, squelching scuffle as they approach, catches sight of something waddling low.

Edal stops. "Did you hear something?"

He nods. "Probably rats." No sense spoiling things.

The next clutch of green bins is the ripest so far, radiating a gag-reflex fog of spoiled meat. Guy holds his breath, widening his eyes at Edal. She puffs her cheeks out in reply, jogs ahead a ways before gulping for air. "Next time, I choose the route."

"Next time?" He smiles. There's just enough light to make out her response—her small mouth mirroring his, the seriousness in her gaze. He should say something. Either that or keep quiet. Women like a man who listens—he's sure Aunt Jan told him that. But does it count as listening if the woman says nothing? If she holds stock-still and watches you through her wide-set eyes?

The voice, when it comes, belongs to neither of them. A high cackle reminiscent of the funhouse, it shatters the uneasy peace. A night-blue Dumpster looms between them and the source—the cackle peaking, breaking off with a harsh, skipping hiss. Guy holds a finger to his lips and motions for Edal to follow him. At the Dumpster's rusted corner, he reaches back and, after several suspended seconds, feels the shock of her hand in his. He draws her up alongside him to see.

There must be a dozen of them, the nearest perhaps three paces from the tip of Guy's boot. He does his best to count while they're holding still, staring back at him. Eleven, twelve—a baker's dozen, all told. Twenty-six ears like white letter *U*s upturned, twenty-six eyes like cherries lit from within. It's the same face over and over: eyes set in a band of black, white brow and snout, dark knob of nose. A clown's face, funny and frightening in one.

The scene is one of reeking plenty. Between the Dumpster and the Precious Pearl's back door, a trio of green bins lie tipped and gutted. One by one, the raccoons sit up tall, showing their moulting bellies, their dark and dangling hands. Guy breathes shallowly, his attention torn between the diminutive crowd before him and the hand still clasping his own.

When one of the larger raccoons relaxes back onto all fours, the others seem to take it as a signal: yes, we're being watched, but the watchers mean us no immediate harm. Soon every one of them is back at work, feeling through the muck. One touches a lump of broccoli to its nose. Another plucks up a crab claw and squeals. Guy glances at Edal. Her lips are parted, her gaze soft—a movie-house expression of uncomplicated delight. He gives her fingers a squeeze, and she squeezes back.

"See that big male?" Her whisper sends a small thrill through the group. "Over by the drainpipe, the one with the fish head?"

The animal in question sits off on its own, gnawing a pointed, silvery skull.

"How can you tell it's a male?"

"Size. And their faces are wider. Broader snouts." Her brow furrows. "It's weird, him being here. Mature males keep to themselves as a rule."

Just then a slighter specimen locates treasure beneath a leafy mound. It tugs hard, dragging a slippery mass into the open, forgetting to respect the corner claimed by the big male. The growl could be a German shepherd's. The young raccoon spins to face the threat, the big male dropping forward, scooting the fish head back between its hind legs. Arching its spine, it lowers its chin to the pavement, flattens its ears and screams. The other turns tail, a banded, quivering target that urges the male to spring. The bite is real enough—the resulting yelp makes Guy wince—but the male lets go almost at once, allowing its victim to scramble away.

"Tough guy," Edal says softly beside him. And then she takes back her hand.

It helps a little that she uses it to point. Beyond the furthest bin, a raccoon is scooping its forepaw deep into a glinting jar. It draws out a handful of something dark, holds it not to its own mouth, as Guy expects, but to the mouth of another—an undersized creature that initially appeared to be part of its haunch.

"See it?" Edal says in his ear.

He does now. Not a kit but a kitten. It's harder to make out than its boldly marked adoptive mother, but Guy knows a tabby when he sees one. Even without the beautiful white belly and paws.

The raccoon digs again into the jar and holds out the takings, but this time the kitten tries to sit up and copy its mother. It fumbles like a toddler in oven mitts, knocking over the jar and rolling it against the raccoon's foot. The mother burbles—a soothing, frog-pond sound—and offers the handful again.

As the kitten nuzzles deep into the cup of the raccoon's hand, Guy flashes on the horses at Riverdale Farm, the way they mouthed the carrots he held out to them, closing their giant eyes. He used to love the little city farm. It's only the far side of the footbridge; why does he never go? He resolves to mention it to Edal, ask if she's ever been.

The kitten's tongue is tiny in comparison with a horse's, rough and persistent—just right for licking a raccoon's nimble digits clean. At last it lifts its greasy face, turning it up into a cut of light from the caged bulb above the kitchen door. Its eyes are golden, fastened on its guardian, charming the next mouthful from the jar.

It's the last mouthful of the night, at least from that particular source. The door of the Pearl sounds a hard click, an alarm that ripples across every stooped and furry back. Light sweeps over their bristling forms as a kid of maybe thirteen fills the door frame, his ankle-length apron stained like a surgeon's gown. He shrieks—a boy's best effort at a yell—and the raccoons scatter, wheeling and humping away. They're gone in seconds, flesh turned to shadow, leaving their mess behind. The adoptive mother is the last of them to disappear, herding the skinny kitten into the night.

The kid glares at Guy and Edal.

"Hi—" Guy begins, but the kid looses a line of rapid-fire

Cantonese, digging violently in his apron pocket and producing a pack of cigarettes. Guy recognizes Export Plain, Uncle Ernie's brand. Uncle Ernie never shook his smokes like that, though, like they were proof of a crime committed, or a hint of retribution to come.

"Guilty by association," Edal says quietly. "Come on."

The kid ups his volume as they turn to go, Edal hurrying her stride comically in response. Guy overtakes her, breaking into a jog, and she lets out a little yelp, a puppyish sound that trips a rush of boyhood in his veins. She's beside him in moments, arms pumping, and then she's off.

There's something wild in the way she runs, a wiry abandon more compelling by far than grace. Guy has his work cut out for him catching up. The tarred length of the alley sounds in his bones; blood beats in his neck, runs like a thaw in his extremities, threatening to flood. When he draws flush with her, she's smiling, showing her teeth. It's all he can do to match her, breasting the invisible ribbon at the alley's end by her side.

They pull up hard between two parked cars, Guy planting his feet side-on like a star forward, feeling the shudder in his teeth. He throws out an arm as a brake for Edal, but she never meets it, seeming to stop as she started, with a spring.

"Not bad." He bends, hands on his knees, breathing hungrily through his open mouth.

She's walking a ring around him, winding down. "I'd've beaten you in another quarter block."

He laughs. "Less."

Still she circles him like the second hand on a clock, moving in and out of view. He straightens, runs a hand through his hair. "Hey, how come you know so much about animals, anyway?"

The question stops her cold. "I don't," she says after a moment.

"Sure you do. The raccoons, the hawk."

There's a sudden stiffness about her. "I grew up in the country."

"Oh, yeah? Where?"

"North."

"Where north?"

Again she hesitates. "Up toward Owen Sound."

"Owen Sound." He should probably leave it at that. "I've never been. I hear it's nice."

She lets out a snort, a sound harsher than he'd have thought her small nose capable of producing. "Yeah, well." She turns, orienting herself toward the lights along Gerrard. "I should be going."

"Oh." Guy feels his face fall. "Okay."

"See you." A tight over-the-shoulder smile.

"Yeah, see you."

She doesn't exactly run, but he can tell she wants to. She can't wait to get away.

It happens naturally enough, Kate and Lily leaving at the same time, standing at the gate with Billy swaying on his feet between them.

"The cats'll be pissed," Kate says as Lily leans in to work the padlock. "I should've been home to feed them by now."

Lily draws open the gate and the three of them slip out into the empty street. "What are their names?" She turns to lock up.

"You won't believe me if I tell you."

"Come on, they can't be that bad."

"I didn't name them."

"Name them what?"

Kate shakes her head. "Smoke and Fire."

"Jesus, did you hear that, Billy?"

"I know, I know. It suits them, though. Smoke's grey and fluffy, and she generally takes her time. She's only got one eye, but she's still the one in charge. Fire's a little on the skittish side. He's—"

"Let me guess, an orange tabby."

"I'm afraid so. They were littermates. They're pretty much inseparable."

"Yeah, yeah, I get it. Where there's smoke . . ."

Kate closes her eyes. Lou-Lou and her corny lines. "Yeah, well, like I said, I didn't name them."

*Who did?* It's the obvious response—the one Kate both hopes for and dreads—but Lily takes a tack of her own.

"Can I meet them?"

"Meet them? Sure."

"Tonight?"

"Tonight?" Kate's heart is suddenly clumsy, knocking wildly in her chest. "Okay."

The walk calms her. It helps keeping her eyes forward, swinging her limbs. Chinatown's quiet for a Friday. Neither one of them speaks, yet an easiness settles in the space between them, as though they've known each other far longer than a handful of days. Billy's presence helps, just as it did when they stood together watching him swim.

"How's Billy with cats?" she asks as they turn onto Withrow.

"Don't worry." Lily lays a hand on his rump. "He'll be good."

Yard after pretty little yard. What if the wilderness really did take it all back one day? Imagine all these gardens trampled. Roofs torn open by gleaming tusks, cars strangled, concrete heaving and splitting apart. Would Smoke and Fire turn feral and attack her, or would they spare her, the way Mowgli spared Messua, the human who had shown him love?

"That was some story Guy read tonight," Kate says.

"Yeah, freaky."

"He do that often?"

"Every night this week."

"Huh."

"I like it," Lily adds after a moment.

"Yeah, me too." She glances up to find they've reached the house. "Well, here we are."

Lily stops on the sidewalk and stares. "This is your place?"

Kate sees what she always does: a simple two-storey row house, the lucky end spot in a line of four. Only maybe it's not so simple, not through the eyes of somebody who sleeps outside. She looks again, noticing the brick path Lou-Lou laid down with a river bend in mind, the blooming lilac, the painted porch with its clapped-out wicker chairs. "Yep," she says brightly, "this is it."

Lily follows her wordlessly up the path, standing on the steps while Kate unlocks the door.

"Come on in." Kate steps inside and slips off her shoes, setting her bag down on the heavy hall stand. It's one of Lou-Lou's better garbage-day finds—scratched and pallid when she dragged it home in the hatchback, now a dark cinnamon colour, glossy to the touch. She glances up to see Lily still standing at the threshold, looking terribly young. "Come in. You too, Billy. Both of you."

"Should I take my shoes off?"

"Only if you want to. Come through to the kitchen, I'll make us some tea."

Kate busies herself with filling the kettle, warming the pot. Cups and saucers is what Mummy would do, and Lily might think it's fun—or it might make her feel out of place. Better to go for a hybrid, teapot and sugar bowl, milk carton and mugs.

She turns to find Lily seated at the kitchen table with Billy gathered close against her. Their eyes meet briefly before Lily glances away. "You live here by yourself?"

"Uh-huh. Just me and the cats." Kate takes a breath. "I inherited it."

*Who from?* is what most people would say next, but again Lily shows herself to be anything but. She nods and rests a hand on Billy's head. It makes sense in a way, given the closed book of her own past. She won't ask. It's up to Kate to give the information away.

"It used to belong to my—" *Housemate.* She comes within a hair's breadth of letting it slip. "—girlfriend."

Lily looks up.

"Lou-Lou. Louise."

No response beyond the unbroken gaze.

"She was older than me. She turned forty not long before . . . I'm—" She has a sudden urge to lie, call herself twenty, even nineteen. "I'm twenty-two. It was never a problem between us," she adds hastily. "She never mothered me or anything like that."

Lily nods.

"We met at the clinic, back when I was still working in Emerg. It was when she brought Smoke in with her eye."

"What happened?"

"She got into a fight, probably a raccoon."

"No, I mean with Lou-Lou. What happened when you met?"

It's like a thunderclap, that name on those bare, chapped lips. "Oh. Well, she'd brought Fire along too. He wasn't badly hurt—just a few scratches—but they'd never been separated, and Lou-Lou said she sure as hell wasn't starting now. Dr. Gupta told her to go back to the waiting room when he realized he'd have to take out the eye, but she said the only way she was leaving was if he tranquilized her too. Lots of people cry, you know, but not like Lou-Lou. She never made a sound, just stood there with the tears running down her cheeks." Kate drops her gaze. "She was so beautiful. She had blue eyes. Really blue—you could see the colour across the room. And her hair was black."

"Like yours."

"Darker. Really, truly black. She wore it in a bob, you know, with those perfect little bangs. I know it sounds weird, noticing stuff like that when somebody's crying their eyes out—"

"It doesn't sound weird."

Kate looks up. "It was crazy. I could barely hear what Dr. Gupta was saying to me. I felt like I was drowning when I looked at her. Like I was going to die."

The kettle stops her from going any further—not the ear-splitting scream she grew up with, but an ascending harmonica hum. Lou-Lou thought about things like that, the sounds a person hears over and over in her home. Kate lifts it from the element, staring for a moment at the glowing coil.

"Down, Billy," Lily says behind her. "Lie down."

Kate turns to see Smoke puffed up double in the doorway, her lone eye wide. Behind her, Fire stands frozen. One or both of them leaking that terrible close-mouthed precursor to a wail.

"It's okay," Lily says softly—to Billy? To Kate's two cats? She slips from her chair onto all fours. "It's okay," she breathes, and this time it's clear she's addressing all of them, every disquieted soul in the room.

Stephen's bench in behind the pine trees is peaceful. The night smells of forest and traffic, and Rosie has wormed her way up beside him to nestle her chin in his lap. The Rottie-shepherd cross was a rescue case, chained in a shit-smeared concrete yard until the cops raided the meth lab she'd been tasked to protect. She flew at Stephen the first time he got close to her cage. By the fifth approach, she contented herself with snarling. By the fifteenth, she was ready to sniff his palm. At first he only dared exercise her in the outdoor pens, but they've been on three proper walks now, though she always hugs in tight against his leg.

He won't see the girl again. *Kyla.* It's the wrong time of day, and anyway, who says this is even her regular route? He closes his eyes and calls up her image, finding it noticeably changed. In his mind she wears little if any makeup. Her long, pale hair is bundled into pigtail braids, still the same sweet stripe at her crown.

It could happen. Say she started work at noon—wouldn't she be heading home right about now? How long is a dancer's shift? How many hours of taking off her clothes and getting dressed so she can take them off again? *Everybody knows Jilly's.* And now Stephen does too. Before returning Tiger to the shelter that day, he made it his business to circle past the brick block at the corner of Queen and Broadview. Larger-than-life women adorned its grubby front—lacy good girls and leather-clad bad girls and schoolgirls in tiny plaid skirts.

He's only ever set foot inside a peeler club once. Somehow it was easier to try new things when you were one of a dozen cologne-soaked, crewcutted young men, fresh from nine punishing weeks of soldier qualification training. The girl on stage was one thing; by the third mug of draft he could just about maintain a comfortable distance from her in his mind. The one who approached him where he sat was another matter. His fellow celebrants howled when she turned to show Stephen her wagging backside, and for a second he thought, sure, bring that tanned ass down. Then what? Would she grind against the fly of his new chinos until he was straining against the seams, until he was—what? Wet in his Jockeys? Wiping up afterwards in the john?

It might have worked if she'd kept her back to him, lowering down on him as though he were a chair—but she didn't. She turned. He'd seen that look before, on a face nowhere near as pretty or painted-up. It was the look Ruby Hopper wore when he caught sight of her through that pitiless crowd.

He pushed the lap dancer away. He had no wish to hurt her—not even her pride—but he had to get out of that chair. She stumbled back as he rose, slapped away the hand he held out to steady her. "I don't feel so good," he said softly.

"What, he's puking already?" Collins, the thickset son of a miner, roared. "Come here, girl. Come and meet a man who can hold his beer!"

Kyla wouldn't do that, would she? Straddle strangers in a crowded bar? It doesn't bear thinking of. He can think of nothing else.

Until Rosie growls. His eyes snap open as her head lifts up off his thighs. Tightening his grip on her lead, he feels a corresponding restriction in his chest. It's his heart, of course, but the sensation is somehow external—a familiar combination of stricture and weight. Stephen knows he's not wearing body armour over his hoodie. Knows it almost to the point of being sure.

It was hard to get used to, eighteen-odd kilos of Personal Protective Equipment whenever you set foot outside the wire—suddenly becoming a larger, harder creature than you actually were. He was glad of the burden the day he took a round in the plate. The impact knocked him back, left him breathless and dry-heaving in the ditch. His buddies thought they'd find him lifeless; they laughed like Stanley Cup drunks when they discovered he wasn't even hit. *Got a furball, Carnsew? Atta-kitty, you cough that fucker up.*

He took the round over and over that night, back safe and sound at KAF, in the snoring, foot-stinking comfort of Bravo Company's Big Ass Tent. Top-bunk trauma every time he closed his eyes; by midnight he felt certain his heart would burst. Not long before reveille, a thought fluttered through between flashbacks. What if the round had hit home—if the spreading bruise on his chest were replaced by an unfathomable hole? Careful what you wish for. It was a virus that got him in the end, but he couldn't help feeling he'd invited it in.

A sound brings him back, footsteps on pavement, someone coming up on him from behind. He presses a hand to his whumping heart. Feels for his C7—not there, not for nearly two years. Rosie's still beside him, but she's no longer lying down. She's crouching, making ready to spring.

"Pardon me . . ."

The voice is foreign, maybe even Middle Eastern. By the time Stephen can find his feet, the dog in his charge is going mental. Who needs an assault rifle? If he were to let go of her leash, Rosie would sing through the air and cut the creeping enemy down.

Only he's not. *Enemy.* He's not.

Stephen blinks, sees the small dark-skinned man backing away with his hands in the air, the beat-up Rapid Courier Corolla idling open-doored in the alley. In the next instant, Rosie leaps from the bench. No longer trusting the leash, he tackles her—her deafening voice in his ear, her teeth mere inches from his human throat. Tear it out, girl, he thinks, go on, but the Corolla's reversing down the alley at high speed, and the retreat of its whining engine dampens the dog's desire to kill.

After a time, she ceases to struggle. The pair of them lie

panting, her breath damp, vaguely rancid, against his cheek. Minutes pass before she softens fully in his arms. Minutes more before he releases her and rolls onto his back in the grass.

For a time the night is still—unnaturally so, as though some great speaker has come unplugged. Then a sound so faint, Stephen mistakes it for the skipping of his own pulse.

*Tht-tht-tht-tht-tht.*

Rosie can hear it too—he can see as much from the cant of her ears—but whatever its source, she's clearly unconcerned.

Stephen squints, looking up through feathery branches to a lamplit patch of night. A bat is circling. A lone bat above him, turning perfect laps.

*Tht-tht-thwwwt-tht-tht-tht.*

There must be a healthy population of them roosting under Toronto's many roofs; he often catches sight of them by half-light, contracting, banking hard. Never like this, though. Never this warm-blooded orbit, this steady, almost soothing, return.

The bat hasn't been awake long. She slept through the sun's fall, its long rays lulling her through the wall of the day roost then rousing her with their sudden withdrawal. She hadn't far to fly before coming upon the night's first offering. The human love of light has its pluses: their buzzing, burning globes draw midges, a living cloud.

Shunning the lamp's core, she circles at the gloomy fringe. It's no great feat maintaining course; a circle is only one wing outflapping the other. Upstroke, downstroke, back and chest. Heat escapes through her wings, rising from the silky black skin.

The echoes tell her where she is. Long waves describe the wider setting—clumps and clutches of trees, the mesh of a human barrier, the staggered backdrop of their many walls. The ground below supports a lone human, lying prone along-side a sizable dog. Both of them quiet, though definitely drawing breath.

Fingers spread, the bat cups the ringing air. Short, sweep-ing waves sing of the details. The faster she sends them out, the faster they come lapping back, flecked with a myriad of forms. Taken singly, the midges are minute, which is why the bat takes them en masse. On every pass she scoops a whisper-ing haul into the membrane surrounding her tail, dips her muzzle into the stretchy pouch and feeds.

And now, a new presence, fluttering at the edge of her keenest field. Another loop and she's certain: this is no muzzy, fumbling school of food, this is a moondust delicacy, a sensi-tive, substantial meal. She stalls, sideslipping from the circle's grip as she intensifies her calls. The moth detects her signal and folds its silvery wings, but the bat is made for such man-oeuvres. She slices down at a mad angle, halting the plain progress of its fall.

The futon might as well be a cement sack beneath her. No rest for the wicked—or if not wicked, then certainly weak. How hard could it be to tell him? *How does she know so much about animals? Funny he should ask.*

She hadn't exactly set out to become a federal wildlife officer. Her career path, though seemingly direct and deliberate, was in fact a series of tentative steps. The summer job at Bruce Peninsula National Park felt like better luck than she had a right to expect; while other kids in her class flogged hot dogs and soft-serve, she led guided hikes and gave bear talks by the light of a blazing fire. The park warden only had to mention the program at Fleming College once. Having been an average student for most of her life, Edal sailed through the fish and wildlife technician course. It only made sense to stay on for the additional law enforcement year—two more terms in her bright little dorm room in Lindsay, far from her mother's mess.

The deputy conservation officer posting came as a happy shock—the only drawback being that she'd be working out of the area office in Owen Sound, which meant moving back to within drop-by distance of home. To be fair, Letty showed up rarely, but when your mother was a scarecrow in a grubby T-shirt, dragging you out to look at her latest carload of crap, one workplace visit was more than enough. When Edal heard Environment Canada was hiring, she told herself only a fool would pass up better job security and higher pay. Not once—internally or otherwise—did she call the new position what it was: a ticket out of Letty's shopping grounds, her insatiable collector's reach.

Five years now she's been wearing the blue and gold badge with pride—so why keep it a secret? Because telling would mean admitting they were right about her in the first place. She is the spy Stephen initially took her for. She is, for all intents and purposes, a cop.

It's a soft night, the air gentle, almost damp. Lily kneels beneath a quarter-moon in the grass out front of her tent, drawing the brush through Billy's fur. She's come to love the little clearing. Maybe no one will ever find it, and they'll be safe here together for good. Or at least until the first big snow.

Billy sighs as she rakes the dark slope of his back. Her arm is getting tired, but she can hardly give up when he loves it this much. He deserves it, too, after being so good with Kate's two cats. It was an uneasy truce, vibrating with mistrust, but it held. The three of them might even come to like each other, given time.

Besides, left untended, Billy's lovely coat would soon degrade to the state it was in when she found him. She was walking the twilit shoulder back from the arena, skates in hand, when he came bounding out of the scrub. They were strangers to one another, yet she felt no fear. It was as though he'd belonged to her since weaning. As though he'd broken her heart by going missing but had finally found his way home.

They were both still babies, Lily not yet twelve, Billy full height but only half as solid as he would become. She laid a hand to him and felt the evidence of neglect—untold twigs and burrs, great clots and shingles of felted fur. After sneaking him into the garage, she smuggled out three cans of Chunky beef soup to keep him busy, and set to work with an old brush of her own. It was the wrong tool for the job. In the end she had no choice but to cut the whole mess away.

Clipped down to a centimetre of fuzz, he could no longer

hide the hunger he'd endured. It may have been what saved him. She'd never dreamt she'd be allowed to keep him, but it turned out the sight of a naked, emaciated dog could touch even a rotten heart. Or it might have been simpler than that. No favour without a price tag. No debt that doesn't come due.

Lily lays down the brush and looks up at the skinny moon, a massive claw left hanging in the sky. She knows what's really up there—the pocked and stony sphere, the earth's fat shadow playing tricks—yet she can't help but believe in what she sees.

Closing her eyes, she works her hands into Billy's neck ruff, feeling for ticks. So far there's been no mention of Mowgli picking parasites off his fellow wolves, but he must have; it wouldn't be fair to keep those clever fingers to himself. Baloo, too—why wouldn't they like bear blood? It's hard to imagine one latching on to Bagheera, though. Piercing that perfect black hide.

She's had a few herself—one in her neck, a few in her armpits and crotch—but in general they seem to prefer the taste of dog. She hates the idea of them clinging to him, forcing their little heads into his flesh.

It was Stephen who taught her how to get them out. The third time she visited the wrecking yard, Guy wasn't around. The pretty-boy who came when she buzzed seemed to know all about her, and leaving would've meant finding Billy's breakfast elsewhere, not to mention going without something to read.

After following Stephen back to the kitchen at a safe distance, she filled the kibble bowl to overflowing then crossed quickly to Guy's room. When she returned with *Never Cry Wolf* in her hand, Stephen was kneeling in front of her dog.

She knew the flush of unreasonable panic she always felt when Billy made a new friend. It turned to shame when Stephen showed her the three black bloodsuckers he'd found.

"You're bound to miss a few in a coat like this," he told her. No way to take that but as a kindness. "You know not to twist them out, right? Don't pop them while they're dug in, either. Just pinch in tight against the skin and pull, slow and steady, until you feel it release."

Having ploughed through Billy's mane, Lily shifts to the rich hunting ground around his ears. Sure enough, at the base of the left one, her thumb stumbles on a swollen nub. She gets in tight with her nails and tweezes, lifts the tick and the skin it's anchored to, and counts off the seconds in her head. At seventy-seven the fucker finally lets go.

She could flick it into the bushes, but what if it finds its way back, crawls up onto Billy and bores into him again? Better to finish the job.

Lily combs the grass, feeling for a suitable leaf. She rolls the tick up in a long, lightless tunnel then crushes the tunnel flat. It's a good method, quick and clean. Not, however, entirely satisfying. Some part of her—a small part wholly within her control—would prefer to do it the dirty way. Press the bloated thing between her fingers. Feel the greedy bastard pop.

# 14

# Ring of Dark Timber

A month passed before Jim Dale came gunning up Edal's driveway again. She stepped out onto the porch as his truck shuddered to a halt, her mind already leading him across the yard to the path that began between the two red pines. She would name every tree they passed, not in a show-offy way but as a kind of conversation, though he would speak little, if at all. Noises would suffice. Closed-mouth sounds of approval, the odd whistle of disbelief. *Stupid.* She didn't know why he'd come, but she could be sure it wasn't to go for a walk.

"Hey there, Edal."

He remembered her name. What was more, he said it as though it were normal, like Donna or Christine.

"Hi, Mr. Dale."

He smiled. "Jim'll do. Your mom and dad home?"

"My mom's working." She hesitated. "There's only my mom."

"That so. Well, come on over here, I've got something I want to show you."

She was dressed like a hobo—baggy cut-offs and her Aerosmith T-shirt with half the band rubbed away. She felt her lack of footwear keenly as she walked toward him. She hadn't thought to slip on her runners when she'd caught sight of the truck, had thought only of rushing out to meet him so he wouldn't see inside the house.

He turned, reaching for something on the passenger seat. When Edal saw him straighten up with a liquor store box in his arms, she felt a tightening in her chest. Books. She couldn't refuse—it was rude and it might hurt his feelings. And anyway, how could she begin to explain?

He set the box down on the hood, loosened its crossed flaps and lifted out a handful of white fur. Edal heard herself squeak. She accepted the kitten without question, folding it to her chest. Up close she could see its eyes weren't exactly a pair—one blue, the other leafy green.

"Somebody left a whole litter on my doorstep. Do you believe that? Six of them. I found folks to take the others, but nobody wanted this little guy."

Nobody wanted the white one? The one with the blue and green eyes? "How come?" Edal said softly.

He took one of the kitten's front paws between a finger and thumb. There were two, maybe three extra toes. "They're all like that. One of the back ones is worse." He let go the paw. "So, what do you think?"

Edal shifted the kitten to one hand and took hold of his splayed paw. He didn't squirm. If anything, he relaxed, surrendering his small weight and considerable warmth, watching her through his mismatched eyes.

"I'll take him."

"What about your mom? You think—"

"It's okay," Edal blurted. "She already said I could get a pet."

"Is that right?"

"For my birthday." Her face felt suddenly raw. She was unused to outright lying; Letty rarely paid sufficient attention to give her cause.

He said nothing, and Edal saw he was making his mind up to come back another time, when her mother was home.

"She says I need somebody to play with," she said quickly.

His mouth changed then, softening in the black circle of his beard. "No brothers or sisters?"

"Nope."

"Neighbours don't have kids?"

"What neighbours?" She squeezed the kitten's paw and felt seven or eight claws slip from their little pink sheaths. "My birthday's next week."

"In that case," he said, "happy birthday to you."

It was the best present she'd had in years. When Nana and Grandpa Adam had been the ones doing the wrapping, the thrill of picking open bows and peeling back tape had been exquisite. Letty's gifts generally came in brown paper bags. Edal wouldn't mind always getting books if she could at least see some sense in the titles her mother chose. She used to try following Letty's line of thought: Nana liked knitting, so maybe she thinks I want to learn how to crochet; or, she knows we do French in school, so maybe she figures I know German too.

A name for the kitten came to her moments after Jim Dale drove off, his arm crooked out the window in a lazy wave. Its paws weren't so strange, especially if you stopped thinking of them as paws. The toes were like petals, radiating from the central pad. She would call him Daisy. Whoever decided all flowers were girls?

Daisy could live in her room. He'd be safe there, thanks to the padlock. It was hard to imagine leaving him alone all day while she was in school. Maybe she could take him along, smuggled inside her Mack. The other kids might make fun of his paddle paws at first, but they'd think his eyes were cool.

Only three weeks remained until summer holidays; after that she could stay home with Daisy all the time. She could play with him in her room when her mother was around, take him out in the yard whenever Letty drove off to clean somebody's house or burn up her wages touring the region's sad little Sally Anns. At some point Edal would own up, appearing with a grown-up Daisy slung around her neck. He'd be heavy by then. She'd wear him like a *lead-weighted fur collar*, the way Jimmy Watt wore Edal the otter the day he carried her back to Camusfeàrna when she'd run away from home. Even Letty would fall for him then.

It was a good plan, one Edal went over and over like an elaborate picture she was colouring in. That first night, she played with Daisy for hours, baiting him with wiggly fingers beneath the sheet. At length he tired of the game and began to groom himself. Edal watched his little tongue work, wondering if a mother had taught him—or if, like herself, he was good at learning things on his own.

Once clean, he began to knead her chest. His claws came out once or twice, but he put them away the moment she tapped his toes. Satisfied, he settled in to sleep, his head cradled in the dip at the base of her throat.

She woke in a strip of moonlight to find him gone. She turned back the yellow blanket, then the sheet with its worn pattern of ferns. Not there. She stood up, careful where she put her feet. After a moment she went down on all fours, dropping her face to the floorboards to look at the world his way.

He wasn't under the bed. Or the dresser, or the little brown desk. She didn't think kittens could flatten themselves like bats to slide under doors, but she opened the closet just in case. Rummaging through the laundry basket, she knew a moment's elation when her fingers met the nap of an inside-out sock. She bit her lip and felt inside her runners, her ankle boots. She delved into the bag of stuffed animals she couldn't quite seem to throw away. Not one of them responded to her touch.

Edal began to hum, a single droning note. She backed out of the closet. The crack beneath the bedroom door was slimmer still, an impossible squeeze. Sitting back on her heels, she saw the dormer window she'd left open. The screens weren't in, not since Grandpa Adam last took them out. But Daisy was too little, wasn't he, to climb up all that way? She crawled closer. Close enough to see the tear in the checkered curtain, the dangling threads. It came to her then, clear as anything: more toes meant more claws.

Edal rose up on her knees and looked out. The slant was steep, but maybe not too steep for a kitten with grip to spare. Surely the curling asphalt shingles would afford some kind of hold. She pictured Daisy slipping and catching himself, inching down toward the volunteer alders that crowded up against the house. In her mind's eye he managed the leap with ease. Landing in leafy chaos, he let the bobbing branch settle before clambering inward to the trunk. From there he made his way to ground level. Down among the coyotes and the foxes. The shadowy minks.

Or maybe he never even got that far.

He would've stood out like a pale invitation against the scabby shingles. The threat could've come swooping from behind, silent wings and saucer eyes, horned head rearing as the talons closed. Poor Daisy, pinned between the tilt of the roof and the sparkling black cavern of the sky.

She could call Jim Dale, summon him from the darkness where she imagined him lying alone. He would come, wouldn't he? And what if he did? He'd find out she couldn't even be trusted to look after a kitten. He'd see her for the stupid kid she was.

Better to go looking for Daisy on her own. She crept downstairs in her pyjamas, slipped on her flip-flops and took the flashlight from its hook beside the door. The porch steps felt off-kilter. The grass licked her ankles and left them wet. As she swung her beam up onto the roof, swishing it to and fro, mosquitoes caught wind of her breath-scent and came to feed.

Daisy was so light—how could she expect to find proof of his passage? All the same, she looped her beam over the yard, searching for pressed-flower prints in every patch of telling ground. In any case, tracks were only one aspect of what *Tracking: The Subtle Art* had referred to as "sign." If the killer had come on foot, there would be a fresh trail through the grass. If it had arrived by air, there might be pellets, regurgitated and let fall from its tree. A feather come loose when it struck.

If it was in fact an owl, there were a few things Edal could be sure of. For starters, it had no teeth; *Ontario Birds* had taught her that. Bird bills were nothing more than overgrown jawbones covered in something like horn. Like the jaws of snakes, they hinged top and bottom to swallow their victims whole.

# 15

# The Chronicles of Darius

Grandmother waited until Darius was old enough to keep a secret before she showed him the book. On the way back from the school bus that day, he told her about the video they'd watched in class, the giraffes and the elephants and, best of all, the pride of lions.

"Pride?" she said.

"That's what they call it."

When they stepped into the warmth, she carried on to his room without pausing to take off her coat. He followed to find her down on her knees on the rug, sliding her hand under the dresser, as though she were pushing a fat envelope under a door.

The paperback came out downy with dust. Grandmother blew across it, sneezed and blew again. Darius looked down on the book's cover. A face like a gold medallion, dark, sparkling eyes above a broad, majestic snout.

"It was her favourite," Grandmother said, stroking the lion's face. "She'd have taken it with her, I'm sure, if she hadn't left in such a rush." She looked up at him. "Shall I read it to you?"

Darius wasn't sure what to say. He was ten—plenty old enough to read for himself.

"He'd kill me," she added quietly. "He'd kill us both if he knew."

Darius bit his lip. "Okay."

He sat on the bed while she took the small, hard chair that belonged to the desk. He had questions, the first uttered before she could even open the book.

"What's a wardrobe?"

She thought for a moment. "It's like a closet, only it stands on its own." She turned to the beginning. "You be sure and listen for the truck."

They weren't far into the story—the four children had arrived at the professor's country house and were upstairs talking— when Grandmother glanced up from the page.

"I've just remembered something."

"What?"

"Your mother—she used to like me to say her name in place of Lucy's. Lucy was Faye."

Her face was soft as an old pillow, puffy and creased. Darius looked down at his hands, lying separate from each other in his lap. "Read it like that."

"You want me to?"

"Yes."

She took a breath. "'"What's that noise?" said Faye suddenly. It was a far larger house than she had ever been in before and the thought of all those long passages—'"

"Grandmother?"

"Yes, Darius?"

"Can I be—" He wanted to say Peter, the older brother who referred to the professor as *that old chap*, but it didn't seem right somehow. Not when Lucy-Faye was the youngest. "Can I be Edmund?"

"Edmund? Are you sure? He has a pretty rough time of it."

Darius nodded.

"All right." She read on. "'—the thought of all those long passages and rows of doors leading into empty rooms was beginning to make her feel a little creepy. "It's only a bird, silly," said Darius.'"

She read the whole first chapter: the children stuck indoors because it rained; the huge house offering up hallway after hallway, room after room. Darius had trouble imagining it—even school had only the one floor. Several rooms in the professor's house were *lined* with books. Faye had sometimes flicked through the magazines at the laundromat, but she'd never brought any of them home. Grandmother had a few *Reader's Digest*s in her knitting basket and the heavy blue book of recipes on the kitchen counter; Grandfather had only the newspaper and the black leather bible beside his chair.

The idea of empty, extra rooms was bewildering. One had nothing in it but a wardrobe, which Lucy-Faye looked into on her own. She rubbed her face against the fur coats it held, then passed through them into a snowy wood. The little man she met there had the legs of a goat and, sticking up through his curly hair, a pair of pointy horns.

"Horns?"

"Yes, Darius." Grandmother met his eye. "Not like that, though. You'll see."

They kept to a single chapter a day; anything more made Grandmother jumpy. She wouldn't chance it on weekends, when they could never be sure of the old man's movements. On Saturdays he might make a quick trip for supplies, or he might stop in at the mill to check up on the relief foreman and be gone for hours. On Sundays, after they'd sat down to buckwheat pancakes and ham, he would read to them from Leviticus or Proverbs or Romans I, often carrying on where the Scriptures left off. The weekend paper supplied no end of inspiration, stories about heathens who had no business coming over here in the first place, government money-grubbers and women who thought they were men. When Grandfather ran out of words, he generally filled his vest pocket with shells and took the twelve-gauge out for a walk. He might be back with a grouse slung over his shoulder in no time, or they might not see him again until Darius was laying the table for four.

All in all, it took them most of October to make their way through the book. Darius could see why Grandmother had warned him against being Edmund, and yet his name grafted easily onto the character's back, as though they were made of the same poor stuff. He understood perfectly when Edmund-Darius couldn't help being spiteful to Lucy-Faye—and later, when the boy in the book followed his sister through the wardrobe and stood calling her name in that unfamiliar world, Darius too grew sullen when she failed to reply.

It wasn't such a stretch to imagine being impressed by the White Witch when she drew up in her sledge. Of course he accepted her gift of Turkish delight, whatever that might be. Of course he told her everything about himself and his siblings—even going so far as to offer them up in exchange for more of the magical treat. Never mind that it had turned him into a red-faced, sticky-fingered thing.

With the passing of every chapter, things grew worse for the little boy. Darius might not have had any brothers or sisters, but he knew well enough what it felt like to be left out. When Peter called his younger brother a *poisonous little beast*, Darius felt the injury keenly and shared in the dark fantasies it spawned.

It wasn't until all four children came upon a talking beaver, though, that Darius slipped entirely under the story's skin. Much of the tale had been foreign to him until then—the endless country house and its treasures, the odd, stilted manner in which the children spoke—but the beaver was Canada's creature. He'd learned all about it in school, even before he came to live in the mountains and saw a dam with his own two eyes. How many times had he dreamt of entering a lodge via its secret underwater passage, of folding his flat tail and curling up wet yet somehow warm? And now he could—only this lodge had a door and a stove and a kitchen table, and it turned out to be another place Edmund-Darius didn't belong.

The beaver lodge was where the children learned about the third element of the book's title. Darius hadn't realized he'd been waiting for the lion on the cover to appear until the beavers brought up his name. He felt a little nervous, like Lucy-Faye and Susan, but at the same time, like Peter, he longed for the King of Beasts to appear. In his heart of hearts, though, like Edmund, he felt compelled to run.

When Edmund-Darius did make a break for it, no one noticed for the longest time. He got a good lead on them, making straight for the White Witch's distant house. Darius felt the saliva well up under his tongue at the thought of the coming reward. It hurt to learn Lucy-Faye and the others never doubted the news that he'd betrayed them; it made betraying them the right choice.

Or if not right, then at least inevitable. Just as it was inevitable that he should grow colder and more miserable and more alone as he approached his protector's house, and that it should turn out to be not so much a house as a castle surrounded by frightening statues—one of which turned out to be a living, breathing wolf—and that the wolf should lead him to the White Witch who, instead of welcoming him like the prince he might have been, mistreated him like the wicked little boy he was.

Edmund-Darius missed the visit of Father Christmas and the picnic of ham sandwiches and tea. Instead he got hard bread and water, and was forced to jam in alongside the witch in her sledge, and ride with no coat through the frozen dark. There was no fooling himself that she was a good queen anymore. You could still try when someone had only yelled at you and called you names, but not once they'd hit you. Not once they'd tied your small hands behind your back.

Lucy-Faye and the rest of them carried on without him, passing out of the witch's winter into the lion's gift of spring. Together they mounted the hill to the great stone table, where they met a host of well-meaning creatures, including the great beast himself.

Meanwhile, the witch had Edmund-Darius lashed to a tree. It came as a relief when she showed him her terrible white arms; the whiz of her knife against the whetstone was like a comforting sigh. He would be out of it now. No matter what else happened, none of it would be his fault. But this was a storybook, so instead of having his throat slit, he was rescued and reunited with Lucy-Faye and the others. Even less credible, he was forgiven by them all.

It was then that the story took a turn. Edmund-Darius was a traitor, and according to the deep magic, the White Witch was owed his blood. The witch knew it, and the lion knew it too. Darius nodded and began believing again.

When the story turned back on itself, and it seemed his character would be saved a second time, Darius wasn't fooled. If he wasn't going to die, it could only mean something worse was bound to occur. Right again. The lion had bought the little traitor's freedom at a terrible price. He would lie down in Edmund-Darius's place and let the White Witch have her way.

She could have done things quickly, cleanly, but Darius wouldn't have bought it if she had. His own character was back at the camp with Peter, so he watched the scene of sacrifice through Lucy-Faye's streaming eyes. Though the lion didn't struggle, the witch had him bound. And shaved. And muzzled.

Again the witch bared her pale, pale arms. Grandmother read the closing lines of that chapter quietly: "'The children did not see the actual moment of the killing. They couldn't bear to look and had covered their eyes.'"

When the witch and her minions left to do battle, Darius assumed the story would follow them back to Edmund. Instead, it held vigil with the girls. Grandmother read slowly, as though she never wanted that sad night to end. At one point she left such a long pause, Darius wondered if she'd slipped into an open-eyed nap. He was about to speak up when she read on.

"'I hope no one who reads this book has been quite as miserable as Susan and Faye were that night; but if you have been—if you've been up all night and cried till you have no more tears left in you—you will know that there comes in the end a sort of quietness.'"

The story was real now, so real it threatened to drag Darius down and hold him under. And then the lion came back to life. It was worse somehow than when he'd been killed—the surge in Darius's chest felt dangerous.

He wanted the reading to stop then, but Grandmother kept on, soft and unrelenting, through the part where the lion—his mane magically regrown—stooped to lick Susan's brow, then on to the passage where he romped around madly with both girls, *tossing them in the air with his huge and beautifully velveted paws.* Darius was a stranger to such abandoned play. Son of a careless mother, he'd started out careful, watching his step long before he came to live under Grandfather's roof.

Grandmother paused to smile at him, and he did his best to smile back. Then she bent her head and gave voice to the sweetest, most painful scene in the book. "'Have you ever had a gallop on a horse?'"

Darius hadn't, of course, but it scarcely mattered; the words made space for him to climb on.

"'Think of that; and then take away the heavy noise of the hoofs and the jingle of the bits and imagine instead the almost noiseless padding of the great paws . . .'"

The story should have ended when the ride on the lion's back was done. True, the statues in the witch's courtyard had to be brought back to life, and there was still the great battle to be fought, but Darius heard that chapter only distantly. Edmund had come good by then. He fought alongside Peter, but Darius found he couldn't leave Lucy-Faye, so he watched with her from the sidelines like the coward he was. There was bloodletting, but not the particular blood Darius longed for. The lion simply rolled over the witch and she was dead.

His own character was gravely wounded. Again he should've died, and again the story saved him—this time by having Lucy-Faye drip cordial into his mouth with trembling hands. The thought of it made Darius's stomach turn over beneath his heart.

Of course the good side won. Of course the four children became kings and queens, and threw a big party for all their new friends. The lion didn't come, but nobody seemed to care. Lucy-Faye and Edmund-Darius and Susan and Peter got to live both lives—the royal one and the regular one they'd left behind in the professor's home.

Darius was barely listening by then. The story had let him loose, and he'd bobbed back up to the surface of his own life— the room, cramped and brown around him, Grandmother with her grey head bent, the old man out there somewhere, due home soon.

# 16

# The City Book

The coyote is the first one Lily's seen in the valley. She's had hints of their presence before now—twists of hair-and-bone shit on the footpaths, the occasional short-lived howl—but they seem to keep a low profile in the city. And now she can see why.

Billy found the body, veering off the footpath with a jerk and crashing into the brush. Lily raised a hand to whistle him back but let it drop. There was something in there. Chances were it wasn't good, but it had to be significant to work on him like that. She stood on the path for several seconds, then ducked to enter the twig tunnel he'd made.

It was dense but passable, patterned shadows and viscous light. She hadn't far to go before she saw Billy humped over whatever it was. For a moment the tail was a ponytail, fluffy and blond. A girl, she thought, jeans down around her ankles—because that's what you find in the bushes, isn't it? Sooner or later, that's what you find.

Now, as Billy noses over the body, hindquarters to head, Lily stands twisting her hands, a fellow mourner watching the widow weep over the corpse. Not that Billy was ever partial to the living article. She can remember standing at her bedroom window one fall evening and seeing him emerge from his doghouse, snout lifting to the breeze. Moments later, a high, mad song came floating. Billy bristled. Watching him, Lily felt her own hair—natural then, long and honey blond—felt it too rise up in its roots.

One coyote, then another, loped into view on the neighbouring field. The first came to a halt, tilting its head back as though its neck were a well-oiled hinge. The sound it offered up was unearthly; Lily felt the thrill run through her, heard it echo in the second coyote's response. Giving voice, it leapt spine-first like a frightened cat. Landed and yelped and leapt again, this time rearing up on its hind legs like a man. The first sprang and gambolled, yodelling. Together they paused, together they broke into movement again, passing the song between them like a bone. Billy kept quiet, puffed and rigid out front of his little plywood house, but Lily pressed her forehead to the glass and whispered along. *Owooo, ow-ow-owooooo.*

Having smelled the whole story, Billy sits down heavily, whining through his nose. Lily takes a step closer to the coyote. Even she can smell it now, the pungent presence of the newly dead. No torn-open throat or belly, no obvious signs of disease—nothing save a raw, swollen look about the nose and eyes. It's rangy, the way they are, though not overly thin. A little moult along the back, but the coat is still fine. Lovely, in fact. Unmarked.

Except there, where the slender foreleg comes to a sudden end.

She sees it now, the patch of darkened earth, probably still wet with blood. She'd like to believe a trap did it; as in so many stories, the wild creature chewed its own foot off to be free. Except a chewed-off paw would leave a raggedy stump, and this one's neat and clean.

Fear rolls like a raindrop down her back. She meets Billy's glistening eye. "Let's get out of here." He looks willing enough, but when she stands, he stays planted, making that crying sound. She drops her voice half an octave. "Billy, come."

He obeys. Thank Christ, he rises and obeys.

**Coyote Cop's Blog**
**Saturday, May 31, 2008**
Well apologies to the vermin-loving coyote huggers among you but its time to talk turkey as they say. Its all very well knowing theres a problem but if you keep on turning a blind eye or the other cheek your not just ignoring the situation your making it worse. Leave it alone people say it will go away. Only thats not the way problems work. Not the big ones. The big ones keep on growing until sooner or later they get bigger than you.

So how do I do it you ask. How do I kill a coyote? Lots of ways. Poison is easy to get hold of but tricky to use in town. Dogs are too good at nosing out baits and once you kill a dog or two accidentally or otherwise you will have all kinds of crap to deal with. Of course certain breeds can be an ally in the cause but there again you run into trouble in the city. A pack of coyote hounds can tear the legs off a coyote in under a minute but it just takes one concerned citizen to hear the baying and your shut right down. Same thing with traps. You might think you can find a trail or two in the Don Valley where people don't go but there's people and then theres people. Nobody gives a rats ass about drunks and junkies most of the time but you can bet there would be all kinds of hell to pay if they started tripping leg-hold traps and losing their stinky feet.

So what can you do? Ever hear of a little something called a go-getter? Its pretty simple. Just a cyanide canister with a detonator attached. You bury it near one of their trails with a rag or a bit of wool tied to the detonator and left sticking up out of the ground. Rub a mixture of meat and musk into the rag and then all you have to do is take up your position and wait. Not too close or you will give away the game. You have to stick around or else you can bet a dog will mess with your set up and it will be the poison story all over again. Besides believe me you will want to be there.

You might be waiting for hours. You might feel your ass go numb or you might even drop off and have to

pinch yourself awake but sooner or later he comes
trotting along that trail. When he does theres no
way he's going to pass up that smelly tuft of rag. He
sniffs. Pretty soon he gets his teeth into it and
tugs. Bang. Cyanide in his eyes and nose and mouth.
Its like he's trying to take his own face off. And
after not so very long he's gone.

Maybe some of you think I'm all talk and no action.
Well maybe you ought to take a look at this.

POSTED BY Coyote Cop at 7:23 AM

It takes Darius several tries to post the photo. He smiles
when it finally appears. It's true what they say about a thousand words.

He quits the browser, rises to close the blinds against the
brightening day. *Trying to take his own face off.* Lying down
on the thin green foamy, Darius finds he can see it, clear as
a YouTube clip—the coyote pawing furiously at its eyes,
grinding its snout along the ground. It's there whether he
shuts his eyes tight or opens them to stare at the ceiling's
stippled dark.

He sits up, blinking. Better. Rolls up onto his feet. Better
still.

He could turn on the TV, but it never seems to soothe
him the way it did when he was small. There's nowhere to go
in the cramped bachelor apartment he calls home. The bathroom scarcely counts; it's little more than a closet with
plumbing. Still, it offers a threshold to cross.

The linoleum is sticky beneath his bare soles. His bladder is far from full, but he manages to squeeze out a stream and a couple of follow-up squirts. Shake it and tuck it away. Now what?

Maybe he needs something to eat. He had the last of the bread last night before heading out, but there should still be a little ham, maybe even a can of beer. He doesn't bother turning on the light—the handle of the fridge door gleams.

There is a beer, and a single pink slice in the package marked *Old-Fashioned Honey-Baked*. Plus one item more. It can't be an hour since he placed it carefully on the middle rack; how can he have forgotten it was there?

He's had trouble thinking clearly about the thing in general—including why he felt the need to take it with him in the first place. He hadn't planned that part; he had the hunting knife on him only because he always does. You have to be ready for close combat when the enemy walks on soundless feet.

The coyote hadn't been dead a minute when Darius heard voices coming through the trees. Teenagers, it sounded like, young love. They were laughing too hard for him to make sense of what they were saying, the boy making drowning sounds, the girl screeching like a hungry gull. They never got close enough for Darius to consider running, but he played it safe all the same, waiting until they moved off before taking the body by its front paws and dragging it into the scrub.

Maybe that was what put the idea into his head—the long bones springy in his grasp, the claws tickling bluntly at his wrists. It was darker than dark inside the maze of brush. He drew the knife from its sheath and did what he had to by feel.

It's the first time Coyote Cop has included a picture. For a moment Stephen can't make sense of the image, his mind rejecting the input of his eyes. It's like one of those bare-bones shots they have in old recipe books—only instead of a sweating sausage roll or a wedge of devil's food cake, the plate holds a bloodied paw.

His heart's already racing when Lily bursts in through the office door.

The whole way here, he's been hoping she somehow got it wrong. Billy leads him into the bushes while Lily stands guard with the bike. No mistake. It's definitely a coyote, definitely vital-signs-absent.

Billy worries over the carcass, concluding his mute appraisal at the tip of the truncated leg. Stephen sways a little, hands braced on his knees. There are flies, some sticking close to the wound, others buzzing in Stephen's ears. The coyote is what it is, a dead, four-legged thing—at least until he stoops to pick it up.

They'd been on patrol for three long, scorching days when the village came into view: another mud-walled maze surrounded by bizarrely verdant fields—acres of grapes, a whiskery tract of what might have been wheat. The place seemed deserted. Definitely emptied of women and children, but as always the question of fighting-age males remained.

The answer came in the crackle of small-arms fire, followed by the shriek of an RPG. Contact was hot and brief, the bird gunners in the LAV laying down cover while the troops on the ground moved in. Stephen scarcely had time to fire his weapon before the enemy was in retreat, a handful of thin, turban-topped backs glimpsed weaving between walls, plunging away into green.

In keeping with his training, Stephen followed a blood trail into the field of vines. *Fighting-age.* The one he found curled up in a furrow might have been anywhere from sixteen to twenty-five; the life there aged them strangely. Whatever his age, he was hugging himself like a kid with a gut-ache— only the ache was the actual red mass of his guts. Again, Stephen did what he'd been trained to do. The enemy weighed nothing—no body armour, no weapon, no boots.

The child in the recruitment poster had lain quiet, gazing up at his saviour with adoring eyes, but the man in Stephen's arms struggled like a goat going to slaughter. Stephen stumbled back through the grapes and the whispering sway of grain, unsure of his balance, his strength—unsure of anything but a need to reach the casualty collection point. The Talib was starting to settle, shock or blood loss or both. Soon he would be co-operating to the full.

"Stephen," said the medic. "Hey, Stephen." Only the medic was holding a bicycle. The medic was a skinny, pink-haired girl.

Stephen stands blinking in the light.

"You found him," Lily says.

"Yeah," he says numbly.

"Come on, put him in the basket. Hurry up."

Kate feels like a fraud. She should be toasting and grinding her own spices—or at least making the trip to Little India to buy fresh. It's not her fault she never learned. On the rare occasion when she ate curry as a child, the food came in Styrofoam containers, and Daddy never finished what was on his plate.

Lou-Lou was the one who introduced her to India in a jar. It soon became tradition: Kate's one night a week to make dinner was curry night. *Mmm, smells good. What are we having, Ms. Patak?*

Opening the cupboard beside the stove, Kate surveys a line of purple labels. The fiery Vindaloo Paste was Lou-Lou's favourite, but Kate will stick with something milder for tonight. Better to play it safe with Lily and her friends.

Lily can't believe what she's reading. "Jesus," she says, coming to the end of the most recent post, "this guy's fucking cracked."

"I know." Stephen leans in over her shoulder. "Scroll down, there's more."

"How long has he been posting this shit?"

"Since Monday. I should've told you sooner."

"You think I don't know there's creeps down there?"

"Well, no, but—"

"You know someplace there aren't any?"

That shuts him up. She reads on until he says quietly, "I've been commenting."

She swivels the chair round to face him. "You have?"

"Yeah, well, soldierboy has. You should take a look at those too."

"Take a look at what?" Guy says, stepping through the office door. Billy rouses himself and goes to greet him. "Hey, Billy-boy." He pats the dog's side. "Take a look at what?"

Lily glances at Stephen, who directs his gaze to the floor.

"Okay," Guy says, "I'll start. I see there's a fresh mound of dirt around back."

Again Lily takes her cue from Stephen, who nods but keeps his mouth shut.

"Well, what is it?"

Lily takes a breath. She found the body, she should be the one to say. "A coyote."

"What? Where did you—"

"You'd better take a look at this." Stephen's voice is calm. It helps steady Lily's nerves.

"Yeah," she says, "pull up a chair."

The three of them read over the whole thing, Stephen reaching for the mouse to guide them, post to comment to post. When they reach the bottom, Guy sits back, running both hands through his hair. "Holy shit."

"I should've said something after the first post," Stephen says. "I thought, I don't know . . . I thought I could get through to him."

Lily laughs, short and sharp. "You think you can get through to a sick fuck like that?"

"I don't know. Maybe." Stephen's face is miserable. "I guess not."

"Lily," Guy says gently, "are you sure it's a good idea, you camping out down there?"

"Maybe she could stay here—" Stephen begins.

Lily stands abruptly. "I can take care of myself."

"We know you can," says Guy. "We know. It's just—"

"I have to get to work."

Stephen steps back to let her pass. "You have a job?"

"Yes, I have a job."

"Where?"

"Yeah," Guy says, "where?"

She wants to say *none of your business*—maybe even scream it—but it suddenly hits her that this is nowhere near true. At the door she turns to face them. "The Precious Pearl, okay? I'm the dish pig at the Precious fucking Pearl." The quaver in her voice only makes her madder. "Happy?"

They nod.

"Good. Come on, Billy, let's go."

*soldierboy wrote . . .*

Buried explosive devices—now where have I heard that idea before? You never did say what this war of yours is about, so here's a theory of my own. You're scared. Never mind that it makes no sense, you're scared shitless of coyotes and you think if you kill them the fear will go away. Well, guess what? The fear doesn't live in the coyote. It lives where you feel it, down deep in those guts you keep talking about. And look what's happening to you in the meantime.

You're the kind of guy who squats in the bushes for hours on end just hoping for the chance to watch a fellow creature suffer a painful and terrifying death. And even then you're not satisfied. You have to mess with the body. Maybe you figure taking a piece of it with you will make that low-down feeling stop. So how's that working out for you? I'm willing to bet, paw or no paw, you're still walking around scared to death.

POSTED AT 10:48 AM, May 31, 2008

She's just out walking—maybe down to Queen Street for a gelato, maybe all the way to Cherry Beach to watch the dogs run. Out walking, nothing more.

Edal turns at Mt. Stephen Street like a streetcar following its rails. At the gate, she presses the buzzer with a trembling finger. Fights a ridiculous urge to run.

This time he appears in the kitchen doorway. He's wearing the rawhide jacket; the fringe work dances as he jogs toward her across the yard. She feels suddenly, sickeningly over-dressed. Navy blue shorts and a white sleeveless top—what is she, a sailor? She misses her uniform. Longs for it. She's never known how to dress.

Guy pats the tow truck as he passes it, as though its blue flank were sensible of his presence, desirous of his touch. Edal steps out from behind the sign, showing herself in full. "Hi."

"Hi, yourself." *Led Zeppelin* shows where the jacket hangs

open, the name in red, the dirigible itself cracked white against black. He draws the key up on its chain, fumbles a little with the padlock—the first time she's seen any part of him unsure.

Stepping into the yard, she finds herself scanning the place for Stephen, uncertain whether she wants him to be there or not.

"All on my ownsome," Guy says behind her, the padlock chucking shut in his hand. "Stephen's out walking his dogs."

She turns to him. "He has dogs?"

"He volunteers down at the shelter."

"Oh."

He tucks the key away. "We ought to get you a copy made."

"What? Oh, no, I—"

"Why not? You're a friend, aren't you?"

She feels her face grow hot. The day's turning close, the air ever so slightly tarry. First smog advisory of the year.

"Come on." He touches her elbow briefly. "I was just going to exercise Red."

It's what she's been hoping for without knowing it. They're halfway across the yard when the phone sounds its bygone peal.

"Shit." Guy wheels and pelts for the office. "Back in a sec."

He banks to take the corner, as though he's got a motorcycle beneath him, or a horse. In his absence Edal becomes aware of the parkway. It would be like living alongside a waterfall, only minus the rainbows, the cool, clean air.

"Sorry," he calls, jogging back. "Pileup on the Gardiner." He runs a hand through his hair. "You want to stick around?"

Edal looks at her feet. She can see herself sitting on his doorstep, getting thirsty, maybe even heat-stroked, while she waits for him to return. Stephen or Lily showing up to find her passed out in the dirt. "I should probably get going."

She lifts her eyes to the zeppelin on his chest. It floats for a moment, then buckles as he twists to shuck off the jacket. He gives it a shake, swings and settles it across her shoulders. "You fly him."

She looks up. "Me?"

"You know what to do, don't you? You watched me."

"I guess."

He raises both hands to the neck of his T-shirt. "It's the same key as the front gate. You'll have to let me out."

It's a simple enough gesture, him lifting the silver chain up over his own head and guiding it over hers. The key settles at her breastbone. She takes it between her finger and thumb.

The red-tail's getting tired. Its wings spread slowly now, grudgingly, and it looks darker somehow, as though its feathers have been oiled. The last few passes, it's glared at Edal with what she can only interpret as rage.

The rawhide drags at her arms. Reaching the door end, she skids and spirals round in time to see the cloud cover part. Light like a knife through grubby wool. It cuts across plumage, a gleaming, seconds-long span, until the hawk contracts to land in its tree. Edal stops, panting hard, hands on her knees. Suddenly the rawhide is unbearable. She straightens to struggle out of its muggy hold.

"Hot?"

Edal lets out a small cry. Stephen stands watching her, just outside the cage. "You startled me."

He blinks, black lashes sweeping. "Where's Guy?"

"He got a call." She pauses, gulping air. "Pileup on the Gardiner."

He stares a moment longer. "Want something to drink?"

The kitchen is cool, a boxy air conditioner humming in the window beside the door. Edal pulls a chair out from the table and sits.

Stephen opens the fridge. "Iced tea okay?"

"Sure."

He watches the drinks in his hands as he approaches, like a child afraid to spill. Placing her glass on the table, he sits down opposite with his own. His cheeks are flushed, but so far as she knows they generally are.

"Thanks." She drinks, ice shunting against her teeth. "So, dog walking."

He looks up.

"Guy mentioned. It's good. They go nuts cooped up in there all day."

He nods, takes a mouthful and sets down his glass.

"How many do they let you take out?"

"Only one at a time. You get the easy ones at first, until they figure out what you can handle."

"You're good with them, I bet." Somehow this is the wrong thing to say; the lashes drop, as though in answer to some internal twinge. "I've seen you with Billy," she adds, "that's all."

His smile comes back halfway. "He's great, isn't he?"

"He's a beauty." Probably best to leave it there. She lifts her glass and drains it.

"Want some more?" he asks, already rising.

Edal's never been good at knowing when people are just being polite. Not enough practice. Better to leave early just in case. "Okay, thanks." It must be the thirst talking, all that moisture she sweated out. At the same time, she becomes aware of a need to pee. "Mind if I use the bathroom?"

He unseals the fridge door. "Go ahead."

It's a small room, uncluttered, surprisingly clean. Paper on the dispenser, almost an entire roll. The toilet's an old one, the bowl yellowed with age, but the seat shows no splashes, no errant hairs. No need to crouch.

The sink and surrounding counter are of a piece, one of those hard plastic slabs with a seashell-shaped depression. A little grime around the taps, but nothing unusual. There's a cake of white soap in a shallow, ribbed dish, a can of Barbasol and two plastic Bics. Two toothbrushes and a pinched tube of Crest in a cheap black mug.

Edal washes her hands. No hand towels—that would be downright spooky—just a couple of what look to be beach towels, one garish as a fruit salad, the other navy blue with orange tropical fish. She lowers her nose to the fish towel—Guy's towel, she decides, the more mature of the two. No funk, not even a hint of mildew. No false-flower detergent smell either. Just towel. Used recently to dry a clean man. She draws another deep breath through her nose before using it to dry her hands.

When she emerges, Stephen is standing beside the table, holding her full glass. "Want to see something?" The look on his face is disarming—he could be ten years old.

"Sure."

He sets the iced tea down and turns, stepping quickly to the bright green door—the door to what is, almost certainly, his bedroom. Not ten years old, Edal reminds herself, twice that. She follows several steps behind him and halts in the frame.

The room is deep like the kitchen, neat and spare. An old four-poster stretches along the far wall, its head lined up with the door that must lead through to the office. Stephen hasn't much to his name. Hooks on the wall dangle T-shirts, a couple of pairs of jeans. Runners and a pair of sand-coloured boots lined up on the floor beneath them. Heavy, lace-up boots. Edal's eyes skip again to the bed. Plain tan sheets, a single grey blanket tucked tight. The pieces shift a moment longer before clicking into place—his knack for silent approaches, his unnerving, straight-backed stance. Even now, as he lowers himself to his knees at the bedside, his movements are quiet and controlled.

For a moment, Edal imagines he's about to pray. Is that what he wanted to show her? Is she expected to join in?

Only now he's on his hands and knees, then knees and elbows, reaching beneath the bed. Whatever the treasure is, it must be fragile; he pulls it toward him with care. Edal steps into the room, peering past his rounded back. A mid-sized dog carrier comes into view. She draws alongside him and kneels.

There are four of them, eyes wide open, hands reaching through the metal grid of the carrier door. Raccoon kits, five, maybe six weeks old. One gives a whickering cry.

"Hey, fuzzballs," Stephen says, and the kits break into a squeaking chorus. "Okay, okay." He shuffles back on his knees and stands.

Edal looks up. "Where are you going?"

"I'll be right back." He turns and slips out the door.

She stares after him for a moment before turning back to the kits. Their cries are working on her, causing her to feel vaguely upset. She considers rising to see what's keeping him, but thinks better of leaving the babies alone. Kits, not babies. For God's sake, they live in a cage under a bed.

When Stephen returns, he's carrying a cookie tin. Standing up in it, like rubber-capped toy soldiers, four undersized baby bottles. He kneels carefully, setting the tin down between them.

"They can all get going together for once," he says softly, handing Edal two bottles. "No squabbling."

He opens the door, the kits spilling out to crowd around his knees. Without further ado, he upends his bottles and guides their little yellow nipples into the two nearest mouths.

"Go ahead," he tells her, and when she does the same for the other two, they latch on with surprising strength. One bunches over onto its side and twists its neck, cheeks and throat pumping. The other rolls onto its back, offering up the smooth maroon pads of its little hands.

When Stephen glances up at her, she can't help but return his smile. "Where'd you find them?"

"Hole in a tree."

"You took them from their den?"

"Well, yeah." His smile fades. "Their mother was dead."

"Are you sure?"

"What do you mean, am I sure? Dead is dead."

"No, I mean, how did you know it was their mother?"

He looks down at the kits, all four of them nursing hard. "I knew."

"It's just, sometimes people mean well, but—"

"They would have died if I'd left them." His voice is still quiet but no longer entirely soft.

"Okay." She focuses on the levels dropping in all four bottles. "Is this cow's milk?"

"No, it's not cow's milk. It's the stuff you give kittens. I know what I'm doing."

"Okay, sorry. It's just—shouldn't you be starting them on solid food?"

"I am," he says sharply. "I will. What makes you such an expert anyway?"

"Me? Nothing. I'm not." A squeal alerts her to the fact that her hand has shifted, popping the nipple from one of her hungry mouths. The kit kneads the air fretfully. "Sorry," Edal says again, and she nuzzles the tip back in.

It would appear Lily's not a fan. She's still picking at her first helping while Guy and Stephen go back for thirds, even though Kate went with a mild-to-medium rogan josh. At least Lily came. Kate thought she saw Edal frown at the mention of curry, and sure enough, she hasn't turned up at all.

"We should have this every night," Stephen says, scooping up a last forkful of rice.

Kate smiles. "You liked it?"

"More than like."

"Ditto," says Guy.

"I meant because of *The Jungle Book*, though," Stephen says. "Indian food for an Indian story."

"I don't know how Indian it is." Kate hears the edge in her voice. "Don't get me wrong, I love the book. It's just not—he's not Indian."

"Sorry." Stephen flushes. "I didn't—"

"No, it's okay."

"We should have raw meat." Lily stands, reaching for Kate's plate. "Antelope, maybe, or monkey. If we want to be like the book."

Guy laughs. "Cut down on the dishes."

"Speaking of which." Stephen rises, takes his own plate and Guy's, and follows Lily to the sink.

Guy stands a moment later and heads for the corner room. Kate's not sure what just happened. She reaches back for her ponytail and holds it. When Billy nudges up against her, it's all she can do not to cry.

Tonight's chapter is uneven. "The King's Ankus" starts off promisingly, but Kate feels her attention begin to wander during the scene in the ancient vault. She has about as much interest in the mounds of forgotten treasure as Mowgli does. When the jewelled ankus catches the wolf-boy's fancy, her mind wanders even more.

Lily's right, *The Jungle Book* is about the animals—at least the best parts are: Mowgli wrestling with Kaa until the great snake tires of the game and sends him sprawling; the pair of them swimming silently together in the *pitchy-black pool.* Kate tunes back in when Mowgli returns to the jungle and meets up with Bagheera. What a thing it would be to go running with a panther—even if it was to follow a trail of corpses, tracking the cursed ankus from man to greedy man.

She's not sure what she expects when the reading's over. Anything but this sprung silence, the four of them staring at the closed book as though they're waiting for it to move.

"Okay." She rises. "Well, thanks again, Guy."

"Any time. Especially if you bring the food."

Billy trundles out from beneath the table to press against her. "Bye, Billy."

"I'll let you out," Stephen says.

"Oh. Okay, thanks. See you, Lily."

"Yeah." Lily's got the book in her hand now. She doesn't look up.

Stephen walks ahead of her to the gate—part gentleman as he holds it open, part warden as he secures it again. "Good night, Kate." His face not unfriendly, but perhaps not as friendly as before.

"Good night."

She's tempted to run home, flip-flops or no. Why she wore them tonight, she can't say—except that they're red and new, and her feet were craving contact with the spring air. The leather rubs between her toes as she walks. She might have to go barefoot part of the way; blisters would mess with tomorrow's run.

At Broadview, she catches herself looking back, hoping to see a pair of inseparable figures, one upright and willowy, the other stump-like on all fours. The street is a void. Three short blocks until it turns back on itself alongside the wrecking yard and comes to an end.

She keeps her shoes on through Chinatown, bends to slip them off as she leaves the coloured light behind. The pavement is smooth enough, but she keeps her eyes down, scanning for a spring smear of dog crap or the warning glister of glass. Which may be why she doesn't hear them coming, why she jumps when Billy's nose meets the back of her knee.

"Sorry." Lily hops off Guy's old bike beside her. "Did we scare you?"

Kate nods, her heart hammering. "A little."

"Sore feet?"

"New shoes."

"Maybe you need physio."

"Yeah, vet tech heal thyself."

Billy walks between them, his fur brushing Kate's bare leg. She lays a hand on his head and lets it ride along.

"You think it's for real," Lily says, "that ankus thing? Do they really stick hooks in the elephants' heads?"

"I don't know, maybe. Probably not anymore."

"Aren't you from there?"

"India? No. My dad is." She pauses. "I've never been."

Is Lily just escorting her home, or is she planning on coming inside again? Last night she spent the whole visit on the kitchen floor, bridging the gap between natural enemies. Maybe this time they should sit in the living room.

"You have to work tomorrow?" Lily says as they take the turn.

"Nope." Kate waits a moment before adding, "How come?"

"No reason." Lily runs her fingers through Billy's swishing tail. "What's it like, anyway? Is it, like, a gym for dogs?"

Kate laughs, then winces, stepping on something sharp. She stops to inspect her heel and finds a pebble, dark and pointed, clinging to her flesh. They're two doors down from the house. She could invite Lily in and describe the rehab centre in detail, just like she did when Lou-Lou asked. Or she could try something new. "You really want to know?"

"I asked, didn't I?"

Kate nods, deciding. "You'd better lock up the bike."

"It doesn't have a lock."

"Okay, then, bring it inside." She tries the heel, finding it only slightly tender. "Come on, I have to get the car keys anyway."

Lily raises her eyebrows. "You have a car?"

"Nice."

It's the first word Lily's spoken since she bundled her dog into the back seat and buckled herself into the front. Silence as they crossed the Gerrard Street bridge. Silence through Cabbagetown, the gay village, downtown. Now, as they idle at the corner of Harbord and St. George, Kate can only assume it's the sprawling campus that's finally prompted her to speak.

"This is U of T," she says. "Maybe you know that already." She pauses. "Are you from Toronto?"

"I meant the car."

"Oh." The light changes, and Kate eases her foot off the brake. "It's nothing fancy. I think it's a ninety-nine."

"It's nice," Lily says again. "It's cute."

Of course it is. Kate loves the little hatchback—why did she put it down? Another red light at Spadina. She slows to a stop. "It was Lou-Lou's."

"I figured." Lily's quiet until the light turns. Then, as Kate touches the gas, "I should learn to drive sometime."

Kate nods, eyes on the tail lights before them. It's as good a chance as any. "How old are you?"

"Me?" Lily spreads a grubby hand on the dash. "Old. Fucking ancient."

It's the last response Kate expects. "No," she says, "seriously."

"Seriously?" Lily turns in the seat to face her. "I'm seventeen."


"'Annex Canine Rehabilitation Centre.'" Lily reads the sign aloud as Kate punches in her access code. "You get any dogs on meth?"

"Har har."

Six digits and they're in, the time of their arrival recorded somewhere, though Kate doubts anyone ever reviews such things. If they do, she can always say she forgot her purse and had to come back. Hell, why even lie? No one's ever told her she can't bring a friend down after hours for a tour. All the same, she's glad the Emerg entrance lies around the corner, out of view.

Bypassing the wall switch, she opts for the gentle glow of the desk lamp. While Lily surveys the room, Billy snuffles over the mat where dozens of his species have submitted to Kate's care. *Doggy masseuse? Daddy's always had a way with words. Is this what you are telling me? Now you are massaging dogs?*

*Not only, Daddy. There's more to it than that. It's a promotion.*

*Promoted to dog-rubber.*

*Vic.* Mummy touched his hand.

*Okay-okay. Congratulations. Many happy returns.*

"What's this?" Lily says, picking up the goniometer.

"That's for measuring girth, say at the hip or the stifle joint—the knee."

Lily nods. "So it's a measuring tape."

"Well, yeah, a fancy one. It's calibrated so you get the same pressure every time."

"Huh." Lily returns the goniometer to its spot on the shelf. It's something Kate's noticed before, this concern for other people's things. Lily dried Guy's chipped plates as though they were finest bone china. Stacked them in the cupboard with care.

Lily inspects a pair of laminated posters: *Canine Skeletal Configuration, Canine Muscular Configuration.* "Hey, Billy, did you know you have occipital condyles?"

Billy looks round at the sound of his name then back to the exercise ball he's nudged into the corner.

"So do you," Kate says.

"Just me?"

"Well, no, me too. We all do." She hears herself and takes a breath. "So. Well, this is the reception area. File cabinets, closet, computer, desk. I guess that's all pretty obvious."

Lily says nothing. Kate looks down at the desk, flipping open the top folder in the pile. Pinky, a chubby pug with a fractured pelvis. Should she tell Lily about him, show her the Polaroid in the file, or just get on with the tour? Billy makes the decision for her, padding down the narrow corridor toward the tank room.

"Billy," Lily says sharply, halting him in his tracks.

"No, he's right." Kate closes the file on Pinky's pushed-in face. "That's next."

She ushers Lily before her, feeling absurdly formal, as though she's just laid her cloak down over a puddle in the road.

"Wow," Lily says. "What the fuck is that?"

Kate comes to stand alongside her. Billy's already on the ramp, nosing the front panel of the tank. "That, believe it or not, is an underwater treadmill."

"You're shitting me."

"Nope. The water takes the weight off. Lets them build up their muscles without the strain."

"Wild." Lily moves to the tank, curls both hands over the faux wood rim and looks inside. "Hey—" She turns, keeping one hand in place like a ballerina at the barre. "Can Billy try?"

Kate should have seen it coming, and maybe some part of her did. No doubt she'd be in trouble if anyone found out. She might even be out of a job.

"Absolutely," she says. "Your wish is my command."

Billy handles the tank like a pro. He stands firm while the water level rises, begins strolling the moment the belt kicks into gear. Lily kneels on the ramp before him, her palms pressed to the glass. "He loves it. Look at him—he fucking loves it. You want to go faster, boy?" She turns her smile Kate's way. "Can he go faster?"

"Sure." Kate moves in to punch the button, stepping back out of habit to gauge how Billy reacts. Not a hitch. His fur waves like seagrass. He lifts each foot distinctly, almost proudly, as though he's marching in a parade. "Perfect."

"What is?"

"Billy's gait. His stride. It's perfect."

The look on Lily's face is heartbreaking—she beams as though she might cry. Kate watches her stand and reach down inside the tank. Watches Billy nuzzle her fingers for a moment before she dips her hand. "It's warm."

"Uh-huh. It helps their muscles relax."

"Plus it's just nicer."

"That too."

The air is damp and doggy. The water's turning murky; this is an animal well acquainted with the silty Don. It's all right—Kate will wipe down the tank when he's done.

"Think he's getting tired?" Lily asks.

"I don't know. Looks like he could go all night."

"Sure, but when do the rest of us get a chance?"

Kate looks up. "Oh. It's not really the same for bipeds. The weight distribution—you don't get the same lift." Maybe it would be different for Lily, though. That delicate neck. Those bird-quill bones in the backs of her hands.

"What if I went on my hands and knees?"

Kate blinks. A single canine freebie she might be able to explain. A teenage girl down on all fours, not so much. Her hand finds the control panel. She spreads her fingers, pressing *Slower* and *Drain* in one.

Billy ends his session cheerfully enough, slowing to a contented stop then squeezing past Lily to bustle down the ramp. Kate reaches for a towel, but he's already shaking, loosing an explosive spray.

"Man," Kate laughs, wiping her face, "he's fast." She stoops to blanket him in the towel, rubbing his sturdy legs, the black barrel of his chest.

The sound of running water makes her turn. Lily's standing in the tank with her hands clasped behind her back. Her vest, her boots and jeans, her man's pyjama shirt—everything lies in a pile. How did she get down to T-shirt and panties so fast? Pink panties—candy pink against the skim-milk skin of her thighs. Kate lowers her eyes.

Lily's feet, submerged now past the ankles, are just as Kate imagined them—sweet, ill-used, in need of repair. She leaves the towel draped over Billy's waterlogged ruff and steps up onto the ramp, checking the seal.

"I closed it," Lily says.

"Okay."

They stand face to face for a moment, perhaps a ruler's length between them. Then Lily kneels and drops forward onto her hands. Kate steps down to stand by the controls. Trains her eyes forward to read the *Pool Rules* Sandi brought in to brighten up the back wall.

> *No swimming unless supervised.*
> *No diving.*
> *No peeing in pool.*
> *Animals with long hair must wear a bathing cap.*
> *Absolutely no cats allowed.*

"Hey," Lily says, "you trying to drown me?"

"Sorry." Kate halts the flow. "You want me to let some out?"

"No, it should be okay." She holds her chin up to keep her face out of the water. The T-shirt has swollen out around her, lifting to show the shallow dimples at the small of her back.

"Ready?" Kate asks.

"Fuck, yeah."

Kate starts the belt, Lily setting off like an infant, wobbly but cocksure. She just fits the tank, her toes kissing the back panel with every stride.

"Faster," she says, and Kate touches the button. *"Faster."*

She's really moving now. "Yeah," she pants, "I can feel it. I'm definitely lighter."

Kate turns to see Billy watching his owner intently through the glass, the towel still hanging around his neck—ready for the sauna, maybe even the ring. When she crosses to the bench, he follows to plant himself beside her and lean. Only then does she see it: the flesh of Lily's left forearm is marked with an angry cross-hatching. Kate sits forward, elbows on her knees. There's a pattern to it, inch-long incisions arranged into groups of five. She feels her stomach shrink, steals a look at Lily's face. She's straining to keep her head up, her expression one of determination, even eagerness. Or is it fear?

"Okay." Kate rises. "That's enough."

Lily makes no protest, slowing as the belt slows, dropping her chin as the water begins to drain. By the time the belt comes to a stop, she can hang her head without drowning, and she does, the T-shirt clinging to her back, revealing her laboured breath. She rises up on her knees. Gets one foot, then the other, beneath her. Kate fetches another towel, fighting the urge to hold it open like a mother meeting her child at the water's edge. Lily reaches out to turn the handle, releasing herself from the tank. The wounds on her right arm are similar but brighter, more recent.

Kate stands at the foot of the ramp, holding out the folded towel. When Lily reaches for it, Kate says quietly, "What are those marks?"

Lily stands dripping, the towel pressed to her chest. "What do they look like?"

Kate should just say it. *Come home with me, Lily. Come and stay.* But Lily has asked her a question. "They look—" She pauses, her mouth suddenly dry. "They look like days."

The Necropolis closed its gates over an hour ago. Luckily, the iron fence is old-fashioned, a line of painted lances more ornament than obstacle to anyone with a bit of jump. Guy grapples over and drops, landing in a crouch. For a moment he feels vaguely feral—a boy raised up in the jungle, befriended by the wild. He had hints of a similar sensation on the way here— once when he stepped onto the footbridge and felt the valley yawn beneath him, then again as he skirted the rustling pungency of Riverdale Farm.

He's never really warmed to the graveyard's official entrance, the quaint little archway with its curlicues of painted wood. It feels more natural entering on the sly. Leaving the street lights behind, he does his best not to tread on any plaques. It's hard to be sure where the dead actually lie in a crowded old yard like this.

The monument stands in the lee of a big spruce, just steps from the central path. He always stops here first, like checking in with the grieving hosts before walking through to where the true wake's going on.

Budding rose bushes cluster about the paired columns, simple stone plinths marked with small commemorative plaques. The first supports a bronze, doll-sized family, the son on his father's shoulders, the mother seated nearby. Guy stands in the path of her unseeing gaze. The bronze parents are young in a way Jan and Ernie never were—Ernie's back already chronic by the time Guy was born. Young in the way his first parents must have been.

He's been to visit their graves plenty of times—all the way out in Mississauga, among a crowd of other dead Howells he never knew. Year after year on the anniversary of the crash. Not since Jan died, though. Not once on his own.

The top of the second column has been left bare. People leave tokens here. Flowers would take up too much room, so most opt for small, smooth stones. One, ideal for skipping, has been etched with rough letters: *LOVE*. Another bears a plump heart in red felt pen. Someone has left a Moosehead bottle cap—the beloved's favourite beer. Guy finds the card-sized plaques that belong to him and bends to read them in the gloom.

IN MEMORY OF
ERNEST "ERNIE" HOWELL
BELOVED HUSBAND AND UNCLE


IN MEMORY OF
JANICE KETTERIDGE HOWELL
BELOVED WIFE AND AUNT


He's brought the usual offering: a pair of lug nuts polished to a shine. He fingers them in his pocket, then draws them out and places them gently on the monument, side by side.

The path carries on from there to turn a sharp right angle, but Guy cuts the corner, walking overland again. At the mouth of a narrow cutaway he stoops to search out the hidden sign. Every year it retreats deeper into the hedge; those who know it's there can still read it, but only just. VALLEY SCATTERING AREA.

Having found it, he stands for a moment, staring down the cutaway's length. The last in a row of houses abuts its western bank. Light spills from an uncurtained study. What must it be like to live there, knowing the dust on your bookshelves—in your lungs, for that matter—is laced with human ash?

He walks downhill, neighbourhood to the left of him, trees to the right. It's a comfort, this small forest let stand when the land might have been sold for plots. Maybe the decision was a practical one, the grade too steep to keep hold of coffins, or even urns.

Slabs and standing stones dot the descent. Loose rows of embedded plaques, the odd tree planted and tended in somebody's name. When Uncle Ernie died, Aunt Jan chose one that was already growing: a strong-looking pine at the edge of the little wood.

"Good view of the intersection," she said. "He'd want to keep up on the new models coming off the line."

Guy nodded. "It smells nice, too."

She didn't scatter her husband so much as tip him out, tilting the lined box and shaking the contents in a rough circle around the base of the tree. "That way, when we want him, we'll know where to look."

Eight years later, not long after he turned twenty-one, Guy fed ashes to the pine's roots again—so he'd know where to find her too.

It's a good place to sit, better than any bench or pew. A carpet of needles beneath him, the steadying trunk at his back. He'll come away fragrant, his clothing sticky in places with pitch.

After a time, he becomes aware of a small irritation—a

pebble digging into his behind. He feels for it, examines it in the deepening dark. It's lighter than stone, almost porous, and so pale it appears to glow. Could it be? A knuckle, maybe, relic of the finger Ernie broke when his wrench slipped—or else one of Jan's twisted, arthritic toes. He closes it between his palms.

Normally he talks to them only inwardly, but here, where their mixed molecules lie all around him, it makes sense to voice his thoughts aloud.

"So," he says, letting his breath out with the word, "there's this girl."

The air is weighted, shot through with telling scent. The coyote rarely strays this far—it lies beyond the true home range. Needs must. The young are cutting their teeth, pouncing on every grasshopper that comes their way. Soon—this night or the next—they will begin to demand real meat.

The coyote has no pack to help her provide; here among the humans, it pays to keep to the family core. Only now, even the mate is gone. When he didn't return from last night's hunt, she braved the late morning and nosed out the most recent of his trails. It ended in a scent-scene of mayhem. A drag mark led her into the nearby brush, where she came upon a redolent patch of his blood. His body was nowhere to be found.

She's been on edge ever since, tempted to seek out a new den site and move the vulnerable pups. As soon as the daylight ebbed, she set out in search of food. So far she's had a squirrel—all gristle and tail—and a few mice gleaned from the roadside grass. Not a scrap of carrion along the shoulder. She crouched until there was relative quiet then bolted to the other side.

Having squeezed under the curled hem of a fence, she trots upcountry toward the cover of the trees. The atmosphere troubles her. Nowhere else has she come across a death-scent this dry. The earth breathes bone with every touch of her paws; even the grass smells wrong, like clumps of indigestible hair. Traces of fire, too, the cool grey silt it leaves behind.

As she enters the trees, the night grows fresher, more easily understood. Moving without sound through the closing flowers, the damp, receptive moss, she doesn't get wind of the human until she's almost upon him. He sits alone with his back against a tree, eyes closed, trusting his surrounds. She watches him for a time before continuing on.

At the crest of the hill, she enters a disturbing scene. The trees stand lonely, surrounded by oddly shaped stones—some her own height, many taller. She hastens her pace. The smell of death runs deeper here, laced with a poisonous strain.

It's a relief to wriggle through the barred gate; now nothing but a narrow road and a pretty little fence lies between her and the reason she's come. Already she can smell the barns.

She leaps the fence. Making her way to the nearest wooden wall, she sniffs along the foundation, seeking the loose board, the crumbling corner, that will allow her in. The cracks leak a mouth-watering mixture of chicken and pig—geese too, but why struggle for a meal when a helpless one roosts nearby? She can hear them, squawking and squabbling in their unease. Her scent has wound its way inside even if the rest of her can't.

The second barn is even more trying, one corner smelling sweetly of rabbits, others heady with goats and sheep—this year's crop among them, rickety-legged kids and lambs. The coyote scratches helplessly at the fragrant base of the door.

The larger creatures have been left out overnight. The dark, heavy-boned horses turn head-on to her as she pads softly past. The donkey follows suit, its long ears switching, reminding her of the rabbits beyond her reach.

In a corral of its own, the cow is lying down. It meets the coyote's gaze through the fence rails, then rolls and heaves up onto its feet. What looked to be part of its blotched body is in fact the soft body of a calf. The mother nudges it until it scrambles to a stand. Not a hope. Maybe if the coyote belonged to a pack, but even then she'd risk getting kicked to death. This is the kind of meat you find, not the kind you fight for. The cow holds her in its brown eye until she turns.

Nothing left but to slope away down to the pond. She might come upon a raccoon feeling for its dinner, or even a sleek muskrat slipping from its lodge. She hasn't had muskrat since the mate brought her one whole, back when this year's litter was new. The gift was fresh when he dropped it on the den floor before her. Still tender, still ever so slightly warm.

# 17

# Ring of Dark Timber

It was summer—no school bus coming to ferry Edal to and fro, nothing to break up the days. Weeks had passed since she'd lost the many-toed kitten, proving herself unworthy of Jim Dale's trust. She told herself she was only out walking, sick of the woods, seeing what else she might see. Redwings in the cattail ditches, deer tracks where the shoulder turned soft. A couple of trucks passed, one midnight blue, the other grey where it wasn't lacy with rust—a young woman in the showpiece, an old guy in the junker. Nobody she knew.

It turned out his place wasn't all that far, only an hour's walk from home. Dogleg Road was more of a track, two dirt ruts scattered with gravel, a healthy strip of growth between. Edal crouched to identify quack grass, black medick, common plantain. She had plenty of time.

It really was a dogleg, and not long past the jog she came to a gravel drive marked with a wood-slab sign. He'd painted it dark brown with yellow words: *Jim Dale Outfitters.* She rested a hand on it before advancing up the drive.

Set back in the woods, the little log house looked more like a home than somebody's place of work. He probably did live on site; it only made sense for a man with no family, and Edal would have noticed if he'd mentioned a wife or kids.

The light was scattered, moving in lazy concert with the leaves and needles that allowed it through. A cone-strewn parking patch stood empty, sprouting weeds. With no truck out front, the place could almost pass for a dwelling from another time, the kind people built when they had to clear the land themselves—the man and his horse grubbing out stumps, the woman stooping to push seeds into the dirt.

The picture windows belonged to the here and now. The one to the right of the split-log steps was curtained, leaving Edal free to make up what lay inside. She kept it simple: a wood stove and a couple of old armchairs, a clean corner kitchen, a door leading through to the pioneer couple's bed. She didn't mean to imagine them in there—the man and his small, strong woman moving together under the crazy quilt.

The left-hand window stood clear. With nobody home, it had the watery look of the aquarium at school.

Edal took the steps slowly and knocked. Nothing but the thousand small sounds of the forest. She looked round to make sure she was alone, then bent over the rail to get her face close to the glass.

It was a tidy office—desk and file cabinet, plus a couple of tall metal cupboards, probably for storing guns. Maps in washed-out colours papered the walls. The only homey part was a half-sized fridge with a plug-in kettle on top. The kettle was crowded onto a metal tray with two jars—coffee and Coffee-mate— plus a sugar bag and three brown, hourglass-shaped mugs.

What would Edal say if he offered her a cup? She'd never tried it, though she knew the smell well enough—fresh and pleasant when the jar lid twisted off, sour on Letty's breath for hours after she'd drunk it down. *Yes, thanks,* is what she would say. Or better yet, *Sure, I'd love a cup.* Stir in the creamy powder and sip and smile.

When she'd touched everything in the room with her eyes—wastepaper basket, ashtray, heavy black phone—Edal drew back to stand again before the door. Her fingers found the knob. She clutched it and turned. Locked.

Something like relief made her knees go spongy. After a moment they hardened up again, and she spun to take the rough-hewn steps in one. Jim Dale probably saw the leap, or at least the landing. He pulled up onto the gravel patch and cut the engine, his rolled-up sleeve at the rolled-down window. "Hey there."

Edal wondered if he'd forgotten her name. "Hi, Mr.—"

"Jim." He swung open his door. "How goes it, Edal? How's that big-foot kitten of yours?"

She stood rigid a moment, as though she'd been slapped or stung. Then she began to cry.

"Whoa, whoa. Hey, now."

She hid her face in her hands. Heard him shut the truck door and come to stand beside her. Then felt his palm on her back. He chose the rounded stretch of spine between her shoulder blades, held still there a moment, then started patting. He kept up a steady rhythm until she was done.

"Want a pop?" he said as she wiped at her eyes. "There's root beer in the fridge, maybe even an Orange Crush."

Edal nodded. No coffee, then. At least not yet.

———

She downed her root beer in silence, then squeezed the can so it dimpled and made hiccuping sounds. Meanwhile Jim stirred up a coffee—black with two sugars—and sat down behind his desk. Finally she looked up and told him about Daisy—the moonlit wakening, the window hoisted high.

"When was this?" he asked.

She considered lying, making up a week or two of the kitten living happily in her room. "The day you brought him." She hung her head. "That same night."

He nodded. "So that's, what, four, five weeks now?"

"I guess."

"Well, you're probably right, an owl or a coyote got him." It helped that he didn't sugar-coat the thing. It made it something they could share. "What'd you say you called him?"

Edal hesitated. "Daisy."

He laughed. "No wonder he ran away."

A week or so later, she walked up his drive to find him unloading sheets of plywood from the bed of the truck. "Hey there," he said.

"Hi, Jim."

"What's the good word?"

"I was just passing," she heard herself answer. It sounded exactly right. "Building something?"

"Storage shed." He hoisted a sheet in both hands.

"Need any help?"

He looked her up and down, as though assessing how much use she might be. "Sure," he said finally, "I wouldn't say no."

# 18

# The Chronicles of Darius

Not long after Grandmother read the last chapter of Faye's favourite book aloud, the old man took Darius with him into the woods. They tramped down country until the light off the river glinted through the trees, then Grandfather forked left onto a one-man path. Darius followed, catching snap-back switches in the cheek. For a time they carried on within sight of the water, then the path peeled off into a thin cover of yellowing trees.

The pond was long and narrow, choked with cattails at either end. Grandfather's duck blind was a simple brush lean-to. Water seeped up through the floor of trampled reeds, brown like the third-round tea Grandmother coaxed from every bag. Soon they were kneeling in a shallow pool. Looking down, Darius counted beetles, a water-skimmer, even a tiny darting fish. He began to fidget, and Grandfather hissed at him to keep still.

Darius had eaten duck several times, aping his grandparents, picking shot from the slippery meat and piling it up on his plate with the bones. He'd encountered the living article too, tails-up in a back eddy, or fat and quacking on the bank—even creaking their watertight wings overhead. Never shot out of the sky, though. The jerk and the wheel and the splash.

He was almost thankful when Grandfather tasked him with wading in after the first floating corpse—his itchy, aching legs were that desperate to move. The weak-tea water rose to his waist, the bottom sucking every step. The duck was a male. Head like a green gemstone, blue medals on its wings. There were five more bodies before they were done, five soaked and miserable vigils while the survivors forgot the fallen and came flapping to land again.

The path home felt different. It held to higher ground, and it seemed longer, too, though that might have been down to the ducks bumping against Darius's back. He wondered if you could wash a winter jacket—Grandmother wrestling the puffy grey mass into the sink and scrubbing—or if the blood would mark his shoulders for good.

They were halfway home when Grandfather stopped in his tracks. He didn't look back, only held up a finger that said *Freeze*. The ducks doubled their lifeless weight. Darius's wet, goose-pimpled legs ached anew.

The old man raised his hand again, beckoning Darius on. He pointed to where the brush showed signs of a struggle, then directed Darius's gaze farther—perhaps ten paces in from the path—to a mound of fallen needles and dirt. A mound with a hoof. A patch of grey-brown hide.

Grandfather used the shotgun's muzzle to part the understorey, taking slow, plunging steps toward the covered kill. Darius longed to keep to the path, but with the old man gone, the beaten earth felt like a seam beneath him, a fault along which the forest might crack. He stooped and followed, boughs grabbing at his feathered load.

Standing over the carcass, Grandfather reached out to tear a branch from its tree. Slowly, almost tenderly, he swept the dirt layer away. The neck was clearly broken, but the head it had carried was whole. No antlers. Only big, stiff ears, a sleeping eye.

"See the neck, boy? Spinal cord snapped clean through." Grandfather flapped his branch at the deer's belly—the pit where its belly had been. "Cougar. Wolves or coyotes go in under the tail. They wouldn't cover it like this, either."

*Cougar.* Darius shaped the word but couldn't sound it. He'd forgotten the real-life woods held lions too.

"Come here, boy." Grandfather laid a hand on Darius's shoulder, bending him low so he could smell the musk of the deer's death, the upsetting fetor of meat on the turn. "Teeth like razors." The branch flapped again. "See how he shaved the hair away before going in?"

Darius saw—the skin naked where it rose away from the cut. What kind of a tooth could be used for shaving? He closed his eyes and saw the massive, neat-eared head, the golden gaze and cotton-ball whisker-puffs. Rubbing with one cheek then the other, the way cats do. Only curling a lip back first, unsheathing a single fang.

The lion in the book had teeth—Darius was certain of that—but there'd been no mention of him using them to razor a hide clean. The only one shorn in that story was the king of beasts himself.

Grandfather turned the branch around, gathering the

greens up in his fist. The broken end made a fine pointer. He poked it into the open deer. "Looks as though he's had the liver. Got up under the ribs too. Heart and lungs are gone."

Darius heard a buzzing sound in his head. The combined weight of the ducks and the old man's hand felt like something sitting hunched on his back. He feared he would tip forward, bury his face in the deer's deep wound.

"Can't be far off." Grandfather's hand fell away just in time. "Hell, he's probably watching us from some tree."

Darius straightened up slowly. If the cat dropped down on them, Grandfather would shoot it. Only Darius couldn't remember him reloading after the last duck hit the pond— and what would birdshot do to a cougar anyway, besides make it mad? The old man could use the butt end of the gun like a club, but Darius had nothing to defend himself with besides the day's haul. It wasn't the most hopeful of pictures, the big cat spitting and lashing its tail, him swinging his clump of ducks.

"Best be going," Grandfather said, letting his branch fall. "Don't want him shaving your belly too."

# 19

# The City Book

It's weird how they've never come here before. From the beginning—before Lily had even heard of Howell Auto Wreckers or the Precious Pearl—she and Billy made a habit of heading east along the footbridge once they'd climbed the stairs from the valley floor. She had an idea there was something called Riverdale Farm over this way, she just never imagined it would be an actual *farm*. Of course, they can't go in—or Billy can't, which amounts to the same thing. They can stand at the fence, though. There's still plenty to see.

"Horses, Billy. You remember those. And that funny-looking one's a donkey. See there, standing all on his own?"

Billy makes a sound in his throat.

"Yeah." She pats his flank. "I know."

Behind them, the happy noise of a neighbourhood park. Now and then the shriek of an indignant toddler, a burst of yapping from somebody's poorly trained dog. Lily was here before any of them, having broken camp at the first grey hint of day. Despite what she told Guy and Stephen, it's hard to sleep knowing the coyote creep's down there. Harder still to lie staring, counting the hours until dawn.

She and Billy could have swung by the wrecking yard, picked up the bike and gone gleaning for birds, but there didn't seem to be any point. She found nothing yesterday morning, and only a single white-throated sparrow the day before. Besides, sometimes it pays to break a habit and try something new. In addition to the farm and the busy little park, they've discovered a graveyard.

The place was flooded with early light when they first arrived, trees and tombstones laying long shadows on the grass. The gates were still locked, so Lily sat with her back to the wrought iron rails and read about Bigwig and the other rabbits busting out of Woundwort's evil warren. She had to wait until they were all drifting downstream on the punt before she could trust the story enough to crack the dragon book and take out her pen.

> That they should feel any relief—dull or otherwise—was remarkable in the circumstances and showed both how little they understood their situation and how much fear Woundwort could inspire, for their escape from him seemed to be their only good fortune.

When the caretaker came to open up, it turned out the graveyard was yet another place where Billy wasn't allowed. They made do with walking the perimeter, staring through the pointed bars.

"'Toronto Necropolis,'" she said, reading the sign. "'Cemetery and Crematorium.' You know what that means, don't you?" She laid a hand on Billy's head. "Any preference?"

He gave a whistling sigh.

"Me too. Cremation every time. Dump us in the Don with the other sludge."

In truth, though, she liked the look of the old grave-yard. She could picture ending up there, if only Billy could come too.


At least it makes sense keeping dogs out of the farm. Billy's as well trained as they come, but even he could lose it if a stray chicken came clucking across his path—and God help him if there were rabbits in one of those barns. As it happens, the fence is as good a place as any for getting close to the cow and her calf. Lily's proud of her dog, the way he keeps his cool when the pair of them come lumbering from their little shed.

The mother's lovely, caramel and cream, with dark, lash-laden eyes. Her calf is almost entirely golden, save for the white splash across its brow. The cow pays close atten-tion to this spot, passing her tongue over it again and again—but Lily feels certain she'd do as much for any calf she'd given birth to, no matter how its hide was marked. And it wouldn't end there. Whatever peril, whatever pred-atory force the world thought fit to provide, the cow would put herself between it and her child. She'd lower her horn-less head and ram the fucker. She'd kick the vicious prick to death.

**Coyote Cop's Blog**

**Sunday, June 1, 2008**

Nothing wrong with taking a trophy. A man ought to take pride in a job well done and anyway it helps to have a reminder of what the fight is all about. Because a coyote is not a feeling in somebodys guts or anywhere else. Its a flesh and blood menace. Its a predator. And when it comes for you it comes on four grey paws. I don't mind admitting that scares me. It should scare you too.

A couple of you wrote saying you didn't know where to find cyanide canisters. I'll post a link down the bottom of this entry but in the meantime I bet you know where to get your hands on some gasoline. Like I said you want to be on the lookout for den activity this time of year. I know some of you have already found promising looking holes. Well here too the trick is to watch and wait. Bring some binoculars if you have them. If you get too close to a den before your ready to make your move the mother will get wind and cart the pups off somewhere else. Watch the main entrance but also keep an eye out for a possible back door. There won't be any sign of digging there. Chances are the only way you'll spot it is if you see one of them dive nose first into the ground.

If the den is active you ought to see pups this time
of year though they won't be straying very far from
home. One or both of the parents will be out hunting
during the twilight hours so midday and the dead of
night are your best bets for finding most of the
family at home. Of course in the city you will want
to go about your business in the dark.

First if you are lucky enough to know where that
back door is block it up. Bring something to cover
the main entrance too. Old car wheels work great
or even shopping carts. Try looking in the river
around the bridges where people like to chuck stuff
in. The riverdale footbridge is a good one. Its
pretty shallow and stuff gets snagged along the
bank. Lots of times its only a tire but if you
get lucky like me you might just fish out the
whole damn wheel. Whatever you use you will want to
stash it in some nearby cover so when you need it
its close to hand. The rest is just common sense.
You have the gasoline and you have the matches. You
pour. You light. When the flames die back enough so
you won't burn off your eyebrows you roll your
wheel into place. If your the type that gets nervous
you might want to make tracks and thats just fine.
What matters is getting the job done. Or maybe your
more like me and you want a little something to
remember your successes by. But who wants to crawl
face first down a skinny smoky hole and what are
the chances theres anything worth keeping down

there anyway? It probably looks like chicken and ribs closed up in the barbecue on high. Besides as you can see theres more than one way to take a trophy. Just roll that big old wheel away and remember to use your flash.

*POSTED BY Coyote Cop at 6:04 AM*

In the office of Howell Auto Wreckers, Stephen sits rigid in the old swivel chair. No sound save the rumble of the parkway, the hum of the computer's fan. The photo floats on the screen before him. At first it appeared celestial, the blacker-than-black circle wearing its halo of eerie light. Now he sees it for what it is—something much, much closer to home.

**soldierboy wrote** . . .
I don't know how long I've been looking at this picture. Long enough to forget the room I'm sitting in and find myself down there in that burnt-out hole. Not now, when it's all over, but then, when the gas came splashing and the den filled up with fire.

Of course, I'm not there. Still, for a while my heart was beating so hard I thought I might die from the sheer terror of it. Can you imagine what it must have been like for the creatures who were down there in the flesh? Because I think you should. I think we all should. And I'm not sure what's wrong with us that we don't.

There's a switch inside every one of us that I guess grew there as a necessary part of survival. How can you drag a fish up out of the river for your supper if you feel the yank of the hook in your own cheek? I get that part. We can't feel for everyone and everything all the time. We'd die of fear or sorrow a hundred times a day. The thing is, it's gotten so we flick that switch off like it's nothing. And, more often than not, we forget to turn it back on.

So I'm asking you, Coyote Cop and everyone else reading this, put yourself down in that den. Bunch yourself up against the back wall with your brothers and sisters. Feel what happens in your chest when the air turns to poison. Then to flame.

Now look at the photograph again.

*POSTED AT 8:19 AM, June 1, 2008*

Chin is a demon with a cleaver. At the moment he's disman-tling chickens, reducing featherless bodies to their elements—bone-white, breast-pink, blood-red. In the lull between bus pans, Lily comes to stand beside him, watching his old hands fly.

"What you doing, no-name-girl?"

"What's it look like? I'm watching you chop."

"Huh." He brings the cleaver down, splitting a thin bird in two.

"Looks easy when you do it."

"Easy. You think easy?"

"No, I think it's hard."

"Huh." He angles the blade, dividing a breast from its fan of bones. "Maybe I teach you sometime."

"Teach me?" The possibility never occurred to her. She's never even touched one of his cleavers. He cleans and sharpens them himself.

"If you sticking round." He glances at her. "You sticking round?"

The rinse cycle clunks to a halt. Ping, the teenage prep cook, is out back smoking, mumbling to Billy in Cantonese. Lily can almost hear the cups inside the dishwasher giving off steam. Her marked-up arms, normally so heavy, feel strangely light, almost papery, inside her sleeves. The butterfly knife, on the other hand, remains leaden. She can feel it in her jeans pocket, dragging that side of her down.

Slipping a hand up under her apron, she digs it out and sets it on the counter. Chin lays the cleaver aside and wipes his chickeny hands on a rag. He takes up the knife, opens it. Tests the blade against his thumb. "Tch."

"Would you—" She pauses to steady her voice. "Could you sharpen it for me?"

"That depend." He looks up. "What it for?"

She meets his gaze. "Protection."

"Protection." He nods. "Okay, sure."

Stephen's made another of his standbys—red lentil soup with chunks of potato, the onions sautéed with cumin and added last thing. Armpit stew, Lily called it when he cooked up a pot a couple of weeks ago, but he noticed she went back for a second bowl.

She makes no comment tonight, setting the table in silence before walking around back with Billy to smoke.

Kate shows up as he's tossing the salad. He looks round to see her standing awkwardly, just inside the door. "Guy said I could stay for supper." Something forced in her tone. "Anything I can do?"

"You could put out the butter, and some of those rolls."

"Okay." She heads for the bathroom. "I'll just wash my hands."

Guy comes in next, engine grease to his elbows. He crosses to the sink and squirts dish soap into his palm.

"You get that pump out all right?" Stephen asks.

"Yep."

"Any sign of Edal?"

He lathers up carefully. "Nope."

Stephen's deciding whether he should say more when Lily steps back inside. A moment later Kate appears, towel in hand. "Hi, Lily."

"Oh. Hi."

Kate pats her thigh, but Billy needs no encouragement. "Hi, Billy."

"Don't be a suck, Billy," Lily says sharply. "Come here. *Come.*"

At the table, Guy stares down at his helping. Kate watches Lily; Lily keeps her eyes on her dog.

"So," Stephen hears himself say brightly, "how was everybody's day?"

"Good," says Guy.

Kate echoes him. "Good."

Lily says nothing, spooning up a mouthful of soup. Stephen hasn't seen her this prickly in weeks—not since she first started showing up at the yard.

"How was work, Lily?" he says.

She shoots him an unpleasant look.

"You have a job?" says Kate.

"Yes, I have a job. Why is that so fucking hard for anybody to believe?"

"Sorry, I just—sorry." Kate lays down her spoon. "Where do you work?"

"Coal mine," Lily mumbles, her mouth full.

Kate blinks. "Pardon?"

"Oil rig."

"Lily, if you don't want to tell me—"

"Slaughterhouse." Lily reaches for a roll and tears it in two.

Not much point trying to make conversation after that. Stephen focuses on his food—yellow soup, green salad, brown roll. Nobody takes him up on an offer of seconds. Lily clears, Kate washes, Guy dries. They could be hooded brothers at a monastery, not a word shared between them as they work.

Stephen lingers at the table, nursing a second glass of milk. No one seems much in the mood for a story, so he's surprised when Guy fetches the book from his bedroom and the other two resume their seats.

For the first page or so, Guy's delivery is uncharacteristically dull. Only when a cry sounds throughout the jungle—the terrible *Pheeal* that tells of *some big killing afoot*—does he begin to do justice to the words. Stephen feels his head grow heavy with dread. The Red Dogs are coming, the monstrous, one-minded pack known as the dhole.

To defeat them, Mowgli will require an intelligence older and more supple than his own. He will require the python, Kaa.

The snake is a tactical thinker with years of experience in the field. The mission he comes up with is risky; as Mowgli puts it, "It is to pull the very whiskers of Death." While Kaa waits in the river below, Mowgli will lead the dhole over the high marble cliffs. Caves are dangerous places, and the cliffs are laced with them. Dripping with dark honey, they're home to the killer hives.

The table is hard, unyielding against Stephen's brow. He knows the man-cub will land unscathed in the water below, just as he knows the dhole will drop through the wakening swarm to the death of a thousand stings. Worst of all, he knows the long fall to the river will be only the beginning. Bees may be smarter than any bullet, but there's no way they'll neutralize every insurgent. There are always those who make it through.

Downriver, Mowgli and the wolves take on what's left of the ravening horde. Guy reads the pages-long battle like a pro, calling up all the dumb lust and horror, the sorrow and the sickening glee.

It's a happy ending of sorts: the dhole are vanquished, victory to the man-cub and his wounded pack. As with every chapter, though, the true conclusion comes in the shape of a song. This one belongs to Chil the Kite, winged scavenger that waits for them all. Guy reads it plainly—no lilting tone, no relentless, thudding hand. "'Tattered flank and sunken eye, open mouth and red, / Locked and lank and lone they lie, the dead upon their dead.'"

When it's over, Stephen lifts his head—lighter now, almost weightless. Lily rises before Guy can even close the book. She slips outside without a word, Billy sticking close, as though she's sewn him to the flesh of her thigh. Kate looks up sharply at the muted clang of the gate. Her expression is painful to behold, so Stephen turns to Guy—only to find he too looks as though someone has died.

Stephen needs to lie down. "Well," he says, standing, "good night."

They answer him with one voice: "Good night, Stephen." Then Guy on his own: "Want another beer?" And Kate: "What the hell."

The apple green door seems to shimmer. He lets his floating head lead him through it to his room. The bed isn't his, not really—it belongs to the old lovers, Ernie and Jan. Lowering himself down beside it, he stretches out long on the floor. The cries start up as soon as he's on their level. He rolls onto his side and drags the carrier out into the gloom.

The kits come tumbling the moment he swings open their door. Three make for the far reaches—one of the greys already fingering the curtain's hem—but the brown runt decides to stick close. Stephen lies back, allowing her to clamber up on his thighs. She waddles away down the length of his legs, pausing to sniff his boots thoroughly before turning and scampering back. Little fingers at his kneecap, his hip bone, his ribs. Her eyes are shining. She comes face to face with him, practically nose to nose.

Guy rarely has trouble getting to sleep; as a rule he's out like a light after a chapter or two. Tonight he reads until the words swim, and still he can't seem to drift off. Not *Ring of Bright Water*—he'll have to leave that one for a time. Maybe even for good.

Aunt Jan used to do the bookwork when she couldn't sleep. In the weeks following Ernie's death, she laid her hands on every invoice and order sheet in the place. Guy could walk round to the office and give it a try—only Stephen handles that end of things now, and ever since Guy followed his advice and bought the computer, the bookwork involves few if any actual books.

He ought to get a lesson on the new system. *This is your place, Guy.* Uncle Ernie with the blowtorch, or the caulking gun, or the plunger in hand. *There shouldn't be a job on the property you don't know how to do.* Besides, Stephen might decide to move on. Which would leave Guy on his ownsome again.

No sense kidding himself. Two evenings in a row now she's stayed away. He should never have loaned her his key, let alone mentioned having one cut; it's enough getting used to the place without thinking he's planning on her moving in. No sense dwelling on it, either, something else Ernie taught him. *The more you feel sorry for yourself, the sorrier you feel.*

Guy sits up. Swings his legs out from under the covers and pulls on the day's dirty clothes. Cocoa. That's what his uncle used to do on the rare night when he couldn't settle. Cocoa and smokes at the kitchen table—Guy always knew by the saucepan left to soak until morning, the ashtray loaded with butts. He'll have to make do with cocoa on its own; it's nearly four years since he lit up.

The air in the kitchen is relatively fresh, a sweet cross-breeze sweeping in through the locked screen door. Maybe he'll step outside and take a few deep breaths. Remind himself of the wider world.

His hand is on the latch before he sees her. She stands still as a doe, looking out over the shadowy sprawl of his yard. He's gentle with the lock, but she hears him and turns sharply. He snaps on the light.

"Oh, God." Her face is pale. "Sorry."

"It's okay." He steps out onto the stoop.

"I should give you your key back."

"Keep it."

"Oh, no, I—"

"Go on, it might come in handy."

She touches a hand to her chest. "What about the chain?"

"Keep that too." He comes to stand beside her. For a time neither one of them speaks.

"I was wondering," she says finally.

"Yeah?"

She points into the darkness. "What's that?"

"What?"

"That thing over by the loader. It looks like—I don't know, like a mouth."

She's right, it does look like a massive, parted mouth from this angle. He can remember the afternoon he helped Ernie make it, marking out the first cut around the belly of the oversized drum while his uncle flipped down his mask and fired up the torch. The following cuts were subtler, made on the oblique down the drum's curved flank. The shape they cut free was lovely. They might well have called it the mouth, but Ernie had another name in mind.

"That," Guy says, "is a half-moon."

"A half-moon." She smiles. "What's it for?"

"Turns the fork into a bucket."

"What?"

"The loader. It turns the forklift into—" He halts, gripped by an idea. "Wait here."

The coveralls hang where he left them, just inside the door. After a quick sniff to make sure they're not too ripe, he grabs them and ducks back outside.

"Put these on."

"What? Why?" But she's already drawing them on, leading with her left foot in its slim canvas shoe, her bare left leg. Soon she's all zipped in. The colour suits her; she actually looks good in grease-stained elephant grey.

He reaches for her hand. "Come on," he says, pulling her after him.

"Where are we going?"

"Just come on." He drops her hand when they get there. "In you get."

He expects her to question him, but she only smiles, stepping blithely into the crescent cup of the half-moon.

"That's it," he says. "Now sit down. Make sure you tuck in your feet."

She arranges herself tidily and looks up at him.

"There's a fresh pack of earplugs in the breast pocket. You better put those in."

Again, she does what he says. He vaults up into the loader and slips on the earmuffs. Two tries before it starts with a hacking roar.

Turning to track in close, he drops the forks so they skim along the ground. He takes it easy slipping them under the half-moon's rusty base, lifts smoothly, only a metre or so to begin. She seems calm enough, but it's difficult to judge from the top of her head.

He tracks upland first, keeping to even ground. At the top of the yard he lifts Edal so she's level with the uppermost layer of wrecks. He trundles past several stacks, giving her a good long look, before lowering the forks again. Shunting round, he tracks over to the tire pile and shows her the highest tire. After that, he heads for the old willow that overhangs the southern fence. He holds her up there a little longer, watching her hands fan through the shadowy curtain of leaves.

The tree's a hard act to follow. Buying time, he eases her down to half height, executes a restrained one-eighty and tracks back to the centre of the yard. He comes close to overlooking the next attraction, just catching it in the top corner of his eye. The true moon is nowhere near half, little more than a sliver left. He raises Edal up to make sure she sees it too.

The key to a great show is knowing when it's over. He lowers her to the ground with care, kills the engine and springs down from the cab. She's already standing by the time he reaches her. Having taken her up in the loader's arms, it's only natural to close her in his own.

Lying two abreast in Guy's skinny bed ought to be a squeeze, but there's no such thing as crowded when a body truly lets go. For the first time ever, Edal understands the mammalian habit of sleeping in clumps—the dug-out dens and warrens, the tree holes packed with tangled limbs and ticking hearts. Her shoulder fits precisely into the red-haired hollow beneath his arm. Her cheek, pressed to his breastbone, receives the beating message therein. Yes, she thinks, she would like nothing better than to live in a cave with this man. The tighter the fit, the better.

It happened fast, the initial kiss like the click of a stopwatch. Edal was first through the bedroom door, catching her finger in the long zipper of the coveralls and crying out. It took her a second to realize the muffled sensation in her head was down to the earplugs, a second more to pluck them out. Guy was awkward too—slamming the bedroom door, wrestling his T-shirt up over his head. It didn't matter, they were graceful enough in the end.

He stirs. She lifts her face to watch him, feels something tear loose inside her when he opens his eyes. This time she's the one reaching for the nightstand. She rips the little packet with her teeth, rolls the condom on with as much care as her trembling allows. He keeps his eyes open as she climbs across him. At no point—not even when the helpless sound escapes her lips—does he look away. He comes staring up at her. "Edal," he says, rocking, "God, I love that fucking name." She folds down to kiss him, long and deep.

The laughter comes when she sits back. It starts innocently

enough, but soon she's making ape sounds, hiccuping hysterically, covering her mouth. Guy beams back at her but doesn't
crack. He works a hand gently beneath her butt to hold on the
condom, the nudge of his knuckles making her shriek. She's
laughing so hard now she could pull a muscle, maybe even
give herself a hernia. Then suddenly she's crying—an unkind
observer might even say bawling—and still, she can't help but
register through the gaps between her fingers, he hasn't so
much as blinked.

"Hey," he says gently, "hey."

"Sorry." She wipes at her eyes. Watery snot threatens to
escape her left nostril, decorate his chest like the path of a
snail. There are no tissues, at least none she can see, so she
sucks it back up noisily. "Sorry. *Jesus.*"

"It's okay."

She takes a shuddery breath. "Christ." She drags the back
of her hand under her nose. "Is there any tissue?"

He feels among the sheets and hands her his T-shirt.

"Really?"

"It'll wash."

She holds the sleeve to her nose and blows.

"Better?"

She nods, balling up the shirt.

No avoiding it—she has to climb off him now. She does
so slowly, careful not to catch him in the balls with her heel.

"Come here." He pulls her close.

"Sorry." She says it in his ear this time.

"What the hell for?" He draws back to look at her. "I've
never felt this good in my entire life."

"Really?"

"Really."

He smells of beeswax—if there existed a subspecies of bee with a rippling coat and dark, magnificently feathered wings. She breathes deeply, drifting to the brink of sleep.

"There is one small problem, though."

She opens her eyes. "What?"

"Condom. It's got to go."

"Oh." Edal hears herself giggle like a fourteen-year-old—like she never did when she was actually fourteen. She rolls back to free him, her bare ass meeting the wall.

He sits up. "You want something to drink?"

"Water, please."

He scoops up his boxers and pulls them on. Twists at the waist to kiss her. "Won't be long."

Edal lies for perhaps a minute in the negligible light before turning on the bedside lamp. Its yellow glow pleases her; she wants to see him properly when he comes back. Arranging the pillow lengthwise against the headboard, she sits up a little, tucking the sheet in under her arms.

On the nightstand, the Kipling lies stacked atop a handful of other books. She reaches for it, intending to browse the chapters she missed, but sets it aside upon spotting the title beneath. She studies the cover closely. It's the edition she knows, boy and otter walking together along the shore. When she looks up again, Guy's standing in the doorway. He's brought a single tumbler for them to share, the way lovers do.

"Your turn," he says, closing the door behind him.

"My turn?"

"Yeah." He sets the water down on the nightstand. "You can read, right?"

"Of course I can read."

He climbs across her to take the side by the wall. "So, read to me."

There are several pages marked. Edal opens to a Juicy Fruit gum wrapper, the flap of a matchbook, an actual book-mark from the library, torn in half to keep two places instead of one. "Where are you up to?"

"Doesn't matter." His hand finds her thigh beneath the covers. "Read something you like."

"Okay." He's patient while she finds the passage. "'For the rest,'" she begins, "'she was a small, exceedingly heavy body inhabiting a rich fur skin many sizes too large for her. It cannot be described as a loose fit; it is not a fit at all. The skin appears to be attached to the creature inside it at six points only: the base of the nose, the four wrists or ankles, and the root of the tail. When lying at ease upon her back the surplus material may be observed disposed in heavy velvety folds at one or other side of her, or both . . .'"

Stephen can't sleep for thinking of them: the dead dogs on the page and the live ones in their cages; the kits safe in their den and the pups burnt to a crisp in theirs. Time and again his mind slips out the window, to where the three-footed coyote lies curled in the ground.

Maybe Lily's right. Maybe there's no getting through to some people. Okay, so he won't comment. Just a quick check to see if there's anything new.

**Coyote Cop's Blog**

**Sunday, June 1, 2008**

See now thats the trouble with ignoring the difference between us and them soldierboy. Before you know
it your putting yourself in their furry little shoes
and forgetting your a man.

And speaking of us and them theres something important we haven't covered yet. The subject in case you
haven't guessed is guns. Of course its complicated
using one in the city. Unless you have some kind of
silencer get ready to cause a stir. And be sure and
plan out your escape route because your going to
have to run.

Those of you who aren't already crackshots will want
to get in some practice before you head down to the
Don Valley or some other ravine in town looking for
a big old pair of ears. You won't get a second shot
at a coyote. Maybe you already have a rifle or even
something smaller you like to use. Well I'm no expert
but for my money theres nothing like a shotgun for
bringing vermin down. Mine is an oldie but a goody.
A Savage double-barrelled 12 gauge handed down to me
along family lines. Nobody taught me how to use it.
I figured that one out all by myself.

*POSTED BY Coyote Cop at 8:31 PM*

Edal's come to the part where her namesake is learning to trust the sea. "'By the end of June she was swimming as an otter should, diving deep to explore dim rock ledges at the edge of the sea tangle—'" She halts, certain she's heard movement outside the door.

"Don't stop," Guy murmurs.

The knock, though soft, is somehow urgent. "Guy?" Stephen whispers harshly.

"Yeah, buddy."

Stephen opens the door. His face is the fragile white of a supermarket egg. He's been crying. Or sweating. Or both. "Oh, hey, Edal." He fixes his gaze on the floor. "Sorry."

"What's up?" says Guy. "You okay?"

"I have to show you something."

"What is it?" Edal lays the book down, losing the page. "What's wrong?"

Stephen looks past her to Guy. "There's a new post." He pauses. "It's bad."

They follow Stephen back across the darkened kitchen, Guy in his boxers only, Edal in T-shirt and shorts. In the office, the computer whirrs. Light from the goose-necked lamp overlaps the glow of the screen.

Stephen stands to one side of the desk while Guy motions for Edal to take the chair. He reads the new entry over her shoulder. "Jesus."

She turns to him. "Who is this guy?"

"You better read the rest."

"All of it?"

"Yeah."

She scrolls slowly down, clicking to skim the comments at the foot of each post. Guy and Stephen move to the couch. The pair of them sit quietly, like men at a funeral. Hands folded in their laps.

After a time, Edal looks up. "Soldierboy—that's you?" she says to Stephen. He nods. "Have you reported this?"

"No."

"You have to. You have to tell the police."

"She's right," says Guy.

"Yeah. It's just, I thought I might make him see—"

"It's gone beyond that, Stephen," she says. "I think this guy's for real."

He and Guy exchange a look.

"What?" she says. "Tell me."

"They found the body," says Guy.

"What?"

"The coyote," says Stephen. "The one with the cut-off paw. We found it and—" He glances toward the back wall.

It dawns on her what he must mean. "And you brought it here."

"Yeah."

Edal thinks for a moment. "You can't tell them," she says finally. "Not about that."

"But wouldn't it be evidence?" says Guy.

"Maybe, but it's an offence to be in possession of illegally killed wildlife. Not to mention all the accidental kills you have buried out there. I'm guessing you didn't report any of those to MNR."

"MNR?"

"Ontario Ministry of Natural Resources. You're supposed to report the acquisition of wildlife killed by natural or accidental causes. They'd get you on the hawk too, and the raccoons. You can't keep wildlife in captivity without authorization, even if it is for the purpose of rehabilitation." She scrolls back up to the photograph of the paw, leaning in for a closer look. "Anyway, the blog alone should be enough to get the police interested. They'll bring MNR in on it. By the looks of it, he's in violation of God knows how many articles—night hunting, using poison, destroying a fur-bearing mammal's den—" She glances up to find them both staring.

"How do you know all this?" Stephen says.

"Good question," Guy says quietly.

"I—" Her mind races then slows. Nothing for it but to tell them the truth. "I'm a federal wildlife officer. On leave. I've been on stress leave."

Neither one of them speaks. After a moment Guy stands and comes to lay a hand on her shoulder. "Why didn't you say something?"

"Like what? I didn't think you'd trust me, any of you. I wanted you to—Jesus, it's pathetic." She looks up at him. "I wanted you to like me."

"Okay, well, mission accomplished." He bends to kiss her, quick and natural, as though he's been doing it for years. "So, seeing as you're an expert, how should we do this?"

She takes a breath. "Stephen should go down to the station first thing."

"Go down there?" Stephen says. "Really?"

"Definitely. If you call it in, there's a chance they'll come here to take a statement. They might start poking around."

Guy gives her shoulder a squeeze. "Does this mean you're not going to turn us in?"

"Who, me?" She tries out a smile. "I told you, I'm federal. And anyway, I'm on leave."

How can they not have heard him coming? Both of them dead to the world until the tent flap lifts.

Billy thrashes awake, lunging into the zipped-up screen as Lily snaps her eyes open and screams. The flash-lit face is nothing like she's imagined. Her mind's eye held an older man, grey buzz cut, bright buttons for eyes. This one is closer to her own age, soft, sad features, brown hair curling like a boy's.

Billy's going berserk—he'll bring the tent down around them any second, barking and snarling, tearing into the screen—but already the light and the face it showed them are gone. Lily throws both arms around her dog.

"Shh, Billy, shh. Stay. It's okay. Stay."

There's no way she should open what's left of the screen and let him give chase. The face was bad enough, but it wasn't all. There was a weapon—a glinting length of pipe, or maybe even a gun—and there was the paw. She saw that too. The sad, silvery paw, swinging down at her like a pendant on its string.

—

Staring skyward, the raccoon works her hands over the river's darkened bed. It's an ideal spot—the current mild, the bank riddled with promising holes—yet so far not a single crayfish has offered itself up to her grasp. Her soft-skinned fingers keep on. Wet hands feel keenly—so keenly, they seem to see. The stars above show more than their own design; a second shadow pattern hovers there, a map of mud and pebbles, twigs and rippled sand.

She feels down into a crevice, hoping for a fan of tail armour, the slim pinch of a claw. She must find something soon; her milk will tell the night's tale, and so far it holds only a swirled strain of snail meat and the tang of a long-dead gull.

The young await her—one for every clawed foot that will carry her back to them. It's a decent den, still smelling of the fox that abandoned it, but well hidden and dry, and warmer than last year's tree. Snuggest of all was the human-made den she stumbled upon one long-ago spring. It stuck straight up out of a roof, and though it was stone-like, it held none of stone's chill. She fit its recess nicely with her brood, a large litter, as befits a cold year.

She lost all save one the day the grey smoke came curling. They'd lived with the thinner variety in their coats since birth, but this was different, so dense it rose like filthy water, drowning their squeals. She ran a mad relay, lunging for the nape of each little neck, depositing one kit after another in the long, leaf-choked ditch that ran along the edge of the roof. Too late. She whuffled over the dead for a time, then gripped the living kit in her teeth and reached for an overhanging branch.

It was easy producing enough milk to feed that surviving kit—a male that grew fat and left her come fall. Not so simple to provide for a denful. Perhaps if she holds still, something will scuttle up out of hiding, or hop down to the river's edge. A starlit fish might even come winding her way.

The current tugs gently at her belly fur. A bat dips down out of the darkness to drink. Skims open-mouthed and rises, banks and skims again.

The stars are the only pattern now, her dark hands hanging blind. She looks down into the water to find points of light winking there too. Come, crayfish, with your fringed underbelly, your pebble eye. Come, sucker-fish, a silver twist for the milk.

There is only this: food and what her body can make of it, the den and its many mouths. In time, when the young leave off suckling and stumble after her in the hunt, every clouded message they drew from the teat will come clear. Barring death, they will grow. The males will wander off, the females may or may not stay. Come the cold, she'll den up until mating time comes again.

This latest litter came of a lone male. Long-lived and tailless, he was the greatest weight she'd ever known. She felt him curve up inside her, push and push and pause. He laid his head down on her back, parting her winter ruff with his snout. She submitted until she was certain, then craned round to face him and snarled. He didn't run, but he didn't linger either. His hind end bulky in retreat, alien to her without its tail.

The water flows with scarcely a ripple. It may be best to move on—in more ways than one. The valley holds many sounds, but there's no mistaking the dumb thunder of a dog.

She's downwind for the moment, the first whiff of it reaching her nose. And now a grainy glimpse of darkness on the move.

Thudding through the understorey, the dog is larger than most. She could hold her nerve and hope for it to pass, but what of the moment when it lollops into the advantage end of the breeze? And what of the human blundering in its wake—its scent arriving now, female, fairly young. Some can be counted on to call off an attack, but just as many take part in the violence, goading their creatures on.

It's a chance the mother raccoon can't take. She drops forward, a lump of weathered wood come to life. Head up, she lays her tail along the surface and paddles for the opposite bank.

It's not exactly a dream; dreams tend to involve movement—some narrative progress, however irrational, from *a* to *b*. The image in Stephen's head is still. He's made the burnt-out den his own, imported it from the files of blogmonster.com to the recesses of his sleeping mind.

He wakes with the sheet up over his face, struggles frantically for moments before finding he can still breathe, still see. The den is gone. The room is dark. Turning his head, he sees the hour spelled out in glowing crimson: 3:49.

He sits up, pausing to get his bearings before standing and dragging on his clothes. Padding barefoot into the darkened office, he stoops to bring up the blog. Nothing new. Which means he's still out there, looking for some poor creature to kill.

Edal's right—Stephen has to tell the police. He'll go as soon as it's light, cross the Queen Street Bridge and cut down to the cop shop at Parliament and Front. They'll take a statement, maybe even sit down with him at a computer and go over the blog. And then what—uniformed officers descend on the valley in formation? Cyber-detectives trace a virtual trail back to the suspect's last known address? Even if they do take the threat seriously, it will take time to organize any kind of response. Meanwhile, Coyote Cop's free to follow his instincts—and it's more than likely he's got a gun.

Stephen should have insisted Lily stay with them, should have made her see sense. Instead, he let her go back down into that half-wild valley, with no more protection than a dog. Billy's a force to be reckoned with, but he's not bulletproof. What if the next desecrated bodies Stephen finds are known to him? What then?

One year in training, six months in country. He may be no longer fit to serve, but that doesn't mean he's forgotten the secrets a soldier knows. Guy and Edal are civilians; they won't understand. Stephen fetches his jacket and boots in silence. Not even the kits wake up to hear him go.

# 2 0

# Ring of Dark Timber

Most girls would have come up with a cover story, but Edal didn't feel the need. Even when Letty noticed she'd been out, she never bothered asking where.

Knocking the shed together used up two visits; painting it dark brown with yellow trim filled a couple more. They worked well together, Jim and Edal, Edal and Jim. She wasn't sure what they'd do once the shed was complete, but she felt certain there would be more.

"I've been thinking," she said one afternoon as she crouched in front of his little fridge, holding the door open to get the good of the cold. "You ought to spruce this place up a bit."

"Uh-huh." He looked up from the binder he had open before him on the desk. "Tell me more."

She turned on the balls of her feet, twisting them against the dirty white soles of her flip-flops. "You could plant some flowers."

"Yeah?"

"Out the front. And maybe some down around the sign." The fridge kicked on, sending a fresh chill down the gap at the back of her shorts.

"What kind of flowers?"

"How do I know?" She reached behind her and felt for a can. "I could come with you to look."

"You could." He turned a page and gave it his attention. "And you could close that fridge door too."

She got busy digging the beds while Jim went to work patching the larger of his two canoes. By the time he was done, she'd made a ring of black dirt around the signpost and two coffin-shaped plots, one on either side of the front steps. She was still on her knees when he came to look over all she'd accomplished. The hair on his bare calf tickled her arm.

She sat beside him on the way to the nursery, the view from the truck cab putting the Chevy's smeared windshield to shame. Together they picked out red and white begonias—Canada's colours, and the blotted-out sun on the tag meant they'd do all right among all those trees. While they were choosing the best plants, Jim accidentally snapped off a stem.

"Careful," Edal said.

He grinned, tucking the prong of fleshy blooms behind her ear.

She knew just what to say. "How do I look?"

He stared down at her, the grin frozen for a moment, then gone. "Pretty."

"You think so?"

"I think," he said, turning back to the plants, "we ought to be getting our butts in gear."

The lady behind the counter was pink-faced, too big for her smock. She let out a noise like a small dog settling when they lined up their trays to pay. "Nice to see dad and daughter doing a project together."

Edal laughed. "He's not my dad." She turned to share the joke with Jim, but found him staring down into his wallet.

"Is that right?" The lady's face had altered, the gentle fat gone hard.

Jim fingered his bills. "What's the damage?" he said, still not looking up.

He didn't speak on the way out to the truck. Edal thought he might say something once they were out of the parking lot, but he held his tongue until they were nearing the turnoff to Dogleg Road. "How about I drop you off at home."

She looked at him. "What about the flowers?"

"You can put them in another day. Or I can."

Edal felt her stomach drop inside her. She'd done something to piss him off. Or else he was just sick of her. It wasn't such a long jump from helper to pest. "It's okay." She reached for her seat-belt buckle. "Just let me out here."

"Don't be stupid, it's not far."

"It's okay, I'll walk."

"Edal." It was his teaching voice, the one she hadn't heard since he stood at the front of her classroom drawing on the board.

"Just drop me at the turn," she said, and when they reached it, he did.

She stayed away for a whole ten days. When she finally set out around noon, after waiting for Letty to drive off to the

Pettigrews' in Owen Sound, she told herself she wouldn't take the turn. Even if she did, she'd double back at the kink in the road.

The beds had already thrown up a fair crop of weeds. No truck, but the begonias were in plain view, still in their flats, set down to one side of the front steps. They looked thirsty and thin. Edal could've used a drink herself, and so, after a long moment spent standing at the foot of the steps, she mounted them and tried the door. Locked. She turned, looking back at the road. Listening hard for his engine, she heard nothing but a squirrel flailing through the canopy, leaf litter shifting with beetles and shrews.

The shed was still a possibility; he often left the open padlock hooked through its loop to avoid fishing for his keys. It was all right to go inside—she'd helped build it, after all. She took down the trowel, then stood still in the dim interior, letting her eyes move over his things.

She started on the beds out front of the cabin, rooting up weeds and laying them aside, replacing them with the plants he'd bought. She did her best to make the flowers look natural, mixing up the colours and staggering the rows, but it was hard with all that bare black dirt. Watering only made it worse, spattering the bright petals with mud.

Having planted four flats, Edal carried the remaining two down to the foot of the drive. She worked on the ring garden for what felt like forever. Time and again she imagined him driving up to find her kneeling in the dirt, saw him leaning out of his window as she rose.

At last she stood to survey her work. The begonias looked rubbery and desperate, a flock of unfledged nestlings anchored in soil. She trudged up the drive and returned the trowel to its nail on the shed wall. Aside from the three ugly beds, she left the place as she'd found it. As though she'd never been there at all.

# The Chronicles of Darius

Darius was thirteen when it happened. If it had been any other chore—carrying the garbage out to the shed, shovelling, checking the snares that ringed the yard—it might have been him who stepped out into that twilit scene. But Grandfather liked splitting the wood himself.

When the back door slammed, Darius stood at its little window and watched. Axe in hand, the old man kicked through the snow to where the woodpile stood in the lee of the shed. He reached for an oversized piece and balanced it on the scarred face of the stump. Hoisted his weighted blade and let it fall.

Now and then the axe met a knot, or lodged in a stubborn streak of grain, forcing the old man to lift the whole works and bring it thudding down. More often than not, though, a single blow was sufficient. Pieces halved and sprang apart. He let them lie where they landed; it would be Darius's job to gather and stack them after he was done.

"What are you doing, Darius?" Grandmother came up

behind him, bringing the smell of the soup she was making with her.

"Watching."

They stood together then, her looking over his shoulder, touching him nowhere save with her breath at the back of his ear. It was a pretty picture they looked out on—tree boughs laden, the yard smothered and still. With no wind, the only movement came from the old man, the axe, the leaping wood.

Except there, on the roof of the shed.

Grandmother saw it when he did—he knew by the sharp inhale, the touch of her breath withheld. It had taken its time finding them; three years had passed since Grandfather had levered Darius down over the deer, showing him what teeth could do.

The length of the beast surprised him. Crouched low, it spanned the six-foot roof, its head at one edge, its muscled hind end at the other. Its tail rose and fell, a slow, shuddery dance. Its back hammocked down like a saddle, a hollow where some lucky child might hold on for dear life and ride.

As was to be expected in those parts, the lion had no mane. No matter. Just like in the story, the shorn face was *braver, and more beautiful, and more patient than ever.* Grandfather didn't see this. He had his back to it. His breaking, straightening back. The three of them—beast, woman and boy—watched the man.

Grandmother didn't say anything—how could she with no air in her throat?—and Darius found he too had no words. He thought of what he might do. There was the shotgun, but he'd never so much as picked it up. *The Lord help you if you lay a finger on it.* There were Grandmother's kitchen knives, which shrank to toothpicks in his mind; and there was the axe, already in Grandfather's hands. Last but not least, there was Grandfather's whipping belt—and wasn't a whip the very thing men used for controlling lions? Men, yes, but boys?

It was then that Grandmother finally made a sound. Not a scream or even a squeal, but a sigh, the air leaving her body the same instant the cougar left the roof. The leap was golden. Grandfather took the brunt of it, the axe shooting from his grip. The impact alone would have been blinding, never mind the talons. *His huge and beautifully velveted paws.*

The cougar bent its head as though it would drink from a stream. Its brave and patient face opened wide. *See the neck, boy? Spinal cord snapped clean through.* It would all be over soon.

Or it would have, if Grandfather had been any other man.

When the cougar closed its jaws, it closed them not on flesh and bone, but on wood. The old man's stand-in spine blocked the bite; more than that, it froze the bite in time. Jammed behind the killing canines, the board held the cougar fast. The cat wrenched and writhed, the old man thrashing beneath it in the snow.

Darius jumped when Grandmother's hand landed on his shoulder. "God," she breathed. "Please, God."

For once the blind bastard in the sky was listening. As luck would have it, He misunderstood.

Somehow, despite the great twisting weight on his back, Grandfather began to crawl. While the cougar panicked, desperate to tear its face free, the old man worked his torn-open shoulders. The axe hadn't flown far. Inch by inch, he wormed toward it. Groped through the snow until one hand, then the other, found the handle's curve. The strength in those wrists was inhuman. The blade shot up dark and glinting, and plunged into the cat's yellow back.

Stretched on his belly, face down in the snow with a six-foot mountain lion bucking like a stallion on his back, Grandfather somehow retained the ability to think. To calculate, even. He lifted the wedge of his blade from the lion's back and shortened his grip on the handle. Swung it down blindly again.

In Faye's book, the children covered their eyes when it came time for the sacrifice. Not Darius. The lion in his story thrilled at the second touch of the axe, turning rigid, almost electric, before it slumped. Darius saw everything: the long, shapely handle of the axe suspended; the blade buried deep in the animal's skull.

For a moment, nothing stirred. Then, like a dark fin surfacing, an arm bent at the elbow sliced up out of the snow.

"God help us," Grandmother said, her fingertips digging under Darius's collarbone.

As they stood staring, the old man levered up on the hand he'd planted. The cat shifted on his back, Grandfather shouldering, heaving, until the body capsized. Now the old man was on top. Still anchored to the cat, snow-caked and spluttering, he kicked like a beetle on its back.

"God help us," Grandmother said again, releasing her grip. "Nothing can kill him."

She'd gone for help—at least that was what Darius told himself. It seemed strange, though, leaving like that, without a word.

He'd turned at the sound of the front door slamming, stood stunned as the truck's engine roared to life. Too late to stop her, he caught only the tail lights winking away down the drift-choked road. Strange. Maybe shock could alter a person, make them thoughtless, even cruel.

If Darius knew anything, it was that his life depended on what he did next. He thought for a moment, decided to pull on his boots but not his coat. A coat would look as though he'd taken his time. His only chance was to be ignorant of all that had transpired, aware of nothing but the old man's roar.

He acted the part admirably, bursting from the back door, stumbling like a mad thing through the snow. "Grandfather, Grandfather!" Drawing close enough to make out the fur-clad corpse, he let out what he judged to be a suitable scream.

"It's all right, boy," the old man said hoarsely. "It's dead." And Darius knew he was in the clear.

Grandfather's eyes were dark in their sockets. He was powdered like a doughnut, leaking a cherry-coloured mess. *What's black and white and red all over?* The laugh caught Darius off guard, bubbling from his lips as he dropped to his knees at the old man's side. He caught it in the nick of time, twisted it into a sob.

*"Agnes,"* Grandfather moaned.

Darius's mind was quicker than he'd ever known it to be. "She was right behind me. She must've gone for help."

The old man let out a sound—or was it the animal beneath him?—a wordless, deflating complaint.

Darius fought back a second wave of the giggles. "What should I do, Grandfather?" he wailed. "What should I do?"

"Get a knife," the old man said through his teeth. "The big carving knife. You know where it is?"

"I'll get it." Darius rose and pelted for the open back door.

*You want the fork too?* Inside, he let himself laugh out loud, covering the sound by rattling the cutlery in the drawer. Closing his hand around the stub of antler that was the knife's handle, he clamped his crazy mouth shut.

He judged it best to say nothing while he followed Grandfather's instructions, opening first the old man's coat, then his snap-button shirt. "Cut it," the old man said of the bloodied undershirt, and then again, "Cut it," referring to the bandage beneath. Darius breathed evenly and did what he was told.

As always, there was the dark, scented presence of spruce. Beneath it, the smell of blood, like a penny fished from a fountain; Faye had always let him fill his sopping pockets, even when another boy's mother said he was undoing somebody's wish. The cougar itself smelled like an abiding secret. Piss and raw pollen and meat. Was this the *rich sort of smell* that came over Lucy-Faye's sister in the book, when the lion rose from the dead and licked her face? Darius wasn't fool enough to imagine the cougar would ever work its tongue again; no denying the sweet, unseemly odour that wafted from the cleft in its head.

He sawed through the bandage, loop by loop.

"Easy, now, easy. Okay, undo my belt. The button too." The old man's breath was smoky and sour, like bacon grease turned yellow in the pan.

He needed help sitting up. Without his board to harden him, he was more plant than man, drooping forward under the weight of his own head. The grey ducktail lifting. The curve of naked neck exposed. Darius flashed on the picture of a different boy—one who could prop his grandfather up with one hand while he reached for a length of split wood with the other. Who could fix his dead eyes on a target and do what had to be done.

It took a lifetime to half stagger, half drag the old man inside.

"Agnes!" he bellowed the first time he stumbled and went down in the snow, taking Darius with him. Then again, as he crashed against the door jamb, "AGNES!"

"She went for help, Grandfather."

They lurched together to the table.

"This is good." The old man fumbled for a chair.

"Shouldn't you lie—"

"I said, this is good." He sagged sideways into the seat. Grabbed the table edge and righted himself, then let his forehead meet the planks with a crack.

Darius worked what was left of the coat down the old man's arms. The shirt was torn to a skein, each shoulder a bundle of ribbons, festive and bright.

"Get the kettle on," Grandfather said. "Get a basin and a bar of soap. And a rag. A clean one from the drawer."

"Yes, sir."

"And shut that door."

"Shut the door. Yes." He slammed it accidentally.

"And put some more wood in the stove."

Washing the wounds took another lifetime. Grandfather's flesh jumped under the sudsy rag, but the man himself held perfectly still.

"Really get in there. Harder. That's right."

Darius was shaking by then, but he could still make his fingers do what he asked. Wrapping the index in a layer of cloth, he pushed the tip in deep.

"Where's Agnes?" Grandfather said to the table planks. "Where is she?"

"She went for help, Grandfather, remember?"

"Help." The old man laid his cheek on the table and fixed Darius with a one-eyed stare. "How?"

Darius looked away, dipping the rag, greasing it against the soap. "She took the truck."

"My truck?"

"Yes, sir." He touched the rag to a gash along the old man's spine.

*"Stupid."*

"What's that, sir?"

"I said, stupid. She'll put it in the ditch."

The old man was wrong about that. It wasn't a ditch so much as a gully—at least, that was the word the RCMP constable used. He arrived not long after sun-up. Grandfather was still hunched over the table, where he'd insisted on spending the night. Darius was on the couch. He'd slept little, flinching awake every time the old man twitched or snored, rising every couple of hours to add wood to the stove. When the sound of a truck engine finally came, the pitch was entirely wrong.

He could picture it, plain as the breaking day beyond the Mountie's back—the truck snout-down in the head-high drift, Grandmother resting her brow on the wheel.

Darius turned in time to see Grandfather lift his head. "What did I tell you?"

"Jesus Murphy," the Mountie said, stepping inside. "What the hell happened to you?"

"Don't you take the Lord's name in vain in this house," Grandfather croaked. "Don't you dare."

It was only later—after Darius had taken the Mountie outside to see the cougar on its back, with the axe in its head and the board still jammed between its teeth; after Grandfather had refused to go into town for treatment, and the Mountie had told him he was sending a doctor out to the cabin whether the old man liked it or not; after Darius had made coffee for both men, and Grandfather had propped himself up and told all about the attack in his own words—that the Mountie let slip exactly where Grandmother had died. Forty clicks south of town. South. Which meant she'd passed clean through help and kept on going.

Darius saw clearly then. He was the chunk of meat you throw back over your shoulder while you're sprinting for the gate. Faye probably would've done the same if he hadn't been clinging on tight to her insides.

Grandfather said nothing about it. Not then, not ever. The story was simple: A cougar had dropped down on him by the shed. Grandmother had gone for help and somehow gone off the road.

It turned out Grandmother had been wrong too. Something could indeed kill the old man, and it only took five years to come.

The time whistled through Darius, stretching him to the height, if not the heft, of a man. He kept his head down in school, hovering at the C-minus line. At home he made the bread and rubbed clean the clothes, served up supper for three every night and scraped the third plate clean when, as ever, the Lord Christ Almighty didn't show. It fell to him to strap Grandfather to his board each morning and release him from it each night. The eyeless skin of the cougar watched them, nailed like a flattened sun to the old man's bedroom wall. With Grandmother gone, Darius took every beating Grandfather had left in him to give. If anything, the scars from the attack seemed to have made him stronger. A man who could kill the king of the forest while lying prone on his belly was more than a match for a skinny sneak of fourteen, sixteen or eighteen years.

It was hard not to blame the old bitch—all those times Darius stood bracing himself over the shithole, taking her share. Five years. She could've stuck it out. Could've held on until the thing that could finish the old man off finally did.

It happened, through some sweet, unfathomable symmetry, out by the winter woodpile. Darius was in Grandfather's bedroom, making up the bed, when his brain registered a silence that had lasted too long. He looked up at the cat skin, and it fixed him with an empty stare. Leaving the top sheet untucked, he walked out into the main room.

The back-door window beckoned. Looking out, he saw the old man lying broken across the split and scattered wood—the attack internal this time. Darius took his coat from the hook and drew it on. Fed each foot into its boot. Pushed open the back door. He advanced evenly, making use of Grandfather's fresh tracks in the snow.

The old man was dead. No doubt about it. Darius had seen staring green eyes like that before. All the same, he approached the body warily, stood over it scarcely daring to breathe. When he finally got up the guts to make contact, it was with his foot. First a nudge with his toe, just by the shoulder, just in case. Then, when the bright eyes didn't blink, he used the entire boot.

# 2 2

# The City Book

The house stands shabby and alone. To begin with, Edal is locked out, her dream-body pacing the porch. She halts at the door, knocks and knocks. Then, just as she's about to begin pacing again, her fist becomes a spout and pours her inside. Little wonder her mother hasn't answered. How could she hear with the door bricked over like that, volumes deep.

Edal listens. Nothing. Then, deep in the heart of the house, something stirs. She's here, still here—the monster in the maze, the child gone missing in the woods. Endlessly patient, Letty Jones lies waiting to be found.

Edal sits bolt upright in the narrow bed. Guy shifts in the covers, reaching out to circle her hips with his arm.

"I have to go." She lifts his hand. "I have to go home."

"Now? It's not even light out."

"Not *my* home. *Home.*"

He withdraws the arm, rising up on one elbow. "What's wrong?"

"Not for long. A week, maybe."

"That's not what I asked."

"Well, a week might be being a little optimistic." She swings her legs out, snaps on the lamp. Yesterday's cotton bikinis lie on the floor by her heel. She bends for them.

"Edal. Hey, Edal, look at me. What's going on?"

"Nothing."

"Turn around for a second, would you?"

She busies herself fastening her bra.

"Why won't you look at me?"

Because now, when she does, it's like being punctured. The air leaves her in a sound, the weirdest, weakest utterance she's ever heard. He waits a moment before touching her.

"I have to go home," she wails.

"Okay. That's okay."

"My—my mother."

"Is she all right?"

"No, she's not *all right*. She's dead."

"Oh, Edal." He strokes her back. "It's okay, I'll come with you. I know all about funerals—"

"No! There is no funeral. Was. She died a month ago."

"Oh."

"I haven't been back." She draws a deep breath. "I haven't— Her ashes are waiting to be picked up."

"Baby." His hand at the base of her spine. "I'll come with you."

"You can't."

"Sure I can. I want to."

"What about Stephen?"

"Stephen will be fine. He knows what he has to do."

She takes a breath. "You don't understand. The house—"

"I can help with the house. Whatever needs doing."

Edal hugs herself. Now or never. "The house is crazy."

"How do you mean?"

"My mother—" She turns to face him. "The house is insane. It's packed to the rafters with books."

"Okay, so she was a reader."

"No, I mean *to the rafters*. There's nowhere to sit, no window she hasn't blocked off."

"Oh." He's quiet for a moment. "Sounds like a big job."

Edal closes her eyes, sees the flat grey face of the family home. "Yes."

"So, you'll need help."

Yes, she will. She does. She looks at him. "Guy, you have no idea."

"What are you talking about?" He smiles. "I grew up in a junkyard, remember?"

Darius is immune to it all—the ticks making their way to his warmest parts, the undead numbness in his legs, even the punishing curl in his back. That's what focus does for a man.

He's been running low on the stuff the last little while. At first he put it down to plain fatigue—the long vigils and shallow daylight sleeps, the bushwhacking and tree climbing and flat-out running through the dark—but he can see now there's more to it than that. There's a reason why generals keep enemy propaganda away from their troops; all that back-chat on the blog has been sapping his purpose, clouding his resolve. He ought to have spotted the problem sooner, but there's a lot to keep track of when you're commander and foot soldier in one.

It's late—so late as to have become early. There's no way he should have been wasting time watching over the girl; he put the whole operation in jeopardy, chanced getting his throat ripped out, and for what? She's nothing to him. No one.

Enough. He's where he needs to be now, the blackened den mouth gaping not ten paces from where he sits. No camera flash to light it this time—only the thinnest hint of dawn. Darius's pupils have long since opened wide to serve him. He can see just fine.

The twelve-gauge lies quiet in the undergrowth beside him, each barrel holding its cartridge close. Not much in the way of a keepsake, but a man makes do.

After Grandfather died, Darius couldn't sell up fast enough. The land had to be worth something, and it pleased him to imagine the cabin dismantled, fed log by log to the sawmill the old man had haunted for most of his life. That was before the notary in town explained to him how property was never really free and clear—how the government kept on taking its cut, and if they didn't get that cut, it became something called back taxes.

Darius has survived for five months on the government's leftovers. If he's careful, he has enough to last out the year. More to the point, he made it all the way to Toronto. Not bad, considering Faye barely made it to Calgary, and Grandmother never even got that far.

Stephen has only two points of reference from which to begin: the stretch of riverbank where Coyote Cop found the wheel he used to block the den; and, perhaps two kilometres north of there, the spot where Lily and Billy discovered the coyote with the missing paw. Hurrying down the footbridge stairs, he can't help but imagine the pair of them lying in that same bank of brush—a sweet, maltreated girl and her loyal companion, together to the bitter end.

Stephen's in enemy territory now. Following the gloomy path, he walks carefully, quickly, upstream.

Darius must have closed his eyes, maybe even nodded off. How else to explain the suddenness with which the coyote appears? She's made of flesh, not smoke. She can't have come winding out of thin air.

The brush where he sits was meant to provide cover, but the animal gazes directly at him, as though he's huddled in an open field. Those bright, inward-slanting eyes. Stepping softly, almost delicately, she positions herself between Darius and the den. He feels for the shotgun, wincing at the resulting crackle of twigs. The coyote startles him by staying put. She watches him bring the butt to his shoulder, watches him tuck his finger in against the forward trigger and sight along the barrels' twinned extent. She doesn't move a hair. Stands motionless as a tree, a naked outcropping of stone.

And then she sits. Still eyeing him, the coyote sits down like a contented dog.

It throws him. It's hard to be sure, holding the creature in his sights the way he is, but he could swear her gaze has changed. Still unwavering, still unnervingly direct, it can no longer properly be called a stare. The coyote is regarding him. Mildly, terribly. For a full minute now. For what feels like his entire life.

He could shoot, if he could control his trembling enough to be sure of his aim. Or he could surprise everyone, including himself, and abandon the gun—leave it to rust away into nothing, rise up and run for his life. The only problem is his legs. A new-born feebleness has come over his lower half, from his belt-scarred buttocks down through his clenching toes. There's an odour to the feeling, a sudden putrid waft. No, nothing so mysterious. It's coming from his own sweat-dampened chest. The paw, resting its black pads against his heart, is starting to stink.

The coyote cocks her head. It's quite a trick, making her meaning known like that without a single word. Darius hears a sound like a faucet coming on. Clouds of steam, the level rising inside his skull. He weighs the twelve-gauge in his hands a moment longer before turning it the right way round.

Stephen spots the den first—a giant's dark eye embedded in the scrubby slope. And now, in the path of the den's black gaze, a sight that makes him catch his breath. A large coyote sits staring into a clump of brush, its coat glimmering in the breaking day. Stephen halts a stone's throw from the scene. Tries in vain to see what it is that has the animal so entranced.

Instead, he hears.

A sliver-thin whimper from the coyote's closed mouth. Then, from inside the leafy cover, the shotgun's deafening blast. The blood, too, seems made of sound; it explodes from the bushes like a scream.

Finally, it's getting light. Not many people on the streets, but it won't be long before the city shakes itself and begins to move.

Lily could use a little more sleep. She tried to make camp again in the valley, but couldn't seem to settle on a spot; nowhere felt hidden enough. She could go to the wrecking yard, lay the mummy bag out on the kitchen floor, or maybe in the office—there's that squeaky old couch. She'd be safe there. Stephen would never try anything, and neither would Guy—she's as sure of that as she ever will be. In some ways it's a bigger risk to find herself standing here.

The neat brick path with the little twist in it. The flowering bush. The paired wicker chairs down the end of the porch. Lily takes the front steps gingerly, Billy light-footed beside her, as though they're pulling a B and E. She swings the duffle bag from her shoulder and lays it down on the bristly brown mat.

No doorbell. She has to close a hand around the heavy brass ring, lift it and knock. Nothing for as long as she can hold her breath. Then a light coming on in the hallway, glowing yellow through the pebbled glass. Footsteps. A pause while Kate looks through the peephole's magnifying eye. Lily lays a hand to the door and feels the deadbolt turn in its works.

Letting himself in the wrecking yard gate, Stephen flashes again on the body in the scrub. It had no face to speak of—scarcely any head—yet he could see there were characteristics they'd shared. They were both young men, both seemingly healthy and strong.

He thought about heaving the remains up onto his shoulder, but there was nowhere to take them, no trained and capable comrade waiting to relieve him of what he'd found. The coyote had simply turned and trotted off. After standing over the body for a long moment, Stephen found himself following suit.

He enters through the office door. On his way past the desk, he comes close to checking the blog. Actually goes so far as to reach for the mouse. *Coyote Cop.* It's like something a kid would come up with—not that *soldierboy*'s much better, even if Stephen did mostly mean it as a sad and ugly joke. What if he'd signed himself *Stephen* instead? Maybe, over time, Coyote Cop would have offered his own name in exchange.

Too late now. Too late to do anything—unless maybe he should still tell the police. It's hard to think straight about it all, hard to be certain what's right. He'll see what Guy has to say when he gets up. Edal, too.

The raccoons cry out to him as he passes through his room. "I know," he says, "you're hungry." No more putting it off—he'll blend some dog food into the morning feed, begin the process of getting them weaned.

In the kitchen, he sees the note, anchored to the counter with the jar of powdered KMR.

> *Hey buddy,*
> *Sorry I can't go to the cop shop with you—gone with Edal to help her sort out some stuff back home. Not sure how long we'll be. I'll call when we get there and let you know. Can you take care of feeding and flying Red? And keep an eye on Lily will you? You know if she needs a place to crash it's fine by me.*
>
> > *Guy*

Stephen reads the note over again, and smiles. So it's official. His friend is in love.

They've been taking it easy, winding through suburbs and brick-and-board towns, bypassing the twelve-lane terror of the 401. They're already through Shelburne, closing in on the Grey County line, when Guy leans across to open the glove compartment. The door drops down, revealing the familiar pinkish spine of a book.

"What," Edal says, reaching for it, "you're going to read while you drive?"

"Not me, you. Come on, there's only one chapter left."

Edal smiles, opening to the spot he's marked. "The Spring Running" takes place two years after *the great fight with Red Dog*—a tale Edal missed and will have to make up for. Mowgli has become a beautiful, formidable young man. The chapter opens with him lying on a hillside in the company of the aging panther, Bagheera. It's the *Time of New Talk*—springtime in the jungle. Soon all his animal companions will desert him to run with their own kind.

"'There is one day,'" Edal reads, "'when all things are tired, and the very smells as they drift on the heavy air are old and used. One cannot explain, but it feels so. Then there is another day—to the eye nothing whatever has changed—when all the smells are new and delightful and the whiskers of the Jungle People quiver to their roots, and the winter hair comes away from their sides in long draggled locks.'"

She pauses, and Guy reaches over to lay his hand on her knee. She looks at him, and he turns to meet her look. Not for long. Just long enough.

They feel the bump together—Guy wincing, Edal letting out a strangled cry.

"Shit!" He brakes hard, the truck fishtailing sickeningly before it judders to a halt. "Shit, did I hit it?"

But Edal's already out of the cab, walking stiffly, miserably, back to what she knows she will find: the shell cracked along its latitudes, blood rising up through the faults. She knows the best she can hope for is that it's already dead—that neither she nor Guy will be obliged to deliver the final, merciful blow.

She can see now it's larger than she thought. This is no pretty, painted thing. Mud-dark and twice the size of the one Letty killed, this can only be a snapping turtle—most likely a female loaded with eggs. She'll have to be careful if it's still alive.

Glancing back, she sees Guy bent over into the back of the cab, doubtless digging beneath their hastily packed bags for his shovel and bin. Yes, she thinks, the least we can do is clean up the carnage, prevent the body from becoming an ugly, unrecognizable smear.

She gets as close as she dares. She was right, it is a snapping turtle, an ancient, weighty mother in search of this year's nest. And she was wrong—the shell isn't cracked, it's perfect. In fact, every part of it appears miraculously unharmed.

Guy's still a ways back, but not so far that he can't read the look on her face. He lets out a whoop. Lets everything drop and comes running, his arms rising up at his sides.

# Acknowledgements

Many thanks to the following individuals for sharing their time and expertise: Sergeant Ben York, B.C. Conservation Officer Service; Gary W. Colgan, Director, Wildlife Enforcement, Enforcement Branch, Ontario Region, Environment Canada; John Almond, Area Supervisor, Halton-Peel-Toronto Area, Ontario Ministry of Natural Resources; Ryan Gold of A. Gold & Sons Ltd. scrapyard in Chatham, Ontario; Mara Sternberg and the staff of the Veterinary Emergency Clinic; Tracy McKenzie and the staff of the Animal Rehabilitation Centre; Lieutenant Commander Albert Wong, Senior Public Affairs Officer, Department of National Defence; Linda Coleman, Communications Advisor, Department of National Defence; Michael Mesure, Executive Director, Fatal Light Awareness Program; Dr. Ronald Brooks, Department of Integrative Biology, University of Guelph; Alan Macnaughton, Toronto Entomologists Association; Ian McConachie, Senior Communicator, Toronto Humane Society; Tara Harper, Bruce Peninsula National Park; Dr. Robin Love; John Routh.

In addition to these walking, talking sources, several books and websites deserve special mention: *Ring of Bright Water* by Gavin Maxwell; *Kipling: A Selection of His Stories and Poems*, edited by John Beecroft; *Watership Down* by

Richard Adams; *The Lion, the Witch and the Wardrobe* by C.S. Lewis; *Wild Animals I Have Known* by Ernest Thompson Seton; *White Fang* by Jack London; *Toronto the Wild: Field Notes of an Urban Naturalist* by Wayne Grady; *A Little Wilderness: The Natural History of Toronto* by Bill Ivy; *The Beast in the Garden: A Modern Parable of Man and Nature* by David Baron; *The Nature of Coyotes: Voice of the Wilderness* by Wayne Grady; *Raccoons: A Natural History* by Samuel I. Zeveloff; *Raccoons: In Folklore, History and Today's Backyards* by Virginia C. Holmgren; *Just Bats* by M. Brock Fenton; *The World of the Fox* by Rebecca L. Grambo; *A Wing in the Door: Adventures with a Red-tailed Hawk* by Peri Phillips McQuay; *Ontario Birds* by L.L. Snyder; *Outside the Wire: The War in Afghanistan in the Words of Its Participants*, edited by Kevin Patterson and Jane Warren; *Fifteen Days: Stories of Bravery, Friendship, Life and Death from Inside the New Canadian Army* by Christie Blatchford; Fatal Light Awareness Program at www.flap.org; Don Watcher at www.donwatcher.blogspot.com; DND and the Canadian Forces at www.forces.gc.ca; the Cardiomyopathy Association at www.cardiomyopathy.org.

My thanks to the Canada Council for the Arts for their support during the writing of this book.

Once again, I'm deeply grateful to the dream team at Random House Canada and Vintage Canada, especially my treasured editor, Anne Collins, who never misses a trick.

Special thanks and welcome to my agent, Ellen Levine.

As always, heartfelt thanks to my beloved family and friends. To my husband, Clive, as much love and gratitude as twenty-one years can hold.

ALISSA YORK's fiction has won the Journey Prize and the Bronwen Wallace Award, and has been published in Canada, the U.S., France, Holland and Italy. Her most recent novel, *Effigy*, was shortlisted for the Scotiabank Giller Prize and longlisted for the International IMPAC Dublin Literary Award. York has lived all over Canada and now makes her home in Toronto with her husband, the writer and filmmaker Clive Holden.

www.alissayork.com